MARILYN LEE

MOONLIGHT
Fervor

ELLORA'S CAVE
ROMANTICA PUBLISHING

What the critics are saying...

❧

Moonlight Whispers

"A fast paced, action filled story." ~ *Fallen Angel Reviews*

"If you're a fan of the whole Dumont clan as well as the Moonlight series, you'll love this book. […] Awesome job!"
~ *Sizzling Romances Review*

Moonlight Desires

"Ms. Lee definitely knows how to turn up the heat and engage a reader's desire and passion. ~ *Just Erotic Romance Newsletter*

An Ellora's Cave Romantica Publication

www.ellorascave.com

Moonlight Fervor

ISBN 9781419955327
ALL RIGHTS RESERVED.
Moonlight Desires Copyright © 2003 Marilyn Lee
Moonlight Whispers © 2004 Marilyn Lee
Edited by Martha Punches.
Cover art by Syneca.

This book printed in the U.S.A. by Jasmine-Jade Enterprises, LLC.

Trade paperback Publication July 2007

Also by Marilyn Lee

ℰℐ

About the Author

❧

Marilyn Lee lives, works, and writes on the East Coast. In addition to thoroughly enjoying writing erotic romances, she enjoys roller-skating, spending time with her large, extended family, and rooting for all her hometown sports teams. Her other interests include collecting Doc Savage pulp novels from the thirties and forties and collecting Marvel comics from the seventies and eighties (particularly Thor and The Avengers). Her favorite TV shows are forensic shows, westerns (Gunsmoke and Have Gun, Will Travel are particular favorites), mysteries (love the old Charlie Chan mysteries. All time favorite mystery movie is probably Dead, Again), and nearly every vampire movie or television show ever made (Forever Knight and Count Yorga, Vampire are favorites). She thoroughly enjoys hearing from readers.

Marilyn Lee welcomes comments from readers. You can find her website and email address on her author bio page at www.ellorascave.com.

Tell Us What You Think

We appreciate hearing reader opinions about our books. You can email us at Comments@EllorasCave.com.

MOONLIGHT FERVOR

ജ

MOONLIGHT DESIRES
~13~

MOONLIGHT WHISPERS
~131~

Author Note

ℰↃ

To Moonlight Fervor Readers,

First, I'd like to thank you for purchasing Moonlight Fervor, which contains the two stories Moonlight Desires and Moonlight Whispers. While the first chapters of these stories are very similar, they are not the same book. Moonlight Desires was originally intended to be a short story. When I yielded to readers' desire to write a sequel to Moonlight Desires, I used much of the first chapter from Moonlight Desires as a way to refresh readers' memories and to make the transition into Moonlight Whispers smoother.

In Moonlight Desires, you'll follow my hybrid shifters Acier and Etienne Gauiter on a wild night as they surrender to the call of the full moon. Moonlight Whispers starts with part of the first chapter of Moonlight Desires before picking up where Moonlight Desires left off. So even though the two stories start similarly, they are different tales, each focusing on a different female lead. I hope you'll enjoy both.

Best wishes,
Marilyn Lee

MOONLIGHT DESIRES

૪૭

Trademarks Acknowledgement

೮೧

The author acknowledges the trademarked status and trademark owners of the following wordmarks mentioned in this work of fiction:

Hell's Angels: Hell's Angels Motorcycle Club, California

Stetsons: John B. Stetson Company, New Jersey

Chapter One

❧

"I really need you to do this for me."

Acier Gautier sat in the living section of his custom-built RV and sighed. The man on the other end of the long distance call had been there for him and Etienne when they'd needed him most—when they'd left Pack Gautier against the Supreme Alpha's wishes and struck out on their own some twenty years earlier. Practically penniless and uncertain how they could manage without the support of the pack, Maurice Williams had become not only literary agent to him but also banker and friend to them both. Acier chose to make his living writing. Etienne made his with the face, physique and charm that drove women wild. Although not pleased by Etienne's choice, Mo had supported them both and they owed Mo a lot but—

"Mo, you know ordinarily I'd love to keep an eye on Raven." He opened the blinds in the living area of the RV and glanced upward.

That night the moon would be full and he would not be at his best. Already he was in prowl heat. His dual needs for blood and sex were at the point where they would soon override all other considerations. Although Mo had known them for some twenty-two years, Mo didn't know what he or Etienne were. He frowned. Hell, even he wasn't sure what they were.

He had always hated being torn between his two worlds, neither entirely wolf-shifter nor fully vampire. Because they were half-breeds and their mother a wolf-shifter, the vampire community had rejected them. He, his mother and Etienne had suffered some lean emotional times before finally being accepted, if not embraced, by his mother's wolf-shifter pack.

He could still remember as a young pup having their mother hold him and Etienne in her arms while she sobbed softly, uncertain what was to become of them. He still carried the mental scars of being neither wolf-shifter nor vampire. Not knowing who their father was did not seem to bother Etienne. In truth, as long as he had a willing woman in his bed, not much seemed to bother Etienne.

Acier, however, felt a burning need to know who had fathered them. Now, at forty, he was determined to learn who they were so he could visit vengeance upon the selfish, uncaring vampire who had sired them and left them to face the world alone.

Once he had called the unknown and despised male to account, he could then return to Den Gautier and take his rightful place as Den Alpha. In his absence, his cousin Xavier handled the day-to-day den business but that was not an ideal situation as the pack members sometimes sought him out in bewilderment, certain that he no longer viewed their welfare as important. This was a situation that could not continue. Each pack member needed to know that his or her concerns were Acier's concerns and that he would overcome any obstacles to assure they were happy and secure.

Besides, he was needed in Pack Gautier. More, he missed the pack. Etienne didn't seem to miss the structure of pack life and since leaving the pack, he leaned more toward the vampire side of their nature.

I am coming for you.

Those words had haunted Acier for the last several months. At a hundred and thirty, Supreme Pack Alpha Aime Gautier was growing old and weary. Acier, Alpha of one of the biggest dens in Pack Gautier, was needed at home to help battle the pack's internal and external enemies. Just as he was about to abandon his search for their father and return to assume the position of Supreme Alpha for which Aime had groomed him for ten years, those words had come to him in a dream, taunting him and had been with him ever since. *I am coming for you.*

He opened his wallet and stared at a small snapshot of a large watercolor portrait his mother had done just before she died. It was a picture of a man with glowing eyes and bared incisors. Etienne, who sometimes exhibited traits of psychic powers, had led him to the picture of their father, an unknown vampire who had impregnated their mother and then disappeared before he and Etienne were born. His jaw clenched. He was not prepared to sit back and wait for the male who had abandoned them to come find them at his leisure. One day he would find him and then…

He snapped his wallet shut and rose. "Now is not a good time for me, Mo."

"I can appreciate that but we're talking about Raven here, Acier. I won't have a moment's peace with her so far from home for the first time, spreading her wings. If you can't help, I'll have to risk her wrath and follow her myself. I can't have every Tom, Dick and Harry sniffing at my baby girl."

He sighed. He had to help. Now that Leon had taken complete leave of his purebred senses, Mo was his oldest and dearest friend. And like Aime, Mo was growing frighteningly frail and old. At twenty-two, Raven was the youngest of the three daughters Mo had raised alone after his wife's death. He had never remarried, devoting himself entirely to his daughters. They were everything to him. He knew if he didn't help, Mo would worry himself into even worse health.

"How long will she be here?" he asked, moving slowly through the RV.

"Two, maybe three weeks, tops. Can I count on you?"

"Yes." He tried not to sound as ungracious as he felt. True he hadn't seen Raven for ten years but how bad could her visit be? They had always gotten along well and he could put his search on hold long enough to make sure Mo's baby girl had a safe and happy two weeks in and round New York City and Philadelphia. If he were lucky, Etienne would show up and take her off his hands for part of that time. When she left, he would resume his search for the soulless bastard who had abandoned them. "Sure. It will be great to see her again."

Mo sighed. "You don't know how big a load this is off of my shoulders. Now I'm counting on you, Acier, because I know she'll be safe with you."

"Of course she will. I'll guard her like she was my own pup."

"What? Your own what?"

Mo sounded shocked and he realized what he'd called Raven. "Just an expression of affection," he said hastily. "I'm glad to help, Mo." He would go on the prowl and be back at the rural trailer park between Philadelphia and New Jersey where he'd spent the last two months by the time Raven arrived. "When is she arriving?"

"She should be there some time this evening."

He paused in the kitchen area. "What?!" Shit! He couldn't have her around while he was in heat and about to go on the prowl. "Mo, that changes everything. You have to call her and tell her to go stay at a hotel for a few days until I come pick her up."

"She's looking forward to staying with you, Acier."

"With me? Mo, I live in an RV with one bed. Etienne sleeps on the floor when he visits. Where is she supposed to sleep?"

"Don't pretend you're living in some pokey trailer with barely enough room to walk around in. I've seen that fifty-foot, half-a-million dollar RV of yours, Acier, with the loveseat bed. She can sleep there. But if you need a few days, just tell her when she arrives."

"Yeah, but Mo—"

"How is Etienne?"

"He's fine. He's just wrapped up filming for the season on the show and he's doing reshots for the adult pay movie I told you about."

Mo snorted. "Movie? Call it what it is, Acier, porn. You write it and he lives it."

He frowned. "It's not porn, Mo. It's literary erotic fiction. And like the vampire and werewolf series I write, of which you're so proud and fond, my screenplays have a plot, three dimensional characters and a sound reason for everything that happens, including the sex. The scripts I write for Etienne are just as good as anything else I write."

"Acier, you are talented whether you're writing novels or smut for Etienne. But this Wyatt Diamond adventure series is just an excuse for Etienne to bang every woman he comes across in every conceivable position."

He smiled suddenly. "He likes sex."

"Now there's an understatement if I ever heard one. Between the two of you, you must have bedded a quarter of the women in any city or town you've been in longer than a few weeks."

He laughed. "I like sex too," he admitted. "And it's hardly our fault if women keep dropping their drawers the moment they meet us."

"There's more to life than bedding an endless succession of women, Acier."

"Maybe so but for now that's what we enjoy most."

"You could both benefit from settling down."

"Marriage doesn't interest either of us at the moment."

"At the moment? The two of you are forty, Acier, not twenty! You need to think about settling down while you're still young enough to enjoy having children."

From Mo's point of view, he knew he and Etienne should have been married and have had a few kids by now but wolf-shifters lived long lives compared to humans. And with their vampire blood, there was no telling what sort of lifespan he and Etienne could expect. Not that he could tell Mo any of that.

"You both need a good woman but I suppose you'll have to reach that conclusion yourself," Mo went on when he remained silent. "Listen, thanks and I'll talk to you about that book of yours that's late in a week or so. Oh, and Treena expects to see you and Etienne at the wedding. Tell Etienne no excuses. And that goes for you too. You've missed entirely too many important milestones in my girls' lives, Acier. We took you and Etienne into our family years ago. Now it's time to act like a family member and start showing up for big family events."

Treena was Maurice's middle daughter, several years older than Raven. "Yeah, we both know it's more than our lives are worth to miss Treena's special day, Mo. I know I've missed some big events but—"

"Acier, there's always a 'but' with you and Etienne. Either we're important to you or we've not."

He swallowed hard, feeling as if the air had been knocked out of his lungs. "You have no idea how much you mean to me, how much all of you do."

Mo softened his voice. "Both you and Etienne mean a lot to us as well, Acier."

He sighed, running a hand over his hair. "Mo, that makes this difficult to say but about Raven—"

"She's been looking forward to seeing you for weeks now, Acier. Please, don't disappoint her again."

"No, I won't but Mo—"

"Tell Etienne I said if he doesn't call me soon, his big behind is mine the next time I see him."

"I'll tell him, Mo, but—"

"Later."

He waited until Mo hung up before slamming his cordless phone down on the small kitchen counter top. He'd been played like a damn fiddle! He rose and paced the area in front of his loveseat, his cock beginning to feel constricted. Stalking to his bedroom, he reached into his pants and removed the support cup he wore over his genitals when he wasn't on the prowl. He tossed the flexible, white triangular cup onto his bed.

As it landed, it made a small, distressed sound.

He walked over to the bed and stroked its back and the small creature that lived to serve him projected a feeling of satisfaction towards him. He smiled. "No, Pen, I'm not mad at you. I just need to be able to breathe. No, you don't restrict my breathing. I just want my cock free for a bit. Okay?"

He felt Pen's acquiescence and sighed. Sometimes his Keddi pets took more work than he felt like putting in to them. Small wonder that living leather pets were forbidden to all except the Alpha Supreme and a small number of wolf-shifters of his choosing.

Having stroked Pen's sensibilities, he sighed and allowed his cock to spread out along his leg. There. That was better. He reached back and removed the clip from his hair and it fell forward around his shoulders. He raked his hands through it, frowning. The closest hotel was thirty miles up the highway. He'd follow Raven there and then go on the prowl.

Half an hour later, he heard a vehicle arrive in his private parking space. Moments later, a rap sounded on his door. He rose from his computer at the small desk in his bedroom and padded through the RV to answer the door. "Yes?"

"Steele? It's Raven."

Remembering a skinny, gangly preteen who use to stare at him with wide, wonder- filled eyes, he smiled and opened the door. He felt an immediate and disturbing reaction in his cock. The woman standing outside was at least five-foot-ten-inches, with curves in all the right places, a pretty face with clear, dark, milk chocolate skin, warm, deep brown eyes and one of the most amazing smiles he'd ever seen. In a word she was breathtaking.

Surely this confident, attractive woman with the sultry voice and seductive smile was not little Raven. His nostrils flared and he inhaled deeply. Under her familiar scent, he caught an unmistakable and highly intoxicating and arousing aroma. As she stood there smiling at him, he could smell her pussy creaming. His cock went hard against his leg and a rush of hot blood flashed up the back of his neck. He felt the call of the full moon.

Chapter Two

ଊ

"*Petite?* Raven?"

She gave him a sultry smile that made his cock harder. "Steele. Long time no see."

This close to his prowling time, when he was in heat, every scent of a woman sent the blood rushing to his cock, turning it into a semblance of the nickname seven-year-old Raven had given him. When told Acier was French for steel, she had immediately begun calling him Steele.

She tilted her head to one side and her long, thick hair fell against one smooth, dark cheek. "So, can I come in?" Her skin looked lovely and smooth. He'd always loved a woman with dark, radiant skin.

"Ah…yes, but you can't stay."

Her eyes widened. "I can't? Dad said it wouldn't be a problem for me to stay until the wedding."

"Until the wedding?! That's not for another two months."

"I know." Her smile deepened. "We have two months to get reacquainted."

"Raven, I have only one bed."

She grinned at him. "Dad tells me it's queen-sized. We can share."

He felt his face flushing at the thought of sharing his bed with her.

"Oh don't look at me like that! It won't be the first time we've shared a bed."

He glared at her. "Are you nuts? You were ten years old and frightened of the storm! There's no storm now, you're not ten and you're not getting anywhere near my bed."

"Don't worry, Steele. You won't even know I'm here."

That wasn't bloody likely. The aroma of her fragrant pussy was already threatening to make his cock explode. If she stayed longer than a few hours, he would be hard-pressed not to toss her onto his bed and fuck her senseless.

Casting a sexy, confident smile at him, she moved past him.

Sighing, he picked up the two large suitcases near his door and carried them inside. The moment the door closed, the smell of her sent the blood rushing to his head and down to his cock. He needed pussy and blood. Quickly. He looked at her standing in the living area, just behind the two mahogany leather captain's chairs in the cab of the RV. A pair of big, heavy-looking breasts strained against her sheer top. Without her bra, her breasts would be more than a hungry mouthful. When bitten into they would taste delightful and have large, dark nipples. His gaze flickered downward. Her long legs were encased in a pair of dark silk pants that showcased her nicely padded rear. The palms of his hands itched as he imagined cupping her ass in his palms as he thrust his cock deep into her fragrant pussy. There were few things half as exciting as making no-holds-barred love to a beautiful, voluptuous woman who exuded sensuality as she did.

"So. Give me the grand tour of this black beauty of yours, Steele."

The only black beauty in sight was Raven herself. Damn but she was gorgeous. "There's not much to see."

"Not much to see? Steele, do you know how many people wished they had houses that cost half-a-million dollars?"

"It was the cheapest one I could find with what I wanted," he said, feeling defensive.

She looked around his living area with its sofa opposite a small loveseat, above which a flat screen TV was built into one wall. He put her suitcase down near the sofa. Beyond the living room area on the left side of the passage was a small powder room. On the right was a laundry area with a stackable washer and dryer and a hide-away ironing board. The passage opened into the kitchen area with cherry-wood cabinets and stainless steel appliances. He followed her as she moved through the kitchen area to stop in front of a cherry-wood door. She opened it, revealing a short, narrow passage with a door on either side, separating the split bath. On the right side was a shower stall. Directly across was a larger powder room with a mahogany and light rose interior.

Beyond the bath was a folding door. She pushed it back revealing his bedroom, dominated by a queen-sized bed with cherry-wood storage cabinets above and on the side of it and a large, tinted window behind the bed and along the side walls.

He looked at her looking at his bed where he'd so carelessly tossed Pen. He sent a silent message to Pen ordering him not to move. Nevertheless, she gave Pen an intent stare, almost as if she suspected he wasn't just a cup for his cock. Finally, she turned to look at him and he smelled her pussy giving off a fresh rush of moisture.

"There's plenty of room for both of us in that bed, Steele."

Her voice was soft and seductive and he sucked in a breath. "No! That's out of the question, Raven."

"Why? What are you afraid of?"

He took a deep breath. "Raven, I'm not some boy you can play games with," he warned.

She tossed her head, sending her lovely dark hair cascading around her beautiful face. "Who's playing games?"

Normally he enjoyed playing sexual games with beautiful women, but he could not afford to indulge his carnal tastes with Raven. Soon, his need for sex and blood would become overbearing. He had to get away from her immediately or he would be hard-pressed not to strip her, lay her on the bed and shoot his aching cock balls-deep in her sweet-smelling pussy with one lusty thrust that would burst through the cherry he suspected she was still saving for some lucky human male. His cock jerked and spread out along the side of his leg like a thick pole. Damn but he ached for pussy, blood and ass. His nostrils flared. Her pussy. Her blood. Her shapely ass.

Her gaze shifted to his groin, slowly taking in the length and thickness of his cock. "Oh…*my.*" When she raised her eyes to his, her full lips were parted and he saw an awareness of his lust in her wide gaze.

He cast a quick glance at Pen, realizing he should not have removed him. Now his lack of control was clearly visible to her. Shame and dismay filled him at the sudden, almost overpowering urge he felt to toss her on the bed and ravish her pussy and her fine looking ass. Two of the most exciting aspects of a woman for him were big breasts and an ass with enough padding to take the pounding he would give it. He was a tits and ass male big time and Raven had both in abundance. And a cherry he'd love to take.

She looked directly into his gaze. "I admit I like to cuddle but I'm not a bed hog. You'll hardly know I'm sharing your bed, Steele. Just give me a cuddle and a friendly lip-lock and I'll drop off to sleep like a baby."

He felt his incisors descending and his lust for blood increasing. But even in heat he shouldn't feel this way about his good friend's baby daughter. If there was one thing he could not do, it was fuck Maurice's baby, even if her pussy was creaming so deliciously and giving off the most incredibly wonderful, please-fuck-me-hard-and-often aroma he'd ever inhaled.

He clenched his jaw. "We're not sharing a bed, Raven," he ground out.

She closed the distance between them and looked up into his eyes. "Why not? We used to when you stayed with us."

"Raven, you were ten years old and afraid of the storm and I was baby-sitting while your father was away at a conference! You were frightened and crawled into bed with me. Don't make it sound as if I bed children!"

She shrugged. "What's your point, Steele?"

"You were not a fully grown woman with...with..."

Her eyes gleamed with merriment and he knew she was enjoying teasing him. "With what, Steele?"

With large, firm breasts he longed to suck and a pussy he ached to fuck. But he could not say that to her even though she was doing her best to goad him into doing just that. He shook his head. It wasn't going to work. He was not going to betray Mo's trust by fucking her.

"I have to go out. Make yourself at home. You'll find everything you need here. The fridge is full and the keys to the door are on the nightstand. I'll see you in a day or two." He swung away from her and stalked through the RV.

"A day or two?" She followed him and clenched his arm. "Steele, wait a minute!"

Her touch seemed to burn through his shirt to his skin, heating it to a quick boil. "I can't."

"I think you've misunderstood."

He looked down into her eyes and saw his own lust reflected there. "No, Raven, I haven't misunderstood a thing. When I return, we'll discuss what hotel you're going to stay at for the next few months, my treat."

She lifted her chin and stared at him. "I'm not going to a hotel. I am staying here with you, Steele."

"No Raven, you're not!" He shook off her hand.

"Steele, please. I need to talk to you. There are things I want to say to you. Don't go!"

"You can say them when I get back but right now I have to go!"

"Don't...please."

He took a deep breath. "I have to go. I do but I'll be back as soon as I can."

"When?"

"In a few days."

"A few days? You can't just leave me here alone while you go off, Steele!"

"Petite, please try to understand, I have to go now. Forgive me." He snatched up his leather jacket from the recliner behind the passenger seat and dug the keys to his motorcycle out of his pants pocket. With his nostrils filled with the sweet scent of her, he quickly left the RV. Outside, he took a deep breath and tried to calm himself. He looked up at the full moon in all its lunar glory. No more time. He had to get far away from Raven as quickly as possible before the urge to satisfy his dual natures with her become more than he could control.

He moved around the side of his midnight black RV and unlocked a large hidden compartment, revealing a gleaming silver and black bike a Hell's Angel would have envied. A few minutes later, with his special prowling kit safely tucked away in one of his side bags, he roared out of the park, his long dark hair flying around his leather-clad shoulders. Acier Gautier, wolf-vampire hybrid, was on the prowl.

* * * * *

From the bedroom window of the luxurious RV, Raven watched in disappointment as Steele, seated on his bike with his glorious dark hair flying around his wide shoulders, disappeared into the night. He was one of the most attractive men she'd ever seen. With his almost silver-gray eyes, big, sleek body and hairy chest, he had always reminded her of a big, majestic wolf. She wasn't quite sure why.

She sucked in a breath as she recalled the incredible fragrance he had emitted. How is it that she had not remembered that about him? His scent had been sort of musky and lusty, highly arousing and totally intoxicating, and the outline of his cock. She ran a hand through her hair, savoring the memory of it seen so long ago. Long and thick as she recalled from the one time she had seen him briefly when she was younger. She'd been hiding in the linen closet across from the guest bathroom intending to spring out and startle him when he emerged from the bathroom. Instead, she had been stunned when he had stepped out of the shower at her house stark naked. To her young eyes, his cock had seemed impossibly huge and she had come to believe her memory had been faulty.

She breathed in deeply, recalling the eye-popping length and hardness of his shaft lying along the side of one leg. Now she knew better. He really was huge. She frowned, wondering why he would have stepped out of the bathroom naked like that in a house full of young girls. Her father would have tossed him out on his rear if he'd ever learned of the incidence.

She frowned. It was so unlike Steele to behave like that. She had never even so much as seen his bare chest before that incident. Was it possible that she had imagined the incident after all? She was no longer so certain.

In any case, she was more determined than ever to have a wild fling with him before she went home and settled down to a job in her father's agency. She sighed. She'd over-played her hand and tipped her cards too early. Having a fling with Steele was going to prove much harder than she had anticipated.

All the endless women with whom he'd shared his bed notwithstanding, she suspected getting him to take her to bed was going to be a hard sell. But she had seen his lust for her in his beautiful silver-gray eyes. His cock had nearly spread out to his knee as he'd looked at her. Clearly, he could stand to invest in a few pair of briefs. Despite himself, he wanted her. And she hadn't waited this long just to have her fantasy denied.

Her first challenge would be getting him to allow her to stay. Once she did that, his lust would take care of the rest. She smiled. Maybe she'd make him a present of some sexy briefs and then make a game of taking them off before they made love. Her heart thumped at the picture her imagination conjured up of her kneeling before Steele wearing only a pair of briefs, about to slid them down his legs and then finding herself staring at his cock within easy reach of her mouth. Oh God, it didn't bear thinking about.

She took out her cell phone and made a call. The phone on the other end was answered almost at once. "Hello?"

"Abby," she sat on the sofa, "things are not going well."

"What's happened?"

The warm, caring voice of Abby Valentine invited her confidence. She sighed. "He took one look at me and practically ran out of the door."

"Where'd he go?"

"To some other woman. Oh Abb, here I am sitting alone, ready and willing to please him and he's out banging someone else."

"Give the relationship a chance, Rae."

"What relationship?" she sighed.

"Well, you told me you *knew* the two of you would be together."

She nodded slowly. Ever since she could remember, there were things she just *knew*. She wasn't sure how or why but sometimes there seemed to be an inner melody or music that came to her and she saw or knew things. At least she thought she did. When she looked at Steele, she felt that inner melody and knew they were meant to be together, at least for a short time. Now all she had to do was convince him.

"I know and I still believe that but Abb, it was so hard to watch him leave knowing he's going to another woman. She's small and petite and she doesn't love him. Why would he leave me to go to her?"

"Small and petite and doesn't love him? You mean he introduced you to her?"

"No. Of course not!"

"Oh! He has a picture of her at his place?"

About to shake her head, Raven paused. She had seen the woman in her mind, in the music. The mind music that she didn't understand and couldn't tell anyone else about without being thought crazy. "No, but you know big men like him almost always prefer tiny, petite women. And here I am practically an Amazon. No wonder he went running to her. He can actually pick her up if he wants to. If he tries to pick me up, he'll strain every muscle in his body."

Abby laughed. "Don't exaggerate, Rae. There's not an ounce of excess weight on you and you're under six feet."

"By two lousy inches. Big deal."

"And I'm sure he's strong enough to pick you up."

"Well, he is awfully big and powerful. Maybe he can," she allowed.

"How long is he going to be gone?"

"Several days."

"You want me to drive up and keep you company?"

"That would be very nice for me but highly inconvenient for you. I'll be fine. I just have to come to terms with the reality that he's not going to drag me into his bed and make love to me as easily as I'd hoped." Despite what her silly mind music had led her to believe. "Well, it was a long drive and I'm a bit tired. I think I'm going to take a shower and have an early night. What are your plans for the night? Got a date?"

"Don't I wish."

Abby was attractive, intelligent and always dressed well. Raven couldn't help thinking that if Abby spent less time watching movies and more time on her social life, she'd have landed a hunk of her own by now. "So what are you going to do?"

"Watch a movie."

She sounded defensive and Raven smiled. "One of the days, I'm going to sit down and watch that Wyatt Diamond series with you and see what the appeal is. I mean, he must be—"

"Oh you wouldn't like him."

Abbey spoke quickly and Raven got the impression she wasn't being strictly above board with her. She decided then and there she was going to find out all she could about this Wyatt Diamond Abby was so taken with that she'd rather spend her time watching him than cultivating a relationship with a real man.

"Wouldn't I?"

"No. I'm sure of it. Listen, Rae, you know where I am if you need me, sweetie."

Although Abby was ten years older than her, they had taken one look at each other when they'd met at a silent movie festival and decided they liked each other big time. Over the next two years they had become firm friends. She nodded. "Yes. Thanks."

After ending the conversation with Abby, she sat wishing she'd been able to talk Steele out of looking for love elsewhere. Her thoughts were interrupted by the sound of a vehicle stopping very near the RV. She frowned and glanced out the window. A dark, luxury SUV occupied the space next to her car. The door opened and a man gorgeous enough to make a woman go damp just looking at him stepped out. He was tall and the expensive dark, tailor-made suit emphasized how well-built he was with wide shoulders, narrow hips and long legs to which his pants clung almost lovingly.

He had chiseled, classically handsome features with a mouth that begged to be kissed and dark deep eyes that suggested to whatever woman he gazed at that she was the only woman in the world worth looking at. Etienne Gautier, Acier's twin brother, quickly started towards the RV.

Chapter Three

ℬ

She ran through the RV, pulled the door opened and threw herself forward. "Tee!"

She was caught in a pair of strong arms and held close briefly before being swung off her feet and easily carried back into the RV.

She wrapped her arms around his neck and covered his handsome, clean-shaven face with kisses. "What the…?" She drew back, pushed the dark cowboy hat off his head and let out a small, scandalized cry. She raked angry fingers through his short, dark hair. "Tee! What is this? Oh my God, Tee! How could you? What have you done to all my lovely locks?"

A pair of smiling silver-gray eyes looked down into hers. He kissed her on both cheeks and sat her on her feet. "Don't look at me like that, Petite Corbeau. I'm forty years old now. It was time to get a hair cut. Besides, now when you want to nuzzle my neck you won't have to push my hair aside first."

"I've never nuzzled your neck!"

He turned a lecherous grin on her. "Well, now you can, Petite, without my hair blocking your access."

Although neither of them had ever really acknowledged it, there had been an undercurrent of sensuality underlying their conversations since her eighteenth birthday. She touched the strong column of his throat. A warm tingle rolled over her and she leaned closer. She sniffed and inhaled deeply, savoring his scent, completely male and wonderfully fresh and sexy. A brief, silent, rhythmic song danced along her senses. Her chi approved of him. And so did she. Smiling, she brushed her lips against his neck.

"Oh that's very nice, Petite."

31

Yes, it was. She opened her mouth and pressed a quick kiss against his skin.

"Hmm." A big hand settled on the back of her head. "Now aren't you glad there's no hair in the way? Just my neck and your sweet, warm lips, Petite."

She kissed him again and drew back to stare into his beautiful gray eyes. "But Tee, couldn't you at least have left it shoulder length?" she wailed. Although he was still one of the most drop-dead gorgeous men she'd ever seen, she knew she was going to miss all that long, dark, silky hair that used to hang around his shoulders underneath an assortment of Stetsons.

He grinned at her. "Afraid not. I was ready to get rid of all of it."

"But Tee, it was so sexy and gorgeous."

He frowned. "So what are you telling me, Petite? That you only loved me for my hair?"

"No!" She leaned forward and kissed his neck again. "I love you period, you big, gorgeous hunk," she breathed against his skin. She licked at his neck and drew away from him.

He smiled and brushed his nose against hers. "That's my Petite."

"Still, I loved you more with hair," she dead-panned.

"Well, as long as you still love me a little bit."

She linked her arms around his neck. "I love you lots, Tee. I always have and I always will."

His warm, tender smile sent a tingle right down to her toes. "I love you lots too, Petite."

She shook off the regret that it was Etienne saying he loved her instead of Steele and frowned. "Still, I'm going to miss your hair."

He laughed. "Don't despair. Sei still has enough hair for both of us."

She nodded. Yes, Steele still had a head full of gorgeous hair. "But he never let me play with his as you did."

He brushed his cheek against hers. "Bear with him, Petite. There's a lot going on in his life right now."

"I've waited a long time to see him again."

"I know, Petite."

"But he doesn't know or care."

He stroked a finger down her cheek. "Yes he does. Don't misunderstand because there are a lot of things occupying his mind. He's always been very fond of you and that's not going to change."

"Are you sure?"

"Yes, Petite. I am very sure."

"Oh...well...okay."

"Now, speaking of Sei, where is he?"

She frowned. "He went out, looking for *love*."

Tiny lights seemed to dance in his gaze. "Ah. And left you all alone?"

She nodded. "He wasn't very pleased to see me."

His arched a brow. "Don't jump to unfounded conclusions."

"Unfounded?"

"Yes, because I know he's very fond of you. Why wouldn't he be?" He took a step back and gave her a long, lingering look. "Holy hell, Raven!"

She flushed. "What? What's wrong? Is my nose shiny or something or...?" She spread a hand over her breasts, afraid her blouse had popped open but found it securely fastened. "What is it?"

"Damn, but you are one stunningly beautiful woman! When I last saw you three years ago, you were a skinny gal with potential, sure, but holy shit, look at those big, bad tits you're wearing."

"I'm not wearing them! They're breasts, not tits, Tee, and they're all natural and all mine!"

"I can see that, my lovely." He circled her slowly, slapping her lightly on her behind.

"Hey!"

"And that ass." His hand lingered on her butt. "Very nice, Petite. What was Sei thinking of leaving you?"

She blushed, liking the feel of his hand palming her behind. "I don't know. I don't think he wants me here."

He gently squeezed the cheek under his palm and surprised her by sniffing the air. "He wants you here all right."

She stared at him. She knew or at least suspected that Steele was "different." Tee was his twin and hadn't she read somewhere that identical twins had identical DNA? So if Steele was different, wouldn't Tee also be different? Although she had never "seen" Tee change, she was suddenly convinced that he could. "How do you know that? Have you talked to him since he left?"

"No."

"Then how do you know that?"

"Not only are we twins but we're very close as well. There are lots of things we know about each other without words."

And she had two months to discover just who or what he and Steele were. That is, if she could convince Steele to allow her to stay. In the meantime, Tee was there with an appreciative gleam in his eyes. And like Steele he was big, handsome, and as sexy as the day was long.

She beamed at him, spreading her arms to give him a better view. "So you think I've turned out all right, Tee?"

"All right? You look good enough to swallow whole, Petite."

Why couldn't Steele have said that to her? It would have made his leaving her to go bang someone else a little easier to take, maybe.

He looked at her and she almost felt as if he was looking right through her skin into her inner being, seeing the hurt she felt. She bit her lip and frowned, drawing mentally away from him.

"Don't take his leaving too hard, Petite. It's not personal. It's just something he had to do."

"Why?"

He sighed. "There is a lot about us you don't and shouldn't know — at least not yet. But trust me, he does care about you. Okay?"

She sighed. "Okay, I guess."

"Good." He extended an arm. "Now enough about him. He's gone and I'm here. Come give me a kiss and a slow grind or two."

"Tee!"

"Don't Tee me. Have you looked in the mirror lately? I'm serious."

"You are?"

"Damn straight. I know a good thing when I see it, even if Sei doesn't appear to. I want to taste those sweet-looking lips and get my hands on that fine ass of yours!"

"Tee!"

"Are you coming or not?"

Why couldn't Steele have given her this type of reception and openly admitted that he found her attractive and wanted her? But then Tee had always been more demonstrative than Steele. And unlike Steele, Tee had actually come back to see her as he had promised. Although they had not seen each other in some three years, Tee had at least kept in touch, calling her every so often to see how she was.

So if Tee wanted to get a little friendly, so be it, as long as he knew how to stop when she'd reached her limit.

She moved to press against him and closed her eyes when he cupped her face between his palms. "No, Petite Corbeau," he said. "Open your eyes and look at me."

Petit Corbeau. Little Raven. The nickname he and Steele had given her so long ago sounded sweet and sexy rolling off his lips, just as it had coming from Steele the last time he had used it. She sighed and looked up at him. It was strange how he and Steele could be nearly physically identical and yet have such different personalities. Had she been this close to Steele her heart would have been hammering and her mouth dry. While Tee was every bit as breathtaking as Steele, he didn't create the same level of havoc in her that Steele did. Not that Tee didn't excite her, because he did. He was entirely too sexy and handsome to leave any woman he looked at unmoved. Besides, like Steele he oozed sex appeal from every pore in his big, gorgeous body.

And she had a feeling he was just as well endowed physically as Steele was. And he might actually want to bed her. Not that she was prepared to go that far. "Tee, what are you doing?"

"I'm about to play with you a little." He brushed the tip of his nose against hers.

She sucked in a breath. "Should we do this?"

"Why not?"

Because she feared what Steele would say when and if he found out. "Tee…"

"Don't worry, Petite. Nothing is going to happen between us that you don't fully want."

She nodded impatiently. "I know that, Tee. I do. I just wish…"

"That I was Acier?"

She felt her face burn but he just laughed and pressed his cheek against hers. "Give me a little kiss," he urged, "and I will chase thoughts of Sei right out of your lovely head, Petite."

She had been infatuated with Steele for such a long time that she did not expect anyone, even the charming and delightfully wicked Tee, to chase thoughts of him from her mind. She looked up into Tee's silver-gray eyes and wet her lips. Okay so she stood corrected. If anyone could drive thoughts of Steele from her mind, it would be the handsome, uninhibited Tee.

There was only one way to find out. She turned her head until their lips met. She felt a pleasant tingle from the contact. Nice but she wanted more. She pressed closer and parted her lips. One of his hands left her face to wrap around her waist and draw her closer. He deepened the kiss, lightly running the tip of his tongue along her lips.

This time she felt a jolt of desire and need. She trembled, her hands splayed flat against his chest. His heart beat strong and fast under her fingers. Knowing she was the cause of the quickening of his breathing excited her.

She parted her lips further and touched the tip of her tongue to his. A combined shudder danced through their bodies. Sighing softly, she slipped her arms around his neck. "Tee, oh Tee."

His other hand drifted down from her cheek to her rear end. She felt his hand sliding over her butt.

"Nice," he whispered, nibbling at her lips. "Oh what a nice ass you have, Petite. Big, soft and yet firm. A nice handful. So nice." He kissed her again. "Hmm. Damn. I'll bet you have a hot, luscious pussy to go with these beautiful tits and this fine ass of yours."

She shuddered. "Tee!"

He sighed and lifted his head. "What? Am I being too crude? Have I embarrassed or shocked you, Petite? Shall I clean up my language? Tell me what you want and I'll do it. I'll do anything to please and delight you, Petite."

It amazed her that she wasn't shocked. She'd always liked Tee but to be making out with him like this and have him talking so frankly to her about her body, she should feel some level of embarrassment or shame. She felt neither. Instead of shocking her, his language turned her on and fueled her already heated passions. "No, I like that you admire how I look and I love how you express it."

"Then what's wrong, Petite?"

"I guess I didn't expect you to want to bang me."

"Bang you? Oh but I don't want to bang you, as you put it, Petite. I want to fuck you. Hard and long. How could I not?" He brushed his face briefly against her breasts. "You are absolutely the most gorgeous woman I've ever met."

Although pleased, she found his words difficult to believe. Men generally seemed to find her attractive but gorgeous? "You're just saying that because you want some pussy."

"No!" He bit lightly into her bottom lip and squeezed her ass cheeks, making her tremble with desire.

His hands on her rear felt so nice. She rotated her hips, pressing her behind against his palms. "No?"

"Oh I absolutely want some pussy but I'm saying it because it's true. You know I never lie to you, Petite. And you are going to give me some pussy, aren't you?"

That was the question. Was she going to go all the way with him?

Chapter Four

∞

"Oh Tee, you're making me so hot and wet." She slipped her fingers through his hair, urged his mouth against hers and greedily sucked at the tip of his tongue.

"I can make you scream with delight," he threatened. "Make love with me, Petite, and you won't be sorry."

Her heart thumped and she wet her dry lips. She kissed his lips. She wanted him. His lips were sweet and hot and addictive. She kissed him again, rubbing her aching breasts against his chest.

"Petite?" he asked softly. "Don't torture me. Tell me you'll give me some pussy."

Her heart hammered and liquid fire burned in her veins. A need and desire for him ignited in her, consuming her. She wanted him. "Yes. I think."

He pressed a warm, tender kiss against her lips. "Don't be afraid, Petite. Nothing more will happen than you want." He cupped her face between his palms and gazed down into her eyes. "I would never, ever do anything to hurt you."

"I know that, Tee."

He had a way of looking at her as if he were looking past any façade she might have erected around her emotions and straight into her heart. He smiled. "Neither would Acier."

She wasn't so sure of that. She knew Steele would never hurt her physically but emotionally? She feared her emotional well-being didn't overly concern him. Even after she had shamelessly thrown herself at him, he had rejected her in favor of another woman. Tee was here now, unashamed to admit to wanting her. Now was all that mattered. Now and Tee, wanting her and her wanting him.

"I don't want to talk about him. I don't want to talk at all. I just want you to…" Her face burned and she averted her gaze. "You know what I want."

"Understood, Petite." He peppered her lips with warm, insistent kisses that engendered a feeling of affection for her while quickly heating up her desires. His lips adored her mouth, face and neck while his hands caressed her body and stroked her passions.

She felt confused and a little afraid. Steele had dominated her thoughts and passions for so long, she had never expected to feel so lustful with another man. Yet she felt hot and hungry for Tee and the satisfaction she knew he could give her, if she allowed it.

Dare she? What would Steele say or do when he learned she had slept with Tee? Would it ruin her chances with him?

Tee's hands drifted up to her blouse. He paused and looked down at her. Under the unabashed desire, she saw tenderness coupled with a willingness to stop at her command in his gray gaze.

The knowledge that he really wouldn't do any more than she wanted gave her the confidence to surrender to her desires. Breathing deeply in an effort to control her pounding heart, she placed her hands over his and pulled them against the fabric.

His smile offered reassurance just before he unbuttoned her blouse. He did it slowly. For each button she allowed him to undo, he rewarded her with a warm, sweet kiss that made her damp, hungry and lusty.

She told herself that she wanted Tee so much because he was Steele's identical twin but she knew that was not true. Tee had a natural charm and allure all his own that were as enchanting as they were irresistible. She wanted him because he was who he was.

With her blouse unbuttoned to just below her bra, he paused and looked down at her. "This is going to get interesting now, Petite. Are you still with me?"

She gasped in a quick breath and nodded.

"That's my Petite." He undid another button. This time instead of kissing her mouth, he lowered his head and pressed warm kisses against the tops of her breasts, peeking out at him from her bra.

The feel of his mouth on her skin sent a delicious tingle through her. She bit her lip and held his head close to her breasts. "Tee."

He kissed her breasts again, his breathing quickening. He lifted his head. He looked down into her eyes and held her gaze captive as he unfastened the last few buttons.

Instead of immediately pushing the blouse off her shoulders, he slipped his arms around her and held her close, brushing his lips against her hair. "Petite, you feel so good in my arms. I want you so badly."

"Take me," she whispered. Even as she spoke she uttered a silent prayer that Steele wouldn't find out. Then deciding that he and Tee were too close for Tee to lie to him, prayed that he would understand when he did.

"He's not the one you need to worry about now," he told her softly. "I am."

She caught her breath and stared up at him. Sometimes she suspected he knew just what she was thinking. "Tee?"

He released her and eased the blouse off her shoulders. Instead of allowing it to fall onto the floor, he buried his face in it, deeply inhaling her scent. What a turn-on to see him so aroused by her scent. She sucked in an aching breath, her desire increasing.

After several moments, he placed the blouse over the back of one of the captain's chairs. Still breathing deeply, he drew her close to him and unhooked her bra. After sniffing at each cup, he stuffed it in his pants pocket and stood back to stare at her, his eyes dark and hot with lust.

She stood before him, bare-breasted, her nipples hard and peaked, her heart hammering. Her breasts were large and firm and she knew she didn't need to be ashamed of them. Nevertheless, she had to fight hard not to surrender to the urge to cover them.

He moved closer and cupped them in his hands, sending a rush of moisture into her pussy. "Damn, Petite, these have got to be the absolute loveliest tits I've ever had the pleasure of holding."

"They're not tits, Tee, they're—"

"The hell they're not. Some women have breasts, ho-hum, others, lucky ones have tits. Oh shit, Petite, but these are tits, tasting tits. I gotta suck these bad girls," he murmured, lowered his head and kissed each breast, slowly laving each nipple with the heat and moisture of his mouth until she felt ready to melt.

Sucking and lapping at her breasts with a greedy enjoyment that took her breath away, she felt his hand at the front of her pants.

Her eyes snapped open and she brought her hands up to close over his, her heart beating so fast, she could barely breath. "Tee, wait please."

He withdrew his mouth from her breast and looked down at her. "Too rough?"

She shook her head.

"Too much too soon?"

He would probably think she was an awful tease but she nodded anyway. "Yes."

"Why?"

"I...Tee...I..."

He sniffed and his eyes narrowed. "Saving the good stuff, your sweet pussy, for Acier?"

She flushed and bit her lip. "Oh Tee! Don't be angry."

"Not to worry, Petite. I won't fuck you if you don't want but I am going to taste your pussy."

"Tee!"

"What? Do you want me to stop? You know you only have to say the word and even if it kills me, and my cock and balls drop off, I'll stop."

She laughed and shook her head. She didn't want him to stop. She wanted, oh, hell, she wasn't sure what she wanted. "No."

"That's my Petite. Trust me. I won't hurt you."

"I know that, Tee."

He gently pushed her hands away and unbuttoned her pants. He knelt and removed her shoes. Then, still on his knees, he slid down her zipper. Rising, he quickly removed her pants, revealing her dark thong panties.

Going back down to his knees, he kissed his way up and down each of her legs until they were wobbly and threatened to collapse under her. Leaning forward, he pressed his face into her thong-covered mound, inhaling deeply.

"Petite, you have such an incredible aroma. I've never smelled anything like it, ever. I have to taste you."

"Tee, don't…"

He looked up at her, his eyes suddenly looking almost gold. "I have to. I promise I won't fuck you but I'm going to eat you. I have to. I have to taste you, Petite. Okay?"

She made a small, whimpering sound that was a combination of reluctance and lust.

He paused, staring up at her. "Petite? It's your call."

"I…"

"Shall I stop?"

If he did, she would probably die a thousand times. "No."

"You're sure?"

She nodded quickly before she could change her mind.

Smiling up at her, he eased her thong off. The center was damp with her excitement and she nearly came when he buried his mouth and nose into the dampness glistening in the fabric.

"Oh Petite. Holy shit! I have to have some pussy!" He stuffed her thong into his other pants pocket. Parting her legs, he growled deep in his throat and buried his mouth against her mound.

A shudder of pure lust thundered through her and she curled her fingers in his short hair, clutching his head close. "Tee, please. I ache. Take away the ache."

"Oh Petite, I'm going to," he murmured, parted her lips and dove into her pussy. She had expected him to eat her slowly so that they could both savor the experience. Instead, he thrust his tongue as far up her pussy as he could get it, closed his big, hot hands over her behind and ate her to a quick, scorching climax that engulfed her entire being.

As she shuddered through the biggest climax of her life, he kept his tongue thrust up her, his mouth over her pussy, eagerly lapping up the copious juices flowing from her like a waterfall.

He kept eating her and she kept coming until she thought she would pass out from the intensity of one climax rolling into another. Finally, when the only thing keeping her on her feet was his strong hands on her behind, he removed his mouth, withdrew his tongue from her and allowed her to slide down to her knees.

She leaned forward, burying her face against his shoulder. "Oh Tee. Tee."

"It's all right, Petite. I'll take care of you." He eased her to the carpeted floor onto her back and spread his big body, still fully clothed, on top of hers. His chest crushed her breasts and his body pressed hers into the carpeting. "Holy shit, Petite. That's the best pussy I've ever had. Damn, it's hot, sweet and so delicious. My cock is about to explode." He sucked at her breasts for several moments, making her toes curl and her back arch before looking down at her. "Holy hell, Petite, I need some of your pussy. Give me some. Please. Let me fuck you."

She looked up at him and felt a fresh wave of desire seize her. She wanted him to fuck her. She wanted to feel his cock buried to the balls inside her aching pussy. She wanted to feel him thrusting inside her and then clutching her butt in his hands as he filled her with his seed, no condom, just hot cock to aching, greedy pussy. At least part of her did. Another part couldn't bring herself to go all the way with him.

"Tee, please," she begged, pressing against his shoulders. "I…I'm sorry but I can't."

She expected outrage that she allowed him to eat her to several orgasms and now was asking him to stop without giving him any satisfaction whatsoever.

"Il était au chaleur et il a eu besoin du sang et un baiser."

She blinked up at him. It took a moment to realize why she hadn't understood him. Although she knew he and Steele spoke French, they rarely spoke it around her and her high school French had quickly been forgotten. "What did you say?"

"I said I need a fuck, Petite."

"I thought you said something about blood too."

"I did but it's not important."

He'd said he needed blood. Not wanted, needed. There was definitely a lot she needed to discover about him and Steele. "I can't go any further, Tee. I'm sorry but I…I just can't."

"Are you sure?"

She nodded. "I'm sorry."

"Oh holy shit, honey!" He pressed a quick kiss against her mouth, rolled off her and lifted them both to their feet.

"Tee, I'm sorry," she whispered.

"Prove it." He lifted her chin and pressed a long, hot kiss against her lips that made her go damper. She gasped and leaned into him, slipping her arms around his waist.

"A little more?" he whispered the question against her lips and then kissed her again before she could respond.

But she did respond with her lips and her body. Opening her mouth, she rubbed her breasts against his chest. He slipped a hand between their bodies and tweaked her nipples until they hardened into aching peaks.

She felt hot and aroused all over again. She wanted to feel his cock. She pressed closer but couldn't feel him. "Take off your jock strap," she whispered. "I want to feel your cock."

"Why?"

She blinked at him. "Why?"

"Yes. Why?"

Chapter Five

❧

"I…I want to hold it and touch it."

"Touch it and hold it?" He lifted his head and looked down into her gaze. "No."

She slid the palms of her hands along his chest. "Why not?"

"I don't take my cup off when I'm with a woman unless I'm going into her pussy. Is that what you want, Petite? Do you want my cock in your pussy?"

She licked her lips. "Yes, yes, I do!"

"But?"

"But I can't, Tee."

"Then why should I take off my cup?"

"Because I want…I need to touch you, Tee. I can't go all the way, but I'll jerk you off or blow you."

"Take me in your mouth and blow me?"

Her face burned. "Yes. if you want."

He smiled and kissed the tip of her nose. "That's a very generous and sweet offer, Petite but what I want and need is some pussy. Preferably some of yours. We could spend the night together and I'll give you a series of long, sensuous fucks you won't ever forget."

She shuddered again, nearly overwhelmed by lust and desire. Part of her did want that but another part wanted only Steele. "No," she whispered.

"Ah, I see how it is with you. You just want to handle the merchandise, get me all hard and hot and then toss me out on my ass with blue balls? Is that the deal?"

She bit her lip and then laughed.

He laughed too and they hugged, shared a warm, sweet kiss and backed away from each other. Although she was naked, damp between her legs and her face was hot, she felt surprisingly comfortable with him. "You're making me sound like a tease."

He moved close and slipped an arm around her shoulder. He gently squeezed one of her nipples. "You are a tease." He kissed her cheek. "But not to worry. A woman as gorgeous as you are can be anything she wants to be."

She looked up at him. "But really Tee, I didn't intend to tease you."

He pulled her close and stroked his hand over her behind. "Prove it. Give me some pussy."

"I'd like to Tee, really I would. I know you know I'd like to but I can't."

"Saving it for Acier? The lucky dog." He gave her shoulder a squeeze. "Listen, if you're firm about not giving me a roll in the hay, I'd better hit the road."

She laced her fingers through his. "Don't leave, Tee."

"I actually came here on business. I'd better go track Acier down. Besides, I am what is known as hot and bothered. I need some pussy, bad. I'd better leave before I toss you onto the floor and take some of yours."

She flushed. "Tee! You wouldn't!"

"Of course I wouldn't!" He kissed her lips lightly, holding her close and grinding his lower body against hers. "But I am tempted," he admitted. "I want you so badly my cock's about to explode. Wouldn't you like me to explode inside you? I'll make your pussy very happy."

"I know you would."

"But no go, huh?"

She bit her lip. "Tee, if you're really in bad shape, I guess we could—"

"Could we?"

"Well, if you use a condom and — "

"A condom? I'm not going to use a condom. If we fuck, I'm coming inside you. No condom."

She bit her lip, her stomach muscles clenching at the thought of Tee fucking her and then flooding her with his seed. "Oh Tee, that would be so…"

He pressed a finger against her lips. "Shhh. I know you want to save it for Acier and I'm all right with that, for now. Maybe later you and I will have a rematch. If we do, I plan to go all the way, Petite. Make no mistake about that. No teasing and then pulling back will be allowed. The next time I have you naked in my arms I will be getting some pussy."

She pressed her lips tightly together, her heart thumping.

"Now, walk me to the door before I change my mind."

"Okay, but you still have my bra and thong," she reminded him.

"And I have news for you, I'm keeping them," he told her. He picked up his hat and plunked it down on his shorn head. "The only way you get them back is to surrender your pussy. No pussy, no underwear. It's the least you can give me."

"Tee — "

"Forget it, Petite. You're not getting them back." He pulled her thong from his pocket and buried his face in it. "Hmm." He surprised her by pressing the cotton crotch between her legs and rubbing it against her pussy.

"Oh!"

He grinned, sniffed at the freshly dampened crotch and put it back in his pocket. "Walk with me, Petite."

She walked him to the front door of the RV. "Tee, would you really have fucked me?"

He arched a brow. "Hell, yeah! You have incredibly good pussy. I could eat you all night long and still not have had enough. And you smell so good."

"You like my perfume?"

He laughed. "I was talking about the smell of your pussy."

She flushed. "Oh. Nice, is it?"

"No! Incredible. No wonder poor Acier left. He was probably afraid of tossing you onto the bed and fucking you senseless." He kissed her cheek. "Listen, I'll see you at the wedding."

"Tee, that's not for another two months!"

"I know but if I see you any sooner, I might be tempted to wrestle you away from Acier and take some of the luscious pussy you're saving for him."

Flushing with pleasure that he was so open about wanting her, she kissed his cheek and then his mouth. "I really do love you, Tee."

He returned her kiss, nipping at her bottom lip and cupping his hands over her ass. "I love you too, Raven, and it's because I do that I'm going to leave now."

"You'll call me?"

"Don't I always?"

"Yes but it doesn't stop me from missing you."

"I always miss you too, Petite." He pressed a warm kiss against each breast, eased her away from the door and left.

Holding up one of the blades in the blinds at the window, she watched him go with regret and big-time second thoughts. Maybe she should have allowed him to fuck her. Lord knew she wanted a fuck in the worse way. As Steele wasn't inclined to bed her, she should have jumped at the chance to make love with Tee who was one big, handsome stud.

But what if Steele had come back and found them together? She had waited too long to ruin her chances with him the first time another handsome hunk squeezed her butt and sucked her breasts. She decided she'd made the right decision. Still, she felt horny and tired after her long drive. With thoughts of Tee still uppermost in her mind, she took a quick shower.

As the cool water cascaded over her head, she breathed deeply, reliving the feel of Tee's hands and lips and tongue on her body, in her pussy, making her climax again and again. Oh man, but he knew how to please a woman. She turned the knob until cooler water splashed over her.

Shivering, she turned the water off and got out of the shower stall. Then instead of putting on one of the sexy teddies from her case, she found one of Steele's shirts tossed across the hamper near the tiny washer and dryer behind the kitchen area and put it on.

She made her way back to the bedroom, stopping often to sniff the shirt to savor his scent. Although it was similar to Etienne's scent, it was also different. In the bedroom, her gaze fell on his bed and onto his cup. She stared at it, trying to put her finger on what was wrong with the cup. For one thing, there were no straps or strings. So how was it held on? She frowned. And if she stared hard enough she could almost believe it moved, breathed almost.

She gave a shake of her head. She was really getting weird. First the mind music that had been her secret for so long and now she was imagining that Steele's jockstrap was alive and a part of him. She closed her eyes, letting her inner music wash over her and she saw the cup clearly breathing, lying in Steele's hand, trembling and upset. She saw Steele talking softly to it, stroking a finger on the small, quivering cup, which now looked like brown, living leather.

Brown, living leather. A part of Steele. So if she touched it, him, it would be like touching Steele. Feeling wicked, she lifted his jockstrap-like cup to her face and inhaled deeply. The scent of him sent a flood of moisture pooling in her. Still holding the cup, she climbed into his bed. His scent lingered, not only in the cup, but in the room.

Taking another deep whiff of the cup, she placed it between her legs, pretending it was Steele's cock about to power its way into her pussy. She shuddered in near ecstasy at the thought. She lay awake for a long time thinking about him, with the cup lying between her legs. She knew he must be with a woman and that certainly tied her stomach into knots. "Oh Steele, please come back. Whoever you're with can't want or need you anymore than I do."

She sucked in a deep, painful breath and sighed softly as the cup seemed to move lightly against her.

* * * * *

After leaving Raven, Etienne drove with the windows of his SUV down and his moon roof open. He felt hot, sexually frustrated and a little amazed. Unlike Acier whose hatred for their unknown father fueled his refusal to embrace the vampire half of their nature, he considered himself more vampire than wolf-shifter. His best friend, Damon duPre, a seventy-year-old full-blood vampire, had schooled him on vampire customs so he understood why he had felt such an unexpected but powerful attraction to Raven. She was clearly Acier's bloodlust which made her very attractive to any who shared the same blood as Acier, including him and Slayer.

Should have stayed and fucked her. Let's go back and fuck.

Etienne turned his head and glanced briefly at the small, brown leather cup lying on the passenger seat of his SUV. He had removed Slayer, his support cup and pet, after leaving Raven. He shook his head. "If we do, we'll have to deal with Acier and Pen."

He felt Slayer's agitation. *Let's go back. Not afraid of Pen.*

Penetrator, Acier's favorite pet, was generally as easy-going as Acier, unless he felt Acier's interests were at stake. Then he became as feral as any wolf-shifter. And although

Slayer was fearless and a more accomplished and skilled shifter than Pen, Etienne knew Slayer was not up to going against the other Keddi.

"I know you're not but I'm afraid of Acier," he said.

You can take him.

He smiled. Slayer was the ideal pet, always certain he was up to any and every challenge, even taking on Acier. Well that wasn't going to happen.

"We're not going back," he said firmly.

Want her.

He sighed, feeling his cock pulsing along the side of one leg as he thought of her, so very beautiful and sweet and too much in love with Acier to allow him to fuck her. He growled softly. "So do I."

He made his living fucking and was rarely without a woman in his bed. Nevertheless, he'd rarely felt the need for a fuck more intensely. There were any number of women he could call who would be only too happy to spend the night with him. A few of them would even welcome Slayer's attentions but he wanted Raven so badly, he was hard pressed not to turn his SUV around and go back and try to talk her into allowing him to stay. He tightened his hands on the steering wheel. He'd never had to beg a woman for sex and damn if he would start now.

Want her. Go back and beg.

Because Slayer was so in tune with him and his innermost needs, he felt the need for Raven as strongly as Etienne did. Still, Acier was the one in the midst of bloodlust. Not him. He had no reason to be led around by his cock. But holy hell, he wanted to fuck Raven as badly as Slayer did.

He and Acier had drifted apart during the last five years or so. They were rarely in the same place for very long and their interests and concerns were very different. After their mother died when they were ten, Aime Gautier, the Supreme Alpha, had been father to them. After they left the pack, Mo had taken Aime's place in their lives as father-figure. He loved both Aime and Mo and felt no particular need to find and punish their father. Since Acier did, they had drifted apart.

From Damon he had learned that vampire fathers were not particularly sensitive or nurturing. On the rare occasions when they managed to impregnate a lover, they often abandoned the resulting offspring without a second thought. The sin Acier could not forgive their father for meant little to Etienne. It was what he expected from a vampire although he had long ago determined that should he ever be fortunate enough to father a child, he would not only stay around but take a very active and loving part in his child's life.

He cast a quick look upward as he drove. The full moon in all its radiant glory dominated the night sky. He raked a hand through his hair, feeling the not inconsiderable pull as it called to him. It had been a very long time since he had surrendered to its power, shifted and run wild with Acier through the woods as they had done as adolescent pups.

Now, for some unknown reason, he almost felt a need to answer the call of the moon. He felt his eyes glowing and his incisors descending. He wanted blood and pussy. And he wanted them in his natural form. He sniffed the air and caught a familiar scent. Acier had passed this way. And he had not been alone. Mingled with Acier's spoor was that of an aroused woman's.

We shift?

He nodded slowly. "Yes, Slayer. I think we will." Any woman Acier took when he was on the prowl would have to be experienced and resilient. Maybe resilient enough to handle two hungry men.

And me?

He shook his head. "No. You know you can't be yourself with any female who is not a shifter."

Want pussy.

He reached a hand down to cup his cock which ached with need. "So do I. When I get some, you'll feel it too," he pointed.

Want some too.

He frowned. Acier was always telling him he was letting Slayer get out of hand and he supposed he was right but he found it difficult to deny his faithful pet anything. He would make sure Slayer shared in the sex that night. It had been a very long time since he and Acier had spent the night with a single woman. He felt a thrill of anticipation. The woman's spoor was strong. He inhaled deeply. He sensed the woman in question would be more than equal to taking on him and Acier for a night of no-holds-barred lust.

Slayer too?

"No, you greedy prick, not you. Tomorrow we'll head for Den Gautier and you can get some loving up close and personal but for tonight you will have to be satisfied to share the experience through me. Now not another word out of you," he warned, sensing Slayer was about to argue.

Slayer subsided in a sulky silence and he frowned. Still, it was a shame they weren't spending the night with Raven. He gave an angry shake of his head. Hell, Acier could keep his mystery woman. If given the chance, he would have happily spent the night making tender love to Raven.

Me too.

"I know, pal, but she wanted only Acier and we'll both have to deal with that." She wasn't the first woman who'd preferred Acier to him and he doubted she would be the last one. But he'd given her the last thought he intended to that night.

He pressed his foot on the accelerator and sent the SUV speeding along the dark, country road, eager to find Acier and his lady of the night.

Chapter Six

&

Lying in Steele's bed, sleep continued to elude Raven. Thoughts of Steele and Tee intermingled in her mind, keeping her on edge and awake. Why had she sent Tee away? And where was Steele? She knew what he was doing but she didn't know how long he'd be doing it.

Given the fact that Steele might be gone for several days, she'd been a fool to deny both herself and Tee. Steele was probably banging some lucky woman senseless while both she and Tee were full of frustration.

She had half a mind to get out of bed and call Tee and ask him to come back and get as much pussy as he wanted. She'd actually sat up in bed when she changed her mind. She liked Tee too much to yank his chain. If she called him back, she'd have to be willing to go all the way and she wasn't sure she was willing.

She sank back onto the bed and lay in the dark, willing sleep to come. When it did, she dreamed of a large, majestic gray wolf with gold eyes padding towards her with a small brown living leather creature on his shoulder. She lay naked on her back in the woods under a beautiful, silver-white full moon. As he approached, his glowing eyes locked with hers, looking deep into her soul, seeking out her most deep-seated desires and needs. As she watched, the creature on his shoulder shifted until he was in the form of a large, pulsing cock.

She made no effort to hide her thoughts and innermost needs. When he looked into her soul now, he, she and his pet were as one. He knew of the song in her chi that controlled her destiny and she knew of the change that took place in him when the moon was full. She knew of it and accepted it and welcomed him in his natural form, him and Pen. But how did she know Pen's name? It must be part of the dream.

She trembled with anticipation as he lowered his handsome head to lick his way down from her face and neck to her breasts. She felt Pen, warm and hard, moving against her body. Her nipples hardened and he gently nibbled at the tips, allowing his tongue to circle each peak. Pen slid off of his shoulder and moved down her stomach, coming to rest between her legs. The muscles in her stomach tightened and clenched. She parted her legs and Pen, thick and pulsing, slid along one thigh and up into her pussy.

She moaned softly, her back arching. He licked his way down her stomach to her pussy where Pen lay one quarter buried inside her. Sighing softly, she parted her legs further and tilted her hips, longing for one of his cocks to slide all the way inside her and take possession of her.

He growled softly, moving in closer. He lapped at the outline of her vagina and touched his tongue to her clit while Pen slipped slowly in and out of her, never going more than a quarter of the way inside. Oh but by the Goddess Caldara, Mistress of the soul song, it felt so good. A jolt of desire shuddered through her. She gasped and thrust her hips forward, hungry for more. Pen slipped out of her and made his way up her body. She felt him against her lips.

She gasped again, opened her mouth and he slipped inside. She closed her lips around him and sucked gently as her lover's tongue sneaked into her pussy. A wave of pleasure suffused her. *Ooooh,* she gasped around Pen's hard warmth.

He laid his big body across her legs and settled down with his tongue buried deep inside her. His tongue felt hot and thick inside her and he had a way of twisting and thrusting at the same time in tandem with Pen that nearly drove her wild. Icy heat radiated all through her, making her toes curl and her back arch until she ached. She reached down and grabbed his head, pulling it closer to her. *Ooooh. Please! More.*

His tongue slithered further up into her. She shuddered through a wave of pleasure and she feared she would explode from the excitement and bliss rapidly spiraling out of control in her. He alternately tongued her with long, leisurely movements and short, powerful thrusts that seemed to pierce her to the core of her being. All the while Pen echoed his movement between her lips, making sweet love to her mouth. Occasionally he withdrew from her altogether so he could lick and gently nibble at her clit, enclosing her in a world of wondrous and liberating pleasure. She felt the song she couldn't control slowly building in the pit of her stomach and spreading its melody all through her. Under the magic of the full moon and in time with the rhythm of her inner song, he ate her to a slow, mind-numbing climax.

As she lay on the ground, writhing in ecstasy, the big gray moved up her body and stood over her. She looked up at him and saw a promise of desire and tenderness in his beautiful golden gaze. There was almost a question there. Her gaze swept down to center on his underbody. The breath caught in her throat and she trembled with renewed anticipation, feeling the song she couldn't control beginning to dance along her nerve endings. The head of his thick, almost bronzed cock peeked out of its sheath at her. A fresh flood of moisture made her damp.

He growled softly deep in his throat, his golden gaze on fire. She could almost smell his excitement as well as his need for her. Yet she knew he would not proceed until she acquiesced.

Let him. Please, Pen begged, pulsing with excitement and lust between her lips. She ran the tip of her tongue over Pen's big, thick head, and delighted as he shuddered in response, trying to hold back his climax. She knew he didn't want to come without his master and she decided not to force him to. This time.

Yes, she whispered. *Make love to me.*

Growling softly, he moved over her lower body, went down on his hunches and shot his cock up into her. Pen thrust forward at the same time and she felt a double dose of pleasure.

Ooooh!

With his penetration came pain. He was big, thick and so hard. The pain was quickly followed by a sense of pure delight. This had happened so many times before and yet each time was like the first. He kept sliding deep into her until she was so full of his hard, hot, pulsing warmth, she found breathing difficult with Pen swelling and filling her mouth.

He paused, allowing her time to get used to being impaled on his heavy, silky length.

She lay still, breathing slowly through her nose, savoring the delight of knowing she was so deliciously skewered on both his cocks. Then she found that she wanted, needed more. She lifted her legs and wrapped them around his body. He withdrew before slowly pushing at her. She gasped and shuddered. He growled slowly and plunged deep into her. She cried out silently, wrapped her arms around his strong neck so her body was pressed tightly against his. He withdrew and lunged forward into her again. She thrust greedily upward to meet him and they fell into a sweet, primal mating rhythm.

The music inside her swelled and throbbed in time with their thrusts. Her pussy clung to his cock and her mouth to Pen making them both fight to withdraw even an inch of it out of her drenched channels, only to thrust quickly forward again.

Pleasure and pain washed over her as her inner song thundered in her heart and in her ears. She was lost in a world that centered around the exquisite satisfaction of their bodies joined together in a ritual as old as time and as joyful as anything she'd ever felt. But it was a satisfaction of more than just body. She felt his care and affection for her with every thrust of his powerful hips, driving both his cocks ever deeper in her. Having him take her this way was far more delicious than she'd imagine.

"*Oooh, oooh,*" she moaned, her legs and arms dropped away from him and she sank against the ground, shuddering through her orgasm.

He rested his front paws on her shoulders and gazed down into her eyes as he thrust up into her pussy with a hunger and fury that exploded her world again and again. She felt his breath, hot and strangely exciting on her face. His cock felt thick and hard as it conquered her pussy as only he could in this wonderful way.

Feeling another climax approaching, she clung to him, keeping her eyes open so she could see his unashamed, feral passion for her in his gaze. She wiggled her behind and kept her groin pressed tight against his. His cock hurt but it was a pain with an underlying sweetness that took her breath away. In a matter of moments, she sobbed and came yet again. Good. Oh so soul destroying good.

He stiffened on her and his cock seemed to swell and grow larger and thicker. His thrusts brought exquisite pain. Pen felt as if he would block her airway with his powerful thrusts. Then he lifted his head, howled at the full moon and blasted a delicious stream of seed deep into her pussy as Pen sent jet after sticky, tasty jet of seed against her tongue and down her throat. He began to withdraw but she moaned in protest and wrapped her legs around him, eager to keep both his cock and every drop of his semen inside her where he and it belonged.

Finally. He was hers, they were one and would never totally be two separate individuals again. Keeping his front paws on her shoulders, he began to make love to her again, fucking her slowly and leisurely this time. Pen echoed his movements. She wrapped her lips around Pen and sucked him gently, savoring his delight in her. The sweetness of his controlled passion held her captive and heightened her desire. Feeling out of control, she wrapped her arms and legs around his body. She thrust herself wildly at him until they came together in a sweet burst of lust and desire that shattered them both while linking them together in a way she'd longed for.

"Steele, oh Steele. Steele!" Raven came abruptly awake, bolting up in bed. The room was dark and filled with unfamiliar shapes. It took her awhile to recall where she was and that she had been dreaming again. Breathing deeply, she lay back in Steele's bed. She closed her eyes and welcomed the memory she had repressed for so long. The memory of waking late one night and looking out her bedroom window as a child and seeing Steele, with a small, brown creature on his shoulder become something other than Steele. Something big and gray with four legs and beautiful golden eyes. She had watched him morph into something that should have frightened her but excited her instead.

Had it been a dream? Or like the memory of the length of his shaft, was it real? She frowned. What had just happened wasn't exactly a dream. And yet it certainly had not been real. She sighed, suspecting that neither was her "vision" of having seen Steele's cock. She had never actually seen him nude or seen him morph. Certainly not when she was a child. So how had she known he could change and his cock was huge. On his visits to her home, she had never thought to look at his groin and even if she had, she was now certain that she would have seen nothing. If he was unwilling to touch her now, he certainly would not have allowed her to see him nude at her home. So how did she know things she had no real way of knowing?

She had two months to find out. Thoughts of him made her feel overheated. She kicked off the cover and unbuttoned his shirt. Her pussy throbbed and without thinking, she reached around in the dark until her hand encountered Steele's cup. She placed the cup over her pussy and gave a startled squeak when it seemed to cling to her skin.

She shot up in bed and turned on the light. The formerly white support cup now looked and felt like dark leather. More importantly, instead of just resting between her legs, it fit snugly over her pussy. And what felt like a thick, moist tongue was actually thrust part way in her pussy.

Gazing down, she saw it move up and down, almost as if it were breathing in and out. She should definitely be afraid. The cup almost seemed alive and sentient, for heaven's sakes. Somehow, she was not afraid. How could she be afraid of something that was a part of Steele? She knew Pen would never hurt her. And having him inside her was almost as nice as having Steele inside her.

Feeling comforted and strangely excited, she turned out the lights and lay back in the bed on her back with her legs pressed close together. She felt the cup, Pen, making soft inhalations against her skin and felt a tingle go through her. With thoughts of Steele making her go damp, she drifted to sleep. As she slept, Pen, who had been reared especially for Acier, continued the gentle inhalations and easy quarter thrusts in her so that even as she slept, a pleasant jolt danced along her body.

* * * * *

Deoctra Diniti, weary and more frightened than she had ever been in her entire one hundred and one years, quietly moved down the back roads of the red-light district of the city. Although the shoulder wound she had suffered at the hands of the vicious rogue vampire Vladimir Madison had healed and she again felt able to defend herself from most threats, she feared she had lost some of her spirit. She had suffered much grief in the last year and a half. Not only had she lost her bloodlust, Mikhel Dumont to a human whore but she had lost her two sisters to the vengeance of Palea and Mikhel Dumont. Worse, she didn't dare return home. Her mere presence would endanger her surviving sisters, respectively twenty-two and twenty-nine.

She felt an ache followed by a terrible anger and emptiness when she recalled her lost sisters, Katrina and

Mitclena. At thirty-eight and forty-two years old, they'd had so much life ahead of them. They had missed so much. They had never blood-feasted or even known bloodlust. To be cut down so cruelly for sins that were not their own. Just the memory of their deaths made her ache deep in her heart.

Remembering the words of Elaina Delmarco, a full-blood with whom she had a strange friendship, she bristled. Despite the other fem's words, she would not, could not, admit that her sisters had been dispatched because of her actions. Although Elaina was older, she considered blood-feasting beneath her and had never bloodlusted. As a consequence, Elaina did not understand the power and might of bloodlust.

To a vampire there was nothing more powerful than the wedding of a consuming lust for blood and sex with a single individual who then became the vampire's reason for living, his or her bloodlust. Despite Elaina's words, whispered to her as they had clung together sobbing over the loss of Katrina and Mitclena, Deoctra knew she'd had a moral right to seek vengeance for the grievous wrong done her. Still, had she known the great price attached to seeking out that vengeance, she would not have taken her precious little sisters with her.

She gave an angry shake of her head. She could not afford to dwell on the past or to wallow in misery. She couldn't help her dead sisters but there were living sisters who needed her. In order to help them, she had to first survive. To ensure that, she must satisfy her hungers. She needed blood and she desperately wanted a hard, hot cock up her ass. She was afraid and depressed and a few nights of having a handsome full-blood fuck her breathless would surely lift her spirits. Such a tryst might even infuse her with the sense of power she found highly exhilarating.

And yet, would she be able to trust that a full-blood wouldn't know who she was and know that both the Dumonts and the Madisons were out to dispatch her? She sighed with regret, deciding she was not yet strong or confident enough to risk seeking out a full-blood or even a latent. It would have to be a human male, she supposed. She spat on the ground in anger. How she longed to be united in lust and bloodlust with one of her own kind. But for some reason, God had chosen to forsake her again. First with the loss of her parents and now this on top of losing Mikhel. Elaina said it was wrong to blame God but who else was there to blame?

Who else could have prevented all the tragedies that had befallen her since the death of her beloved parents? It was all well and good for Elaina, surrounded by a loving family, to insist Deoctra had brought some of the grief in her life on herself. Elaina had never known any real pain or hurt so she did not understand how Deoctra felt.

She heard the squeal of wheels behind her and turned quickly, crouching. From that position, she propelled her body up into the air just in time to avoid being run over by some lunatic human on a motorcycle with long, dark hair flying loose and wild.

"Human whore!" she spat out angrily as she landed on her feet. "You will pay dearly for your recklessness."

The driver wheeled the bike around and came to a stop, facing her, putting down the kickstand.

Staring at him with the big, gleaming silver and black bike between his long, muscular, leather-clad legs, left her almost breathless. There was something about a handsome man with long, dark hair wearing leather and riding a bike that she found incredibly erotic and irresistible. She wet her lips and felt her desire blazing. The driver was tall and powerfully built. She guessed he was roughly six-foot-four-inches and about two hundred twenty pounds. Waves of long dark hair cascaded around wide shoulders. A pair of thick, sinfully long lashes adorned silver-gray eyes that burned with unmitigated lust. His mouth, with its full, sensual bottom lip, taunted her, heightening her passions. She cast her gaze downward. A thick cock, almost as long as her forearm, lay along the side of one of his legs. God Almighty, what a weapon!

Her nostrils flared and the blood pounded in her head. His monster cock was emitting the most incredible aroma. Inhaling it, she felt her pussy gushing and her behind begin to tingle. She had found her lover for the night. She looked at his cock again, pulsing along his leg almost as if it possessed a life of its own. Maybe she'd keep him for a few nights. A cock of that magnitude would take some time to savor and fully enjoy.

"Human. I will take you to my bed for a night or two of passion beyond your wildest dreams," she told him, putting a hand down to rub against her aching pussy.

"I wouldn't count on that, honey. I have quite an imagination," he pointed out in a voice that was both deep and hypnotic. It sent tingles of lust through her, causing her to go damp.

Although he exuded sensuality like only one other full-blood vampire she'd known, she knew he was not a vampire. At least, she didn't think he was. And yet he wasn't human either. Of that much she was certain. Whatever he was, she didn't much care for his attitude. During their brief time together, she would teach him to respect his betters while she gave him the thrill of what might be a very short life.

She walked over to the bike and boldly cupped her hand over his cock. "I am Deoctra Diniti, full-blood vampire."

"You announce that as if I should I be impressed."

Her eyes glowed and she resisted the urge to backhand him off the bike and across the road. If she beat him, he would be in no shape to stand the fucking she was going to give him. Nevertheless, she would teach him a little respect.

"You will be before the night is over," she warned. "For the next few days and nights, I will be your mistress and you will become my lustful and obedient slave."

He annoyed and angered her by tossing back his handsome head and roaring with laughter. She snarled and slapped him hard several times. His laughter ceased and he surprised her by catching her hand in his as she attempted to slap him again.

She jerked her hand away and rewarded him with yet another slap. This time she struck him just hard enough to show him who was in charge. She had no desire to mar his handsome face. "Do we understand each other now, human?"

His eyes burned with angry lights that she found highly arousing. The thought that he might challenge her sent a brief surge of desire soaring through her. If he chose to challenge her, she would blood-feast on him. If he survived, he'd show the next full-blood who's path he crossed the proper respect. If he did not, so be it.

In the end, he lowered his beautiful lashes and inclined his head slightly. "As you wish."

"Yes," she said confidently. "It will be exactly as I wish. Be mindful of that and you may yet live a little longer."

He inclined his head again.

Chapter Seven

❧

Even as he acquiesced, she suspected he would bear watching. There was a raw wildness about him that intrigued her. His hair, so dark and thick, covered his handsome face. That she did not want. She reached out a hand and brushed the heavy curtain back and palmed his cheek. "I have a small quiet cottage near here deep in the woods. We will go there and I will undress you and discover the secrets of your big, beautiful body and fuck you again and again, all night long. This night you will know joy beyond compare in the ass of a full-blood vampire."

"I want some pussy."

"You'll take what I give you and show the proper respect or else. Is that understood?"

He breathed in deeply but remained silent, as befitted an inferior in the presence of a superior being. Yet his masculinity called to her.

Unable to resist his allure, she leaned forward and kissed his mouth, sucking at his full, sensual bottom lip and rubbing her hand along his thick pole. His cock jerked against her fingers and she caught her breath. She glanced around. The road was deserted and dark except for the light provided by the full moon. The trip back to her place in the woods would take but twenty minutes but her behind tingled and she was impatient.

She had been too long without cock and she would wait no longer. She tugged at the back of her clothing and the hidden buttons there opened and she felt the warm night air on her bare ass. Yes. Good, but not good enough. She quickly removed the one-piece cat suit. She stood before him naked and proud, confident he would find her petite body with the small, firm breasts, tiny waist and dark, hair-covered pussy, irresistible as many men, human and vampire before him had.

He made a low growling noise in his throat and she felt gratified. It was as she thought. Any non-vampire male would be highly honored by the opportunity of fucking a full-blood fem like her.

Tossing her cat suit on the seat behind him, she eagerly unzipped his pants and slipped her hand inside, greedy to feel his weapon.

Her fingers encountered one of the biggest, thickest cocks she had ever felt. Licking her lips and filled with lust, she stuck her other hand inside and carefully, almost reverently drew his shaft from his pants. It was a thing of absolute beauty, thick and long with a big dark helmeted head. Oh the depths a cock of these proportions would reach and the joy it would bring her. She swallowed, feeling almost faint with hunger to be ravished by that monster.

Holding his hot, heavy dick in one greedy hand, she stuck the fingers of her other hand into her creaming pussy. She then thrust first one and a second creamed finger up her rear to lube it. She loved having her ass banged and didn't need much lubrication.

She withdrew her fingers and stared into his silver-gray gaze, baring her incisors and allowing her eyes to glow with lust. "I will have you now on the way to my cottage."

He put a hand down to rub his cock, which was fully and so gloriously erect. "Where is your cottage?"

"It is back up this road. Take a right at the fork and continue until you see a small cottage with a tiled roof amongst an opening in the trees. That is where I will fuck you all night, my handsome one."

"Then let us hope it will be a long night," he said, his voice almost a growl. "Because I have a powerful need for sex."

"It is a need I will totally satisfy, my handsome one." She pushed his hand away and palmed his cock. "Tonight you will experience carnal pleasure as never before."

His cock jerked in her hand and his eyes burned with a light of lust that nearly took her breath away. She breathed in deeply. The aroma from his cock was incredibly intoxicating.

She had to taste him. "But first a little taste of your cock." She leaned down and kissed the head of his dick. It pulsed and shook against her lips, leaking small streams of pre-cum. *Hmm.* Delicious. She loved the smell of the seed of a handsome, well-hung man.

Licking and slurping greedily, she cleaned his cock head. Purring softly, she ran her tongue along the big head, delighting in the taste of him against her tongue. This close the lusty smell of his cock made her nipples tighten.

She gently compressed her mouth and inched forward, slowly sucking a few inches of his shaft between her lips. There were few things more wonderful than swallowing a big, hot piece of cock. His shaft was tangy and luscious, reminding her somewhat of Mikhel Dumont's lovely weapon. Her pussy creamed as she remembered the rare times she had joyfully blown her lost bloodlust. She had never expected to meet another male with a cock to compare to his in sheer deliciousness. And yet this cock was just as sumptuous. It was certainly bigger and thicker.

Closing her eyes and pretending she was with Mikhel, she wrapped her lips tight around his shaft. Palming his balls, she licked and sucked his cock, savoring the taste and texture of him.

The sound of his deep-chested groans excited her already heightened passions and she increased the pressure of her mouth, sucking hard. Good but she needed more cock. She eased more of his shaft into her mouth. Nice. Very nice. Beyond nice. Wonderful.

A big hand descended on the back of her head and the next thing she knew her mouth and throat were filled to the brim with hot, pulsing cock. Feeling almost feral and consumed with cock-lust, she sucked strongly on his shaft while gently squeezing his balls. He made grunting noises and thrust his entire cock down her throat.

She closed her eyes and sucked harder. She felt his whole body tremble and delighted in the knowledge that he was about to come. Her pussy throbbing with need, she continued to suck and pump him until he shuddered and began blasting a flood of cum against her tonsils and down her throat.

Gagging, she gave up trying to get away and began swallowing as quickly as she could but he came and came until the overflow trickled down the side of her mouth. With her face pressed tight against his pubic hair, she felt almost as if she were in danger of being suffocated. What a lovely, lovely feeling.

Finally, he released his grip on the back of her head and breathed deeply, his cock still hard and in her mouth.

Trembling with a monumental surge of cock-lust, she peeled her lips off his shaft. Licking the seed from her lips and chin, she lifted her head. He lay back against the high seatback. His silver-gray eyes glittered with a lust as old as time. She found the depths of his lust quite alluring. She could not recall ever being fortunate enough to encounter such unmitigated passion. Excellent. He would need to have a strong sex drive because she intended to ride his cock all night long. When he went limp, she had ways to get him hard again, even if he didn't want to cooperate. In fact, it might be rather exciting to take him against his will.

She reached out and casually ripped open his shirt. A mass of dark, curly hair adorned the wide expanse of his chest. She ran her fingers through it. It felt silky and at the same time rather coarse. An exciting combination. She inhaled quickly and looked up at him. "Now, my big cock-slave, we fuck," she told him.

He reached out and cupped his hands over her breasts. Tingles of pleasure shot straight down to her cunt. He tweaked her small nipples before stroking his hands down to her stomach and then over her ass. Feelings of sensual delight assailed her. She felt almost lightheaded. She had to have him inside her soon. But for now she had other needs.

"I'll have a taste of your cock now, slave." Sighing in anticipation, she turned, lifted her leg over the bike and then shoved down.

The big head of his cock pressed against her ass. A wave of heat and need shuddered through her. The last time she'd had a really big cock up her rear end, Serge Dumont, Mikhel's younger brother, had fucked her. Serge had a big dick and that fuck outside a girls' school in Boston had been one of the hottest and most enjoyable fucks of her life. She had a feeling the coming fuck would rival if not exceed that fuck.

This strange, handsome male's cock was even bigger than Serge's and she suspected the night would be wild and wickedly delicious. Just contemplating what delights the night would bring made her hungry and so ready to feel herself being nearly split by his huge cock.

He groaned and grabbed her hips with his big hands. Before she could tell him to go slow so she could savor the slide of his cock into her, he gave a rough, powerful pull on her hips and the head of his dick plowed into her ass.

"*Aaahhh!*" she gasped and involuntarily lifted her hips.

But he shocked her with a quick, powerful yank down.

"Oh God!" she cried out as he shot his large, hot shaft balls-deep into her rectum with one unbelievably painful movement.

With her ass feeling as if it were about to burst, she collapsed back against his chest, gasping and sucking air into her lungs. She closed her eyes, almost afraid to breathe. She needed a few moments to adjust to having her ass invaded by such a big, thick shaft.

It was an opportunity she didn't get. Before she could voice her wishes, he released his kickstand and keeping one black leather-clad arm firmly around her tiny waist to hold her behind tight against his groin, he sent his bike roaring down the road and his cock pounding in and out of her stuffed ass.

"*Ahhh!!*" She shuddered as a wall of white-hot pain sliced through her. Allowing the fingers of one hand to stray from her waist, he found the entrance to her cunt and began finger fucking her while roughly rubbing his thumb against her clit.

She moaned and attempted to lift herself off his lap to get a respite from the dick so mercilessly hammering the tender tissue of her ass. Growling in protest against her ear, he pulled his fingers out of her pussy and clamped his arm around her waist again, dragging her ass back down onto his torpedoing cock.

Although it hurt, she loved rough and sometimes painful sex. So even while she squirmed in an apparent attempt to get away from him, she was loving every second of their fuck.

With the full moon over head, her ass stuffed full of the biggest cock she'd ever had, the warm night air brushing across her bared breasts and creaming pussy and the motion of the bike under them, she gave up the struggle of trying to climb off him and surrendered to the pain that had become an almost unbearable pleasure. She longed for him to slap her ass until it was red and stingy but somehow couldn't bring herself to let him know how much she loved pain with sex.

She closed her eyes and lay back against him moaning in agony of unadulterated bliss as he drilled his hot cock up her ass with a speed and power that belied the possibility that he might be even remotely human. Whatever he was, he was giving her ass the most staggering fuck she'd ever had. He pounded his pole up her with a force that nearly took her breath and left her writhing in pain while drowning in the most succulent pleasure.

God Almighty, she'd never felt anything this shattering and totally consuming.

The fingers of his big hand found her cunt again and he dug them inside with little regard for whether they brought pleasure or pain. She gasped and tried to jerk away. It had been a very long time since she'd felt anything other than her own fingers in her cunt and his felt like miniature steel poles slicing through her. It had been entirely too long since she'd had anything even remotely like a cock in her cunt. The last time she'd had anything inside her had been the night she had confronted Mikhel in the hotel room with his human whore. After a fierce fight, she had managed to impale herself on Mikhel's wonderful cock. While his cock had not been as large as Serge's, it had been the sweetest shaft she'd ever had inside her.

She had savored his beloved cock for several brief but wonderful moments. Although he had initially resisted, he had eventually succumbed to the pleasure of her pussy. While his human whore looked on in horror, she and her bloodlust had fucked with a passion and fury as only two vampires could. Oh her Mik—

"*Ahhh!*" Her thoughts of Mikhel were shattered when the male under her gave a particularly violent series of brutal thrusts up her ass that caused the night stars to explode inside her head. Her incisors appeared and her eyes glowed and she screamed in agony and desire as she came, drenching his fingers in the juices that flowed freely and copiously from her body.

Letting out a low animal like growl, he rotated his powerful hips and dug his cock as deep up her ass as he could get it and blasted her full of jet after jet of his seed.

She cried out again, squirming on his lap, eager to receive every drop of his seed and to keep him buried deep and hard inside her. There were few pleasures as enticing as feeling her insides being liberally hosed down with the seed of a big, rough male who appreciated the joy of fucking a really good piece of fem ass.

The bike swerved along the road as they both came, moaning, groaning and fighting to hold onto their shared ecstasy for as long as possible. Finally, his cock stopped jumping and pumping in her and she emerged from her frenzy of satisfaction.

Feeling relieved that her ass was about to get a break, she slumped back against him, breathing deeply and waited for him to withdraw the monster he called a cock from her rear end.

But instead of giving her a needed respite even after he came, he kept his arm clamped tight around her waist and continued to pound her now battered ass so hard and furiously, it began to burn.

"Oh!" she moaned. "Oh God!"

His only response was to bite into the back of her neck and thump her ass harder. Pain sliced through her, quickly followed by a bliss that nearly destroyed her reason. She shuddered and felt her cunt and ass catch fire again. Fighting through the waves of pain, she cried out, dug her hands into his strong thighs and thumped her hips up and down with piston-like power and speed.

"Shove it all the way up me! Now! Give it all to me!"

He fucked his large cock up into her bruised ass like a male possessed and she, caught in the grip of a hunger for cock and pain like none she'd ever felt, filled the night air with her cries of distress and joy. And still he fucked on and on until she repeatedly exploded on his rampaging cock.

Finally, when her ass burned so badly she doubted she could bear anymore, he lifted her body with one hand and withdrew his cock from her busted ass. She moaned in agony and slumped back against him, tears streaming down her cheeks.

"I will kill you for this!" she warned.

"You'll kill me for giving you what you demanded?" He pressed his warm lips against her ear and laughed. "I look forward to you trying, bitch!" He licked the side of her neck. "We've arrived." He brought the bike to a stop and put down the kickstand. "Will you kill me now or after we have another fuck, bitch?"

Bitch. She had killed the last human man who had dared call her bitch. Yet the word on his lips sent a licentious thrill through her. She suspected he hadn't intended it to be a compliment but her pussy creamed and she knew she would have to have this male at least for the night. After that she would kill him for his insolence and daring to fuck her nearly senseless.

"Do not make the mistake of forgetting who you are dealing with," she warned. "I hold your life in my hands."

"Don't count on that!" he shot back. "My life is in my own hands."

She bared her incisors. The arrogant bastard would have to die, after she'd had her fill of him.

She reached a hand between their legs and fondled his cock, still hard. It would be a crime against the entire female universe to harm a male in possession of such an addictive cock, particularly when he wielded it with some force and authority. No, she decided rather reluctantly. Killing him was out of the question but beating him was not. Perhaps she would blood-feast on him.

She knew Elaina would advise against it, counseling that it was not morally right or just for a vampire to take a physically inferior person and nearly drain him of blood while fucking him into a stupor. Her lips tightened. Elaina was not around to caution her and she had needs. In addition, he needed to be taught to respect his betters.

Chapter Eight

ಐ

Acier sat on his bike, watching the small, petite vampire alight. The cheeks of her tight ass looked enticing in the glow of the full moon. His hands itched as he thought of how nice it would be to slap those tiny, round cheeks as he fucked her. Her ass was made for slapping and fucking. He thought of another ass, bigger, rounder, darker. Raven's. His cock hardened and he swallowed as he wondered what it would be like to fuck Raven's ass. Oh God, how he wanted her. He could almost taste his need for her.

But he could not touch Raven. He dared not. He had to make do with this woman. He sighed with regret. The aroma of the fem's aroused cunt carried on the winds of the gentle breeze reached him. He inhaled deeply, deciding his lot wasn't so bad. His cock was ramrod hard, his balls tight and filled with cum.

The appetizer they had shared on the road had only increased his hunger for blood, pussy and ass. And although if given a choice, he would have chosen the sweet, sultry temptress he had left behind over this arrogant and self-important fem bitch who actually thought he'd tried to run her over, the call of his dual natures had to be satisfied.

He was still struggling to learn to control his conflicting natures. Sometimes he was successful, sometimes he was not. If he were to lose control and shift and become rough with a female, better it should be this full-blood fem than Raven, sweet and delicious and unfortunately off-limits to him. His cock threatened to explode as he thought of her. God, he'd never wanted any woman more.

"Move your ass, slave and get inside. I want some more cock."

He pulled his thoughts back from contemplating Raven's smooth dark beauty to find the fem standing in the doorway of the small cottage. Her legs were parted and he could see a steady stream of his cum oozing along the side of one creamy thigh from her ass.

He clenched his jaw, fighting back the urge to shift into his natural form, charge her, tumble her to her hands and knees and pound her ass shifter-style while he howled at the moon. He wasn't into taking any woman by force, even this arrogant fem but the thought of subduing her held definite appeal. Only one thing would make this better, if Etienne were there with him to share in the sexual bounty of the coming night.

His balls hardened at the thought. He and Etienne had not shared a woman in a very long time. Both their sexual appetites were so fierce, any woman they shared would have to be something more than human.

"I do not intend to wait all night while you daydream, slave. Move your ass or I will move it for you!"

He narrowed his gaze and compressed his lips. This fem was starting to get on his last damned nerve. If he weren't so horny and in such need he would roar away on his bike and find another, more agreeable woman to spend the night with. But needy shifters couldn't be choosey. And she'd already demonstrated that she could take a hard, rough fucking.

He turned his bike off, grabbed his keys and slowly padded on the balls of his feet across the ground to her, his cock sticking out of his pants and beginning to drip pre-cum. He was going to fuck her ass but good. When he finished with her she would barely be able to walk. He would show her who the fuck was in charge.

When he reached her, she enclosed his cock in a small, tiny but strong hand. Gritting his teeth, he allowed himself to be led inside with her hand wrapped firmly around his cock as if she thought he would try to escape before she got another fuck. The greedy bitch should be so lucky.

Once inside the lushly furnished bedroom, she moved around him in a swift dark blur pulling his shoes and clothes off until he stood in front of her wearing nothing but his protruding cock. "I think you will do for a night or two," she told him.

He had no desire to spend more than one night with her. He narrowed his gaze and stared silently at her.

Licking her narrow pink lips, she moved across the room to the big brass bed where she lay with her legs splayed open, giving him a perfect view of her cunt. "Come eat my pussy, slave!" she commanded.

His nostrils flared.

When in heat, the tang of a willing pussy always drove him a little nuts. And here was a woman he didn't need to fear hurting. He could and would fuck her as hard as he liked. The thought sent him quickly across the room to join her, lying between her legs on the huge bed. Closing his eyes, he took several long moments to deeply inhale her scent. Rather nice and cock arousing.

But he had drooled enough. It was time to fuck and suck. He growled and slipped his fingers into her pussy. She felt warm and damp, ready for action. He felt his eyes begin to glow and his incisors descending as her scent engulfed him. He finger fucked her roughly. When she started to moan and jerk her slender hips off the bed, he fastened his mouth over her clit and sucked hard.

"Oooh! Oh yes! Suck my cunt and make me come, slave!" she cried, clutching her hands against the back of his head and smashing his face into her groin. Fighting to keep from shifting, he sucked and licked and thrust his fingers into her pussy until she wrapped her thighs around his head and began gushing into his mouth.

Unable to control himself completely, he allowed his tongue to shift and pushed his shifted digit deep into her cunt, lapping up all the pungent juices flowing so freely from her climaxing pussy. The smell and taste of her kept his cock rock hard. He had to stick it into a willing receptacle. Now. As she laid moaning and shuddering through her climax, he rose over her, parted her cheeks, ejaculated into her puckered hole and ignoring her wet pussy, thrust his cock up her ass with a powerful movement.

"Oh God Almighty!" she cried, her glowing eyes flying open. "That hurts so good!"

She attempted to push him off of her but he pressed his full two hundred twenty pounds on her tiny body that couldn't weigh much more than one hundred and ten pounds tops.

"It's about to hurt even more, bitch!" he told her and drove his cock up her ass again. He'd had tighter asses but none he could fuck this deeply and roughly without worrying about doing serious damage to his partner. Without being vain, he knew the length and thickness of his cock had few equals either among human males or the members of Pack Gautier. He knew his lovers got off just a little more knowing how big and thick he was. More importantly, he knew *she* was getting off on the size of his shaft and didn't really want him to stop until she had come again.

She had asked for this and damn if he wasn't going to give it to her. Holding her small wrists tight in his hands above her head, he grunted with satisfaction as he rotated his hips and fucked his full, aching length up her, fighting his way into her warm, moist, tight ass. Shit. It felt good. He thrust in deep and hard. Hmm. Nice. Very nice.

"Ahhh!" She gasped, her entire tiny body shuddering. "Your cock is so hard and stiff!" She tried to jerk her hands loose. He was about to retain his grip when he decided against it. He didn't want her to learn just yet that he was her physical match for strength and stamina. He pretended to gasp in surprise when she pulled her wrists away.

Her palm, making contact with his cheek several times in rapid succession as she repeatedly struck him, stung. He got even by ramming his cock up her ass so hard and fast, she moaned and collapsed back against the bed, her eyes widening, her mouth parting and her body trembling wildly. "Oooh! Oooh!"

He took advantage of her surrender to shove his cock balls deep up her tiny hot ass. Damn. It felt so good to have his entire dick slamming into her. He was going to bust her tiny little ass open. He felt his climax building. Turning them over so she was on top, he grabbed her slender waist in his hands and began bouncing her up and down on his long shaft. As he jerked her down, he shot his dick up into her. Damn good. She had a fine piece of ass for a fem.

As he lay on his back with her above him, her delicate ass still firmly impaled on his cock. Releasing her waist, he rained his palms down on her tiny cheeks, slapping them hard and fast until they quivered and she went wild on top of him, screaming and grinding herself on his cock.

"Ahhh! Ahhh!"

He bit into her neck and fucked on, working hard towards his orgasm. He smelled her pussy creaming and rolled them on to their sides so he could stab his fingers into her cunt and brush her clit.

"Ooooh!" she screamed and drenched his fingers as she came in a blast of heat, pussy juice and wonderful fragrance.

Growling deep with a sense of animal satisfaction at the obvious pleasure she received at the end of his cock, he fucked on, drilling her rear with a gusto and delight that drove him over the edge and shattered her into yet another climax. He came quickly, flooding her with his seed.

"Ooooh," she moaned, her ass muscles clamping down on his shaft and milking the last drop of seed from his cock.

He rolled over so that he lay atop her again. He groaned and shuddered and laid his weight against her. She was so tiny he had the sensation that if she weren't a hard-as-nails fem, he would have crushed her. But she was what she was and he had no need to worry about damaging her—at least not permanently.

With his cock still in her ass, he lazily pinched her small nipples until she snarled in protest and slapped his hand angrily. "Sadist! Take your big paws off my breasts and your monstrosity out of my ass!" she ordered. "Now, you insolent fucker. Remove it!"

He complied but only because he needed a piss. Slapping her ass hard enough to make the small cheek turn red, he started to ease his cock out. When it had finally cleared her quivering ass, she whirled and slapped him across his lips. "Do that again and I will kill you where you lay, slave! I am Deoctra Diniti, full-blood fem and I am in charge here! Forget that again at your peril!"

He stared at her, his stomach tight with the effort not to shift and show this bitch the error of attacking one of his kind. Still, if she hit him one more time, he would shift and rip her throat open and feast on her blood.

"Strike me again, bitch, and you won't live long enough to spout that vampire shit of yours!" he warned. He rose and headed across the room to the door.

She sucked in her breath and he turned to find her staring at him, fingering her pussy, her dark eyes gleaming with an almost unabated lust. His threat turned her on. Greedy bitch! He turned and padded out the room. As he left, he noted that there was an interesting contraption attached to the wall to the right of the door. He knew just what to do with it.

In the bathroom, he urinated, thinking of Raven. What was she doing? Was she thinking of him? God, how he wished he were with her. He gave an angry shake of his head. No! He could not, he would not fuck her! He was lucky that Mo was almost like a father to him. He could not betray Mo's trust.

He took a deep breath and stared at his reflection in the mirror. His eyes, as they sometimes did when he was in heat, had turned a deep gold. He glanced down and saw that his lower body was covered with pelt from his thighs down to his feet or rather, his paws. He still retained most of his humanoid form, at least for now.

Not that he was a wolf in the traditional sense as humans thought of wolves or werewolves. Although the moon did have an undeniable effect on him, unlike the other members of his pack his age, excluding Etienne, he did not have to shift at the full moon. He supposed he could thank the vampire part of his nature which made him strong enough to control his desire to shift. But when he was in heat, as now, he didn't always want to control the shift. He was a wolf-shifter. And when he was in heat, he wanted everyone, especially his lovers, to know what he was.

He tossed his head, sending his hair flying around his shoulders. The fem who thought she could enslave Acier Gautier was about to learn better.

Padding back into the bedroom, he found her curled into a fetal position, sleeping. Good. He had a surprise for her. He went outside to retrieve his prowling kit from his side bag and tensed, his nostrils flaring.

"I am Acier Gautier, Alpha of Den Gautier. Show yourself, beta!" he ordered softly, catching the scent of one of his kind in the surrounding woods.

A small, red she-wolf with patches of red on her head, ears and legs padded into the circle of the moonlight with her tail down and her head bowed in submission as befitted a beta in the presence of an Alpha.

I am Zoe'Achon, beta under Supreme Alpha Aime Gautier. He has dispatched me to warn you that Den Alpha Leon de la Rocque is coming to challenge you for the position of Supreme Alpha-in-waiting of Pack Gautier.

He frowned. Why hadn't Xavier come to him with this news? Was there also trouble brewing in Den Gautier that kept his second-in-command too busy to report to him? Shit. Xay was more than competent to handle most den problems, or cousin or not he wouldn't have chosen him to lead his den in his absence. It was probably time he took care of his own business and gave up the fruitless search for his sperm donor father. It was times like these that he missed having Etienne around. Alone, he had never met a wolf-shifter who could stand up to him. With Etienne, he had never met even an entire rival den willing to go up against them.

But he and Etienne had long ago realized that their diverse interests would keep them apart for long periods of time. Nevertheless, it would be nice to have Etienne around more. Still, Etienne had made his choice and Acier himself had other considerations now.

This was a fine time for Leon, his hitherto life-long friend, to get delusions of grandeur. And it wouldn't be much of a contest. Leon, a gray like Acier, and one of the biggest of the purebreds in all the dens that comprised Pack Gautier, was one hundred and twenty pounds in wolf form and thirty-five inches tall. Xay was one hundred and forty pounds and thirty-eight inches tall. Acier, a hybrid gray, was one hundred and eighty pounds and forty-five inches tall in the *au naturel*. In human form Leon, one of the tallest of the Alphas at five-foot-eleven, while not exactly slender, was no physical match for Xay who was six-foot-two and nearly one hundred and ninety pounds. Neither of the other wolf-shifters were a match for Acier nor Etienne in size, speed or power. Acier could sustain incredible speeds for long distances. Etienne was the only other wolf-shifters who was a physical match for him and these days he rarely shifted.

Thanks to their vampire blood, although he and Etienne had occasionally encountered a wolf bigger, they has always been more powerful, faster and when the occasion demanded, more vicious. So even though he was not a purebred he was a natural to be Supreme Alpha when Aime could no longer carry on. If he so desired. And if he didn't, Xay, a purebred gray, would make a better Supreme Alpha than Leon who tended to think more of himself than he should. Etienne had long since made his lack of desire to be even a Den Alpha clear. If Leon didn't care to have his purebred ass kicked in front of his den, he had better come alone.

"You have delivered your message, beta. Return to the Alpha Supreme and convey my greetings and good wishes for his continued health and tell him I, like all in the pack, am his humble servant."

Yes, Alpha. Keeping her head bowed and her tail down, the beta vanished into the night.

He watched her go. The time was fast approaching when he would have to make a choice between continuing to pursue a father who did not wish to be found and ascending to Supreme Alpha. He might even have to consider abdicating his Den Alpha status in favor of Xay but that would be more difficult than giving up the status of Supreme Alpha-in-waiting. He fiercely loved the shifters in his den and would gladly die to protect each and every one of them. Entrusting their welfare on a permanent basis to anyone else would feel like abandoning them.

Chapter Nine

ഇ

He caught the scent of the fem's pussy and his nostrils flared. But that was a choice for another day. This night was made for fucking and feasting. And fuck he would. If Leon knew what was good for him, he had better not arrive before he finished his fuck-feast. As an Alpha he was easy-going, allowing the shifters in his den to make most of their own choices as long as they didn't get out of hand. But they all knew better than to interrupt him in the midst of a fuck-feast, all save Etienne who marched to his own drummer regardless of what tune the band played.

Thinking of his twin, he smiled, then sighed. He missed Etienne and the puphood romps through the woods in their natural forms they'd shared. He heard the approach of a vehicle and tensed. He was in no mood to have his night of lust interrupted.

A big, dark luxury SUV appeared on the narrow road in front of him. His felt a surge of delight as he caught the scent of the driver through the open moon roof.

"Pup! It's good to see you!"

He hurried forward as the SUV came to a quiet stop and Etienne got out with a big smile on his face, his arms extended. "Sei! I've been missing you!"

They embraced and pressed warm kisses on each other's cheeks before Acier stiffened and abruptly pulled away. "Etienne! What the fuck have you done?"

* * * * *

Etienne sighed and considered Acier in silence for several moments, uncertain how to respond. Acier was the older twin having been born an hour ahead of him during a difficult birthing that had nearly killed all three of them. Although Etienne was in fact two inches taller and about ten pounds heavier, in every way that counted, Acier was the "big" brother who had always strove to shield and protect him. Not that he'd needed much protection. Now he sensed a barely leased anger in Acier, directed toward him. He thought guiltily of Raven's underwear still stuffed in his pockets. Perhaps he should have given them back to her after all.

He shrugged. "What do you mean, Sei?"

Acier's eyes narrowed and for a moment Etienne thought he would pull Raven's underwear from his pockets. Acier leveled an angry finger at him. "You know exactly what I mean. I can *smell* her scent on you, pup."

Acier's meaning when he used the term pup was arbitrary. Sometimes he used it affectionately, sometimes when he was angry, like now. He stifled a sigh. It was a good thing he and Raven hadn't gone all the way or he would have had a rough time peeling Acier's fingers from around his neck. "I suppose you're talking about Raven."

"You suppose right, Etienne! I can smell her satisfaction on you! You have about two minutes to explain why you touched her."

There was an air of menace emanating from Acier that he had never expected to find directed at him. "Or?" he asked quietly.

"Explain what you've done and there will be no need to answer the *or* part."

"And if I choose not to explain? What? You'll beat my ass?"

Acier raked a hand through his hair. "Etienne! Why the fuck did you touch her? How could you?"

"Why shouldn't I have? She's an adult and there's no relationship between the two of you. She told me you didn't even so much as give her a lousy hug. Why the hell should it bother you if she and I pleasured each other?"

Acier's eyes glowed, his lips parted and his incisors appeared. "Etienne! She's Mo's baby! He entrusted me with her care! How dare you wait until I leave and sneak in there and fuck her? Explain your actions. Now, Etienne!"

Etienne decided he had teased Acier long enough. If he didn't 'fess up soon, he really would have to worry about Acier shifting and going feral on him. He put a hand on Acier's arm and promptly had it shaken off. He sighed. "I did not fuck her, Acier."

"She came, Etienne! I can smell her satisfaction on you!"

He shrugged. "Of course she came. Every woman I set out to please comes, Acier. You know it but that does not mean I fucked her. I didn't. Use that nose of yours and you'll realize that although she came, I did not."

Acier stood silently, bouncing on the balls of his feet as he did when he was about to attack. Etienne took a step back then stopped. He and Acier had never had a physical confrontation. And they wouldn't now. They did not keep secrets or lie to each other. They were too close. Acier would know that he spoke the truth.

Acier sighed and allowed his shoulders to relax. "Even so, pup, you shouldn't have touched her!"

Pup, spoke with that under current of warmth Acier always saved for him alone. They were all right with each other again. "Acier, she came a long way to see you. Hell, you know she wanted more than just to see you and yet you left her to come here. How do you think that made her feel?"

"You think I wanted to leave? I had no choice. She's Mo's baby. What the hell do you think he's going to say when he finds out you've been playing with her?"

He sighed. He was no more eager to incur Mo's wrath than Acier's. "I know he's going to want a piece of my ass but she was feeling lonely and unwanted, Sei. She needed cheering up. I cheered her up."

Acier's right hand shot out and clamped against the back of his neck. "What did you do to her?"

"I-I ate her and I sucked her breasts but I kept Slayer on. I didn't fuck her, Acier."

He could feel Acier probing his mind, something he had not done in years. He offered no resistance, leaving his thoughts open to the male who was so much more than a brother and twin to him. Acier was part of who he was.

"I can't believe she let you undress her and—"

He jerked away and shook his head. "What the hell kind of shit is this, Acier? She has as much right to enjoy sex as anyone. Why the hell shouldn't she? After all, you're here fucking for all you're worth and she knows it and yet you expect her to just sit there waiting for you to come back? Why the hell should she?"

Acier took what sounded like a deep, tortured breath. "You don't understand, Tee. I-I feel… I can't explain how I feel about her. I…"

He nodded. "I know, Acier and because I do know I didn't press her for a fuck."

"Press her?"

He shrugged. "Well, she found me charming and sexy and wanted to give me a fuck but she has a real need for you. I told her I'd fuck her later."

"The hell you will!"

He grinned. Poor Acier in the grip of bloodlust with no clue as to its full power or allure. "I think she's a Willoni, Sei."

He saw the surprise in his twin's eyes. "A Willoni? You mean one of those mythical female masters of the song that Aime used to tell us about when we were pups?"

"Yes. They see and know things by means of their mastery of their soul song."

"No. Raven is human."

"According to Aime, so were the Willoni once upon a time. And she knows you can shift."

"No she doesn't."

"Yes. She does. I've seen it in her mind."

"I've never shifted around her."

"And yet, she's seen you shift. Not only that, Sei, but she saw your cock when she was just a kid."

To his surprise, Acier blushed. "The hell she did!"

"It happened when you were getting out of the shower at Mo's house. She was hiding in the linen closet, planning to surprise you when you stepped out of the shower naked."

"Have you lost your damned mind, pup? Do you know what Mo would have done to me if I'd ever been foolish enough to let one of the girls see me nude? It never happened. I always took my clothes in the bathroom with me because I knew Kiki had a crush on me," he said of Mo's older daughter, six years older than Raven. "Kiki was always coming onto me and I made damned sure I didn't do anything to encourage her or cause Mo to beat my ass. Finally, I decided to stay away from her completely."

He digested that in silence. "Ah. So that's why you stopped going to visit?"

"Yes. I…The last time I visited, Raven was only twelve but Kiki was eighteen and so damned tempting I knew I couldn't trust myself around her anymore."

He nodded. He'd been tempted by Kiki as well. And like Acier had somehow managed to resist her, only just. "It's too bad Raven didn't know that."

"How could she? Was I supposed to tell her or Mo that I couldn't come visit because Kiki kept throwing herself at me?"

Etienne knew how well that would have gone over with doting Daddy Mo. "No, but Raven knows you can shift."

"No she doesn't. She never saw me shift because I never shifted when I visited them and she damn sure never saw me naked."

"I'm not saying she has mastery over the song, Sei, but at the very least I think she's a Willoni initiate."

"How can that be? There are no Willoni on earth."

"Some would say there are no North Shifters on earth and yet Packs Gautier and LeMay are here, along with sundry other smaller, insignificant packs. The Willoni can be here too."

He shook his head. "She's human, Etienne."

"I'm not saying she's not but she knows about your ability to shift and when she looked at me, she knew I could shift also. "

"Hell, Tee, she can't even sing!"

He laughed and curled his fingers in Acier's hair. "Maybe not, but she knows about us. I saw a very clear memory in her mind of her seeing you shift."

"I'm telling you it never happened."

"And I'm telling you she saw it. Since you've never shifted around her, how else could she know what we are?"

"I don't know," Acier admitted.

"If you tell me it never happened, I know it didn't. And yet she knows. The only way she could is if she's Willoni." He frowned suddenly and glanced over his shoulder. "Who's inside?"

"Some full-blood who thinks she's God's gift to mankind."

Etienne felt Slayer's excitement as his cock hardened. He'd had his share of human latents and even an occasional half-blood but never a full-blood. "So? How about it? Is the bed big enough for four?"

"Four?"

"Slayer's in the SUV and he's in great need, as am I."

"Well he's not coming out to play."

Etienne watched as Acier went over to his SUV and spoke to Slayer. "I will tell you this just once, Slayer, behave yourself and stay inside."

Although Etienne sensed his pet's desire to rebel, he wasn't surprised when Slayer replied with quiet respect. *As you wish, Alpha.*

For all his bravado, Slayer was aware that as Alpha-in-waiting, Acier demanded and deserved a healthy dose of respect.

Still he felt bound to speak up on Slayer's behalf. "It doesn't seem fair, Acier."

Acier turned and walked over to him. "What doesn't seem fair?"

"That you should leave Pen home to play with Raven while forbidding Slayer to have any fun."

Acier frowned. "Unlike Slayer, Pen knows how to behave himself when left alone. When was the last time one of my shifter lovers awoke to find Pen between her legs pounding away for all he's worth? Answer? Never. Can you say the same for Slayer?"

Etienne shrugged. "So he gets a little frisky now and then. He knows he can't shift and fuck any female who isn't a shifter. Which is more than you'll be able to say about Pen after tonight."

"Pen will not touch, Raven."

"The hell he won't but you'll find that out for yourself. Right now I'm more interested in who's inside."

Acier stared at him. "She's an arrogant bitch who thinks she's superior."

"What do you expect? She's a full-blood. They're arrogant by nature."

"So I've noticed from Damon."

He grinned. "Damon's all right."

"I'm glad you think so. I think he needs to be knocked on his ass."

He shook his head. "I wouldn't try it, Sei. We're strong but a full-blood has incredible strength."

Acier shrugged and Etienne knew he wasn't convinced he couldn't take Damon. He inclined his head towards the cabin. "So? Am I invited?"

"Why would you want a piece of her?"

He shrugged. "*Because* she's a full-blood. I've never had the pleasure of fucking a full-blood. And to be able to do it with you would make it extra special. Do you think she'd mind?"

"No, I don't."

He felt his heart thumping in anticipation. "I see you're prepared."

Acier glanced down at the prowling kit in his hand and arched a brow. "She has a bondage rack along one wall. I plan to do unto her before she does unto me."

The thought of having a full-blood fem at their mercy, sent a jolt of lust straight down to Etienne's cock. The rush was so powerful, the urge to shift was impossible to ignore. He allowed the lower part of his body to shift. He looked into Acier's eyes, certain his were just as glowing and golden.

Acier peeled back his lips, revealing his incisors. "Now we feast."

Etienne undressed quickly, tossing his clothes into his SUV. Ignoring Slayer's pitiful cries that he wanted pussy, he padded on the balls of his feet and followed Acier inside. The full-blood lay on the bed. The breath caught in his throat as he looked at her. She was small, dark and stunningly beautiful with small tits, a flat stomach and a cute little ass. His gaze shifted to the vee between her legs and lingered on her pretty pussy.

A wave of lust thundered through him, almost making him dizzy. He felt a feral urge to rush across the room, turn her on her back and thrust his full, aching length balls deep in her with one thrust.

Instead, he decided to let Acier have her alone for a while. He knew Acier would get off on his watching. *You first, big brother.*

* * * * *

Turned on by the thought of Etienne watching, Acier allowed the heat and lust in him to take over. He grinned and began making his preparations. When he was finished, he allowed more shifting to take place until the only part of him that wasn't covered with his pelt was his face and his cock.

He padded over to the bed. Resisting the urge to leap on it and drill her tiny ass again, he lifted the sleeping fem up in his arms. She made a small sound of pleasure and cuddled against him. Dipping his head, he lapped at her breasts, tonguing her nipples until they tightened. A pity they were so small. Hardly more than a hungry mouthful. Thinking of another pair of breasts, big and full and enchantingly dark, he carried her over to the wall by the door where he'd left his prowling kit. It was time for the fuck-feasting to begin in earnest.

* * * * *

Deoctra woke quickly to find her ass full of cock, which was a lovely way to wake. She realized immediately that she was standing with her legs spread and her arms extended over her head, facing the wall. All her limbs were bound. A big, heavy, body thumped against her as a thick cock drilled her rear. She was bound to the bondage rack along the wall near the door. The same rack she'd had built hoping to bind Mikhel as she rode his delicious cock, driving them both wild.

Without turning her head, she knew the biker she had picked up earlier that night owned the sweet dick spearing her with such unmitigated vigor. He was really giving it to her, just as she loved it. Slamming his powerful hips into her, sending her breasts smashing against the rack and a wave of exquisite pain through her with each upward thrust of his shaft into her ass.

The pain was intense. The pleasure even more so. She wanted more. She wanted to reach back and grab his hips and encourage him to fuck her harder and deeper. She wanted that monster cock driven up her with enough force to split her ass in two. Tugging at the restraints around her wrists, she frowned. They wouldn't budge. She pulled again with the same results.

There was no way any leather could hold even a latent, let alone a full-blood vampire. And yet she was held fast. How could that be? For one of the few times in her life, she found that she was not in control. It was a frightening thought and an exhilarating feeling.

Controlling the only part of her body she could, she slammed her behind back at him. He grabbed her waist in strong hands and held her still and began to drill his cock in her ass with a speed and force that left her gasping for breath and screaming in pain as he rotated his hips and rammed his cock up into her.

The pain felt so good she had to be free to participate more fully. "Remove the restraints!" she ordered, wigging her behind wildly, eager for deeper penetration.

He licked the side of her neck, growling softly and continued to fuck her. She moaned and leaned as far back as the restraints allowed as her climax built quickly and powerfully. As it did, she cried out and eventually began to scream. Her screams seemed to inflame him. The louder she screamed, the harder he pumped his huge cock into her ass.

The only concession he made to her comfort was the occasional release of seed he pumped in her to keep her lubed, much as a vampire was capable of doing.

She felt his big body pressed tight against hers begin to tense and she knew he was reaching his own peak. He gave a particularly powerful thrust up into her that shattered her completely.

Sobbing and moaning she came wildly, her pussy gushing, her breasts crushed against the rack. Her orgasm was sustained so long that it rolled right into another one. He growled, bit into her neck and came, pumping his seed deep in her rear.

She closed her eyes and pressed her cheek against the rack, catching her breath. Her ass felt almost raw and still he kept his hard dick up her. He possessed a vigor a half-blood would envy. Still, she longed for more but she needed blood. "Release me," she gasped.

"I think not," he whispered.

"Release me now or I will kill you!"

Her breath hissed out in an angry sigh of relief when he finally drew his cock out of her tender rear. He made no effort to be particularly gentle and she shuddered, gritting her teeth. She would kill him so slowly for his outrageous insolence. "Now untie me or face the wrath of a full-blood vampire!" she warned.

Instead of releasing her, he kissed a path down her back to her ass, sending quivers all through her. He kneeled between her legs and she gasped as she felt his tongue, unnaturally long, snaking into her cunt.

She bit her lips and closed her eyes as a flood of heat shot through her. Holding her ass in his warm palms, he tongue fucked her for several sweet, torturous minutes that kept her teetering on the edge of ecstasy. Her climax washed over her as he brushed his moist, heated tongue against her clit. She lost her mind in a burst of total pleasure. He gripped her hips, clamped his mouth over her cunt and lapped up her pussy juices with a gusto that sent a satisfied jolt through her. Finally a non-vamp male who appreciated a good piece of pussy.

Chapter Ten

ॐ

When he was satisfied he had devoured every drop of her juices from her quivering outer lips, he rose and pressed his body tight against her. He thrust forward, slamming every inch of his huge dick up into her pussy. The same cunt had not felt cock since she had managed to impale herself on Mikhel so long ago.

It felt so good, tears of lust and joy filled her eyes and ran down her cheeks. "Fuck me!" she screamed, wiggling her ass against his hairy groin. "Fuck me!"

Clasping his big hands over her breasts, he pressed closer and fucked her deep and hard, reaching depths that had never felt cock. The delight thundering out from her cunt and all through her left her bereft of the ability to think. Her world centered around the dick balling her as she'd never been balled.

As he withdrew all but the big head of his shaft, he rotated his hips, bent his knees and then thrust up with a fury and passion that caught them both up in a sexual frenzy. She could feel his big body tensing and straining behind her as he groaned in time with his forward thrusts. He hammered at her with a wildness that was so totally pussy-destroying.

Waves of heat and hunger rolled over her and she sobbed with the sweetness of the release rapidly approaching. Her climax was just a breath away. It would take but a few more lustful thrusts and she would lose her mind in an agony of satisfaction.

Without warning, he suddenly groaned and pulled out of her. She cried out in protest and tensed, waiting for the returning thrust. It didn't come. She turned her head and looked at him, eyes glowing and incisors bared. "Why have you stopped?"

Holding his pussy-coated cock in his hand, he arched a brow at her. "There's something you want from me, honey?"

She sucked in an angry breath and yanked furiously at the restraints which held her tight. The bastard intended to make her beg for it. Well she wouldn't. "There's nothing you have that I want, human."

"It should be clear to you by now that I am no more human than you are." He gave her an insolent smile and shook his cock at her. "And if you're sure I don't have anything you want, I'll just say good night and go to bed."

Her body was on fire and her pussy ached. She had to have that cock back in her. She had to. Or she would surely die. She caught his gaze. "Slave. I command you to fuck me!"

He shook his head. "Your vampire shit won't work on me, honey. If you want some cock, you're going to have to come right out and beg for it."

She burned with rage and need. Her need overcame her rage. Later she would make him pay with his life. But for now, she had to have his cock in her. "I…I require your cock," she said, turning her head so she wouldn't have to watch his triumphant smirk. She would have the last laugh.

"I didn't quite hear you," he said, his deep voice filled with amusement.

"Please. Put your cock back in my cunt," she said, her stomach tight with rage.

"Well, since you ask so nicely, bitch."

He moved against her back. She felt his cock slide between her legs and she wiggled wildly, trying to get it in her pussy. He stood still, making no effort to help. "Stupid bastard, put it in!" she begged.

He laughed, licked at the side of her neck and shot his dick up into her pussy.

"Ooooh yes!" she moaned, her cunt cradling and welcoming the monster cock back. "Yes!"

"Ah yes, bitch," he groaned, grinding his groin against her ass so he could get as much cock in her as possible. "Hell yes!"

He wrapped one arm around her waist, cupped the other over her breasts and began a wild, delicious fuck that had her sobbing and screaming and coming in a matter of seconds.

Rutting into her like she was a two-dollar crack whore, he came, shooting what felt like a pint of seed in her. She moaned and squeezed him, milking the last drop out of his cock. Then she felt his mouth against the side of her neck. Moments later, incisors pierced her skin and she came as he fed on her.

He ingested her blood as he gave her pussy one of the most mouth-watering, slow fucks imaginable. She lost track of how many times she came. He came with her more than once and still he feasted on her pussy and her blood like a vampire possessed.

Finally, he withdrew his incisors from her neck but kept his cock buried deep in her pussy. "I need blood," she told him.

"Would you like some more cock?" he asked.

"Yes."

He licked her side of her neck. "How would you like to be doubled fuck?"

She shuddered and then froze, suddenly aware that they were not alone in the room. Although she couldn't see the other occupant, she could now feel him. Why she hadn't felt him before surprised and dismayed her. The other male projected an air of hunger and lust that made her go damper.

"I will take you both and make you my slaves," she threatened.

He laughed softly and finally drew his dick out of her drenched pussy. She lay with her face against the rack, feeling weak from her lack of blood and totally overwhelmed by the countless times she'd been fucked.

"Who…what are you? Tell me or I will kill you."

He laughed again and slapped her ass cheeks so hard they stung. "We've been over that. You keep threatening to kill me and you won't get anymore of Steele here."

"Steele?" She opened her eyes.

He waved his stiff cock at her. "You haven't been formally introduced yet, but this is Steele."

"And who are you?"

He leaned close and licked her neck where he'd fed. "I am the male who made you beg for my sugar dick. I am Acier Gautier, Den Alpha of Pack Gautier, both your master and your better, bitch."

* * * * *

Acier felt her body stiffen and smiled.

"Pack? You're a werewolf?"

He laughed. There had always been a wildness and a hunger to treat a lover roughly that he attributed to the vampire side of his nature. With this fem he had been able to fully explore it and he was pleased to feel the desire receding. But not completely. He still had a few hours of darkness left in which to dominate her.

"Do you believe in such creatures? I am a shifter whose natural form is that of a wolf. I am not a werewolf."

"Whatever you are, release me."

"I think not. And you can struggle all you like. Those restraints will resist even your strength. It would take a vampire much older and stronger than you to break them."

"They are not leather."

They were from Boreias, one of the fringe planets of Aeolia, the ancient home of the North Shifters who had founded Packs Gautier and LeMay when they had been exiled to Earth many thousands of years earlier. Or at least the technology to raise them was of Boreian origins. While the leather in the restraints was somewhat sentient, it did not possess the level of intelligence that Pen and Drei, his other pet did. "Actually, it is a form of leather but enough small talk. I think it's time you saw me as I truly am."

He dropped to all fours and shifted. When the shift was complete, he moved around to her left so she could see him in his natural form, that of a big gray wolf with gold eyes.

"Oh God! You are a werewolf."

He sensed her revulsion and felt the fur on the back of his neck bristle. He was prouder of his wolf nature than he was of his vampire side. And this haughty fem was about to be taught a lesson.

He moved around her and drew his tongue along the rounded mounds of her tiny ass.

"I do not fuck animals!" she warned.

But her cunt was giving off the most enticing aroma. While part of her wanted to be repulsed by being licked by a wolf, the hereditary enemy of her people, another part of her was aroused. It was that part he meant to exploit.

I am not an animal! he snapped, projecting the thought directly into her mind. *I am a sentient being who happens to have the natural form of a wolf but I am not an animal. Do not make the mistake of calling me one again.*

Although she did not respond verbally, he felt a silent, albeit reluctant acceptance of his statement.

Convinced she wanted him to continue, he sniffed appreciatively, savoring the aroma of her fragrant pussy. It had a nice odor but nowhere as sweet as the one Raven produced. Pushing thoughts of Raven from his mind, he licked at her cunt.

"Oh! Oh!" she moaned, her small body trembling.

She pushed her pussy against his stroking tongue and gushed into his mouth. His nostrils flared and his cock throbbed. He had to have some more pussy and some ass.

Rising onto his back paws, Acier moved behind the fem, located the entrance of her pussy and thrust his dick deep into her. "Shall I stop?" he said with a growl.

"No!" The greedy bitch's pussy grabbed his cock in a vice-like grip and held and massaged it as he fucked into her. In a matter of moments she was sobbing with joy as she thrust her tiny ass back at him. He paused and then continued and they fell into a natural fuck rhythm as old as time.

"Fuck me!" she screamed. "Oooh God, fuck me, wolf! Give it to! Give it all to me, you big hairy bastard!"

She had fairly good pussy and she could take a pounding like no other female he'd ever fucked. So, happy to oblige, he fucked her like she was a beta she-bitch, rutting his cock into her with little regard for her pleasure. Alpha-like, thinking only of his own pleasure. He closed his eyes and allowed himself to be totally ruled by his cock. He fucked her hard and deep, growling and occasionally bending his head to nip at her shoulders.

Her pussy was as good as her ass and he fucked her in a frenzy. Her cries of pain and pleasure mingled with his growls and groans and they fought each other for their satisfaction. She gave as good as she got, slamming her small, tight ass back at him as he propelled his hard shaft as deep in her as he could get it. And shit, it was good. Wild, rough and good.

His balls tightened and his cock exploded. He hosed her pussy down with a load of cum. Then he laid against her, panting as she reached her peak and squeezed his dick tightly as she came.

For several moments they remained joined, both catching their breaths. Finally, he knew it was time. He removed the restraints. Even a fem needed an occasional break. And he could feel Etienne, standing near the door, panting with his cock dripping his seed, about to burst with need.

He licked at her neck, gave one final thrust into her pussy and finally drew his dick out of her warm, tight body. Moving back, he looked at the restraints and they opened.

Her knees buckled and she would have fallen but he shifted his hands and feet to humanoid form and picked her up in his arms. She looked up at his wolf face and shuddered then surprised him by pressing her cheek against his pelt covered chest.

"I require blood," she whispered.

He carried her to the bed and laid her there. She seemed weak. Although he felt no emotional attachment to her, he knew she could no more control her nature than he could control his. Notwithstanding the fact that she had started the night intending to dominate and probably kill him, he was satisfied that she now knew he was the head Alpha in charge. As he did with errant den wolves who had been subdued and bowed to his supremacy, he felt inclined to be gracious in victory.

But first he had to take care of Etienne.

"My brother would like to meet you," he told her.

She turned her head and looked at Etienne, standing half-shifted in the doorway. She sucked in a breath and inclined her head slightly.

He shifted his right arm and extended it as Etienne crossed the room and climbed onto the big bed with them.

Eyes glowing, she grabbed his arm and sank her incisors in and began feeding. As he watched, Etienne, lifted one of her slender legs and thrust his cock up into her behind.

He watched the look of rapture on Etienne's face as he began his slow but hard fuck, rotating his hips and grinding against her ass. He could feel Etienne's pleasure through their bond and shared it.

He closed his eyes and leaned back against the bed. The vampire in him enjoyed the sensation of having a female ingest his blood. A mental picture of Raven filled his thoughts and his cock hardened as he thought of what it would be like to have Raven ingesting his blood as he tenderly fucked her virgin pussy.

He hadn't had a virgin since he had taken the virginity of one of the beta she-wolves of Leon's den who had come to him in heat, needing a good, hard fuck. Although he made it a point never to fuck any of the she-wolves from his own den, he had no problem with fucking one from Leon's.

But you are not going to fuck Raven, he reminded himself. He was supposed to protect her, not fuck her. And Etienne had done enough damage when he had sucked her pussy. He sighed and reached down to fondle his cock. Thoughts of Raven had him hard again. His cock needed some attention.

He maneuvered on the bed so that his cock was in arms length of the fem, still feeding while Etienne licked her neck and fucked her hard and fast.

"Touch me!" he ordered.

Fuck off!

Chapter Eleven

ഌ

"Wrong answer," he told her, grabbed her by the hair and pulled her away from his arm.

He grinned as Etienne clamped an arm around her waist and moved with her, keeping his cock buried deep inside her.

He saw the surprise in her eyes at his strength. And resignation. Finally the bitch was beginning to understand he was not some weak human male she could play with and kill when it suited her. "I said touch me!"

Her eyes burning with resentment and fury, she reached out a hand to his cock. He closed his eyes and lay back against the bed, breathing deeply. He was pleased but not surprised when she abruptly mounted him and impaled herself on his cock with Etienne still buried to the balls in her ass. Few females could resist his wishes after he fucked them.

He lay unmoving under her, enjoying himself as she twisted and groaned and thrust herself up and down on his shaft in harmony with Etienne's thrusts. Shit, it was pleasant to have a submissive bouncing off his cock while his brother pounded her rear.

It had been a long time since he and Etienne had taken one female at the same time. When they did, he usually liked to be on top, thrusting downward as Etienne lay underneath, torpedoing his cock upwards. His senses overwhelmed with lust and pleasure, he allowed himself to drown in the sensations rolling over him.

He longed to fuck her hard and rough but he knew Etienne wanted the fuck to last. He smiled, sharing his twin's bliss at having his cock in the tight, warm ass of a full-blood fem. Etienne was fully enjoying his first fuck with a full-blood fem.

He allowed her and Etienne to control the pace of the fuck. More than once he had to fight to hold back his climax because he knew Etienne wasn't ready to come. Finally though, when he was about to lose control, he felt the same realization in Etienne.

Linking their minds, they continued fucking her in concert until she gasped and screamed, shuddering between them as she came. Only then did he and Etienne release their control and come together in her.

He didn't linger in her. As he pumped the last of his seed into her, he lifted her off his cock and laid her on her stomach. He rolled onto his side and watched as Etienne, covered her small body with his, bared his incisors and sank them into the side of her neck.

She moaned and shuddered to yet another climax as Etienne fed on her. Still inside her, Etienne rolled onto his back and cupped his hands over her small breasts and finally removed his incisors from her neck. Her small body slumped against his. With a gentle kiss pressed against her neck, Etienne lifted her and eased his cock slowly out of her rear. He settled her onto her side, stroking her breasts as he did.

Acier watched, surprised at Etienne's gentleness. If ever tenderness was wasted on a female, it was with her.

You're wrong, Sei. She needs tenderness more than any woman I've ever met.

He frowned. Etienne was letting the fact that he'd just fucked a full-blood for the first time go to his head but he kept his opinion to himself. If Etienne wanted to cuddle her, so be it. In the meantime, he found he was still hungry.

He moved behind her and rubbed his cock against her cheeks. If she resisted, he would respect her wishes and withdraw. Instead, she moaned, squirmed and rolled onto her stomach with her tiny ass teasing him. His cock jumped to attention. He parted her cheeks and shot his cock up her rear end. Resting his weight on his arms, he alternated between fucking his cock into her ass and her pussy with an animal-like lust that he suspected thrilled and titillated her as much as it did him.

She went wild, screaming and moaning so loudly he wondered if the walls would tumble down around them. And when she came, her orgasm was so intense and prolonged, it triggered his. He collapsed his body on top of hers and thrust wildly, filling her pussy with his seed.

Then, finally feeling sexually sated, he nipped her neck and pulled his cock out of her drenched pussy. She made a small sound of protest and looked at him with glowing eyes still full of lust.

But he'd had enough. He wanted to fall asleep thinking of Raven. He inclined his head slightly in Etienne's direction. Even before he'd moved to the other side of the bed, Etienne had taken his place. He rolled onto his back and lifted the fem onto his cock.

Acier watched with an arched brow as they began a long, leisurely fuck that was so hot and passionate, it kept his cock hard. He was hard-pressed not to climb on her back and thrust into her quivering ass but he felt a disturbing connection between her and Etienne as they fucked.

He frowned. No. He and she had fucked. She and Etienne were making love.

He massaged his cock and came twice before Etienne finally pulled out of her and lay on his side facing her. She moaned in protest and curled her body against Etienne's chest pelt, nearly purring. Etienne shifted positions until he lay behind her. He slipped his cock in her pussy. She reached a small hand back and rested it on his pelt-covered thigh. They drifted to sleep, still joined.

Acier sucked in a disturbed breath. Oh damn! He hoped Etienne hadn't fallen for her.

He waited until he was certain she was asleep and then he reached out to Etienne. *Tee? We need to talk.*

He slipped off the bed and padded out into the night. Moments later, a yawning Etienne joined him. "What's wrong, Sei?"

"Tee, you can't fall for her."

Etienne's eyes widened. "What? Fall for her? Sei, are you nuts? Do you know who she is?"

"Yes. Deoctra Diniti."

"Yes. She's wanted by the Walker-Dumonts out of Boston."

"Who are the Walker-Dumonts?"

"They are a vampire family consisting mostly of new full-bloods but the matriarch is a powerful vampire with a long memory."

"What do these vampires want her for?"

"They want to kill her."

Acier was surprised to feel a strange resistance to the idea. "Why?"

"Damon said he didn't know. It had something to do with her not knowing when a bloodlust went bad."

"Bloodlust." He spat on the ground. "Vampires and their shit. Small wonder it lands them in trouble."

"Sei, it's not shit, as you should know by now."

"Me? Why should I know?"

Etienne clamped a hand on the back of his neck and stared into his gaze. "Because you are in the midst of it with Raven."

"No! Tee, you know I don't believe in that vampire shit."

"Whether you believe it or not is beside the point. Why do you think your desire for Raven is so strong and consuming? She's your perfect partner, Sei. No matter now hard you try, you won't be able to resist her for long. You're going to have to have her."

"I'll touch her when hell freezes over, Tee!"

Etienne shook his head and kissed both his cheeks. "It's all ready frozen over, Sei."

"No, I don't want to talk about Raven. I want to talk about you and the fem. You mustn't fall for her. She's wicked. I've felt—"

"Not to worry, Sei. I know exactly what she is and what she's capable of and my heart is in no danger. She fascinates me but she is not my bloodlust. In fact, I only came to tell you Leon was on his way."

"Yes. I know. What I don't know is why Xay didn't come to tell me himself."

"He was going to but he has his hands full with several of the teenage pups so I told him I'd come."

He tensed. "What's wrong?"

"Nothing Xay can't handle, Sei," Etienne assured him.

"Are you sure? Maybe I should return to the den."

"I'm positive, Sei. Xay can handle things. If not, I'll help out. You go do what you need to. Now, about Leon. Shall I stay around and kick his ass for you?"

He laughed and hugged Etienne. "No. I can handle Leon. So why don't you shove off?"

Etienne shook his head. "Sei, I promise you, you have no need to worry about my falling for Deoctra."

"You were very tender with her."

"She's been through a lot lately. As we fucked I could feel this great wall of pain and anguish inside of her, washing over her like a tidal wave. She's done a lot of shit in her time but she'd paid dearly for her mistakes."

"Etienne, have you lost your mind? I've never met a female with a darker soul."

"I know, but she can be redeemed, I think."

"By whom? Etienne, I will not allow you to fall for her. I forbid it. Do you understand?"

Etienne laughed and hugged him. "Not to worry your long, pretty hair, big brother. I told you I have not fallen for her. And to prove it, I'm going back inside to shower and then Slayer and I will be on our way. Okay?"

Acier caught part of a thought sent to Tee from Slayer and frowned. "Just see that the way does not carry you anywhere near, Raven, Etienne."

Etienne shrugged. "Slayer meant no harm or disrespect, Sei. You know he respects you, as I do."

"Just as Pen and I respect the two of you, Tee. Just keep that sex-crazy pet of yours away from Raven."

"Fine. We won't go near her and if it'll make you happy, we're outta of here now without even a shower."

"That's not necessary. I don't want you to feel as if you're not welcome, Tee. I just…"

"Don't want me falling for her." Etienne laughed and slapped his cheek. "I haven't."

"I can feel a certain regard from you for her, Tee."

He shrugged. "She's my first fem. Sei. If you had more respect for our vampire heritage, you'd know how awesome it is to fuck a full-blood fem for the first time. I'm a little awed by that and I admit that I feel a sort of tenderness toward her because of all she's suffered. She's recently lost two younger sisters."

"Why? How?"

Etienne shrugged. "Okay. It was as a result of her own actions mostly but still, Sei, imagine losing me."

The thought of losing Tee for any reason sent a chill of fear and anguish through him. "I can't imagine losing you. If I did, I'd probably die too. Losing you would be like losing my heart."

Etienne smiled and kissed his cheeks. "I couldn't live without you either, Sei. That's part of how Deoctra feels at the loss of her sisters. She's been through a lot and I can sympathize but I am in no danger of falling in love with her. Okay?"

He nodded. "Okay."

"And just to demonstrate that I'm serious, I'm leaving."

After Etienne had showered and left, Acier felt horny again. He got back in bed and curled his body against the small, slender body of the fem. He lifted one of her legs, ejaculated into her cunt and eased his cock inside her. Although he longed to get a last hard fuck, mindful of Etienne's concern for her, he contented himself with falling asleep inside her.

Chapter Twelve

ℰℭ

Deoctra woke to find a hairy arm draped over her waist. Memories of the night before returned and her stomach muscles clenched and she wanted to puke. She, a full-blood vampire had allowed herself to be taken by a… She glanced over her shoulder and shuddered at the wolf face lying on the pillow next to her. She wasn't sure what he was. She knew without looking around that the other werewolf was gone. She stifled a sigh. As he had fucked her, he had made her feel strange, almost as if he were making love to her instead of fucking her. She had enjoyed both fucks but of the two males she would have preferred the other to remain. Maybe when things settled down she'd seek him out.

She gave an angry shake of her head. She was behaving like some silly human female who'd had her first piece of cock. She and the second werewolf had not made love. They had fucked. She had enjoyed being banged by two of the biggest cocks she'd ever seen but there was no need to lose her perspective. It had been wonderful and delicious but it had been sex. Nothing more.

Still, she couldn't stifle a sigh of regret that the other male had gone. She glanced back at the one still lying behind her. He had a lust for blood and sex that rivaled her own and he was part wolf. If not a werewolf, then what?

His cock, semi-hard, still speared her cunt. Although revolted by his appearance, she was loath to separate herself from his wonderful shaft. She lay still as a startling realization struck. For the first time in some thirty years she had not awakened longing for Mikhel Dumont. She glanced at the fur-covered arm over her waist. This male and his twin had done something that none of her many other lovers had managed to do before. They had fucked away her endless ache for Mikhel Dumont, something she had not thought possible except at the end of the cock of one of his siblings. She had never heard of such a thing happening. Even fucking Serge Dumont, delicious as that had been, had not been enough to cure her lust for Mikhel. Yet now it was gone. How could such a thing happen?

She decided that the how was just not important. What was important was that she was finally free! She gasped in a deep breath and tried to blink away the tears that welled in her eyes. Could it be true? Yes! Yes! The ache was gone and she was free! Her eyes filled with tears she could not hold back.

He woke as she sobbed softly. He licked her along the back of her neck and engaged her pussy in a gentle fuck that brought another unaccustomed flood of tears along with a warm and yet invigorating climax. Afterwards, he fed briefly at her neck, withdrew from her pussy and rose from the bed. She remained there as he padded into the bathroom, reveling in her new-found freedom.

Her future was suddenly alive with the possibility of a new bloodlust, this time a full-blood who was not hampered by human blood, which tended to cloud reason. Although she had adored Mikhel and suspected, as her first and only bloodlust, he would always hold a special place in her heart, his human blood had led him astray. What other explanation could there be for him to prefer a human whore to her? Her half-formed planned of seeking out Acier's twin was discarded. Whatever he was, he was not the full-blood to which she was entitled.

Another thought brought a fresh wave of tears to her eyes. She could call to Tally and Smo and have them join her. They would stay far away from the Dumonts and Madisons and finally the nightmare would be over. Finally. Finally! She had her life back. She could live again.

* * * * *

Acier stepped out of the shower and stood in front of the medicine cabinet. He dried his hair as best he could and stared at his face. His human face. The one Raven knew. Raven. He closed his eyes and leaned his forehead against the mirror. With the coming of daylight, the passion that had nearly controlled him with the arrival of the full moon had become manageable. Now he could face Raven without worrying that he would ravish her the moment they were alone together.

He dried himself and went back into the room to find the fem up and heading for the bathroom. It amused him that she avoided looking at him as they passed. He suspected her easy acquiescence of the night before to both him and Etienne now shamed her. He resisted the urge to shift fully and push her against the wall and suck on her small breasts, clutch her tiny ass and take a quick rough fuck in the *au naturel* just because he could.

He did not maintain control of his den by being mean-spirited. Besides, his hunger for sex was quite manageable this morning. He walked over to his backpack and removed a pair of briefs. He extended a hand in the bag and called softly. "Come." Drei, large and white, jumped into his hand and gave a satisfied sound as he settled over Acier's cock. He wasn't going to allow Raven to see him shamelessly displaying his dick again.

He pulled on a clean shirt, a pair of pants and a small leather-like clip from the pack. He raked his fingers through his still-wet hair, drew it to the back of his head and secured it with the clip. He then moved over to the bondage rack and extended his hands. "Keddi. Come." The restraints loosened and flew into his palm. "Good boys," he told them softly.

He felt their pleasure at his praise. They lived to serve his needs but found great delight in heartfelt, sincere praise. He blew softly across them and felt a tingle of delight from them as he placed them in a special compartment in his kit.

His nostrils flared and he lifted his head as he caught a familiar scent. Taking the pack with him, he swiftly left the house and found a man with short blond hair and green eyes emerging from the woods.

He secured his backpack to his bike before leaning back against it with his arms crossed. "Leon. What brings you out so early?"

The other gray stopped within a foot of him, his nostrils flaring, his eyes widening. "For the love of God, Acier! I waited out here all night listening to you and that brute of a brother of yours rutting into that whore like there would never be another full moon. And I still smell pussy. Don't tell me you're still fucking! Don't you ever get enough?"

He shrugged. He and Etienne's sexual appetite had always caused a stir in the pack. All the males of Pack Gautier were renown throughout the North Shifter world for their larger than average cocks. Nevertheless, the males of his pack were envious of the enormous size of his and Etienne's dicks as well as of their ability to totally satisfy many partners in one night. The beta she-bitches were eager to offer themselves as willing sacrifices on the altar of his and Etienne's nearly always hard and hungry cocks.

If he listened to his cock he would still be inside banging the sweet little ass of the fem. But the moon was no longer full and he did not intend to be controlled by his vampire-driven desire today. "I imagine you did some fucking of your own during the night, Leon."

"It was the full moon and there were a few willing females available," he said defensively. "I took what pleasure I could, as was my right."

He curled his lip. Leon hadn't changed one damn iota. Still making allowances for himself while condemning others for the same "sin" of which he himself was guilty. "What do you want?"

"I want to appeal to your better nature, Acier. Whatever could be said about Etienne, he at least knows enough not to aspire to be Alpha Supreme."

He narrowed his gaze. "What the hell do you mean whatever could be said about Etienne? Are you insulting him?"

Leon struggled. "It's no secret that he can't keep his cock in its sheath for more than half an hour. His cock rules him but he knows his limitations. I appeal to you, Acier, remove yourself from consideration for Supreme Alpha. When I ascend to the position, I will ensure you are allowed to run your den as loosely as you do now. But under me Pack Gautier will be lean and ready to face all challenges both within and from out of the pack."

He stared at Leon, reminding himself that Aime would not look kindly on his kicking Leon's ass on a whim. Otherwise, those remarks about Etienne would have been sufficient for him to beat Leon's scrawny ass. "You're wasting your time, Leon." He forced a smile. "I'm half vampire, remember? I have no better nature and you know the way to remove me from consideration is not with reason. If you wish to challenge my status as Supreme Alpha-in-waiting, shift and let the contest begin."

Leon tightened his mouth. "There will come a time, Acier, when your bulk and brute strength will not suffice to win the day," Leon warned. "There are shifters in Pack LeMay who are bigger and no doubt more vicious than you and Etienne and they will be coming to take on Pack Gautier."

"Let them come, Leon. I fear no one, regardless of size."

"And that lack of fear will be your undoing, Acier, but I am determined that you will not take Pack Gautier down with you."

"I am always going to be what I am and it's the vampire half of me that makes me stronger, faster and more powerful than any other Alpha in the pack. No one takes anything from me, Leon. Not you or any shifter from Pack LeMay. If I should choose to stand aside, it will be my choice, not yours. Now unless you are prepared to issue a challenge I will be honor bound to accept, you're holding me up."

"Acier —"

"And it's time you remembered whose presence you are in," he warned, his nostrils flaring. "I am not just a fellow Den Alpha you may be overly familiar with at will. As Supreme Alpha-in-waiting, I require more submission from you, Leon. Show it or I will beat your ass until you do!"

He watched Leon's fair skin flush red, but the other Alpha bowed his head ever so slightly, although his eyes still glared at him.

As he considered if he should beat Leon's ass on general principle, Leon tensed and looked past him. Without turning he knew the fem Deoctra had come outside. He watched her and Leon take each other's measure. Leon's eyes began to go gold and his nostrils flared and Acier knew he could smell the remnants of his and Etienne's seed in her and was aroused. For all his talk of finding him and Etienne inferior, Leon had always loved sampling their leftovers.

The smell of pussy full of his or Etienne's seed always made Leon reckless. Now he stabbed a finger in Acier's direction. "I will not wait forever, Gautier. The time will come."

Gautier? After he'd just warned him to show more respect? His nostrils flared but he decided not to beat Leon to a pulp in front of a stranger. "I'm a little busy at the moment, Leon, but I will send Xay to see you."

"Send your beta at his own peril."

"Double team him at yours, de la Rocque and I will go through you and your den males like a tornado tearing out all your throats," he warned. "Don't fuck with me or my den wolves, de la Rocque, or Pack Gautier will lose Den de la Rocque!"

He sensed a surge of fear in Leon and nodded. "You make sure Xay is treated well when he visits, de la Rocque, or you will answer to me in a night that will be long and painful and your last one alive!"

"You tell your beta to show me proper respect when he comes and maybe he won't get his ass kicked."

Acier narrowed his gaze. He doubted Leon could take Xay in a fair fight and he sure as hell had better not double team him. "Treat Xay with the respect he deserves as my second-in-command or I'll send Etienne next. Or maybe we'll come together. We'll delight your females and kill your males. Treat Xay properly or die, de la Rocque."

Without another word, Leon shifted to a big gray with his cock out of his sheath, turned and padded into the woods.

"Who is he? What is he?"

He turned to look at the fem. "He is a purebred gray who is arrogant enough to think he can take what I have."

"And can he?"

"No!" He shook his head. "The smell of you seems to have sent him back into heat and made him lose his grip on reality."

Her dark eyes glowed and her incisors descended. "Is he mated?"

"He wasn't the last time I checked."

"He has a big dick."

"Of course he does. He's a shifter from Pack Gautier. We all have big dicks."

She smiled and reached down to fondle his cock.

Drei, sensing his mood, immediately shifted out of the way. He tried not to squirm as he felt Drei sliding down his thigh to cling to his right ankle, panting softly. "Nowhere near as impressive as yours but still very nice."

He ground his cock against her hand and she unzipped his pants and slipped her small fingers inside, under his briefs and over his flesh which hardened in her fingers.

Smiling up at him, she dropped to her knees and gave him a quick blow job that was so expertly done that he came in a matter of moments. She licked his cock clean, pressed a lingering kiss against its head and put it back into his pants. She slid his zipper up and looked at him with glowing eyes, incisors bared. "A little blood, my handsome hunk?"

He nodded and when she leapt on him, he wrapped his arms around her and held her as she briefly fed at his neck. When she'd finished, she lifted her head and pressed a lingering kiss against his lips. "Where is the handsome one?"

"We're identical twins," he pointed out, holding her in his arms.

She grinned at him and he caught a glimpse of a warm female who liked to tease. "He's much better looking," she told him.

He laughed and opened his arms so abruptly she landed on her small ass. "So get him to hold you."

She sprang to her feet and clutched his arms. "I could kill you if I wanted to."

He shook his head. "I wouldn't be too sure of that. I know Etienne thinks vampires are superior physically to us but I am not convinced. And what I do not believe is not a fact."

She shook her head. "You are very young. You have much to learn."

"I know enough."

"I have to go now. Perhaps we'll see each other again."

"Would you like that?" he asked.

"It matters not whether we do or don't." She grinned suddenly. "Although I would not mind seeing your handsome twin again."

He laughed. "I'll tell him."

"Do." She glanced towards the path Leon had taken. "In the meantime, I think I'll go introduce myself to your purebred friend."

"You do that but do not make the mistake of interfering in my business."

Her eyes narrowed. "Or?"

"Or you'll be sorry. The fact that you are a full-blood vampire won't help you any if you fuck with me, fem!"

Eyes glowing, she bared her incisors.

He bared his. "It's not very polite to backhand a woman you've spent the night fucking but then I'm not always polite," he told her. "Fuck Leon if you like but do not get involved in pack business, which is my business. Do I make myself clear, fem? Or would you like a demonstration of my power?"

"Do not threaten me, Gautier!"

He remembered how he had awakened to find her sobbing and softened. "It was friendly advice."

"I'm a vampire. Why should werewolves or whatever you are, interest me? I have no wish to be your enemy."

"Nor I yours," he admitted.

She put a hand on his arm and stretched up to press a quick kiss against his mouth. He parted his lips and their tongues touched, sending a nice tingle through him.

He shuddered and decided he had to have a last fuck. He unzipped his pants and she quickly stripped and leapt at him. He caught her in his arms and thrust his cock up into her pussy. She wrapped her legs around his body and her arms around his neck. Kissing and nipping at each other's lips and necks, they fucked standing up. Keeping one arm wrapped around her tiny waist, he used his other hand to rain sharp blows on her ass that increased both their pleasure.

She moaned and whimpered as he spanked her small ass again and again. Finally, she sobbed, her pussy convulsed on his cock and she came, screaming with pleasure. The wild convulsions of her pussy set him off. He came twice, flooding her tight pussy with his seed.

As she lay against him, shuddering through her second climax, he opened his eyes and saw Leon standing at the edge of the path, his big cock out of his sheath ejaculating, panting rapidly as he watched them.

He kissed her neck, fondling her ass. He smiled as she gasped. He had no doubt her ass was rather tender. He palmed both of her cheeks, gently easing her pussy up and down on his cock. "That was good," he told her.

She lifted her head and smiled up at him. "Yes, almost as good as sex with your handsome brother."

He laughed and rewarded her insolence with a gentle slap on her ass.

"Ouch!"

"There's someone on the path who'd like a fuck," he whispered.

She glanced over her shoulder and he felt her pussy tightening around his cock as she saw Leon watching them. She turned back to look at him. "I'll give him the fucking of his life."

"I don't doubt it."

"But first, give me a goodbye kiss."

He bent his head, thought of Raven, and kissed her cheek instead of the lips she offered.

She stared at him for a moment before shrugging. "Your loss," she told him.

He groaned as she climbed off of his cock. He told himself another fuck was really out of the question. Nevertheless, he still wanted pussy.

Leon let out an angry growl and turned and padded into the woods.

As before, she used her mouth to clean his cock before she turned and flashed into the woods, following the path Leon had taken, her pussy creaming as she ran.

He grinned. Old Leon was going to be in for a hot day and night in the old woods.

Drei, trembling with lust, slid up his leg and settled over his cock, breathing in deeply and licking the last of the fem's juice from his cock. "Gently," he said. He had no desire to have Drei get him all hard and hot again.

Want to suck.

Since Drei was a part of him, having Drei suck him to a climax would be like masturbating. While he had nothing against it, he wasn't in the mood. "No," he said softly but firmly.

Drei sighed and settled over his cock.

"Good boy," he told him, heaping praise on him.

Trembling with pleasure at the praise, Drei became still and quiet.

Acier smiled again as he noted a new calmness within himself. The night before and all his life he had felt a need for constant sex with endless and varied partners that he attributed to his vampire blood. The wolf side of him wanted to be tender and loving with a single mate. Now he felt as if he had exercised those demons and could be as loyal and faithful as Aime had been to his mate of the last sixty years.

It was out of his system. He thought of Raven. At least he hoped so.

At the beginning of this feast, the moon and his vampire nature had called him. He had responded. Now he felt a call of a different kind. The call of the woman named Raven. He could no more resist her call than he had been able to resist the moon. He got on his bike and headed for home and Raven.

Chapter Thirteen

❧

It was early morning and the RV park was still and silent. Returning from his night of lust, Acier quietly glided his bike behind the big, black, sleek RV. He owned a medium-sized ranch house in Arizona but as he was rarely there, the RV functioned as home most of the time. Feeling too tired to put the bike away, he knelt down and secured it by lacing slender leather-like links through the spokes of the wheels. "Keddi. Guard," he said softly.

He received a silent acknowledgement from the Keddi and rose.

Retrieving his soiled clothing of the night before from a side bag, he unlocked the front door of the RV and went inside. The interior was dark and cool but he immediately saw that Raven was not on the sofa that folded out into a full bed. Her suitcases still sat where he had left them the night before and her blouse was across one of the passenger seat captain's chairs. He tightened his lips. No doubt Etienne had put it there when he undressed her. He tossed his leather jacket across the recliner and padded through the RV, pausing at the hamper to toss his soiled clothing inside.

Then he opened the door separating the bathroom and bedroom from the rest of the RV. This part of the RV was in total darkness but he had no problems seeing. He made his way to his closed bedroom doors. He quietly folded them back and sucked in a breath at the sight that greeted his eyes.

Raven lay asleep on his bed on top of his comforter. Although she wore one of his shirts, it was open and her entire luscious body was exposed to his ravenous gaze. Her body was dark, sleek and lovely with wonderful, rounded curves.

Her breasts were large and firm with wide, dark nipples and luscious looking areolas which beckoned his mouth and tongue. Her stomach was flat, her legs long and shapely. When he saw Pen laying over her pussy, obstructing his view of her treasure, his cock threatened to explode.

As he watched, he saw Pen lying between her legs breathing in and out. Raven moaned softly in her sleep, her hips lifting involuntarily off the bed. Acier closed his eyes and reached out to Pen and stiffened as he got a very clear picture from his pet of part of his body shifted into the shape of a tight, pulsing cock, thrusting gently, but insistently inside Raven's pussy.

Acier moistened his lips as he felt his Pen's pleasure and delight in himself as Raven's juices began to flow over his cock head. It was a gentle climax but Pen was proud of having induced it.

Drei stirred against him and he knew Drei was sharing the experience with him and Pen.

Good, take more, Drei urged. *Take more, Pen.*

Keeping his eyes closed, Acier parted his lips and felt the warm, sweet taste of Raven's juices as Pen continued to gently thrust into her. His heart thumped and his cock began to feel constricted. Drei, breathing deeply and closing over him, wasn't helping any.

"Oooh. Oooh yes, Steele. Yes. Love me. Please."

His eyes opened and heat rose up the back of his neck and blood shot down to his cupped cock as he listened to Raven's words. Was she dreaming of him making love to her when it was in fact his lusty little pet? The Keddi took their personalities from those they lived to serve. Pen, Drei and Slayer had been known to enjoy the occasional taste of pussy separate from their masters. Etienne's pets in particular were a lusty lot, inclined to jump at every opportunity for a quick fuck. If left unattended for too long, Slayer in particular had been known to go out looking for sex. More than one female shifter had awakened to find Etienne's lusty bunch between her legs enjoying a meal of sweet pussy. Like Pen, upon occasion, Slayer had been known to even ejaculate into a willing lover.

In the past, Acier had occasionally allowed his pets to pleasure a willing lover but Raven was special and he did not intent to rape her by means of allowing Pen, who had become a part of him, to take liberties not freely granted. "Enough, Pen!"

He moved quietly into the room and extended a hand. He felt Pen's reluctance. *More? Please Alpha?*

A little more, Alpha? Drei pleaded on Pen's behalf.

He tightened his lips. Pen and Drei, his favorite pets, only called him Alpha when caught misbehaving. His pets were becoming as greedy for sex as were Etienne's unruly brood. The next thing he knew he'd had to keep them locked up when there was a female around.

Just a little more? Please Alpha, Pen pleaded.

While it was temping to allow Pen to continue because he could share in the pleasure, he shook his head. "I said enough, Keddi. Come. Now!"

With a reluctance that was palatable, Pen broke away from Raven's pussy and jumped into his hand. His small pet trembled in his palm and Acier stared at him, realizing for the first time how much Pen had become a part of him and yet how different he was. He could feel Pen's hunger for Raven , a hunger that matched his own consuming passion for her.

Need her, Pen pleaded. *Want more.*

Acier stood at the bed, breathing in deeply as he looked down at Raven's jewel, nestled among a mass of dark curls and glistening with her fragrant juices and Pen's seed. The greedy bastard had ejaculated in her. His nostrils flared as the aroma of her overwhelmed his senses. "So do I," he admitted softly. "But we will not take her without her permission."

Have to have her, Alpha. Please.

No, my faithful pet. No.

She wanted. Placed Pen between legs before sleeping. Didn't take without permission, Alpha. Wouldn't take without permission. And didn't go too far in, didn't need to. She came and Pen came. Felt good. Good pussy but didn't break anything, Alpha.

He knew Pen spoke the truth. Thank God he hadn't taken her virginity. "I know you would never do anything to hurt her, Pen." Nevertheless, she was asleep. Ignoring the lust he fully shared with Pen and Drei and fighting the urge to caress her, he contented himself with lifting Pen to his nostril and sniffing him. Pen was redolent with the smell of her. He placed Pen over his nose and nearly got lightheaded from the scent of her pussy. Breathing deeply, he backed away from the bed and sat heavily on the single padded chair in his bedroom, his gaze locked on her.

He dared not touch her, but God help him, he couldn't make himself stop looking at his real live sleeping beauty. She was the most perfect and beautiful woman he'd ever seen. And she was off limits to him.

He took a final inhalation of Pen before guiltily pushing Pen under the chair. Sniffing his pet was only making him hornier. "Stay," he warned Pen.

He longed to remove Drei, whose agitation he could feel, free his dick and masturbate as he watched her sleep but knew he mustn't. So he sat and watched her and burned with lust and longing the likes of which he'd never experienced. His sexual appetite had always caused a stir in the pack. He was larger and thicker than any other wolf in the pack except maybe Etienne. And at the full moon, his need for sex was viewed as abnormal by the pack. The males envied his size and stamina. The females happily lined up for a chance to mate with him.

While he never mated with females from his den, he considered females from other dens fair game. Still, he had never experienced a stronger need for a particular woman. That he should feel this intense and unbearable longing for

Raven distressed him. That Pen and Drei should share that need distressed him even more. He had no wish to watch his faithful pets and companions writhe in an agony of need he felt all too deeply himself.

He sighed. He supposed he would have to consider the possibility that Etienne was right. Raven was special because she was his bloodlust. His bloodlust, the one woman neither he nor his pets would be able to resist. And yet he must resist. He could not take her.

Must take her, Alpha. Pain unbearable. Need her, Pen begged.

Silence! he snapped. He felt Pen's and Drei's distress at his harsh tone and immediately relented. He stoked Drei through his pants and extended his hand. *Come,* he called softly. Pen immediately appeared from under the chair and somersaulted into his palm, where he lay panting.

Did not mean to make Alpha angry.

"I'm not angry at you or Drei, Pen." He stroked Pen's soft, quivering body.

I'm sorry. Didn't take without permission. Wanted Pen between legs. Put Pen there and held Pen there. Didn't take without permission or hurt. Didn't break anything.

I know, Pen, but we can't take a woman while she's asleep. Do you and Drei understand?

No. Wanted Pen to take.

Maybe so but even if you don't understand we don't take women who are asleep.

Slayer does, Drei pointed out.

Damn that greedy Slayer. He was going to have to have a heart-to-heart talk with Etienne about him. He was not going to have his wild behavior influencing Pen and Drei, who were well behaved and obedient most of the time. *But you and Pen are my pets. And we do not take sleeping women. Is that understood?*

Yes, Alpha.

Drei?

Yes, Alpha.

Now, all he needed was to convince himself of the same fact. He longed to rip Drei away, tear off his clothes, join her on the bed and fuck her awake. He sighed and closed his eyes. How the hell could he possibly manage to keep away from her for more than a few moments at a time? Drei and Pen were in such a state because he was. After having ravished the almost insatiable fem all night long, he shouldn't feel this level of need for Raven that was almost painful. Almost? It was painful.

Hurt, Alpha.

He nodded, breathing deeply. *I know, Pen. I know.*

Please fix? Pen pleaded.

Want her, Drei added. *Need her. Let have. Just a little. Please, Alpha.*

No. You both know Mo. He would kill us if we touched her.

Not afraid, Pen boldly told him.

Alpha can take him, Drei added. *Not afraid to die. Want her bad.*

As did he. Oh God help him. He sighed. He knew his pets shared his respect for Mo. If they were talking about taking him, they, and he, were in much worse shape than he'd ever been in. He suddenly knew Etienne had been right. He didn't know if this was bloodlust he felt or not. Whatever it was, he was firmly in its grip. He could see no way out.

It would only be a matter of time before he found it impossible to resist Raven. Not that he would go down without a fight. But he knew in his heart that he would be going down. Sooner or later he would have to have her. His heart thumped and he wet his lips. Probably a lot sooner than later. He looked at her and swallowed painfully. God help him, if the raging hunger in his cock and his pets were any indication, it was going to be a hell of a lot sooner.

MOONLIGHT WHISPERS

ജ

Chapter One

∽

"I really need you to do this for me."

Acier Gautier sat in the living section of his custom-built RV and sighed. The man on the other end of the long distance call had been there for him and Etienne when they'd needed him most—when they'd left Pack Gautier against the Supreme Alpha's wishes, and struck out on their own some twenty years earlier. Maurice Williams had become not only literary agent to him, but also banker and friend to both him and Etienne. They owed Mo a lot, but—

"Mo, you know ordinarily I'd love to keep an eye on Raven." He opened the blinds in the living area of the RV and glanced upward.

That night the moon would be full and soon his dual needs for blood and sex would be at the point where they would override all other considerations. Although Mo had known them for some twenty-two years, he didn't know what he or Etienne were. He frowned. Hell, even he wasn't sure what they were. Because they were half-breeds, the vampire community had rejected them. He, his mother, and Etienne had suffered some lean emotional times before finally being accepted, if not embraced, by his mother's wolf-shifter pack.

At forty, he was determined to visit vengeance upon the selfish, uncaring vampire who had sired them and left them to face the world alone. Once he had called the unknown and despised male to account, he could then return to Den Gautier and take his rightful place as Den Alpha. In his absence, his cousin Xavier handled the day-to-day den business, but that was not an ideal situation as the pack members sometimes sought him out in bewilderment, certain that he no longer viewed their welfare as important. The den needed him home.

I am coming for you.

Those words had haunted Acier for the last several months. At a hundred and thirty, the Supreme Pack Alpha, Aime Gautier was growing old and weary. Acier, Alpha of one of the biggest dens in Pack Gautier, was needed at home to help battle the pack's internal and external enemies. Just as he was about to abandon his search for their father and return to assume the position of Supreme Alpha for which Aime had groomed him, those words had come to him in a dream, taunting him.

"Now is not a good time for me, Mo."

"I can appreciate that, but if you can't help, I'll have to risk her wrath and follow her myself. I can't have every Tom, Dick, and Harry sniffing at my baby girl."

He sighed. Like Aime, Mo was growing frighteningly frail and old. At twenty-two, Raven was the youngest of the three daughters Mo had raised alone after his wife's death. He knew if he didn't help, Mo would worry himself into even worse health.

"How long will she be here?" he asked, moving slowly through the RV.

"Two, maybe three weeks, tops."

He hadn't seen Raven for ten years. Still, how bad could her visit be? They had always gotten along well and he could put his search on hold long enough to make sure Mo's baby girl had a safe and happy two weeks in and around New York City and Philadelphia. If he were lucky, Etienne would show up and take her off his hands for part of that time. "It will be great to see her again."

Mo sighed. "You don't know how big a load this is off of my shoulders. Now, I'm counting on you, Acier, because I know she'll be safe with you."

"Of course she will. I'll guard her like she was my own pup."

"What? Your own what?"

Mo sounded shocked and Acier realized what he'd called Raven. "Just an expression of affection," he said hastily. "When is she arriving?"

"She should be there some time this evening."

He paused in the kitchen area. "What? Mo, that changes everything."

"She's been looking forward to seeing you for weeks now, Acier. Please, don't disappoint her again."

"No, I won't, but Mo—"

"Tell Etienne I said if he doesn't call me soon, his big behind is mine the next time I see him."

"I'll tell him, Mo, but—"

"Later."

He waited until Mo hung up before slamming his cordless phone down on the small kitchen countertop. He rose and paced the area in front of his loveseat, his cock beginning to feel constricted. Stalking to his bedroom, he reached into his pants and removed the support cup he wore over his genitals when he wasn't on the prowl. He tossed the flexible, white triangular cup onto his bed.

As it landed, it made a small, distressed sound.

He walked over to the bed and stroked its back, and the small creature who lived to serve him projected a feeling of satisfaction towards him. He smiled. "No, Pen, I'm not mad at you. I just need to be able to breathe. No, you don't restrict my breathing. I just want my cock free for a bit. Okay?"

He felt Pen's acquiescence and sighed. Sometimes his Keddi pets took more work than he felt like putting in to them. Small wonder that living leather pets were forbidden to all except the Alpha Supreme and a small number of wolf-shifters of his choosing.

Having stroked Pen's sensibilities, he sighed and allowed his cock to spread out along his leg. There. That was better. He reached back and removed the clip from his hair and it fell forward around his shoulders. Half an hour later, he stood at the door of the RV staring in amazement at the woman smiling at him. She stood at least 5' 10", with curves in all the right places, a pretty face with clear, dark, milk chocolate skin, and warm deep brown eyes.

His nostrils flared and he inhaled deeply. Under her familiar scent, he caught an unmistakable and highly intoxicating and arousing aroma. As she stood there, he could smell her pussy creaming. His cock went hard against his leg and a rush of hot blood flashed up the back of his neck. He felt the call of the full moon.

"Petite? Raven?"

"Steele. Long time no see."

She gave him a sultry smile. This close to his prowling time, every scent of a woman sent the blood rushing to his cock, turning it into a semblance of the nickname seven-year-old Raven had given him. When told Acier was French for steel, she had immediately begun calling him Steele.

"You can't stay."

Her eyes widened. "Dad said it wouldn't be a problem for me to stay until the wedding."

"Until the wedding? Treena's not getting married for another two months."

"I know. She's my sister, remember?" Her smile deepened. "We have two months to get reacquainted. Don't worry, Steele. You won't even know I'm here."

That wasn't bloody likely. The aroma of her fragrant pussy was already threatening to make his cock explode. If she stayed longer than a few hours, he would be hard-pressed not to toss her onto his bed and fuck her senseless.

Casting a sexy, confident smile at him, she moved past him.

Sighing, he picked up the two large suitcases near his door and carried them inside. The moment the door closed, the smell of her sent the blood rushing to his head and down to his cock. He needed pussy and blood…quickly. He looked at her. A pair of big, heavy-looking breasts strained against her sheer top. Without her bra, her breasts would be more than a hungry mouthful. When bitten into they would taste delightful and have large, dark nipples. His gaze flickered downward. Her long legs were encased in a pair of dark silk pants that showcased her nicely padded rear. The palms of his hands itched as he imagined cupping her ass in his palms as he thrust his cock deep into her fragrant pussy. There were few things half as exciting as making no-holds-barred love to a beautiful, voluptuous black woman who exuded sensuality as she did.

He took a deep breath. "Raven, I'm not some boy you can play games with," he warned.

She tossed her head, sending her lovely dark hair cascading around her beautiful face. "Who's playing games?"

Normally, he enjoyed playing sexual games with beautiful women, but he could not afford to indulge his carnal tastes with Mo's baby girl. He had to get away from her or he would be hard-pressed not to strip her, lay her on the bed, and shoot his aching cock balls-deep in her sweet-smelling pussy with one lusty thrust that would burst through the cherry he suspected she was still saving for some lucky human male. His cock jerked and spread out along the side of his leg like a thick pole.

Her gaze shifted to his groin, slowly taking in the length and thickness of his cock. "Oh…my." When she raised her eyes to his, her full lips were parted and he saw an awareness of his lust in her eyes.

She looked directly into his gaze. "I admit I like to cuddle, but I'm not a bed hog. You'll hardly know I'm sharing your bed, Steele. Just give me a cuddle and a friendly lip-lock and I'll drop off to sleep like a baby."

He clenched his jaw. "I have to go out, but the fridge is full and the keys to the door are on the nightstand." He swung away from her and stalked through the RV.

135

She followed him and clenched his arm. "Steele, wait a minute! I think you've misunderstood."

He looked down into her eyes and saw his own lust reflected there. "No, Raven, I haven't misunderstood a thing. " He snatched up his leather jacket from the recliner behind the passenger seat and dug the keys to his motorcycle out of his pants pocket. With his nostrils filled with the sweet scent of her, he quickly left the RV. Outside, he took a deep breath and tried to calm himself. He looked up at the full moon in all its lunar glory. No more time. He had to get far away from Raven as quickly as possible before the urge to satisfy his dual natures with her became more than he could control.

He moved around the side of his midnight black RV and unlocked a large hidden compartment, revealing a gleaming silver and black bike a Hell's Angel would have envied. A few minutes later, with his special prowling kit safely tucked away in one of his side bags, he roared out of the park, his long dark hair flying around his leather-clad shoulders. Acier Gautier, wolf-vampire hybrid was on the prowl.

* * * * *

It was early morning and the RV park was still and silent. Returning from his night of lust, Acier quietly glided his bike behind the big, black, sleek RV. He owned a medium-sized ranch house in Arizona, but as he was rarely there, the RV functioned as home most of the time. Feeling too tired to put the bike away, he secured it by lacing slender leather-like links through the spokes of the wheels. "Keddi. Guard," he said softly.

He received a silent acknowledgement from the Keddi and rose from his position by the bike.

He entered the RV. Raven was not on the sofa that folded out into a full bed. Her suitcases still sat where he had left them the night before and her blouse was across the passenger seat of the captain's chairs. He tightened his lip. No doubt Etienne had put it there when he undressed her the previous night. He tossed his leather jacket across the recliner and padded through the RV, pausing at the hamper to toss inside his soiled clothing from the night before.

He opened the door separating the bathroom and bedroom from the rest of the RV. This part of the RV was in total darkness, but he had no problems seeing. He made his way to his closed bedroom doors. He quietly folded them back and sucked in a breath at the sight that greeted his eyes.

Raven lay asleep on his bed on top of his comforter. Although she wore one of his shirts, it was open and her entire luscious body lay exposed to his ravenous gaze. Her body was dark, sleek, and lovely with wonderful, rounded curves. Her breasts were large and firm with wide, dark nipples. The luscious looking areolas beckoned his mouth and tongue. Her stomach was flat, her legs long and shapely. When he saw Pen laying over her pussy, obstructing his view of her treasure, his cock threatened to explode.

As he watched, Raven moaned softly in her sleep, her hips lifting involuntarily off the bed. Acier closed his eyes and reached out to Pen. He stiffened as he got a very clear picture from his pet as part of his body shifted into the shape of a tight, pulsing cock, thrusting gently, but insistently inside Raven's pussy.

Acier moistened his lips as he felt his Pen's pleasure and delight in himself as Raven's juices began to flow over his cockhead. It was a gentle climax, but Pen was proud of having induced it.

Drei, covering his cock, stirred against him and he knew Drei was sharing the experience with him and Pen.

Good…take more, Drei urged. *Take more, Pen.*

Keeping his eyes closed, Acier parted his lips and felt the warm, sweet taste of Raven's juices as Pen continued to thrust gently into her. His heart thumped and his cock began to feel constricted. Drei, breathing deeply and tightening over him, wasn't helping any.

"Oooh. Oooh, yes, Steele. Yes. Love me. Please."

His eyes opened and heat rose up the back of his neck. The blood shot down to his cupped cock as he listened to Raven's words. Was she dreaming of him making love to her when it was in fact his lusty little pet? The Keddi took their personalities from those they lived to serve. Pen, Drei, and Etienne's pet, Slayer had been known to enjoy the occasional taste of pussy separate from their masters. Both Pen and Slayer had even been known to ejaculate into willing lovers.

In the past, Acier had occasionally allowed his pets to pleasure a willing lover, but Raven was special and he did not intend to rape her by means of allowing Pen, who had become a part of him, to take liberties not freely granted. "Enough, Pen!"

He moved quietly into the room and extended a hand. He felt Pen's reluctance. *More? Please, Alpha?*

A little more, Alpha? Drei pleaded on Pen's behalf.

He tightened his lips. Pen and Drei, his favorite pets, only called him Alpha when caught misbehaving. His pets were becoming as greedy for sex as were Etienne's unruly brood. The next thing he knew he'd have to keep them locked up when there was a female around.

Just a little more? Please, Alpha, Pen pleaded.

While it was temping to allow Pen to continue because he could share in the pleasure, he shook his head. "I said enough, Keddi. Come. Now!"

With a reluctance that was palatable, Pen broke away from Raven's pussy and jumped into his hand. His small pet trembled in his palm. Acier stared at him, realizing for the first time how much Pen had become a part of him and yet how different he was. He could feel Pen's hunger for Raven, a hunger that matched his own consuming passion for her.

Need her, Pen pleaded. *Want more.*

Acier stood at the bed, breathing in deeply. He looked down at Raven's jewel, nestled among a mass of dark curls and glistening with her fragrant juices and Pen's seed. The greedy bastard had ejaculated in her. His nostrils flared as the aroma of her overwhelmed his senses. "So do I," he admitted softly. "But we will not take her without her permission."

Have to have her, Alpha. Please.

No, my faithful, pet. No.

She wanted. Placed Pen between legs before sleeping. Didn't take without permission, Alpha. Wouldn't take without permission. And didn't go too far in…didn't need to…she came and Pen came. Felt good. Good pussy, but didn't break anything, Alpha.

He knew Pen spoke the truth. Thank God he hadn't taken her virginity. "I know you would never do anything to hurt her, Pen."

He longed to remove Drei, whose agitation he could feel, free his shaft, and masturbate as he watched her sleep, but knew he mustn't. So he sat and watched her and burned with lust and longing the likes of which he'd never experienced. His sexual appetite had always caused a stir in the pack. He was larger and thicker than any other wolf in the pack except maybe Etienne. Many in the pack viewed his need for sex at the full moon as abnormal. The males envied his size and stamina. The females happily lined up for a chance to mate with him.

While he never mated with females from his den, he considered females from other dens fair game. Still, he had never experienced a stronger need for a particular woman. That he should feel this intense and unbearable longing for Raven distressed him. That Pen and Drei should share that need, distressed him even more. He had no wish to watch his faithful pets and companions writhe in an agony of need he felt all too deeply himself.

He sighed. He supposed he would have to consider the possibility that Etienne, who leaned towards the vampire side of their heritage, was right. Raven was special because she was his bloodlust…the perfect mate that the vampire half of him craved. His bloodlust…the one woman neither he nor his pets could resist. Yet he must resist her.

Hurt, Alpha.

He nodded, breathing deeply. Drei and Pen were in such a state because he was. After having ravished the almost insatiable fem the previous night, he shouldn't feel this level of need for Raven that was almost painful. Almost? It was painful.

I know, Pen. I know.

Please fix? Pen pleaded.

Want her, Drei added. *Need her. Let have. Just a little. Please, Alpha.*

No. You both know Mo. He would kill us if we touched her.

Not afraid, Pen told him.

Alpha can take him, Drei added. *Not afraid to die. Want her bad.*

He knew his pets shared his respect for Mo. If they were talking about taking him, they, and he, were in much worse shape than he'd ever been in. He could see no way out.

Chapter Two

🔊

Raven Monclaire woke from an erotic dream to find a drop-dead gorgeous man with long, dark, wavy hair, thick, sinfully long lashes, steel gray eyes, and a full, sensual bottom lip, sitting in a chair in the bedroom of the RV staring at her. Although seated, it was clear he stood well over six feet tall and was very muscular. She glanced at his groin. The long, thick cock he had so proudly displayed along the side of one leg the night before, was now clearly cupped.

Cupped? She frowned. Thoughts of the cup he'd left on the bed the previous night brought memories of a strange living leather-like pet called Pen. She had dreamed of this Pen and Steele with her in the woods, making love to her together under a beautiful, full, silver moon.

Both males had taken her with a lust and hunger that made her cry out in ecstatic delight in her dream. Now there he sat, watching her silently. The look of lust in his dark eyes had an immediate effect on her. She went damp and moist between her legs—legs she suddenly realized were splayed wide, revealing her pussy.

Although she had planned to seduce him, her face burned and she looked wildly around for the cover to yank up over her body. She quickly realized she was lying on it. Considering she planned to tempt him into bedding her and she had already allowed his twin brother Etienne to give her the most incredible oral sex the night before, she was being unduly modest. Now was a good as time as any to start her conquest of Steele. Trying to slow her pounding heart, she sat up and stretched, aware that the action exposed her breasts more fully to his gaze.

She forced a smile. "Oh, Steele, you're back. You look exhausted. Had a good time last night?"

He looked at her with eyes almost gold but remained silent, his lips pressed into a tight line. She tilted her head. She could feel his hunger for her. Her heart thumped. If she didn't blow it, she felt sure she was only hours away from having him succumb to her. Whoever he had been with the night before had only served to increase his sexual appetite. She planned to be the lucky recipient sharing his bed come evening.

She frowned suddenly, closing her eyes and seeing a vision of Steele with a small, dark woman in a remote cabin. The woman was somehow bound to some type of bondage rack along one wall. Steele, part Steele and part big gray wolf from her erotic dreams, stood behind the woman, lustily thrusting his huge, thick cock up the tiny woman's rear end.

A flood of anger, jealously, and lust overcame Raven and she snapped open her eyes, willing the vision away. Ever since she had been young, she had somehow seen and known things she hadn't seen and couldn't know. She knew Steele had spent the previous night with a woman who was not human. If her visions were to be believed, Steele and Tee were not quite human either. She wet her lips. Was she herself fully human? A question for another time, she decided. For the present, Steele was back and she planned to seduce him before the night was over. She was going to drive thoughts of that tiny woman from his mind.

She slipped out of bed, closing his shirt over her breasts. The action left her thighs and most of her bare behind exposed. She felt something trickling down the inside of one of her legs. The muscles in her stomach tightened as she realized what it was and who must have shot it into her. Oh Lord. It had not been a dream or a night vision. One of Steele's pets, Pen, had fucked her and come inside her.

She looked at Steele, still seated in the chair, watching the progression of his pet's seed down her thigh. There was no sign of the small, sometimes white, sometimes brown, living leather creature called Pen. Steele must have put him back on, which was why she could no longer see Steel's incredibly big cock. She longed to ask about Pen, but she wasn't supposed to know about him.

Besides, Steele looked almost feral. Although not afraid of him, she decided now was not the time to challenge or push him.

Instead, she reached down two fingers to wipe Pen's seed from her thigh. Catching and holding Steel's gaze, she popped her fingers into her mouth and sucked them. "Hmm," she murmured.

His breathing became somewhat erratic, but he remained silent.

She removed the fingers from her mouth, slipped them inside her vagina to scoop up more of Pen's seed and licked them clean. "Hmm," she said again. "Heavenly. Hmm. I seem to be a bit of a mess. I should head for the shower."

He didn't respond, just sat staring at her pussy, breathing deeply.

Heat suffusing her whole body, she walked over to the chair and looked down at him. "You look rather hot and uncomfortable, Steele. Would you like to join me?"

He tore his gaze away from her pussy and glared up at her, dragging his lips back to reveal even white teeth. For a moment, she fully expected him to snarl or growl at her.

She stroked her fingers over his hair and leaned down to press her lips close to his ear. "I think I still have some cum in my pussy. Would you like to stick your tongue and your fingers inside me and clean it out for me?"

"You mean like you allowed Etienne to do?" he snarled.

There was no mistaking the accusatory tone in his voice. Instead of angering her, his response excited her. She laughed softly and lightly bit into his earlobe. "There's no need to be jealous of Tee, Steele. He kept his cock in his pants. I'll let you

143

do more than I allowed him to do. You can stick your tongue, your fingers, and your cock inside me. You can have all the pussy you can handle."

He wore softly in French and jerked back in the chair. "I can smell Etienne on you! Get the fuck away from me, Raven!"

Now that was definitely not the response for which she'd been hoping. She sighed and straightened. If he could smell Tee on her, he could just as surely smell Pen on her. She'd better wash both scents off. She'd work on Steele after her shower.

"There's no need to get so testy, Steele. So you can smell Tee on me. I might not be able to smell her on you, but I know what you did last night and who you did it with! So don't come off so damned self-righteous about what happened between me and Tee." *And Pen.*

Without waiting for his answer, she left the bedroom, aware that he still watched her. In the shower stall, she stood under cool water for several moments. Then she lathered up, rinsed off, and did her best to wash away all traces of Pen's seed. When she finished, she wrapped a towel around herself and walked through the RV, turning on lights. In the living room, she picked up her biggest suitcase and carried it back to the bedroom.

She saw immediately that she wasn't going to be able to tease Steele anymore. He sprawled across the bed, snoring softly. He had removed his shirt and shoes, but still wore his trousers and socks, although she thought he had removed his cup because she could see the outline of his cock against his leg. Even flaccid, it was big. How good would he feel, fully aroused inside her?

She glanced across the room to the dresser and saw not one but two small white cups adorning the top. She could detect faint, but unmistakable movements as they breathed in and out. Wetting her lips, she walked over to the dresser and looked down.

All movements halted abruptly. They were roughly the size of both hands cupped. Currently, they were shaped much like the jockstraps they purported to be. She knew they were so much more. She also, suspected they needed to breathe.

"It's all right," she said softly. "Breathe."

They continued to hold their breaths. Uncertain how long they could go without breathing, she reached out a hand and stroked the back of the cup nearest her fingers. It was slightly bigger than the other one. Somehow she knew this was Pen, who had made love to her so sweetly the night before.

"Breathe," she said again.

She heard one quick inhalation and then both pets began to breathe naturally. She continued to stroke Pen. "You're Pen," she said. "You kept me company and made me very…content last night. Thank you."

She turned her attention and her finger to the back of the other pet. "And who are you, my handsome little one?"

He is Drei and I am Pen, Alpha Keddi, the first cup told her, projecting his thoughts directly into her mind.

For some inexplicable reason, she seemed to have a rough idea just what a Keddi was. How, she didn't know. She had never known her mother and there was a lot she needed to learn about herself. Chiefly, why she knew what Steele and Tee were capable of shifting into and yet had no fear of either of them.

"Alpha Keddi? To Steele?" she asked softly.

He is Alpha-in-waiting.

For what? That was the question, but for the moment, she was content with what she had learned. She now knew Steele was definitely not human. She became determined to make him become the Steele of her erotic dreams when he came to her in the shape of a big, beautiful, gray wolf with golden eyes full of lust, love and devotion for her.

She bent and kissed both pets and felt them trembling against her lips.

Give more pussy? Pen asked.

Give Drei some pussy? Please? Drei pleaded. *Already gave Pen some. Give Drei some. Want pussy bad.*

As she watched, both pets levitated off the drawer top and glided down, coming to rest in front of her lower body. Hovering there both began to shift until they took the form of two long, thick, quivering cocks with precum glistening on the ends of their cockheads.

She wet her lips. Lord, she was losing it when these two luscious looking pets could make her hot with their demands for pussy.

Give pussy.

Now, Pen demanded, gliding under the towel. She had to bit her lip to keep from crying out when she felt Pen's hard, thick warmth against her pussy. Drei rose slowly and paused near her mouth.

She trembled and knew she would be hard pressed to deny theses two little pets anything, but the cock she wanted most at the moment, belonged to the handsome hunk asleep on the big bed.

She kissed Drei's head. "Not now, but I promise I'll give you both some pussy later."

Drei pressed forward, trying to work himself between her lips. *Want fuck now! Not later.*

Before she could speak, Pen shot out from under the towel and hovered in the air near Drei. *Keddi! Stop! Not proceed without permission! Alpha said so and so do Pen.*

Drei immediately drew back and hung near her face, projecting an air of remorse. *Drei not mean make mad.*

Forgive him? Pen pleaded on his behalf.

She smiled and pressed a quick kiss against both pets' shafts. "I'm not angry and I promise I'll give you both some pussy. Not now. Not today, but the time will come when you'll both get to make love to me."

Quivering with excitement and lust, both pets glided through the air and settled back on the dresser top. Both began to shift and to her amazement, rather than shifting into the white cups, they took the shape of miniature gray wolves with tiny golden eyes.

Oh Lord, was she losing her mind? "How do you do that?" she asked.

Pen answered. *We are the Keddi of Boreias*, he said, as if that explained everything.

Boreias. She had never heard the word, but she suspected it had great meaning for her and Steele. She turned and looked at him, still asleep on the bed. He must have worn himself out making love the night before. Did he have a special woman in his life? His women never lasted more than a couple of months, but she had once heard her father tease him that he couldn't go more than a few days without sex. Maybe…if she were lucky, he had to have it every day.

She removed the towel and dressed slowly, keeping her gaze on the bed. He didn't stir. When she was fully dressed, she opened the large wardrobe built into one corner of the room and pushed her suitcase onto the floor. She would unpack later, after she had convinced Steele to let her stay.

She walked over to the bed and leaned down to touch his hair which lay across the bed. She brushed her fingers along his cheek. "I couldn't sleep for thinking about you last night and wondering who you were with." She kissed his cheek. "I'm so glad you're back. If you want sex, I'm willing and eager to give it to you."

His eyes snapped open and she found herself staring into his silver-gray gaze.

Chapter Three

ഌ

"Oh!" She jerked back. "I thought you were asleep!"

"I was, but I'm a light sleeper." He sat up.

Just how light? Had he heard her promise to allow his Keddi to sleep with her? Her face burned at the thought. "So…you heard what I said?"

"Every word," he assured her.

She swallowed and ran a tongue across her lips as she looked at his wide chest covered with a mass of dark hair. She pointed a hand over her shoulder. "I'm about to make breakfast, then I thought I'd unpack."

"Don't bother."

"Making breakfast? Aren't you hungry?"

"Don't bother unpacking. You can't stay here, Raven."

"Why not?"

He rose and advanced across the room to look down at her. "You'd better understand something about me, Raven. I am not some boy with whom you can play games. You are not staying here. Period."

She stared up at him. "I am staying."

"The hell you are! After breakfast, I am taking you to a hotel. Your father trusts me and I am not going to touch you!"

She moistened her lips. This close, he nearly overwhelmed her senses. She had never wanted a man— him—more. "Nobody asked you to!"

"The hell you didn't! You think I don't know when a woman is coming on to me?"

She flushed. "You're overreacting, Steele. If my sleeping

in your bed bothers you so much, I'll sleep on the sofa in the living room."

"You'll sleep in a hotel, Raven! And it's time you called me Acier! *Ah-see-á*. My name is not that difficult to pronounce. You're not seven anymore."

"No I am not, but I prefer Steele. And I am staying right here with you!" She stepped away from him. "I don't care whether you like it or not, I am staying!" She turned and headed for the kitchen, pushing buttons to open the blinds at the windows as she went.

He followed her. She turned and they faced each other in the kitchen area. He looked different than he had the previous night. Then his hair had hung across his broad shoulders, he'd worn leather pants, his chest had been exposed, and his cock had been prominently displayed along one leg. His hair was drawn back and he wore a pair of well-made khakis. Yet she detected an aura of leashed power and the wildness of the huge gray wolf in him. She liked it and she intended to push him into being his true self with her.

"You can't stay, Raven."

"Steele, do you remember the last time we saw each other?"

He considered her in silence.

"I do, even if you don't. I was twelve and you promised me I could always depend on you and believe your word. Do you remember how I cried when you left that last time? You gave me a hug, kissed my cheeks and my nose, and you promised you'd be back to see me. Do you remember that?"

He nodded. "Yes, but Raven—"

"Well, you never came back and I grew tired of waiting. So here I am and here I am staying until I get good and ready to leave, Steele."

He sighed, his eyes softening. "Raven…honey…Petite, I did mean to come back to see you, but things got in the way and—"

"And your promise to me wasn't important enough to keep?" She blinked back angry tears. "Do you have any idea how much time I spent waiting for you to come see me like you promised? I used to sit by the phone for hours waiting for it to ring. When it did, it was never you asking to speak to me. Never, Steele! The promise that meant so much to me meant nothing to you! Do you have any idea how much that knowledge hurt?"

"Oh, honey, you must know that's not true."

"All I know is you didn't keep your promise to me, Steele."

"I'm sorry! I didn't realize it meant so much to you."

"Well, it did!"

"Honey!" He cupped a palm against her cheek.

She turned her face into his hand and kissed it, bringing her hands up to caress his biceps. She looked at him with tears misting her eyes. "I waited and waited, Steele, but you never came or even asked to speak to me when you called Daddy. You just forgot all about me...like I didn't exist and wasn't important."

"Raven! Honey, that's not true!" He drew her in his arms. "Sweetheart, I promise that's not true."

"I needed you to come back to see me as you promised, Steele." She pressed her face against his shoulder and clung to him, stroking her hands along his bare back, deliberately trying to stoke his passions.

He drew in a sharp breath and pulled away from her. "Raven, I know what you want and what you're trying to do, but—"

"It's what you want too!" she challenged. "Tell me it isn't! Tell me you don't want to make love to me, Steele. Look me in the eyes and tell me so I believe it, and I'll go. I'll go, Steele, and I won't ever come back."

She watched his apple's Adam bob up and down. "I am not going to touch you, Raven."

She reached down to link the fingers of one hand through his. "It's what I want more than anything, Steele. I know you want it too."

He pulled his hand free and stepped away from her. "It's not going to happen!"

"You can deny it all you like, but I know you want me as much as I want you. So why not?"

"Your father is one of my oldest and dearest friends. I am not going to betray him by sleeping with you!"

"I am not a child."

"I didn't say you were."

"Then what's your point?"

"I am eighteen years older than you!"

"Don't you think I knew that when I came here, Steele? It doesn't matter. I made sure I was old enough before I came after you. I'm a legal adult! I don't need my father's permission to take a lover!"

"I'm sure you don't, but I will not be the lover you take!"

"No?" She lifted her chin. "Well, maybe Tee will."

He leveled a finger at her, his eyes darkening dangerously. "You stay the hell away from him, Raven. I won't have him hurt."

That stung. "You think I'd hurt him?"

"To get your damned way? Yes! His feelings for you are too deep for you to jerk him around trying to get back at me. I'm warning you, Raven. I will not allow it."

Her face burned. "I would never hurt Tee and you shouldn't overestimate your charms and my interest in you, Steele."

He glared down into her eyes. "I'm not overestimating anything. I know exactly what you want from me," he told her coolly.

She moistened her lips. "Then give it to me," she said

quietly, swallowing her pride. "Please. I've waited a very long time for it."

His tone had softened when he answered. "You're an incredibly beautiful, sensual woman. You're sexy as hell. You don't need to beg any man to make love to you."

She shrugged. "It's not any man I want. It's you, Steele. But as you said, you already know that."

"I'm too damned old for you. Go find yourself a man your own age who doesn't count your father amongst his best friends."

"I want you, Steele. I always have."

His spread his hands, a helpless look on his handsome face. "Petite, honey…I cannot touch you! It would kill your father if I did."

"And what about me, Steele? Don't my feelings count for anything? I'm an adult. I have the right to choose my own lovers."

"As do I, Raven and I choose not to sleep with my friend's daughter." His eyes turned cold as twin, frozen pools. "I don't mean to be harsh and I would never want to hurt you, but you need to understand that I cannot and will not sleep with you."

Looking into his gray gaze, she saw no trace of the desire she'd seen previously. He meant it. She had wasted the last four years of her life longing for him in vain. She meant nothing to him and never would. The closest she'd probably come to having him sleep with her would be having Pen and Drei make love to her.

She gulped in a deep breath. "So you want me to go?"

"Want?" He shook his head. "No. Need? Yes. I need you to go for both our sakes."

She told herself twenty-two was too old to cry, but she felt just as abandoned as she'd felt so long ago when she'd realized that he was not going to come back. "Fine! You want me gone? I'm gone, Steele and you won't ever have to worry about me chasing you down again!" The tears stinging her eyes, ran down her cheeks. Brushing them angrily away, she turned and started towards the bedroom.

"Raven! Wait a minute!" He caught her hand.

She pulled it away and stared at him, angry at her inability to stop her tears. Crying like this would only make her seem more immature in his eyes.

"Oh, honey!" He clasped her hand and pulled her into his arms, holding her close. "Don't cry, sweetheart. Please. I didn't mean to hurt you."

She balled her hands into fists to keep from stroking them over his back again. "Release me! I don't need or want your pity, Steele!"

Instead of releasing her, he lifted her chin. "Look at me, Petite."

She opened her eyes.

He stared down at her, his eyes, not quite gray and not quite gold. He cupped his palms over her face. His lips parted and she saw the tip of his tongue. He bent his head. She closed her eyes, her heart thumping wildly as he brushed his lips against her mouth, sending a tingle all through her. "It's not pity," he spoke against her mouth.

He outlined her lips with the tip of his tongue, sending a rush of moisture between her legs. Lord, she had to have him. "Steele…please."

He nibbled at her bottom lip. "Oh, honey, I would…if only you weren't so young and innocent and Mo's baby girl."

She pressed closer in his arms, moving her lips and her hips against his. "I'm an adult, Steele!" She deliberately rubbed her breasts against his chest. "I'm a fully grown woman with needs."

"I know, but I can't…" Even as he whispered the words, his hands moved over her back and his lips settled against hers. He kissed her softly and slowly. Heat and need filled her. She nearly melted when he urged her lips apart and sucked the tip of her tongue into his mouth.

She closed her fingers in his hair, savoring what she hoped would be the first of many kisses shared with him. His lips became insistent and feverish against hers. She sensed a leashed passion in him that frightened and excited her. Oh Lord, to have him inside her, big and hard, and thrusting deep with unbridled passion, branding her and claiming her as his woman. His woman. Steele's woman.

He cupped a big hand over the back of her head and deepened the kiss, sucking at her tongue and making her ache for his cock. She pressed closer to him, rubbing her sensitive breasts against his chest. She slid her hands down to his hips and pulled him closer. She felt him, hard and long against her. She moaned against his sweet lips. Oh Lord, he was about to finally make love to her.

Still kissing her, he slipped a hand between their bodies and cupped her mound. His palm seemed to burn through her clothes and she shuddered, almost light-headed at the thought of how close she was to finally being bedded by him.

"Oh, Steele," she whispered against his lips, stroking her fingers over his tight buns.

She felt his fingers fumbling with her zip and her knees shook. "You're so young and sweet…so delicious." His fingers found their way into her pants, pushed her thong aside, and brushed against her pussy.

"Oh!" she gasped as he slipped a finger inside her. "Oh…oh, Steele!"

He slipped a second finger in. His fingers felt thick and hard and left her longing for his cock. Raining kisses over her cheek and neck, he gently pumped his fingers inside her. "Oh honey, you smell so sweet…so hungry for cock."

"Not just any cock…your big, thick cock, Steele. I want it inside me…I want you to thrust it in deep and fuck me senseless."

She could tell he liked her wanton words. His fingers thrust deep and rough inside her while his thumb rubbed her clit.

Imagining his fingers were his cock, she moaned, and creamed them.

He nipped her bottom lip and fumbled with her pants again. The band loosened around her waist. Moments later, his other hand cupped over her butt. "Steele! That feels so good. I love the touch of your hands on my bare flesh."

He laughed softly and slapped her bottom, then caressed it. With one hand on her behind and the fingers of the other hand thrusting gently in her, she shuddered and creamed his fingers again.

"I can smell your excitement and pleasure. Damn, I'd love to eat you!"

"Then do it, Steele." She ground her hips against his hand. "Take me. Do me. I'm yours! Always has been, always will be. Eat me! Suck me! Fuck me!" She reached a hand between their bodies to close over his cock. "Oh Lord, Steele, I'm aching for you…my pussy's aching for your cock. Take me! Please? Fuck me!"

He stiffened suddenly and lifted his head to look down at her. "Fuck you?"

"Yes! Please! I'm dying for your cock!"

"Oh, shit! We can't do this!" He groaned and pulled away from her, withdrawing his fingers.

She watched, her stomach muscles clenching with tension and heat as he slowly licked his fingers clean of her juices. "We have to!" she cried angrily.

He pulled his fingers from his mouth, his face flushed. "No. You came here a virgin. I am not going to send you back to Maurice deflowered — at least not by me."

Maybe all wasn't lost after all. If he was resisting so hard because he thought she was a virgin, she knew how to deal with that. "Really? Well, what if I told you I didn't have a lot of experience, but wasn't a virgin?"

She saw the surprise on his face and nervously wet her lips. They stood staring at each other in silence for several long moments.

"You're not a virgin? Is that what you're telling me?"

She flushed. "How many twenty-two year old virgins do you know, Steele?"

Instead of being relieved, his eyes darkened like cold gray pools. When he spoke, his voice was a snarl. "Who the fuck dared to touch you?"

"What?"

"Who was it? Tell me so I can tear his goddamned throat out!"

His almost animal-like ferocity shocked her. "You'll do no such thing!"

"Did the bastard hurt you?"

"That's none of your concern!"

"Who is he?"

"Steele, I don't need you going mental on me."

"How the fuck can you not be a virgin, Raven?!" he demanded, looking and sounding as if she had mortally wounded him.

"What do you expect?" she asked defensively. "I'm twenty-two, Steele!"

He touched her cheek. "But you're so young and sweet...how could you give it up so easily? Didn't Mo teach you how to keep your damned legs closed?! How many men have fucked you?"

She flushed, her lips quivering. She resisted the urge to slap him. "Who the fuck do you think you're talking to, Steele?"

"I'm talking to you!" His lips trembled and for one awful moment, she expected him to call her a bitch or a whore.

"How dare you try to make me feel cheap? I'm not some

tramp you can talk to any way you like!"

"Shit!" He hauled her in his arms and kissed the top of her forehead. "That wasn't my intention, honey. I promise it wasn't. I just…the thought of you with…" He stepped back and blew out a deep breath. "How many men have you been with?"

"What?"

"You heard me. How many cocks have you had?" he demanded, his voice raw with emotion.

She stared up at him. He was in pure demanding Alpha mode. Looking into his eyes, she no longer doubted that he was the Alpha male. Now was not a good time to taunt or tease him. "Just one," she whispered.

"What is his name and where does he live?"

"Why?"

"I'm going to kill him."

Noting the lustful fury in his gaze, she decided he was serious. She felt a thrill of fear and excitement. "But…why?"

"Because no one sleeps with my woman except me!" he roared angrily. He curled his fingers in her hair. "Do you really think I'm going to allow some stupid bastard to get away with taking what was rightfully mine? I'll rip his heart out with my bare hands and feed it to him."

His woman? So he was ready to admit she was his…at least for now. She wet her lips, trembling with excitement. "So this changes things between us. Doesn't it?"

He looked at her, his eyes slowly going gold…that lovely, dark shade of gold like the wolf in her fantasies. She stroked a hand down his arm to link her fingers with his. "So what are we going to do? Are you going to let me stay?"

"I don't know. Tell me who you slept with."

"His name is not important. I don't want him hurt… I won't have him hurt."

"I'm not going to hurt him."

"You're not?"

"No! I'm going to kill the motherfucker, not hurt him!"

"He's not important. You are. I don't want to talk about him. It was just sex… I wanted a little experience when I came after you. He did me a favor. Okay?"

He stared silently at her.

She squeezed his hand and smiled up at him, feeling as if she'd won the first battle. He'd already wavered in his insistence that she had to leave and he'd called her his woman. "I'll sleep on the sofa and I promise I won't walk around naked in front of you until you're ready to take me."

He didn't respond.

She leaned forward and kissed his mouth, rubbing herself against his cock. "So. What do you want to do today?"

"Fuck you!" he growled.

Feeling triumphant, she smiled, linked her arms around his neck, and ground herself against him again. She shuddered as a tingle of joy danced through her. "Oh Lord, that can be arranged, sweetie."

He snarled and pulled away from her, leveling an arm with the finger pointed. "Don't you call me sweetie in that tone and I've already warned you not to play games with me, Raven."

She sighed. This Alpha nonsense was going to present quite a problem. "Fine. There's no need to bite my head off, Steele."

"I am not fucking you. So fuck off!"

She sighed. Getting him into the sack was going to take a lot of blood, sweat, and tears. But get him there she would. He had already admitted that he thought of her as his woman. She would capitalize on that sense of possessiveness.

Nevertheless, there was a wildness about him that suggested now was not the best time to push him. She shrugged. "I'll unpack after breakfast."

Eyes still glowing gold, he said nothing.

"So, would you take my other suitcase into the bedroom?"

He turned and stalked silently toward the living room and snatched her suitcase off the floor.

"Hey, be careful with that," she said. "It's new. I got it for graduation...you sent it to me along with diamond studs, remember?"

He curled his lips back over his teeth. She blinked and shook her head as he padded silently pass her with the suitcase. Whoa. For a moment there she had almost thought he had vampire incisors in his mouth! He was something of a werewolf, not a vampire.

She reached over to turn on the overhead lights, but they were already on!

Chapter Four

෨

Acier circled the small space in his bedroom waiting for Mo to answer his private line. He did on the fifth ring. "Hello."

"Mo, I need to talk to you about Raven."

"What about her? Didn't she arrive safely?"

"Yes." He spoke quickly to alleviate Mo's fears.

"Then what's wrong?"

He glanced at the closed bedroom doors. He could hear Raven humming in the kitchen. "She's…all grown up, Mo."

"I know. She's twenty-two."

"And she's grown out and around—a lot. She has…all these…" curves and big breasts he longed to suck on and bury his face between. His cock stirred.

"What's your point, Acier?"

"She…she can't stay here."

"Why not?"

He'd been dreading that question. How was he supposed to admit that she was coming on to him and that he would not be able to resist her much longer? In some ways, he felt as beta when talking to Mo as he did when in the presence of the supreme Alpha, Aime Gautier, who had given him and Etienne his last name when they were cubs.

"She's beautiful, Mo and…" Sexy and as horny for him as he was for her.

"And she wants you?"

He stopped pacing. "What?"

He sighed. "She wants you and is determined to have you."

"I didn't say that!"

"But that's what this conversation is leading up to. Isn't it?"

Mo didn't sound surprised. Acier frowned. "You mean you knew how and what she wanted before she left home?"

"Knew for certain? No. She wasn't foolish enough to let on to me how she felt about you. Suspected? Yes. She hasn't talked about much of anything but you for the last couples of months. You've always been a hero in her eyes."

"Shit, Mo!"

"What did you say, Acier?"

He compressed his lips. He was too damned old to still feel so beta with Mo. "It slipped out," he said warily.

"I thought it must have."

He sighed. "If you suspected how she felt, why didn't you tell me?" He bit back the urge to tell Mo that he'd seen her nude and felt a lust that threatened to totally consume him. Forget admitting that Etienne had performed oral sex on her.

"You know how headstrong she is. I tried to talk her out of going to see you, but she is her mother's child. She was insistent. So I hoped that once she arrived and found out you were not interested in her, she'd brood for a few days and come home."

"Well it didn't work out that way, Mo!"

There was a long silence, then Mo sighed. "Are you telling me you are interested in her, Acier? Sexually? You have a sexual interest in my baby girl?"

"Mo…I need you to convince her to leave."

"Or?"

He closed his eyes and leaned his forward head against one of the door panels. "Or I can't be responsible or what happens."

"She's my baby, Acier!"

"I know that! But I can't control the feelings she invokes in me. I…there are things about me you don't know, Mo."

"I know you run through women like water and I don't want my baby treated like one of your throw-away tramps you picked up in a bar or a back alley!"

"It's not by choice, Mo. I have needs a…normal man wouldn't have…needs I can't always control."

"What are you trying to tell me, Acier?"

"Mo, I am…different from normal men."

Mo sighed. "I've always suspected as much about you and Etienne, Acier."

Something in Mo's tone roused his interest. Raven was like her mother? Who had her mother been? And in what way was she like her mother? Tee had said Raven was *Willoni*. Since Mo was not, that would mean her mother had been *Willoni*. Exactly how had Raven's mother died? He frowned, remembering some of the tales Aime used to tell. Or had she died?

He would find out. But for the moment, he had other concerns. "I need you to get her to leave, Mo."

"I tried to convince her not to go in the first place. She left home determined to… I reminded her that although you might look under thirty, you were actually forty. I even pointed out that you never stayed with one woman more than a few weeks, but she wouldn't listen to any of my arguments. Like her mother, she has strong sexual urges and needs. She's bound and determined to get you into bed."

His nostrils flared. Mo made him sound like a sex maniac. "Well, if she doesn't leave, she'll get her wish and then some!"

"Acier! Don't you hurt my baby!"

"I cannot resist her, Mo. I've tried, but I can't."

"She's only been there one night, Acier. How hard have you tried?"

"I've done my best, Mo. I'm not quite… Please

understand."

"So you're telling me you're going to…"

"I'm telling you I can't resist her much longer."

"Try harder, damn you!"

"Mo…I have tried…if she won't leave…would you have me throw her out?"

"You throw my baby girl out and you'll have to deal with me, Acier."

"Then get her to leave…if you don't want it to happen between us…"

"She won't listen to me where you're concerned, Acier."

"Mo, I can't begin to tell you how much I value our friendship. I don't want to damage our relationship or betray your trust…"

Mo sighed and when he spoke, he sounded old and tired. "Acier, I know that. Just…try not to break her heart. When you move on, I don't want you to leave her shattered like you have so many others."

That stung. "I never willingly hurt any woman, Mo! I just can't control how I feel sometimes."

"And this is what's going to happen with her? You'll take her and discard her when you're finished?"

"No! You don't understand, Mo. I don't think I want to move beyond her. I've never felt this way about any other woman."

"You always move on, Acier."

Not this time. "Mo—"

"I don't want to talk about it anymore. You were the one man I thought I could trust with her."

He sucked in an aching breath, feeling as if he had taken a direct shot in the brain or heart, one of the most effective ways to kill one of his kind. "Mo, if necessary, I would die for you. You know that!"

"Yes, Acier, actually, I do know that. You'd die for me but you won't stay away from my daughter."

"I would, Mo, if I could... I can't...I can't explain it... I just... If she stays, I..."

"She's a virgin."

He frowned, recalling that Pen had told him he hadn't broken anything. Of course he hadn't since she wasn't a virgin and there was nothing left to break. Still, he suspected it was more than his life was worth to point out that she'd already surrendered her virginity to another man. "I'm sorry, Mo."

"Be gentle with her and treat her kindly, Acier, or you will have to answer to me."

"I will, Mo. I won't hurt her. I promise."

"I have your word you'll treat her kindly and with respect?"

"Yes!"

Mo sighed. "I'll hold you to that, Acier. If you send her back to me shattered or broken—"

"I won't."

"And you'd better not send her back pregnant either!"

"Mo, I—"

A dial tone sounded in his ear.

Oh, shit! He needed a cold shower and a long ride on his bike to think. Ten minutes later, he stood in the shower stall, holding the handheld spray nozzle over his head. The cold water pouring over his body did little to alleviate the stiffness in his cock. What the hell was he going to do? Even though Mo had finally given his tacit approval for him to sleep with Raven, he felt like scum wanting her.

Why the hell did he have a thing for Mo's daughters and them for him? Ten years earlier, he'd nearly gone all the way with Raven's older sister, Treena. He'd just come out of prowl heat and he'd been standing naked at the bedroom window, fondling his cock in Mo's house when the bedroom door opened and closed. Turning, he'd seen Treena, her lovely dark, naked body leaning against the closed door.

"Acier, I have someone who wants to meet you," she'd whispered.

"Who?"

She parted her long, lovely legs, reached down and drew back the folds of her labia, revealing the pretty, pink, pussy inside. "My pussy! Don't be shy, handsome. It's tight, hot, and wet for you. Come on in and say hello."

"Treena! Get out of here!"

"Not until I get what I want. I'm tired of you ignoring me and pretending I don't exist. I'm nineteen now and I want you!"

"You're nuts if you think I'm going to touch you!"

"You're nuts if you think I'm leaving this room before I get what I came for...some cock." She locked the door and walked across the room and curled her soft fingers around his cock.

His cock had jumped to attention and he lost his mind. Without another word, he swept her up in his arms and carried her to the bed. Lying on top of her sleek, beautiful body, he kissed her, while fondling her large, firm breasts. She had returned his kisses and eagerly parted her legs. Kneeling between her trembling thighs, he'd pressed his cock against her pussy.

"Fuck my pussy with your big, hard cock, Acier! Drive that big, white pole up my chocolate cunt, baby and get your first taste of sweet, hot black pussy," she whispered.

He'd been with black women before. Hell, he and Etienne had been with women of nearly every race. But he had to admit to having a special fondness for black women with their sleek, smooth dark skin, big breasts, and big asses.

Treena's crude words sent him over the edge. But at the back of his mind was the acknowledge that Mo would kill him if he found out. Still, unable to resist his lust for her, he had slid several inches of his cock into her. He encountered her cherry and froze.

She wrapped her arms around his neck and bit his lip. "Do it. Take it! I've saved it just for you, Acier! Plunge that big sweet dick of yours into me and take my cherry!"

That had brought him back to his senses. He'd jumped off the bed, put her out of the room, closed the door, and spent the night masturbating. Despite Raven's tears and Treena's begging glances, he had left the next morning. Although he had promised Raven he'd return, he knew he couldn't…or he'd end up banging Treena until she couldn't walk.

He had avoided disaster with Treena and now found himself in a worse situation with Raven. With Treena he'd felt nothing but lust. With Raven he felt so much more. How could he resist her? Somehow, for the sake of his friendship with Mo, he had to.

Yet if Etienne were right, he could neither help nor continue to deny his feelings and his very real need for her. He sighed and shook his head. The only way he could see out of the mess he was in, was going back on the prowl for a woman to satisfy his needs. Then maybe he could return without fear of fucking Raven until she could barely walk. Shit! He was not going to touch her! No matter how much they both wanted it.

He dried off, slipping on the pajama bottoms he had brought into the stall with him. Stepping into the hall, he stepped right into Raven—naked except for a tiny thong that barely covered her fragrant pussy.

His chest brushed against her breasts. Her nipples tightened and his cock jumped to instant, rigid attention. Before he could stop himself, he shot an arm around her waist. He pulled her close. He curled his fingers in her hair, and pressed his mouth against hers, parting her lips with a hunger and passion he could no longer control.

Her lips were warm, sweet, and welcoming under his. He kissed her again and again, holding her close and drowning in her touch...her warmth...her aroma...her taste. No other woman had ever had this wonderful, almost painful effect on his senses. He wasn't sure what was happening with her, he just knew this was so much more than lust. Raven was his mate...his woman. He had to have her.

She trembled against him and he pressed his groin against her, allowing her to feel the hot, thick length of his cock. He knew the size and width of his erect shaft aroused most women who saw or felt it throbbing against them. And sometimes, like now, it seemed almost alive...as if it had a mind and will of its own. It ached to be inside her and he fought to hold on to a modicum of control. Even if she weren't a virgin, he wanted their first time to be very special and memorable for her. He didn't want to rut into her with wild abandon and hurt or tear her open.

He slipped his hands down to cup her lovely ass in his palms and rubbed his cock against her pussy. It felt so good he knew he was only seconds away from coming.

She gasped against his lips and slipped her fingers into his pajamas. One hand grabbed his ass, the other curled around his cock.

"Ahhh! Petite!" He groaned out her name and his cock exploded.

"Ooooh." She moved her hand from his cock and sucked his seed from her fingers.

With the rest of his seed spilling down his leg, he swept her up into his arms and carried her to the bedroom. He gently put her down before he kneeled before her. Breathing deeply, he wrapped his arms around her waist, pressing his face against her stomach, mere inches from her sweet, fragrant pussy.

"Tell me to stop now and I will. Let this go any further and I'll have to have you," he warned, trembling with need, not only for her body, but for her blood.

She stroked her hands over his shoulders, making him

burn. "I've waited a very long time for this. I don't want you to stop." She fumbled with his clip and freed his hair. "I want this, Steele. I want you."

He wanted her so badly he felt as if he could barely breathe. He released her and slowly pushed her thong over her hips and past her mound.

She stood before him completely naked. He pressed a long, hungry kiss against her mound, breathing in deeply to savor her scent—musky and exciting and yet fresh and innocent. He decided she must have lost her virginity recently because she still bore the intoxicating never-fucked scent of a virgin.

She was so beautiful. He looked up into her gaze and saw fear and excitement. God help him, he was about to give her what she wanted. "Petite?"

She nodded, breathing deeply.

He rose and exposed his cock, rigid and still fully aroused. Her gasp at the sight of him, heightened his passions. Still, he felt compelled to offer her a last way out. "Is this what you really what?"

She nodded again. "Yes…oh, yes, Steele, I do."

Urging her back onto the bed, he lay on top of her. He ground himself against her pussy, savoring the delight the contact brought. Then he cupped her breasts in his hands.

"You have such lovely breasts."

"You want to taste them?"

"Hell, yeah!" He bent his head and sucked them. They were sweet and delicious. He bit gently into each one, while exploring the nipple with his tongue.

He could smell her creaming. The aroma of her desire for him was almost palatable. He dragged his mouth from her luscious, ripe breasts and pressed his hardened cock against her pussy.

"Oh God!" she moaned.

He detected a note of fear in her and struggled to regain control of himself. Without being unduly vain, he doubted if her one lover's cock had been half his length or thickness. He suspected, for all her eagerness, she wasn't really ready to be fucked by him. But he had to have some satisfaction. Growling in frustration, he forced his body up and off hers. After drinking in her lush curves with his eyes, he kissed his way over her breasts, down her flat stomach. He parted her legs, exposing her lovely treasure.

He kissed her there, parted her fragrant folds and looked down into her. The outer lips were dark and pouty, the inside ones pretty and pink. He had never seen a more luscious pussy. Contemplating the delights awaiting him within, his cock exploded again. He grabbed it and came on her stomach. Giving him a shy, but encouraging smile, she scooped up some of his seed and spread it over her pubic hair. She spread the remainder of his seed between her pretty, pink, pussy lips.

"Do me! Please. Make love to me, Steele and fill me with your seed."

"Mo will kill me if you get pregnant."

"I'm on the pill, Steele."

He sighed in relief. That was one load off his mind because he was going to have to come inside her. "If I fuck you now, it's going to hurt far more than you're going to be able to bear."

"I don't care!"

"I care. You're the last woman I want to hurt." Besides, at the rate he was going, he'd come the moment he entered her before he gave her any satisfaction. His lack of control was damned embarrassing.

She stroked his cheek, smiling at him. "Do what you need to do."

He turned her on her stomach, parted her large, supple ass cheeks, slid his cock between the two lovely mounds, and slowly began fucking his aching shaft back and forth between her sensuous, beautiful flesh.

He was so excited, it only took a few strokes between her warm cheeks before he felt his climax rapidly approaching. He pulled back, quickly turning her over. Shuddering with pleasure, he blasted her clit as he came.

"Oooh!" She moaned. "Oh, Steele. I have to feel you inside me. Come in me." She reached out to clutch his cock between her hands and inserted his head inside her pussy. Shuddering with a combination of lust and tenderness, he continued coming, until his seed spilled from her to trickle down one smooth, dark leg.

The desire to shove forward so more of his aching shaft found a home inside her was difficult to overcome, but he managed to resist it. He pulled away from her, spread her legs wide, and lay on top of her. Grinding his cock against her, he slipped his arms around her to hold her close. He kissed her neck. "Oh, honey! You're beyond sweet!"

She stroked her fingers through his hair. "Oh, Steele, why didn't you fuck me?"

He nipped her neck, fighting off the urge to feed on her. "Don't worry! I will! Just not today, honey."

She curled her fingers in his hair. "Why not?"

He sighed. "There are things you need to know before we take that final step."

She kissed his bottom lip. "I know all I need to know."

"No. You don't. For one thing, you need to know you are now mine and I will share you with no one…not even Etienne."

"I don't want anyone but you."

He lifted his head and looked down at her. "I know you want Etienne, little liar. I can smell your desire for him, and his for you goes off the scale."

She grimaced, then gave him a wicked smile. "Okay, so I do want him. How could I not? He's so warm, sweet, and sexy…almost as sexy as you are, Steele. Maybe you'll give us your permission to make love."

"Never!" he assured her.

She smiled at him and he swallowed slowly, his conviction wavering. There was a lot he would do to make her happy, but he would not share her.

"We'll see." She smiled at him again, making his cock stir. "You'll make love to me soon. Yes?"

"Soon. Very soon. I can smell your pussy and I want it…I need it…I need you. I'm going to fuck you like you've never been fucked."

Her smile was a combination of shyness and hunger. He sighed. He was going to need to go back into the shower and jerk off several times to keep from rutting into her like she was his first fuck in years.

He kissed her lips lightly and rolled off her and on to his stomach.

She kissed his shoulders. "Are you hungry?"

"Yes."

"What do you want?"

He rolled over and looked up at her. "Pussy…lots of it and all yours."

She laughed, brushed her breasts against his chest, and jumped off the bed. He ran after her and caught her in his arms, pressing his cock against her tight ass. "Oh, honey, when I take you, it really is going to hurt."

She shivered in his arms and pressed her head back against his shoulder. She slipped a hand between their bodies to fondle his cock. "I know that, Steele. And I want it to hurt. I want every thick, hard inch of you inside me, pumping deep and forcefully…stretching and hurting me."

"Oh, hell! I need some pussy!"

She turned in his arms, curled her fingers around his cock, and smiled up at him. "It's yours for the taking!" She held his cockhead against her mound. "Feel how much I want you."

He cupped her ass and pressed forward. She parted her legs and he slipped between the lips of her vagina.

"Hmm." She moaned and lifted her mouth for a kiss.

He lowered his head, kissing her hungrily as he eased forward. Another inch or so slid inside her hot moist body. He shuddered and bit into her bottom lip. Lord, he wanted to fuck her long and hard all night long…night after night…week after week…for an eternity.

"I'll be as gentle as I can."

Her soft hands held his shoulders. "I know. But painful or not, I want to fuck you, Steele. I'm going to fuck you…all ten inches of you."

"Bigger," he murmured against her lips. "Much bigger than that."

She jerked back and stared at him wide-eyed. "And thick and hard as steel to boot! That's enough cock for two guys."

He laughed and kissed her again. "And it's all yours."

"Is it, Steele? Is it really all mine?"

"I know what you're thinking, but you're wrong. It's all yours, Raven."

"Well, last night you weren't all mine."

He sighed and drew away from her. "I had to leave last night."

"And you went out whoring."

He raked his hands through his hair. "Yes," he said shortly.

She leaned forward and brushed her lips against his nipples. "And tonight?"

"Tonight I'm all yours, honey."

"And the small, dark woman you were with last night in that cabin?"

He stiffened. "How do you know who I was with last night?" For a moment he had the unwelcome thought that Etienne had disobeyed him and returned to spend the night with her. He quickly dismissed the thought as unworthy. Etienne did not break promises he made to him or anyone else.

"It doesn't matter how I know, I do know, Steele and I want to know if you plan to see her again."

"No! I know it's not gallant to admit, but she meant nothing to me. It was just sex. I sometimes need a lot of sex, Raven. I need you to understand that before we go any further."

"What if I tell you a need a lot of cock?"

He felt a knot of hunger and rage in his stomach as he wondered how many men she'd been with. How many men had crawled between her long, luscious legs and taken pussy that she should have saved for him? She had said just one, but how many men could resist her after having kissed her sweet lips? "I'll give you as much cock as you can handle."

She reached out and fondled him, gave a little jerk on his cock, and then pressed herself against it. "And what if I want more than one night?"

"You can have as many nights as you like."

"I have a lot of lust that needs satisfying, Steele."

He leered at her. "I have a lot of cock."

She laughed, pressing a quick kiss against his mouth. "So you do." She licked her lips. "I'm a little messy. I'm going to take a shower. Want to join me?"

"If I join you in that small space, we'll spend the next few weeks taking sponge baths because the shower stall will be totally destroyed."

Her eyes gleamed. "Do you want me that badly, Steele?"

He hesitated. Was it wise to admit how desperately he needed her? "Well, I…I mean I—"

"Steele! Either you do or you don't. It's not rocket

science."

"I…yes."

"Hold that thought, handsome."

"What? You work me up and then tell me to hold that thought?"

"I'm feeling the need for a bath."

He sucked in a breath. "Does being with me make you feel dirty?"

She widened her eyes. "Don't be silly, Steele. My wanting a shower has nothing to do with feeling dirty. Why should it? We haven't done anything to feel dirty about. So don't stress on me. Okay?"

Why the hell did he allow her to have her damned way about everything? He shrugged. "Okay."

She smiled and kissed his cheek before leaving him alone in the bedroom.

He got back in bed, rubbing his cock against the cover. Then, thinking of her, he fell asleep, his nostrils filled with her scent. His dreams were far from pleasant. He dreamed of the nameless vampire who had fathered him urging him on and then fleeing as he drew closer.

He came awake abruptly, his senses alert, his nostrils filled with the smell of one of his kind…his pack…young and afraid. He bolted up in bed.

Raven, who had been sitting, fully dressed, in the only chair in the room with Pen and Drei on her lap watching him sleep, jumped. "What's wrong, Steele? Did you have a bad dream?"

"I have to go out for a while."

"What?"

He closed his eyes briefly and reached out to the lone cub. *Little one, I am coming. Wait for me.*

He received a timid response. *Yes, Alpha. Please come quickly. I'm afraid.*

Without looking at Raven, he pulled on his clothes and ran through the RV. She followed him and grabbed at his arm as they reached the door. He turned to find her staring up at him with a stricken look on her face. Oh, hell. She must think he was going to another woman.

Chapter Five

ဢ

He recalled that she'd had Pen and Drei, who now hovered in the air around them, on her lap in their natural forms. He would have to tell her what and who he was. "It's a member of my den. She's young, alone, and afraid. I have to go to her, honey."

"I'll come with you."

He shook his head. "No. I have to go alone."

"Why? Is she one of your lovers?"

He tightened his lips. "I do not sleep with members of my own den. I'm entrusted to guard and protect them, not fuck them!"

She caught her breath. "So it's true…you are a werewolf."

"No," he said shortly. "I am not what you'd call a werewolf! But I don't have time to discuss this now, Raven. She needs me."

She touched his chest, then her own. "So do I."

That admission warmed him, but his first duty was to his lost cub. "But you are not alone nor afraid."

"Does that make my need of you any less important?"

He sighed. "We'll talk about this when I return."

She lifted her chin. "So she's more important to you than I am?"

He shook his head. "Don't try to make me choose between you and her. As you've been at pains to point out since you arrived, you are an adult. She's young, afraid, and alone."

"Well…I guess that answers my question. As usual, what

I want or feel doesn't matter to you."

He decided she had deliberately misinterpreted what he'd said, but he didn't have time to play games with her. "We'll talk about it when I get back. Would you like me to leave Pen and Drei with you?"

"Why? How...how long are you going to be gone?"

"As long as it takes."

She tightened her lips. "And if it takes all night?"

"Then I will see you in the morning, Raven."

"And you expect me to sit and spend another night waiting for you?"

"Yes. See that you are here...alone when I return."

Her eyes fairly shot off sparks. "Are you nuts?"

"No. I'm the damned Alpha male in charge around here, Raven." He knew he sounded harsh, but he didn't have time to sugarcoat the truth to make it more palatable for her. He would do that later when he returned.

"Fuck you!"

"That's what I intend to do to you when I return!"

They traded stares for several moments. She looked angry and hurt. He resented her clear lack of trust. When he returned they would have a lot to discuss.

"I'll be back as soon as I can." He touched her cheek.

She slapped his hand away and lifted her chin. "Ask me if I care."

"You'd better care and your ass had better be here when I return!"

He snatched his keys from the living room and left the RV with Pen and Drei beside him. He knew he was leaving a very unhappy Raven behind, but his first duty had to be to his lost cub. He would find her and make sure she found her way safely home. Then he would explain to Raven that although his den members were important to him, so was she.

"Pen, Drei, find our lost cub," he instructed and watched them, in their natural form shoot through the air until they were nearly an invisible blur.

* * * * *

Raven listened to the sound of Steele's bike leaving the RV park in disbelief before she stormed through the RV to the bedroom. There was a lump of anger and hurt lodged in the pit of her stomach as she pulled her suitcases from the big wardrobe.

Damn him if he thought he could treat her like some hussy off the street. After packing her cases, she sank down onto the bed, taking deep breaths. She needed to calm down before she could trust herself to drive. She stretched across the bed, burying her face in the pillow where Steele had lain. It bore his scent and she inhaled deeply, longing for him. She closed her eyes. *Steele. Oh, Steele.*

The sound of a car pulling into the spot next to the RV aroused her. She sat up and went to look out the window. A tall, well-dressed man emerged from a big SUV. Slightly over six feet, he had short blond hair, sky blue eyes, was well-built, and was so handsome he was almost beautiful. She guessed he was roughly twenty-five or thirty. He walked with all the confidence of an exquisitely handsome and sexy man to the RV. A regal gracefulness about him conjured up thoughts of a majestic gray wolf. Was he, like Steele and Tee, a shifter?

She closed her eyes and somehow knew this man presented no danger. When he knocked, she walked through the RV and opened the door. "Yes?"

His lips parted and he started at her, his blue eyes making a brief assessment of her. Without being vain, she knew he liked what he saw. "Hello. I'm looking for Acier."

He had a warm, deep voice that would send tingles through a woman…had she been fancy-free. At the moment, her fancy was entirely centered on Steele. Nevertheless, this male was the most physically handsome man she'd ever seen and it was difficult not to moisten her lips and stare at him. "Steele isn't here."

"Steele?" He smiled, revealing perfectly straight gleaming white teeth. "You must be Petit Corbeau."

She nodded. "How did you know?"

He shrugged his wide shoulders. "Both Acier and Etienne talk incessantly of you."

She extended her hand.

He took it between both of his, lifted it to his mouth and kissed it. "I am Xavier Depardieu, Acier and Etienne's cousin. It is a great pleasure to meet you. May I be informal and call you Raven or is it to be Ms. Monclaire and Mr. Depardieu?"

She smiled, deciding immediately that she liked him. "Call me Raven and you are?"

"Call me what my close friends do, Xay."

"Xay." She stepped away from the door. "Come in?"

He cast a long look at her. He projected a wall of desire at her and she sucked in a breath, taking an involuntary step back.

He tightened his lips and gave a regretful shake of his head. "If Acier is not here, I need to go find him. There is urgent business I need to discuss with him." He paused, still holding her hand. "Are you staying here long?"

That was a good question. "I had planned to stay for a few weeks," she said carefully.

His blue gaze flittered over her face and she saw an unmistakable gleam of interest in his eyes, although it was muted now. "Acier carries your picture, but it does not do you justice. In it you are a child. You have become a breathtakingly lovely woman. Perhaps, when my business with Acier is complete, I will be fortunate enough to see you again, Raven."

Had she not spent so much time longing for Steele, she was sure she would have instantly fallen under the spell of

Xay's undeniable charm and sex appeal. He was so incredibly handsome. Although flattered by his obvious interest in her, she felt no desire to flirt with him as she had with Tee.

She gave him a brief, polite smile. "It was nice to meet you, Xavier."

He arched a brow. "You are spoken for?"

"Yes…by Steele."

He immediately released her hand and stepped away from her. "I beg your pardon. I intended no offense."

"None was taken, Xay."

He inclined his head. "I won't impose on you any longer."

"Hey, wait a minute. I say Steele and I are…a couple and suddenly I'm chopped liver?"

"You are off limits." He inclined his head again. He turned and walked back to his SUV.

She closed the door and leaned against it, frowning. Acier carried her picture with him? When she was a child. Big deal. She frowned and looked at her watch. He'd been gone three hours. She'd give him another hour to either call or return before she decided what to do.

Two hours later, she tossed both suitcases into the trunk of her car. Uncertain where she was headed, she drove out of the RV park. If he wanted to go chasing after young girls, fine. He'd just better not expect her to be waiting like a dutiful, hard-up hussy when he returned.

Ninety minutes later, she checked into a small hotel in Philadelphia. Once in her room, she picked up her cell phone and made a call.

He answered on the fifth ring, his voice low and muffled. "Yeah?"

She couldn't decide if he sounded drowsy or is she had interrupted him with a woman. She paused and spoke in a rush. "I need to see you."

"What is? What's wrong? Where are you? Are you all right? Tell me and I'll be on my way."

She told him. "I need to see you now. Please."

"What are you doing there?"

"I had to get away from Steele. Will you come?"

There was a noticeable pause before he spoke. "Yes. I'll come, but you need to talk to him."

There was nothing to say. Her wants and needs were always going to be unimportant to him. "How long will you be?"

"I'll be there in an hour. Just wait for me."

She nodded. "Okay," she nodded and hung up. There, it was done. She'd called him and there would be no turning back now. Steele had his chance and he'd blown it. He could thank himself for this.

A little over an hour later, the man she intended to spend the night with walked into her hotel room. Dressed in an expensive dark suit with a cowboy hat covering his head, he was tall, with wide shoulders, narrow hips, and long legs. His classically handsome features were chiseled. She ached to kiss his mouth and lose herself in his dark gray eyes.

Although, except for his hair, which was now cut short and worn close to his head, he was a virtual mirror image of Steele, she had never had any problems telling the two apart.

He closed the door, tossed his hat onto the bed, and engulfed her in a bear hug. "Ah, my delicious, Petite." He licked her neck, sending a tingle all through her. "What's gone wrong? Sei still out on the town?"

She wrapped her arms around his neck and clung to him, trembling, close to tears. "No. He came back early this morning, but now he's gone again…maybe for the night. So I left and I'm not going back. He didn't want me there anyway." She turned her face against his shoulder and kissed his chin. "Will you spend the night with me and make love to me, Tee?"

Etienne Gautier stiffened and quickly pulled away from her. He raked a hand through his hair and studied her in silence for several long moments. "Tell me what happened to make you so unhappy."

"I told you…he's gone again and expects me to sit waiting for him. Well, I don't care who he thinks he is. I don't plan to spend another moment waiting for him. Are you going to stay with me or not?"

He sighed. "I can't think of anything I'd like more than to spend the night with you, Petite."

She heard the longing in his voice, but saw the regret in his eyes. "But you're not going to, are you?"

"No, I'm not. I can't."

"Why not when we both want it?"

He stroked a finger down her cheek. "Well, I want it, but you don't really want me to spend the night. You just want to get back at Acier."

She shook her head. "That's where you're wrong, Tee. I do want to spend the night with you. And it has nothing to do with getting even with Steele."

He sighed. "I guess I do know that and I fully share your desire and need, Petite."

She placed her hands against his chest. "Why won't you stay and make love to me?"

He took her hands in his and kissed each of her palms. "I've never wanted a woman as much as I want you, Petite. I don't just want you…I need you, but I can't, sweet. I can see looking in your eyes that you know what we are. Acier isn't just my twin brother, he's the Alpha-in-waiting of our entire pack. And you, my sweet, are his bloodlust. To sleep with the alpha's woman is to invite death."

"His bloodlust? You're making him sound like a vampire!" she protested.

He cupped her palms between his hands. His lips

brushing lightly against hers, sent a tingle of desire through her. "There are things you need to know about us that it's not my place to tell, Petite. Acier should be the one to tell you."

She drew away from him. "He has nothing to say I want to hear, Tee."

He sighed. "Don't be too hard on him, honey. At the moment, he has the weight of the pack on his shoulders. And honey, it's not a light load."

She tossed her head angrily. "So I should be content to be pushed aside for another woman?"

"I can't believe that's what happened, Petite. I know how he feels about you. I know he didn't leave you for another woman."

"Yes, he did. He gave me some line about some young cub who was afraid and needed him."

He arched a brow. "And you didn't believe him?"

"No! I know how he spent last night."

"He told you about last night?"

"He didn't need to." She lifted her chin. "As I'm sure you know, Tee, I sometimes…know things I haven't seen. I saw him with a small, dark woman, who although she looked human…wasn't. I saw you with her too. Apparently you both found her far more attractive than me."

He shook his head and cupped her face again. "That's not true, Petite, with either of us. And I think you know it's not. You're angry and hurt because Acier had to leave you again."

"He didn't have to leave, Tee. He chose to leave. And I chose not to allow him to jerk me around."

"Raven, you are his bloodlust…his one perfect mate who he will forever love and need. Go back. Wait for him and let him explain."

She shook her head. "No! If you're not interested in spending the night with me, I'll find someone who is!" She snatched up her car keys and fanny pack from the bed and headed for the door.

He followed her, caught her arm, and turned her gently to face him. "Don't do anything you will regret and for which Acier will have a hard time forgiving you."

She stared at him. "Are you serious, Tee?"

"Yes. He won't forgive your sleeping with another man."

"Tee, I love you."

He bent his head and pressed a long, slow kiss against her mouth that made her hot and wet. "I love you too, Petite. You have no idea how much I do."

"I don't mean as a family friend."

He licked her neck and cupped her breasts in his hands. "That's not what I mean either. When I say I love you, I mean as a man loves a woman."

"Then stay with me, Tee. Please."

"I can't, Petite. He won't forgive either of us."

She pushed him away. "But I should forgive him for last night?"

He raked a hand through his hair. "I know that sounds unfair, but last night meant nothing to him."

She had a sudden vision of Tee with the same dark woman. "Did it mean anything to you?"

He shrugged. "I won't deny that it was a somewhat…special experience, but spending the night with you would have meant far more to me."

"And yet you won't spend tonight with me?"

"I can't. Last night I didn't know how Acier felt about you. Tonight I do know." He sighed. "Since you already know so much, I might as well tell you that Acier and I are hybrids."

"Half-human and half-werewolf? I know that."

He smiled. "We're not werewolves, sweet. We are shifters."

"But you shift into wolves."

"Yes…mostly, but Acier and I are also part…vampire."

She sucked in a breath, recalling the incisors Steele had bared at her earlier that day. "Aren't you even remotely human?"

He shrugged. "Maybe very remotely. Our mother was a shifter whose natural form was that of a wolf. Our father was…is…a full-blood vampire. Hence we are hybrids. Although I consider myself a vampire and Acier considers himself a shifter, we both have to acknowledge both sides of our heritage. You, Petite, are Acier's bloodlust. No matter what you do or who you sleep with, he will come after you, but he will not be a happy shifter when he finds you."

She compressed her lips. "Are you implying I should be afraid of him?"

"Never! But any man you sleep with is going to have a very short life expectancy."

"Tee, don't be so melodramatic. He's not a killer."

"Don't make the mistake of underestimating his passion and possessiveness, Raven or some unfortunate man will suffer. Acier is a shifter. We mate for life. He will kill to protect his interest in you. Don't make him do it."

It was just as well she hadn't been bowled over by Xavier's charms. But Tee's assertion presented another question. "If I mean so much to him, why did he leave me again?"

"If a member of his personal den is in trouble and needs him, he had to go. He *had* to. There is nothing more important to an Alpha than a member of his personal den. Don't ask him to choose."

"He already made his choice, Tee."

"Raven, honey, please. Go back and wait for him. He has so much on his shoulders right now. Please don't add to his burden. If you trust me, trust me when I tell you he needs you more than you can begin to imagine. He will never be truly happy without you."

"That argument might have moved me…had he made it instead of you." She gave him an uncertain smile. "Now please leave and promise me you won't tell him where I am, Tee."

He shook his head. "Honey, don't ask that of me."

She lifted her chin. "Ask? I'm not asking. I'm demanding. Do not tell him where I am. Promise."

"I…that's a promise I can't make, Petite. I can't sit around and watch him worry about you when I know where you are."

"Then when you leave, I'll leave. Then you wouldn't know where I am."

"But you'll never trust me again. Will you?"

She shrugged. "I'll trust you, but not to the same level as I did when I called you."

He sighed and raked a hand through his hair. "Please. Don't make me choose between the two of you, sweet. Go back."

"No!"

"Damn, you're stubborn. Look, let me call him and you can talk to him."

"There's nothing to say, Tee. I don't mean anything to him. He makes promises he never keeps then he leaves me and expects me to wait for him with no explanations. Well, I'm no man's toy." She pulled the door open and nodded towards it. "Thanks for coming and goodbye, Etienne."

"Don't you give me that Etienne shit!" He shoved the door closed and pulled her into his arms. His mouth crashed down on hers. Cradling her body close, he kissed her with a hunger and passion that made her knees buckle and her pussy wet.

She clung to him, greedily accepting his kisses. She made no protest when he swung her around so that her back was against the door with his big body pressing close to hers. "I love you!" he whispered.

She curled her fingers in his short hair and stared up at

him, her heart pounding. "Oh, Tee...what are we going to do?"

He groaned and pulled away from her. "Nothing. You belong to Acier."

"I do and I love him so much I ache with it...but I want you too."

"That's not possible." He touched her cheek. "I will try to keep your secret, Petite, but he is more than my twin brother. He's a part of who I am. I can't sit back and watch him suffer." He leaned down and kissed her on the corner of her mouth. "We both love you desperately, Petite. Please don't doubt that."

"Then promise you won't follow me, Tee."

"That I promise, but I am warning you, Raven. Stay away from other men."

"He doesn't own me."

He arched a brow. "I can smell him on you. Trust me, Raven, he owns you and he will not share you. But it's a two way street. You own him too." His nostrils flared. "And I can smell Xavier on you as well. You've met him?"

She nodded. "He came looking for Steele, but he didn't come in. He said he had to find Steele."

He tilted his head and studied her face. "You found him attractive?"

She shrugged. "He's beyond attractive, but I think you know I prefer my men with long dark hair and gray rather than blue eyes."

"My hair is short, Petite."

She touched his cheek. "But everything else about you is perfect, Tee."

He sighed. "I'd better leave before I give Acier reason to beat my ass."

She reached down and cupped her palms over his buns. "Nice ass," she told him. "Very nice ass."

He laughed and palmed hers. "Yours is very nice too."

"So is my pussy."

He shuddered and shook his head. "I have to go. Remember, you mean a lot to Acier."

Fat lot of good it was doing her.

He leaned down, she parted her lips and he kissed her slowly, savoring the taste of her lips and lightly sucking her tongue. Her heart pounded and her pussy gushed. Finally, she pulled away from him. "If you're leaving, leave. Don't make me wet and needy and then walk away."

He kissed her cheek and left. She waited half an hour before checking out of the hotel. Three nights later, as she lay sleepless in another room in a small New Jersey hotel, she had a sudden, startling vision of Steele sitting in the chair in his darkened bedroom with his head in his hands, whispering her name with raw despair. Pen and Drei hovered around him in their natural forms, their small heads hung in dejection. *Raven. Petite. Where are you? How could you leave when I need you so badly? Where are you?*

And from Pen and Drei, *Come back. Please. Miss you.*

Need you. Hurt bad. Come back.

Their combined despair reached out to her across the miles separating them. Their misery merged with hers and overwhelmed her. She bolted up in bed. Tee had been right. Steele did need her…badly. So did Pen and Drei. She needed them. She jumped out of bed and packed her suitcases. About to leave the room, she recalled their despair. She decided to call to let him know she was on her way back. When he didn't answer his phone, she almost changed her mind about returning. But she wanted to go back to him and give him a chance to explain his behavior. And she wanted to hold Pen and Drei and reassure them.

She arrived back at the RV park just before four a.m. Using the keys she had taken with her when she left, she let herself inside and made her way along in the dark to the bedroom. She pulled the doors open and gasped. Steele stood facing her. His eyes glowed and even in the dark, she knew his incisors were bared. "Where the fuck have you been?!" he demanded. "If you've been with another man, I swear I'll rip out his throat and tear his heart into little pieces!"

Pen and Drei hovered around, joyfully licking her face. Ignoring Steele, she held Pen and Drei and pressed reassuring kisses over their small bodies. "It's all right," she whispered to them. "I'm back."

They quivered in her palms as they projected feelings of love, warmth, and a desire to cherish and protect her. She kissed them again before releasing them and looking up into Steele's angry gaze. "Hi."

"I asked where the hell you've been!"

"No. You asked where the fuck I'd been. That's nastier than where the hell I've been, Steele!"

"Don't fuck with me, Raven! I am not in the mood for any shit from you!"

Before she could come up with a cool retort, he groaned and pulled her into the bedroom and into a painfully tight embrace. His mouth crashed down on hers.

His desperate embrace made it difficult to enjoy the kiss fully. And she did not like being manhandled, but decided not to struggle or complain. She wanted to ease the anguish she felt roiling in him. She soon questioned her decision not to object when he stripped them both naked, swept her off her feet, and tossed her on the bed. Before she could object, he pinned her down with his body. It happened so swiftly any lingering doubts she possessed regarding his vampire blood vanished.

Alpha, don't hurt, Pen pleaded.

Don't want hurt, Alpha, Drei added.

He stiffened on her. After a moment, she felt him softening. "I wasn't going to hurt you," he told her, staring down into her eyes.

She sighed, almost certain that if not for Pen and Drei's plea on her behalf, he very well might not have softened. Even now she could feel the rage barely held in check under the surface.

She lifted a hand and stroked his face. It was dark in the room, but his eyes still glowed. "Then why the vampire display?"

"You need to know and accept me for who I am."

"That goes for you too, Steele. I am not going to be your puppet. I have a mind of my own and I intend to keep it that way." She pushed at his shoulders. "Now get the hell off me. I'm tired and I want sleep. I am not in the mood to be manhandled tonight."

He immediately rolled off her. Heart thumping, she turned her back to him, settling on her side. She touched her breasts. "Pen. Drei. Come sleep with me," she invited.

Seconds later, a small furry body pressed against each breast. She sighed with pleasure when Pen and Drei each closed a mouth over a nipple and began sucking contentedly. It was almost as nice as having Steele suck her breasts.

"What about me?" he demanded.

"What about you?" she challenged. "Unlike you, they waited for an invite."

"I told you not to play games with me," he growled. Moving swiftly, he slid his big, naked body against her back. Feeling the heat and hardness of his cock, the muscles in her stomach tightened, but she was determined not to give in to him. He slipped an arm around her waist and eased several fingers inside her pussy.

She bit her lip and tossed her head back against his shoulder. "Not tonight, honey, I have a headache," she whispered.

His shoulders shook and to her delighted surprise, he buried his face against her neck and laughed. She could feel his tension easing.

He bit lightly into her neck. "I really wasn't going to hurt you, Petite."

"You were very angry, Steele."

His arm tightened around her waist. He gently stroked his fingers inside her. "I'll never get so angry that you need fear me. Never."

"Tee said you were in love with me."

"Etienne should stay the hell away from you and mind his own damned business!"

"So? Does that mean he was wrong?" she asked in a small, anxious voice.

He licked the side of her neck. "You're my woman."

"And?"

"And what? Isn't that enough?"

"I don't know."

"Well, it had better be because I intend to take your pussy, your heart, and your blood, Petite."

With Pen and Drei still eagerly sucking at her breasts, she turned in Steele's arms and pressed her pussy against his hardened cock. "You and your big dick can take everything I have," she whispered, parting her legs. She reached down and rubbed his shaft against the entire length of her vagina. "But tonight I'm too tired too fully enjoy it. Just hold me tonight?"

He tightened his arms around her and brushed his lips against her neck. "Yes," he whispered, and settled his body against her. "I'm just so…relieved to have you back. Don't ever leave me like that again, Raven."

She responded by lifting her head, inviting a kiss. He bent his head and devoured her lips.

"Tee says you love me," she whispered against his lips.

"He talks to damned much," he growled softly, nibbling at her mouth.

She sighed. Maybe he wouldn't admit he loved her

because he didn't. Then again, he hadn't said he didn't love her either.

Chapter Six

ഗൗ

She woke alone in bed the next morning. She pulled a calf-length nightshirt over her head and headed for the kitchen and the heavenly aroma of brewing coffee.

Steele, wearing only a pair of pajama bottoms turned to face her as she neared the stove. Pen and Drei, lapping up coffee from a saucer on the counter, floated up to kiss her cheeks. She kissed each of them before slipping her arms around Steele's neck and smiling up at him. "Morning."

His gray eyes darkened as he looked down at her. "Petite." He wrapped his arms around her and buried his face against her neck. "Oh, Petite, I need you."

She felt his cock stirring against her and her heart thundered in her chest. She knew the time she had longed for the last four years was just moments away. She was all at once excited and frightened. His cock swelled against her and she reached down to draw it out of his pajama bottoms.

In the light of morning, his erect shaft looked huge. She wet her lips and heaved it in her hands. She found his size and girth both frightening and fascinating…wonderful and weird. She raised her gaze towards him. "Steele," she said softly. "Make love to me."

He turned his head briefly to look towards Pen and Drei who hovered in the air around them. "Keddi, stay," he ordered.

No, Alpha. Want come.

Want share of pussy!

"Let them come, Steele."

Yes. Let come, Alpha.

Please, Alpha. Want come. Want share of pussy.

"Well, neither of you are getting any."

Alpha selfish.

Alpha mean.

"Alpha not sharing," he retorted. "Now for the last time, Keddi, stay." Ignoring their strident protests, Steele put his arm around her shoulders and walked her toward the back of the RV. As he pulled her into his bedroom and closed the doors, she was already damp. She pulled away from him, reaching for the hem of her nightshirt. By the time they reached the bed, she was naked. She fell back against the mattress and spread her legs wide. She smiled seductively at him. "Come on in, big boy."

"You're sure?"

She pointed at her splayed legs. "Does this look like I'm not sure? Stop being noble and get your ass over here before I rough you up!"

He pulled off his pajama bottoms and joined her on the bed, lying in her arms, between her legs. He moved against her, kissing her with a gentle hunger. She clung to him, trembling with obvious need and longing for the moment when he would push his cock deep into her body and make her his.

"Raven, there's someone I want you to meet."

"What? Now?"

"Yes." He nibbled at her neck. "Now."

She stiffened under him and pushed at his shoulders. "What? Are you nuts, Steele?"

He laughed and nipped her bottom lip. "He's been aching to meet you since you arrived."

She thought of Xavier and flushed at the idea of him being in the RV with them. "Well, I don't want to meet him! Not now, Steele."

"Right now, Raven." He lifted his body, grasped his cock,

and eased the head into her pussy. "Raven, baby, meet Steele."

"Steele?"

"It's his name," he told her.

She laughed. "It's what he is too. Steel hard."

"Would you like to meet him?"

"Can you say, hell yeah?"

He smiled and pressed gently forward.

"Oh, my God! Steele!" She looked up at him with glazed eyes. "I'm so happy to finally meet you."

"He'd like to get even better acquainted with you, Petite."

She stroked her hands over his shoulders and wiggled her hips. "Oh, I'd like that too, Steele. Don't stand on ceremony. You feel something you like? Come all the way in and take it, big boy."

Heart thundering in his chest, cock so hard it ached, Acier inched forward. Although she wasn't a virgin, he didn't want to hurt her. He encountered an unexpected barrier. She gasped and he froze, a chill shooting through him. "What the fuck! Why the hell did you lie to me? You told me you weren't a virgin!"

"I didn't lie to you, Steele. I only said what if." She stroked her fingers along his cheek. "In your heart of hearts, you must have known I would save myself for you, Steele."

He groaned. "Oh, shit, Petite. This changes everything."

She licked her lips and smiled at him. "No, it doesn't. Didn't you know this was where we would end up the moment we saw each other again?"

"Your father trusted you to be safe with me."

"Daddy knows why I came here. He knows how I feel about you. There were guys I found attractive in college, but I held out and I saved myself for you, Steele. Go ahead. Take my virginity. It's yours."

He overcame the primordial urge to thrust forward and

burst through her cherry. The thought that she had withstood her own desires because she wanted to share this moment for him, touched him and sent him over the edge. Mo was going to have to kick his ass because there was no way he could stop now. "You've saved it for me. Give it to me, Petite."

Her hands clenched on his shoulders. "I want you to take it."

A sudden desire seized him. "Before it's gone, I want to taste it."

Her eyes widened. "Taste it? Your tongue can't get it there."

"Oh, don't be too sure of that, Petite." He kissed her sweet, warm lips before pulling out and sliding down between her legs. Cupping her ass in his hands, he titled her hips, and slipped his shifted tongue up into her pussy until he encountered the thin membrane guarding the entrance to paradise. He slowly ran his tongue along it, delighting in the proof that no other man had bedded his woman.

She shuddered. "Oh, Steele, I can feel that. How are you doing that?"

Her pussy smelled so good. She felt good. He began licking at her cherry, savoring the aroma and taste of it.

She moaned and pressed forward against his tongue.

Once started, he couldn't stop. Closing his eyes, he continued lapping at her cherry, driving her into a frenzy. She gasped for breath and squirmed on the bed. She closed her long dark legs around his head. And still he licked.

"Steele!" She curled her fingers in his hair and gave a small yank. "That's enough of that! Get up here and take it! Please!"

He gave her cherry one final lick, shifted his tongue back to its humanoid shape, and slide up her lush, beautiful body. Kissing her slowly, he eased his cockhead into her. "Come on, baby. Give it to me," he whispered against her parted lips.

"No. I want you to take it."

"It'll be easier on you, if you give it to me, Raven."

She looked down between their bodies and he could sense that she enjoyed the contrast of their skin colors and that his cock looked like a pole protruding from her pussy. He knew the sight of his pale cock in her dark pussy was an erotic and arousing sight for her, just as it was for him.

"If I take it, I'm going to really hurt you."

"Given the size of your cock, it's a sure bet it's going to hurt whether I give it to you or you take it." She stroked her fingers through his hair. "Steele, I've dreamed of this moment for such a long time. I know it's going to hurt, but I want you to take it. Take it, Steele. Hurt me!"

Her words acted like an aphrodisiac, increasing his lust for her tenfold. "Okay, but baby I need you to understand that once I get past your cherry, I'm not going to be able to stop until I get all my cock in you."

"What? You'll have to stop and give me some time to adjust."

"I won't be able to stop."

"You'll have to. It'll hurt too much, Steele."

"It'll be over quick."

"It'll be over quick? Steele, you can only take my cherry one time. Don't you want to savor and enjoy the moment?"

He licked the warm skin between her breasts. "Of course I do."

"Then be gentle and give me time to adjust once you're inside me."

"I'll try, but you have no idea how much I want and need you, baby." He pressed a tender kiss against her lips.

She slipped her arms over his shoulders and parted her mouth.

He eased his cock forward and stopped at her cherry, his heart thumping wildly. His need to take her virginity warred with his desire to have her surrender it freely and gladly.

"Meet me halfway, Petite."

She bit on his bottom lip and lifted her hips. He pressed down and his cock tore through the thin tissue. A wonderful, madding fragrance greeted his entrance into her sweet pussy. It overwhelmed him, urging him to surge forward to capture his prize completely.

She gasped in pain and he froze, halting his forward lunge. He held her close and kissed her lips. He wanted to whisper sweet words of love and endless devotion, but the feelings washing over his cock were too good. He had to have a little more pussy. He pushed slowly forward until she lay sobbing softly under him.

He kissed her again, stroking his hands over her big, luscious breasts. "It's almost over, Raven." He moved his lips against hers. "Honey, just hold on a little longer."

She tore her mouth away from his and nodded wordlessly.

He eased his hips forward until he felt her public hair against his and knew he had all his cock in her. He shuddered and closed his eyes. There was nothing sweeter than this special moment with this special woman. She made the countless lovers who had come before her but a distant memory. From this moment on, there would be no other woman for him.

She was so sweet and brave. He knew he was hurting her. She tried not to squirm and to remain silent, but he felt the tension in her body and ached each time a small whimper of pain left her lips.

The wolf in him wanted to stop and comfort her, but the vampire wouldn't allow it. The two parts of his nature warred. The vampire side emerged victorious. Devouring her warm lips, he crushed her big breasts under his chest. He thrust into her moist, tight heat with a force that left her gasping against his lips and trembling in his arms. He bottomed out in her.

"Oh God, Steele!" She raked her nails down his back.

He heard the pain in her voice. Caught up in a powerful vortex of love, lust, and desire that he could not control, he could not stop. His passions and unrelenting need drove him on.

Sucking on her tongue, he propelled his cock deep into her virginal pussy, delighting in how tight, hot, and moist she felt. His senses were awash with joy and bliss. He'd never imagined making love could be so wonderful. He'd never made love. Because he'd never been in love before. This was the first time.

"Raven. Oh, Raven!" he moaned her name, lost control, and exploded, filling her with his seed.

Groaning, and trembling, he collapsed on top of her, burying his face against her neck. A wave of need overwhelmed him, making it difficult to breathe. He lay against her, longing for her with a hunger that had nothing to do with sex or lust.

Her hands clutched at his back. "Oh, my God, Steele! Is that it? Is it finally over? After you finished?"

He stiffened. "Am I finished?" He lifted his head and stared down at her.

"Yes!" She hit a balled fist against his back. "Are you?"

"Damn it, Raven! You certainly know how to burst a man's bubble. Didn't you enjoy it at all?"

"No, I did not, Steele! You try having a pole ramming up you like a jackhammer and see how much you enjoy it. And don't give me that wounded little boy look. Your cock is too big for you to have such a fragile ego."

He clenched his jaw. "The size of my cock has nothing to do with my feelings, Raven. You think because I have a big cock, I have no feelings?"

She lifted a hand and stroked her fingers across his cheek. "Oh, come on, sweetie. I didn't mean to wound you."

"Raven, it's gauche to ask a man if he's finished. Trust me, no matter the size of the cock, such a question wounds the

199

male ego in ways you can't imagine. You thoughtless little—"

"Watch your mouth, Steele and don't you whine to me about wounds," she told him. "How do you think my poor stretched pussy feels? Very wounded and stretched way out of shape. But you don't hear me whining, do you?"

They gazed into each other's eyes and then both laughed.

She sobered and brushed her lips against his. "I didn't enjoy it, Steele, but I'm very glad it happened."

He sighed, disappointed she had felt nothing but pain. "Are you?"

"Yes. Yes, Steele. As painful as it was, it's a memory, I will cherish with great delight."

"Good. Then you won't mind that it's about to happen again."

Her eyes widened and she pressed against his shoulders. "Wait a minute! Let's talk about this."

"What's to talk about?" He ejaculated into her, to make his remaining in her more comfortable. "I'm already inside you. Fuck now and talk later," he told her and began fucking her again…gently this time.

"Oh, hell!" She raked her nails down his back, but didn't attempt to push him away.

He kissed her and touched her thighs, her breasts, reached between their bodies to touch her clit. He rubbed his thumb against it and she moaned. Her pussy convulsed briefly around his cock and he came again, thrusting deep into her as he filled her with his seed.

Oh, hell, he had no control when he was inside her.

She sucked in a breath and pushed against his shoulder. "Steele, oh God! Take it out."

"I can't, baby. Not yet. I have to have a little more pussy. I have to. God, Raven, I'll die if you make me stop now."

She raked her nails down his back, this time drawing blood. "Oh, damn it, Steele! It hurts like hell!"

"I know, Petite and I'm sorry. Forgive me. Please. And just let me have a little more, pussy, Raven. Please, baby."

She balled a fist against his shoulder and hit him. "Oh, damn, Steele!"

"Baby, please."

"Don't you even care that you're tearing me up and I want you to stop?!"

He froze on her then pushed his body off hers, resting his weight on his extended arms. He stared down at her, his heart pounding, feeling as if he'd had ice water poured over his heated body. "God, Petite! I'm sorry! I...I..."

Instead of hitting him or pushing him off her, she put her hands on his hips, and jerked down at them. He resisted, shaking his head. "Brace yourself, I'm going to pull out!"

"No!" She cupped her hands over his ass. A jolt of lust shot through him and he stiffened, afraid he was about to come prematurely again.

She stared up at him and finally nodded. "Like I can deny you anything you want when you're stretching me so deliciously like this. Come back and make love to me. I'm your woman, Steele. You have needs?" She extended her tongue between her lips. "I'm here to satisfy them...you'll never have to seek pleasure from another woman."

"I never will, Petite."

She smiled. "Good. Then come take some of your pussy, sweetie."

Filled with a lust he couldn't contain, he lowered his body onto hers, captured her lips, and had her for a third time. He kissed and touched her, tried to stroke her passions and infuse heat into her body. But she remained tense, scraping her nails down his back as he fucked her pussy and sucked on her tongue. It was as his climax approached and he despaired of her ever enjoying their first prolonged fuck that he felt her hips jerk up against his in time with his downward lunges. Her moans softened and became pleasing to his ears.

Instead of scraping the skin off his back, she began to caress his shoulders and hold him. She slid her hands from his back to his ass. Holding him there, she eagerly and deliciously began to fuck him back, her luscious pussy greedily clinging to his raging cock.

Fighting to retain control long enough to make sure he pleased her, he gritted his teeth. He slowed his movements inside her and held her close until she gasped and shuddered against his lips. Then, a long, low cry of ecstasy escaped her lips, and her pussy shattered around his cock.

"Oh God!" She moaned. "Oh God, Steele...oh, Lord! I...oh, God! This is how I knew it would be! So good...such a big...good...cock...such good cock! Oooh! God, you make me and my pussy feel so good and so glad to belong to you!"

He buried his lips against her neck, raking his incisors against the tender skin as he came, shooting jets of seed into her already drenched pussy.

She tightened her inner muscles around him, wrapping her legs around his body, intensifying his climax.

"Oh, shit! Paradise!"

"Good pussy will take you there every time," she teased.

Overcome with emotion, he couldn't speak. He lay against her, feeling weak and trembling.

She held him, stroking her fingers over his shoulders and through his hair. "It's all right," she whispered. "I have you, sweetie and I'll never let you go."

Later as he lay on his back with her sprawled across his chest, still impaled on his cock, he wondered how the fuck he could explain this to Mo. He had busted Mo's baby girl's cherry wide open and found he could not bear to take his cock out of her. To make it easier for her to allow him to remain inside her, he kept ejaculating in her, another fringe benefit of his vampire nature.

She signed softly and kissed his shoulder, seemingly content to remain on his semi-erect shaft. "Steele, I'm going to miss you like crazy when I go home."

"For the wedding?" He stroked a hand down her hair. "I'm invited too, you know."

"I know that! I meant when I go home and you're on the road doing whatever you do. You know when things get back to normal."

He curled his fingers in her long hair and lifted her head. "What do you mean normal? You and me together is normal."

"Now? Yeah, but not once I get back home and you hit the road again."

He put his hands on her hips and lifted her off him.

She gasped as his cock left her body.

He laid her on her back and leaned over her, staring down into her eyes in the darkened bedroom. "When I leave here, you are coming with me."

She slid off the bed and walked towards the bedroom door. He noticed with a sense of pride that she walked as if she'd recently had something large and very hard between her long, lovely legs. At the doors, she turned to look at him. "I have a life and plans, Steele and neither includes driving around the country while you chase God only knows what or who."

He rose and went to stand in front of her, staring down at her. "Then why did you come here and keep at me until you got what you wanted if you didn't plan to stay with me?"

She shrugged. "I couldn't help myself. I thought I was in love with you."

He swallowed slowly, feeling as if his heart had ruptured. "You thought you were in love with me? And you're telling me now you're not?"

"I don't know... I thought... I don't know, Steele. My feelings right now are confusing."

Oh, shit! He had hurt her so badly when he'd taken her, she no longer wanted him. How the hell was he going to make amends? He felt his incisors descending and knew his eyes glowed. She was sadly mistaken if she thought he was going to let her go anywhere without him. Even so, he decided now was not the time to go Alpha on her. She was very young, he had hurt her, and she was probably scared, in addition to being confused. They could get past this as long as he didn't lose his temper.

"All right," he said. He stroked her cheek. "But you will stay with me until the wedding?"

She placed her hands on his chest, and leaned into him, her pretty face turned up towards his. "Yes. Oh yes, but after the wedding, we'll go our separate ways, Steele."

The hell they would! She was his and he kept what belonged to him. "All right, Petite." He bent his head and kissed her lips. "Now go shower before the smell of you drives me nuts and I have to have you again."

Her dark eyes lit up as she looked up at him. "You still want me?"

He slipped his arms around her waist, drawing her close to him. "Maybe just a little."

He shuddered when she ran her soft palms over his ass. "Oh Lord, Steele, you are huge. It's a wonder I can still walk."

He feigned a frown. "What the hell? You can still walk? I must be losing my touch." He grinned and swept her off her feet and into his arms. "But not to worry. That's a situation we can quickly remedy."

She balled a hand into a fist and hit his shoulder. "Oh, no you don't! Put me down!"

He kissed her instead, licking at her warm lips. "Give me some more pussy."

"You've had all you're getting today! Now put me down!"

"After you give me some more pussy," he teased, biting into her bottom lip.

She stroked her fingers through his hair. "Steele!" She pinched his nipples. "I said put me down!"

Before he could respond, the doors were wrenched open and Pen and Drei, both in wolf form shot into the room and hovered in the air around his head. He considered them with an arched brow. They were several times their normal size. Their bodies quivered with rage. Their ears were up, their tails stiff, their eyes glowed, and their incisors bared. They were in battle mode, ready for a no-holds-barred fight.

Chapter Seven

❧

Alpha put down! Pen ordered.

Now!

Not let Alpha take pussy without permission! Pen told him.

Won't let Alpha hurt.

"Oh, no, darlings, we were just playing!" Raven told them. She looked up at him, a warm, adoring look in her dark eyes that made him feel all goofy inside. "Alpha would never hurt me or take me without my permission."

"Never," he assured her.

She smiled and kissed his lips. "Thank you for making my first time everything I thought it would be."

"I hurt you."

"Like hell, but I loved every second of the pain, sweetie. Every second."

Alpha not hurt? Pen asked.

"No," she assured him. "Alpha never hurt."

Pen and Drei bowed their heads, allowing their ears and trails to droop. *Alpha not be angry with Drei. All Pen's fault*, Pen said. *Made Drei come.*

Not all Pen's fault, Alpha, Drei countered. *Not make Drei come. Came willingly.*

Neither of his pets had ever challenged him as they just had. That they had confronted him in battle mode told him how deeply their feelings for Raven ran. Hell, maybe Etienne was right. Maybe there was something to this bloodlust vampire shit.

"I'm not angry with either of you," he told them. "You

did well in coming to her aide when you thought she was being threatened."

Raven pressed against his chest and he gently set her on her feet.

She touched her breasts. "Come," she spoke softly to Pen and Drei.

They immediately flew over to her. Drei settled against her body and closed his mouth around her nipple, sucking contently. Pen shifted into a large golden penis, and worked his way between her legs and into her pussy.

"Oh!" She gave him a wide-eyed look.

"Greedy little bastards!" He bared his incisors. "Send them both packing."

"Oh!" she said again, as Pen slid deeper into her pussy. "Ohhh. I don't think so." She stumbled over to the bed and lay on her back, her eyes closed as his two greedy little pets began to fuck her.

He watched for a moment as Pen thrust deep into her pussy, then closed his eyes. Acier could feel Pen's delight as he pushed into her tight pussy that was still full of his seed.

Good pussy, Alpha, Pen moaned to him. *So tight, hot…so good.*

Want some pussy too, Pen, Drei said. *Get out and let Drei have some.*

Wait turn, Keddi, Pen told Drei coldly and sank himself so deep into Raven's pussy that she shuddered and gasped with pleasure.

"Oh God, Pen! You feel so good!"

Pen has big cock and give good fuck, he told her in a proud voice.

"Very good fuck," she moaned. "Don't stop."

Acier frowned. The little conceited bastard was having a ball—in his woman!

Pen's woman now too, Pen countered. *About to fill with Pen's seed. Get pregnant.*

In your damned dreams, little greedy bastard! he snarled.

Undaunted, Pen fucked on, eliciting soft moans of pleasure from Raven. He couldn't have any more pussy, but she was more than willing to let the blasted Keddi fuck her silly.

Feeling mean-spirited because he begrudged his two faithful pets the pleasure Raven was clearly willing to share with them, Acier headed for the shower.

As the cold water poured over his head, he vowed that he was going to have to give Pen and Drei a stern warning about staying away from his woman. Damned if he were going to share her with the two greediest bastards ever born.

When he returned to the room after a long shower, Raven lay on her back on the bed, asleep. Pen, in his natural form, lay against her breasts. Drei, in the shape of a big, thick cock, lay half buried between her legs, in her pussy.

He sighed. Damn. After this he would never be able to keep them away from her. He sighed again, climbed onto the bed, eased her on her side, and slid his body behind her.

She pressed back against him, whispering his name. Content, he cuddled her close and fell asleep.

* * * * *

"What's wrong with you two sad sacks? I told you what to do. Do it and stop moping. You're bringing the spirit of the place down."

Etienne, pacing in front of the floor to ceiling windows of his condo with Slayer perched in his natural form on his shoulder, paused to look across the room. Sprawled on a long, plush, burgundy leather sofa was a tall man with dark auburn hair, green eyes, and chiseled features that were almost pretty. Although Damon duPre was his best friend, sometimes the other vampire annoyed the hell out of him with his air of knowing it all.

He frowned. "You know what Acier has before him. How can you expect me to sleep with his woman and add to his problems?"

Will fuck for you.

Etienne turned his head and looked at the small, gray wolf perched on his left shoulder. "Slayer, the last thing I need is for you to go off and try to sleep with Raven. Not only will Acier be furious, but Pen will do his best to kick your little hairy behind all the way back to Den Gautier."

Slayer bristled. *Not afraid of Pen. Can take him.*

He knew his favorite pet Slayer had the will to take on Pen, but he wasn't so sure he had the skill and strength. Excluding Dominator, Supreme Alpha Aime's Alpha Keddi, Pen was the oldest living Keddi in their pack. Although generally mild-tempered, Etienne knew Pen would make a formidable enemy and he had no interest in seeing Slayer humbled or humiliated by the older, stronger Keddi.

"It would be unseemly of you to best an Alpha Keddi in battle, Slayer. Would you want to humiliate Pen in front of those who are supposed to obey him?"

Slayer sighed, his tail and head drooping. *No. Pen best Alpha Slayer ever served under. Not unfair or unjust. Always fair.*

He knew Slayer was comparing Pen to Dominator. Dominator was an arrogant bastard who took joy in making the Keddi under him miserable. Etienne touched a finger to Slayer's head. "We'll find our own bloodlust and ravish her until all three of us are exhausted."

Will enjoy, but will still want Petite.

Etienne nodded. He shared Slayer's fear that even meeting his own bloodlust wouldn't dampen his hunger and need for Raven. Memories of how sweet eating her pussy had been haunted him, and his cock ached every time he thought of how much he wanted to sink it deep inside her.

Damon bolted to his feet and stalked across the room to stare at him. "Have either of you been listening to me? She's

Acier's bloodlust. Neither of you can help wanting her. Acier is going to have to deal with that being part of our vampire heritage."

"We're hybrids, Damon. Acier rejects his vampire side."

Damon clasped his hands on his face and stared into his eyes. "Etienne! Stop banging your head against a brick wall! Acier will have to accept his vampire side and that will include his knowing and accepting that his bloodlust will be irresistible to both you and Slayer. Stop fighting your natural urges and go bed that woman."

His nostrils flared as he recalled the enticing aroma of her sweet pussy as he'd eaten her.

Yes. Let's go fuck, Slayer said eagerly.

He drew away from Damon. "No! He's about to have all kinds of problems on his hands. I'm supposed to help him, not compound his problems."

Damon sighed. "Etienne…listen…whatever Acier faces, you face, right?"

"Yes."

"And whatever threatens you, is on my hit list! I will stand with you both…no matter what."

Etienne nodded. For all his faults, Damon was fiercely loyal to his friends. "I know, Damon, but I've seen something that…I'm not sure Acier can handle."

Not worry. Alpha can handle anything, Slayer said.

Etienne had a great deal of confidence in Acier and his ability to protect the pact against most obstacles, but the half-dream, half-vision that he couldn't quite remember left him fearing for his brother's safety.

"What? What did you see?"

He shook his head. "I don't know. I just don't know."

"Whatever it is…I've got your back, Etienne."

He nodded. "I know." But would that be enough? At seventy, Damon was young as vampires went. For the threat facing them, Etienne suspected Acier and the pack might need more help than a young vampire could provide. And maybe he knew just who could provide the needed assistance…the father who had abandoned them. From what their mother had told them, he was a centuries old vampire. Even if he had no wish to know them, he surely wouldn't stand by and watch his sons be taken out by a superior force.

"I know that look. What are you planning, Etienne?" Damon asked.

"I think Acier's right."

"About what?"

"Our father…we have to find him."

Damon raked a hand through his hair. "Do you think that's a good idea? You know we vampires do not make ideal fathers. You and Acier might be the last people he wants to meet. Some vampires have even been known to slay their own offspring."

Etienne shook his head. "No. Even if he wants nothing to do with us, he won't try to dispatch us."

"How do you know that?"

"Mother was a shifter with a second sight far more developed than my own. She wouldn't have slept with a male capable of killing his own offspring."

Damon shrugged. "Okay. I'll give you that one since you're usually right about these things. How do you plan to find him? Acier has been looking for twenty years with no success."

He arched a brow. "Yes, but Acier hasn't been looking in the right places and he doesn't have the benefit of being able to see things as I do. I'm going to find him and make him help us."

"Oh, I can just imagine Acier's face when you tell him you're going to ask for your father's help."

He grinned. "Who says I plan to tell him?"

Damon laughed. "Sneaky. I like that in a vampire. How can I help?"

"You can take me deep into the community."

"You're sure? You've always resisted really going into our community."

He had resisted immersing himself fully into the vampire community because he didn't want to risk becoming alienated from Acier who would always consider himself a shifter.

"I won't now. I have to find our father. Acier needs him."

"And you?"

He shrugged. "It would have been nice to have him around when we were younger. But now?" He shook his head. "I don't need him now on an emotional level, but Acier does."

Damon placed a hand on his free shoulder. "If your father proves difficult when we find him, I've got your back. And if that's not enough, my brothers will stand with us."

Etienne thought of Damon's brothers, both close to two hundred years old. As far as he was concerned, Damon's brothers were borderline nuts. Damn, he hoped he didn't need their help.

Damon's lips twisted into a slight smile. "Hey! Watch what you're thinking about my brothers!"

Etienne grinned. After nearly twenty years of friendship, he and Damon knew each other well. "Let's face it, Damon. You look in the dictionary under nuts and you'll find a picture of those two."

Damon laughed. "Maybe so, but they are good brothers who have never let me down."

"I know and Acier has never let me down. So I have to come through for him. He's always put me first. When we left the pack against Alpha's wishes, Acier did without a lot of things so I could have them. In college he worked two jobs so I wouldn't have to work at all. I was selfish then and let him sacrifice so I wouldn't have to. But no more. It's time to pay him back for some of what I owe him."

Damon shrugged. "That's what big brothers do…make sacrifices for their younger siblings."

Yes. And Acier had done it extremely well and unselfishly. "It's my turn to be unselfish."

"So, we'll find your father…assuming he's still alive of course."

Etienne frowned, closing his eyes briefly. "Oh, he's still alive."

"How do you know that?"

"I just do."

"Finding him would be a heck of a lot easier if you knew what he looked like."

"I do."

Damon arched a brow. "How?"

"Our mother left a picture of him."

"A picture? Then he's not nocturnal?"

Etienne considered. From what Damon had told him there were basically two breeds of vampires, nocturnal and diurnal. Generally, the nocturnal cast no reflections and could not be photographed. The diurnal, scornfully called Reflects by the nocturnal, not only cast a reflection, but could actually be photographed. There were other breeds Damon said were too rare to worry about running across in a dark alley.

"I supposed not," he said slowly.

"No matter. This picture…where is it?"

"It's actually a snapshot of a watercolor our mother did. Acier has it."

"Then we'll get it and go find the bastard."

"That won't be necessary. I can draw it from memory."

"Good. Then we're halfway there. Now, what are you going to do about Raven?"

"Nothing!" He whirled away from Damon. "I've already

told you I will not add to Acier's burden by trying to sleep with her."

Damon shrugged. "Okay, little vampire. I guess you'll just have to find out the hard way just how powerful a force bloodlust is."

Even as his body ached for Raven, he stubbornly shook his head. He would not bed her. He looked at Slayer. "Let's go get some pussy."

Slayer rose up on his hind legs, his cock popping out of its sheath. *Always ready for pussy. Go see Jean-Marie? Smells good and has good pussy. Let Slayer fuck pussy often.*

He longed to go see Raven, but since that was out of the question and Jean-Marie was close, he nodded. "Yes."

He looked at Damon. "There are some female members of Den Gautier living about and hour and a half drive from here. Slayer and I are going to go calling on them. Want to come?"

Damon shook his head. "Maybe another time. There's this sexy, well-rounded woman I saw last week I want to bed."

Etienne gave him a weary look. "Is she a vampire?"

"You know I like mortal women."

Damon's lust for young, human virgins troubled Etienne. In the years he'd known Damon, he'd lost track of how many virgins Damon had deflowered. Etienne enjoyed virgin pussy as much as the next vampire. Still, Etienne had never taken any woman's virginity without her full consent and permission.

"Yes, Damon, but—"

"Mortal women are so much more…exciting. They have such…fresh, delicious blood and such tight, hot pussies. And they're young and fresh enough to fully appreciate a man who knows how to love them."

Etienne sighed. "Damon—"

Damon held up a hand, shaking his head. "I don't want or need a lecture from you, Etienne. I know how you feel and you know how I feel about the subject. I am what I am."

"I know, but there's no need to take a woman against her will. There are too many vampwhores around for that."

"Yes, but I want someone young and fresh, not a jaded vampwhore who parts her legs and bares her neck for any and every vampire who looks her way."

Etienne ran a hand through his hair. "Ok. Slayer and I are going."

Damon nodded. "Call me when you're ready to start looking for daddy dearest."

Etienne nodded. Pussy first, then he would set out to find their father. Their errant father would help Acier or he would have to deal with Etienne.

And Slayer and Karol, Slayer added.

He nodded. Although his Keddi were not as battle ready as were Acier's, he knew neither Slayer nor Karol would let him down.

* * * * *

Two hours later, he and Slayer arrived at a large ranch-style house in rural Pennsylvania. A tall, pretty brunette with dark, smiling eyes, and a beautiful face opened the door and grabbed his hand. "Etienne!"

He smiled. "Jean-Marie! You're looking lovelier than ever."

"And you are as handsome as I remember. What brings you here, Etienne?"

"We're lonely."

Her dark eyes danced over his face before looking beyond him to Slayer. "Ahhh. You've brought Slayer, too. Oh, Slayer, you grow more handsome each time I see you. Come in my lusty little lover. Come in both of you."

Slayer, in his natural form, sailed past Etienne and sank his incisors into Jean-Marie's neck. Lying against her shoulder, he fed, his cock resting against one breast.

Etienne stepped in and closed the door, turning his gaze towards Jean-Marie Aumont and Slayer.

"Slayer, you handsome, devil, I have missed you, my little love." She moved back against the wall beside the door. Closing her eyes, she sighed with pleasure, stroking a finger over Slayer's cock.

His thirst for blood partially quenched, Slayer removed his incisors from her neck and moved up towards her mouth, his cock now thick and hard. *Need fuck bad. Give pussy?*

"When have I ever been able to deny you pussy, my little love? Come. Fuck the pussy that will always welcome you with joy and pleasure, *mon amour.*"

Etienne watched, as without the slightest hesitation, Jean-Maria lifted the hem of her short skirt to reveal a pair of long, shapely legs and a beautifully bare, hairless pussy that made his cock ache.

Shifting quickly until his body was a large, ebony-colored cock, Slayer sailed through the air and slammed himself deep into her pussy with one powerful thrust.

"Ooooh!" Shuddering and moaning, Jean-Marie slid down the wall to sit on the floor with her legs open. She looked down and watched Slayer thrusting greedily into her pussy. Each time Slayer pulled himself almost all the way out of her body, Etienne saw his ebony flesh covered with her copious juices.

His own cock hardening, Etienne dropped to his knees beside her and kissed her.

Moaning, she turned her head and parted her lips, eagerly sucking at his tongue.

As they hungrily kissed each other, he unbuttoned her blouse. Her large, firm breasts spilled into his hands. Cupping and pinching them, he continued devouring her lips.

Through the bond they shared, Etienne could feel Slayer's pleasure as he slammed himself deep up into Jean-Marie's warm pussy. Feeling ready to burst with sexual hunger, Etienne pulled away from her lips, rose, and quickly tore off his clothes. Naked and fully aroused, he dropped down to the floor and eased Jean-Marie onto her side.

Kissing her neck, he moved behind her.

She moaned and leaned back against him, shuddering with pleasure as Slayer continued pounding her pussy. Etienne gently parted the cheeks of her tight ass, thrusting his cock against her butt. Easing her rectum open, he ejaculated into her bottom. He waited a moment for his seed to work its way into her butt, then he pushed the head of his shaft up into her body.

"Ooooh!" she cried out as his huge cock began the invasion of her warm ass. She reached a hand back and urged him forward. "Oh, Etienne! More! Oh God! It's been so long since I've been double fucked. Slide every inch of your cock up my ass. Take me deep and hard!"

That was all the encouragement he needed. Cupping one hand over her breasts, he shot his hips forward, shuddering as his cock sank balls deep in her tight bottom. Damn that felt good. He closed his eyes and cleared his mind of everything except the need to come.

She cried out with bliss as he dug his cock deep into her luscious bottom. "Yes! Yes! Ooooh, yes!"

Etienne was so frustrated that it only took a few deep, powerful thrusts in her before he felt his climax approaching. Determined not to come before she did, he sank his incisors in her neck, found her clit with his free hand, and fucked her hard and furious in time with Slayer's thrusts.

She tightened herself around his cock with such force he nearly came on the spot. He held off and shot his shaft deep in her. Suddenly she shuddered and cried out. With her ass cheeks quivering wildly, she came with the passion and fury of which few human women were capable.

She filled the house with the sounds of her cries of

release.

Holding her tight, Etienne continued to drill her butt as she lay gasping and moaning with bliss. Reaching out to touch Slayer's mind, he knew his Keddi was finally ready. Moments later, he and Slayer came together, exploding in unison in her body, setting off a mini-climax in her.

After they'd all come, they lay on the floor, still joined, none of their hungers quite satisfied. As Etienne was about to start another hungry fuck, Slayer eased out of her pussy and hovered in the air near his face.

Go find own woman. Want all to self.

"Slayer, there's no need to be selfish," she protested, gently squeezing her ass around Etienne's cock. "Etienne fucks a very mean piece of ass."

Jean-Marie's ass belongs to Slayer. Tee find his own ass and own woman. Not share anymore. Want ass and pussy for self.

Although he was far from satisfied, Etienne was used to Slayer. He knew Slayer would gladly die defending him, but when it came to sex, Slayer was not a team player, unless he was on the receiving end. He laughed, kissed Jean-Marie's neck, and eased out of her warm rectum. "Thank you," he whispered.

She rolled over onto her back, parting her legs. Her eyes glazed over as Slayer, still shaped like a long, thick ebony shaft, sank balls deep into her pussy.

"Oh! Oh Lord, yes, Slayer! Yes! Fuck me! Take me as only you can!"

Leaving his greedy little pet to hog Jean-Marie's pussy, Etienne rose. Hopefully one of the other women were home. He looked up and saw a naked petite blonde with blue eyes and large breasts, coming down the hall towards them.

He smiled. "Briquette!"

"Etienne! And you've brought that lovely, delicious cock of yours!"

Unmated shifter females were sensual women so valued because they were unashamedly passionate and ever ready to give a den member a good, hard, no-commitment-required fuck.

He grinned. "Yes. Would you like to say hello, my lovely?"

"Yes!" She ran down the hall towards him.

If only it was Raven rushing towards him, eager for his cock. He pushed the thought away and caught Briquette in his arms. Kissing her lips, he drew her down to the floor, rolled her onto her stomach, spread her legs, and thrust balls deep into her young, wonderful ass. She was younger and tighter than Jean-Marie who was twenty-five. Unlike most shifter females, Briquette's rectum was self-lubricating so he gave her a long, rough fuck with no fear of causing her pain.

She lay under him gasping with pleasure, eagerly thrusting her hips up so that he could sink as deeply as possible into her bottom. She was tight, warm, and his passions quickly reached the point of release.

As he was about to come, he worked the fingers of one hand into her tight, heated pussy. She gave a series of lusty screams of pleasure and writhed on his cock as her fragrant pussy gushed. Damn he loved a woman who practically howled when he fucked her. Sinking his fingers and his cock deep inside her body, he shot his seed inside her as she convulsed around his fingers and climaxed.

He gave her a moment to recover from her orgasm before he eased out of her bottom. He turned her on her back, lifted up her hips and sank his still hard cock deep into her tight ass again. Oh, damn, but that was nice.

"Oooh, Etienne!" She wanted to wrap her arms and legs around him, but he needed a hard, unrelenting fuck to keep thoughts of Raven at bay. Extending his arms to keep most of his weight off her petite body, he slid in and out of her bottom with a speed and fury that drove them both over the edge of passion in minutes.

This time when he shot his seed in her, he sank down on top of her. As he fed at her neck, enjoying the feel and taste of her blood, he allowed her to wrap her arms and legs around him.

"Oh, Etienne, I've dreamed for ages of your returning to take my ass like this!"

"Happy dreams, my lovely!"

The next fuck was gentle and tender. The one following that, fast and furious. When they finally drew away from each other, the hall was fragrant with the scent of sex. He lifted her in his arms and carried her down the hall to her bedroom. With the sounds of Slayer and Jean-Marie still fucking near the front door tickling his ears, he curled his body against hers. As he fell asleep, his thoughts turned to Raven. Oh, damn, but he wanted her.

Chapter Eight

۞

Acier. I am on my way.

Acier bolted up from a sound sleep and jumped from the bed. Pen and Drei, still resting against Raven's body shot into the air, hovering near his head, their small bodies quivering with excitement.

Raven, yawning and stretching, stared at him. "Steele. What's wrong?"

He scrambled into a pair of pants and pulled on a shirt. "Raven, he's here."

She blinked at him. "Who? Who's here? Tee?"

He heard the excitement in her voice at the thought of seeing Tee again and stifled a sigh. He supposed he was going to have to learn to deal with her desire for Tee.

"No. Get up and get dressed. It's Aime."

She slipped out of bed and wrapped her arms around his neck. "Aime had better be male."

"He is."

"A relative?"

"No. He's the Alpha of our entire pack."

"I thought you were the Alpha."

"Only in-waiting and of my personal den. Our pack, Pack Gautier, is comprised of many dens. Aime is the leader of our entire pack." He kissed her lightly and drew her arms from around his neck. "Dress, Petite. Quickly. We must not keep him waiting."

He saw a rebellious glint in her eyes and tensed, then sighed when she quickly nodded. "Okay."

221

He kissed her cheek and rushed through the RV with Pen and Drei flying near his head.

At the kitchen sink, he stopped and washed his face. He raked his hands through his hair, gathered it behind his head, and arrived at the RV door just as a knock sounded. He took a deep breath and opened the door.

A tall, heavily built man with shoulder-length hair stood outside the RV. Although his hair was silver, his face remained unlined. On his shoulder sat one of the largest miniature gray wolves Acier had ever seen.

Just behind him, stood three equally heavily built men with short dark hair. Surprised that Aime now had three bodyguards, Acier dropped to one knee. Pen and Drei dropped down on either side of his legs. He lowered his head. "Alpha, I live to serve."

"Acier, my pup. It does my old ailing eyes good to see you." A large hand settled on his shoulder. "When have you ever lived to serve anyone? Humility sits uneasily on your shoulders, as well it should on one who would lead our entire pack. Rise, my pup."

He rose to his feet, but kept his head bowed. "You honor me with your presence, Alpha. But if you wanted me, you had but to summon me."

Aime waved a large hand. "We have traveled a long way to see you. Invite us in, Acier"

"Of course." He backed away from the door. Aime entered, followed by his bodyguards. All three men were just over six feet and looked like seasoned warrior shifters. Acier nodded at them.

Each man dipped his head slightly in silent acknowledgement of Acier's status as Alpha-in-waiting.

Aime sank down onto into one of the captain's chairs and waved to the sofa where his bodyguards sat. Aime looked at Pen and Drei, who still stood on the floor, their heads bowed.

"Rise, Keddi."

Pen and Drei rose, moved through the air to hover in front of Aime's shoulder, and bowed their heads to Dominator. *Alpha, we live to serve*, Pen told Dominator in a quiet respectful voice.

Drei much younger than Pen, and seeing the Supreme Alpha Keddi for the first time, seemed overwhelmed. He remained silent, his body quivering with excitement.

Pen, Drei is fully grown. You have done well with him. I am told you have done equally as well with Slayer. As Karol is with the pack, I know you have done well with him.

As a rule, the Earth-bound Keddi were prone to speak in short, terse, ungrammatical sentences. But in the presence of the Supreme Alpha and his Keddi, they spoke proper English.

You honor me with your praise, Alpha.

Acier felt Pen's pride at the words of praise from Dominator and smiled. Dominator was an arrogant bastard, and unlike Aime who ruled with a firm but fair hand, Dominator wasn't known for showing the Keddi under his supervision much consideration or respect.

Acier often wondered why Aime didn't rein in the little bastard. He had watched Dominator mistreat other Keddi, but had made it clear to him that Pen, Drei, Slayer, and Etienne's other Keddi, Karol, were not available to be treated unfairly. He let both Aime and Dominator know when he became Alpha Supreme, Pen would become Supreme Alpha Keddi.

Dominator flew off Aime's shoulder and hovered in front of Pen. *Come and talk with me, Keddi*. He looked at Drei. *You may come as well, pup.*

Acier stepped in their path and looked into Dominator's dark eyes. *Treat my friends well*, he warned.

Dominator flew around him without answering, heading towards the bedroom. After a moment of indecision, Pen and then Drei flew after him.

Aime arched a brow. "You still do not like Dom."

"He's unkind and unfair and I will not have Pen or Drei

treated that way."

Aime inclined his head. "It is well for you to look out for their welfare, but I think you will find that Dominator has changed. He regrets that his past actions will make him unlikely to be able to retain his status as Supreme Alpha Keddi when you ascend to Alpha Supreme."

"Even if he had not been unfair to other Keddi, Pen would still have been my choice for Supreme Alpha Keddi."

Aime inclined his head. "It is your right. There are lots of options available to you. You should choose wisely." His nostrils quivered. "You have a woman here."

There was a hint of censure in Aime's voice. "Yes."

"You've mated with her. Have you given no consideration to mating with Chanel Parre'?"

Acier had known for some time that Aime would look favorably upon a union between him and the small, petite blonde with the ice-blue eyes he had known since they were both cubs. She had followed him after he left the pack. Young, brash, and overly impressed with his status as Aime's choice of him to leave the pack, he had been arrogant and selfish. He had briefly taken her as his lover. He had quickly become bored with her and had sent her back to the pack.

They had parted on good terms and it troubled him that she had never mated permanently with another member of the pack. At the back of his mind was the uneasy thought that he had hurt her so that she refused to allow another male to fully possess her.

"I can't, Alpha. The woman with me now is my mate."

Aime sniffed the air, his brows furling. "She is not fully human."

"That's what Etienne says."

"Where is she?"

"Right here."

Acier tensed. Raven, her skin still glistening with drops of water, appeared in the living area wearing a one-piece pantsuit that made him hard just looking at her. She looked beautiful and strangely regal.

She had that glint in her dark eyes that made him uncomfortable. He was almost certain she would say something Aime would consider disrespectful. Instead, she delighted him by walking up to Aime and curtsying. "Alpha Supreme, you honor us with your presence."

Acier watched Aime smile. "*Willoni*. It is a mutual honor." He extended his hand. "Come and tell me which Goddess you serve."

Raven's brows furrowed for several moments. She gave him her hand and sat beside him. "I don't know."

Aime patted her hand. "It is of no consequence. Acier tells me you are his woman."

She turned her head and looked at him, a secret, intimate look in her gaze. "We'll see."

Acier swallowed several times, longing to sweep her up in his arms, take her back to bed, and fuck her until she realized just who the hell she belonged to. Instead, he turned his gaze back to Aime. "What brings you so far from home, Alpha?"

"Leon de la Rocque and Pack LeMay."

He frowned. Surely Leon had no dealings with Pack LeMay, the archrivals of every shifter in Pack Gautier. "I've seen him and sent him on his way, but what has he to do with Pack LeMay?

Aime nodded, for the first time looking a little frail. "Leon has enlisted the aid of an off-world shifter called Tucker Falcone who has aligned himself with LeMay."

Acier stiffened. "Off-world? What does that mean?"

"I know you do not much put faith in the old legends, Acier, my pup, but they are legends for a reason. This Tucker Falcone is a Heoptin Shifter. Tell me what you know of such beings."

225

Acier searched his memory. As a young pup, he like all other youngsters of the pack had sat at Aime's feet as he told tales of the old days. "Ah…there is some confusion where we originate. Some say Earth is the original home world, some say shifters evolved on the planet called Boreias, a fringe planet of an alien world called Aeolia.

"If memory serves, Heoptin was the God of Bliss and Passion whose home was the Blue Desert on Denhari, on Boreias. I think you said he had vampires and shifters who served under him. Heoptin vampires were known for their extraordinary skills as healers while the shifters were known for their viciousness in battle."

Aime inclined his head. "Then you did listen as I talked. Leon has aligned himself with a Heoptin Shifter. He will come to seek you out."

Acier shrugged. "Let him come. I'll be waiting."

"He is not an ordinary shifter, my pup."

Acier tightened his lips. "I am not an ordinary shifter either." He bared his incisors. "I'll be waiting when he comes."

Aime sighed and nodded at the tallest of the bodyguards who had accompanied him. "You know Bakone?"

Acier nodded. As a young pup he had looked up to the big shifter, dreaming that he would one day be as tall and strong. "Bakone is known to all in Pack Gautier…known and revered."

"Bakone is indeed a legend among shifters." Aime rose. "Dalone, Rayton, and I will be on our way."

Acier stiffened. "And Bakone?"

Aime arched a brow. "Why, he will remain here with you, of course. When the Heoptin comes after you, you must not face him alone."

"I will face him alone. I do not need or require a bodyguard. It will make me seem weak."

Aime swung around to face him. "I have two. Would you

assert that I am weak, pup?"

Acier bowed his head. "Of course not, Alpha."

"Then Bekone will remain with you and defend you with his life. You are not yet ready to face this shifter alone."

"You doubt my bravery, Alpha?"

"Never, but it is not a question of bravery. You have no idea who or what you really are and I will not have you killed. I am old and long for the time when I will be free to roam the home territory with my mate without the burden and worry of the pack on my shoulders."

The finality in Aime's words invited no further debate. "As you wish, Alpha."

Aime turned to kiss Raven's hand. "Little *Willoni*, there are dangerous and frightening times ahead. Do not fail Acier."

She lifted her chin, her eyes glittering. "I will not. When this Heoptin comes, he will find himself also facing Ravanni Monclair, of the order of Modidsha, she of the Barren Hills Clan on Stone Mountain, in the land of Wind Swept Valley. I am she who commands the enchanted barrier and will allow no harm to be visited upon those I value."

Aime seemed pleased. "Ahhh. She who commands Bentia, the enchanted barrier. You are young yet, but one day, you will be a force to which many will bow. I thought perhaps, you did not serve the Goddess Caldara. I had thought maybe you were an acolyte of Amisha of the Golden Hills Clan, but I see you are more than a mere acolyte."

Raven blinked, a confused look in her eyes. "I...I don't know why I said that. I've never heard of Modidsha or Amisha or any of that other stuff I just said. I don't know anything about enchantments or barriers. I...I'm human."

"No, my child. You are not! You are confused. You must find your spiritual guide. When you have, with you by his side, Acier will be nearly invincible."

Acier stared at him. "I'm not invincible, Alpha. I'm sure, like any shifter, I can be killed."

227

Aime arched a brow. "Ahhh. But as you said, my pup, you are not any shifter. Have you never wondered why I choose you to lead the pack after me when I might have chosen any number of purebred shifters?"

"Yes," he admitted. As he and Etienne had grown up with Leon and other shifters of their age range, everyone had been sure Leon or Terrone would be chosen to succeed Aime. When it became clear Terrone preferred other males to females, everyone had thought Leon would be chosen. Aime's announcement that he had chosen Acier had stunned everyone, except Etienne, who had just smiled and given Acier an I-told-you-so look.

Aime clenched a hand and placed it over his heart. "I am Aime Gautier, descendant of those who served Dioptin, he of the eternal sight. When I saw you playing as a pup, the vision came to me who you were and what you would one day be to our people."

"Alpha?"

"You will truly be Alpha Supreme for running through your veins is the blood of one of the oldest vampire lines in existence."

"Who?"

"Why, you are a descendant of Heoptin himself. True, there are those on Earth with a stronger blood tie to his line of vampires, but none combines that tie with your ties to those descended from Dioptin. Your mother was a distant relative of mine, although I did not learn that until recently."

Acier felt as stunned as Raven looked. "Do you know who my father is?"

"No, but you will find him."

"And when I do—"

"You will listen to his story before you try to kill him," Aime told him. "Things are not as you might imagine."

"He abandoned us!"

"Perhaps…perhaps not." He sighed. "I grow weary and long for my den." He looked at Bekone. "Come. You are not needed here after all."

Bekone looked at Acier and inclined his head. "Should you have a need it would be my honor to surrender my life while protecting the Alpha-in-waiting for the good of Pack Gautier. I am yours to command, Alpha."

Acier nodded, humbled that the shifter he'd grown up admiring and longing to be like was so willing to offer his life in his defense. "Thank you."

"Dom!" Aime called, turned, and walked from the RV.

Dominator flew out the door behind him and alighted on Aime's shoulder.

Acier closed and locked the RV door. "Pen, Drei."

Both pets flew from the bedroom and hovered around him. From Pen he sensed surprised pleasure. From Drei he sensed suppressed excitement at having finally met the Supreme Alpha Keddi. He could detect no evidence that Dom had mistreated them.

Alpha! Dominator is almost as impressive as Pen! Drei told him.

He looked at Pen and saw his chest puffing out. Dominator was right. Pen, who had taught and raised Drei, Slayer, and Karol, had done a great job. "Well done, Pen."

He touched both of their heads. "I am very proud of you both."

He felt their pleasure. He touched them again and then turned to look at Raven, who still looked stunned.

He sat beside her and took her hand in his. "Petite?"

She looked at him. "Steele…I am human…aren't I?"

He tipped up her chin. "I don't know and I don't care. I just know you are my woman."

She pressed close to him and he hugged her. "Steele, you will be all right…won't you?"

229

His arms tightened around her. "Of course I will. Maybe a normal shifter would have a problem with a Heoptin shifter, but I am not normal... I have a distressing amount of vampire blood running through my veins."

She wrapped her arms around him. "If he hurts you, I'll kill him. I swear it!"

"I'll be fine, Petite. Don't worry about me." He brushed his lips against hers.

Her mouth immediately parted under his and his cock hardened. Still kissing her, he cupped a hand between her legs. "I need some pussy," he whispered.

"Funny you should mention that because I just happen to have some pussy I've been told is very good."

"It's excellent." He smiled against her lips. "So you going to give me some?"

Her response was to reach down and cup her hand over his cock. "For a man who claims he wants pussy, you waste an awful lot of time talking instead of doing."

Laughing, he swept her up into his arms and rose. He looked at Pen and Drei. "Stay."

Want pussy, Drei protested. *Coming.*

Keddi, stay! Pen snapped, moving in front of Drei.

Leaving Pen to deal with Drei, Acier carried Raven down the hall to his bedroom. He undressed them both quickly. Kissing and clinging to each other, they tumbled onto the bed their lips locked together.

Lying on top of her, he kissed her slowly, deeply, enjoying the taste and feel of her lips. He longed to thrust into her and fuck her until she couldn't walk. He reminded himself that she had recently been a virgin and she must be sore. Damn, but he still wanted her so badly, the hunger nearly took away his breath.

She stroked her fingers through his hair. "So take some."

He stiffened, lifted his head and stared down at her. "Did

you just…read my mind?"

"I…I don't know. Did I?"

He rolled off her and sat up. "What do you remember about your mother, Petite?"

She sat up, her eyes looking wide in the dark room. "Not much…she died when I was five and Dad used to get so sad when he talked about her we stopped asking."

He drew her against him and slid down in bed with her in his arms. "I don't think she's dead, Petite."

She trembled against him. "She has to be. Dad wouldn't lie to us."

Mo was definitely big on the truth. "Maybe he doesn't know the truth. Haven't you ever wondered why you don't share your family's last name?"

"Dad said Mom begged him to name me Monclair. He said he didn't know why, but he loved her so much, he did as she asked."

"The Monclairs were from the Barren Hills Clan on Stone Mountain on Wind Swept Valley." He stroked a hand down her back. "I believe Etienne was right. You are *Willoni*."

"No! I'm human, Steele, like my sisters and my father."

"You are *Willoni*, like your mother…and you are mine." He tipped up her chin and kissed her lips.

She slipped her arms around his neck. He lifted his body, located the entrance to her pussy, and slowly pushed forward.

She gasped against his lips, her body warm and welcoming. With her holding him tight and shuddering under him, he made tender love to her, easing his cock in and out of her tight, moist, warm pussy with an aching slowness. The feelings of joy and a pleasure that was almost a pain overwhelmed him as she eagerly accepted his cock back in her with every downward movement of his hips. He had never wanted or needed a woman more. No other woman had made him feel this unbearable tenderness and need to please, protect, cherish, and love her.

And feed on her. With his eyes glowing, he bared his incisors and looked down at her. She opened her eyes and she smiled up at him, tilting her head, exposing her neck.

With a soft growl, he bent his head and bit into her neck. Her blood, warm and sweet rushed into his mouth. A feeling of ecstasy nearly overwhelmed him. Holding her in a tender embrace, he fucked her gently, but deeply, feeding on her sweet, addictive blood, but holding back his own release until she had come several times. Only then did he fill her with his seed.

His climax, the most powerful one he'd ever had, was so long and intense, his eyes watered, and before it was over, she had come again. When his heart stopped hammering, he lay on his side, his cheeks wet. She lay behind him, stroking his fur and whispering softly to him that it was all right.

Somehow, without conscious effort, as he made love to her, he had fully shifted to his true form. And she had accepted and welcomed him.

He rose from her arms, urged her onto her hand and knees, pressed his body behind and over her back, and thrust deep into her pussy.

She gasped. "Oh God, Steele! Yes!"

Leaning over her back, he cupped his paws over her lovely breasts, bit into her neck, and fucked her hard and deep, feeding on her with a gusto he had never expected. Their fuck was hot and explosive. They both came within minutes. When they had, he lay his still shifted body on top of hers and fell asleep with his cock buried balls deep inside her drenched, no longer virginal pussy, her blood on the fur around his mouth.

Chapter Nine

ഇ

Raven woke hungry the next morning. Although her body ached and her pussy was sore, she felt wonderful. She turned onto her side. Steele, shifted back to his human form, slept on his stomach beside her, his long dark hair covering his handsome face.

She brushed it aside to find his cheek, kissed it, and got out of bed. She found the shirt he'd worn the night before on the floor by the bed and took it to the shower with her. She took a quick, cool shower, allowing all she had learned to run around in her head without trying to make much sense of it. Aime had said she needed to find her guide.

Just how could she do that when she had no idea who her guide was? She closed her eyes, slowly swaying from side to side. A picture of Abby jumped into her mind. Abby!

She got out of the shower, pulled Steel's shirt on over her damp body, and rushed to the kitchen. She paused, smiling. Pen and Drei sat on the counter top. Pen lapped up black coffee while Drei devoured a slice of raw bacon.

"Hungry guys?"

Already ate, Pen told her, finishing his coffee. *Drei cooked.*

She noted several broken eggshells in the wastebasket near the counter, along with an empty bacon package.

Drei looked up at her. *Want breakfast?*

The idea of the two of them cooking breakfast intrigued her. "Yes."

Drei gobbled the last bit of bacon and flew towards the refrigerator. She smiled and walked into the living room area of the RV. She picked up the cordless from an end table.

233

Moments later, she had Abby on the phone. "Hello?"

"Abb…who am I?"

She heard Abby draw in a deep breath. "You know?"

"I don't know what I know. People keep telling me I'm something called a *Willoni* and last night when talking to someone…I started sprouting some stuff about being someone called Ravanni of the Barren Hills Clan and something called an enchanted barrier. While I was in the shower…it suddenly occurred to me that I had to talk to you. What's going on, Abby?"

"You are ready to learn who and what you are, Raven. Where are you? I must come to you immediately."

"I'm with Steele."

"I will be there in a few hours."

"Abb, I'm scared."

"Don't be. I will explain everything when I arrive. Hang on, little *Willoni*."

As she hung up, the smell of sizzling bacon made her wet her lips. She put the phone down and returned to the kitchen area. She stopped, her eyes widening. Both Pen and Drei had shifted into humanoid form. When they turned to look at her, she found herself looking at two minimum versions of Steele, right down to the long, dark hair and thick cocks.

Drei hovered near the frying pan on the stove with a tiny spoon in his hand as he poked at the bacon and eggs cooking in the pan. Pen held a coffeepot in his hand, filling a cup.

Breakfast ready, Pen said. *Like eggs over easy?*

She liked them cooked — long and well. "Yes."

Pen pulled out a chair in the dining area and she sat down. Moving so quickly it was difficult for her to keep them in her sight, Pen and Drei, quickly set a plate in front of her and filled it with several pieces of bacon, two eggs over easy, and two pieces of lightly buttered wheat toast. Pen filled a glass with orange juice and sat it next to her.

She arched a brow. "Orange juice?"

He shrugged. *Have to eat good.*

Feeling a little apprehensive, she lifted a forkful of eggs to her mouth. It was delicious. She looked at Drei. "These are great. Who taught you to cook like this?"

Alpha.

"I didn't know Steele could cook."

He can't! Pen quivered with indignation.

Didn't mean that Alpha. Drei pointed at Pen. *Meant that Alpha.*

Pen puffed out his small, muscular chest. *Taught Drei how cook good.*

She smiled at him. "Handsome, a good lover, and you can cook? I think I'll keep you around for awhile."

Pen's handsome face flushed. *Pen stay.* He moved through the air and sealed his promise with a gentle kiss on her lips.

Drei joined him, kissing her too.

"I love you both," she told them.

"What a charming, sight."

She looked up. Steele, wearing a pair of boxers that did nothing to conceal his cock, crossed to the table. She lifted her face and he kissed her mouth.

"What about me?" he murmured against her lips. "Do you like me too, Petite?"

She answered with her heart. "No. I love you."

"And well you should." He pinched her breasts and sat across from her, locking his gaze with hers.

She took a sip of her coffee, holding the cup in both hands. "Do you love me?"

"I need you...I have to have you. Let that be enough, Petite."

"I want love, Steele."

Pen loves.

Drei too.

She tore her gaze away from Steele's. "Then maybe I'll spend the next two months with you guys."

Steele's right hand shot out and closed around hers. "Please, Petite. All this vampire shit and bloodlust stuff is new to me. A few days ago, I thought of you as a little girl… Give me a little time to adjust."

She had a lot to accept herself. "Okay, but don't think I'm going to wait forever, Steele. I'm not going to stay with a man who refuses to say he loves me."

She watched his eyes narrow. "Love is just a word."

"It's a word I'm going to want to hear from your lips fairly soon, Steele."

He lifted her hand to his mouth and kissed the back of it. "I can't live without you. Isn't that enough?"

She shrugged. "I don't know," she whispered.

He kissed her hand again and she convinced herself she saw a gleam of love in his eyes.

Alpha want breakfast? Drei asked.

"Yes."

Drei moved towards the stove, Pen moved towards the refrigerator. *Bacon and eggs?*

"Yes…and lots of pussy."

To Raven's amazement, both Drei and Pen laughed. *How Alpha want pussy?*

Steele grinned. "Hot, slick, tight, and full of my cock."

All three males laughed again and Raven flushed. She rose and slapped Steele's shoulder as she walked passed him. "Eat, then shower and get dressed. My guide will be here in a few hours and you'd all three better keep your cocks under cover. Better still…all three of you brutes…get lost!"

With the sounds of their laughter ringing in her ears, she

stalked from the kitchen. Her stomach rumbled. She stalked back to the kitchen area and snatched her plate away from Steele, who had stretched out a hand towards a piece of her bacon.

"Two little pigs and one big one!" She called over her shoulder and retreated to the bedroom to eat her breakfast and call her father.

"Dad, what can you tell me about Mom?"

"Not much beyond the fact that she was the most beautiful woman I'd ever met and I lost her all too soon."

She sighed. That didn't help much. "Why did she want me named Monclair and not Treena and—"

"She wasn't their mother."

Raven wet her lips. "What? I never knew we had a different mother, Dad!"

"It didn't seem important. Their mother died a few years before I met your mother and she died when you were only five. After losing the only two women I'd ever loved, I knew a third marriage was out of the question."

So he had not married again because he was afraid of losing a third wife to death. Of course Steele didn't seem to think her mother was dead. "What was Mother like?"

"She was a warm, beautiful, caring woman...just as you are. I wish you could have known her, baby."

"So do I."

"Raven...about you and Acier..."

"I love him, Daddy!"

"And does he love you?"

She closed her eyes and lied. "Of course he does."

"Then you're happy with him?"

"Yes. Dad, Abby is on her way so I have to go. I'll talk to you soon."

"I love you so much, baby."

"I love you too, Dad."

As she dressed, Pen and Drei, still in humanoid form came into the bedroom with a box of chocolates and flowers.

Her mood brightened and she smiled. That Steele was a darling and a fast worker. She placed the chocolates on the dresser top and she plucked the card from between the roses. Her smile vanished when she saw the name on the card.

"Why is he romancing you?"

She looked up. Steele, his eyes dark and dangerous-looking, stood in the doorway.

She sighed. "I thought you sent them."

"Why did he send them?"

She looked down at the card again. *Even if he doesn't admit it, he loves you, Petite. And so do I. Etienne.*

She shrugged. "Probably because he knows you won't. He says you love me. Do you?"

"I need you."

She sighed. That was probably as good as it was going to get with him. Was it going to be enough? She wasn't sure.

Almost as if he sensed some of what she felt, he walked into the room and put his arm around her. As she turned her face against his shoulder, he took the card from her hand. "Do you love him, Petite?"

"Yes," she admitted. She lifted her head and looked up at him. "But you're the one I can't imagine living without."

"I would gladly die to protect him, but I am not sharing you with him. I don't give a fuck how much you two love each other. Is that clear, Raven?"

"Tell me you love me and I'll never look at another man. Keep telling me love isn't important, Steele, and I might find a need to seek it elsewhere."

His arm tightened around her waist. "And I might have to kill the unfortunate bastard you take up with."

"And what if that man is Tee?"

He shook his head. "It won't be. No matter how much he loves you, he wouldn't do that to me."

She sighed. "No. He wouldn't…and neither would I. I wouldn't pit you two against each other for anything." She touched his cheek. "I'm sorry I even suggested it."

He buried his face against her neck. "Please…don't insist I say words that have no meaning for me. I want you and I need you. I can't live without you. Let that me enough, Petite. It's all I have to give."

And yet she needed so much more. So where did that leave them?

* * * * *

Etienne stood in the doorway of the upscale bar and lounge in the society hill section of the city. The large room before him was filled with scantily clad vampires, male and female, dancing close together in the nearly dark room. Although he couldn't actually see it, he knew many of the club goers were having sex. He could hear the sounds of cocks sinking into pussies and asses all around them. The air was fragrant with the smell of sex and blood. What a delicious aroma.

"Hey, you two in or out?"

Etienne glanced over his shoulder. A vampire bouncer stood just outside the door, behind Damon.

Damon gave him a push and he walked into the club. He pointed towards the bar along one wall where a beautiful, buxom brunette sat. "That's Kalista. We'll start with her. If she doesn't know him, she'll at least know which direction to point us."

He nodded and made his way towards the fem.

She turned on the barstool, watching their approached. Her dark eyes settled on Etienne. After a moment, her gaze dropped down to his groin.

Just knowing that a full-blooded fem was looking at his cock with lust in her gaze, made him hard. His cock quickly spread out along the side of one leg.

Because Slayer was in full lust mode, he had left him behind, buried to the hilt inside Jean-Marie's willing pussy, fucking her to climax after climax in a frenzy of lust.

He saw the fem lick her lips as she pulled her gaze away from his groin and looked into his eyes as he and Damon stopped near her. "Damon, who is this handsome young vampire-like hunk?"

Etienne smiled and bowed his head slightly. "Etienne Gautier, at your service, ma'am."

She offered her hand. He took it in his, brushing his lips against the back of it.

She smiled, revealing her incisors. "You are a well put together young man, Etienne Gautier. Tell me, are you any good with that wicked-looking cock hanging so blatantly against your leg?"

"Oh, hell, yeah!"

Her smile widened and she rose. She was nearly as tall as he. She wore a dress with a low-cut bodice. The skirt ended well above her long, shapely legs. In true fem fashion, she reached out and cupped her palm along his cock. "Oh my, but you have a large, lovely cock." Keeping one hand over his cock, she placed her other hand on his arm. "Let's go to the back and fuck."

His blood pressured soared. He was about to fuck a second full-blood fem in just over a week. Damn, but his ship had definitely come in. "Hell, yeah."

As they turned towards the back, Damon clamped a hand on his arm. "Wait just a damn minute, Etienne. We didn't come here to fuck. We came here on business."

His lust nearly at full force again, he swung around and glared at Damon, bearing his incisors. "Get lost, Damon!"

"Fuck you!" Damon reached in the breast pocket of his jacket and pulled out a detailed sketch. Damon leaned past him and extended the small picture towards Kalista. "Do you know this vampire?"

Kalista gave it a brief, but thorough gaze. "Maybe. I'm going to lay Etienne and then we'll talk about him." She gave Damon a cold look, took Etienne's hand in hers, and led him towards a closed door behind the bar.

He followed her down a long hall dotted with doors, behind which he could hear lustful fucking going on. At the end of the corridor, she opened a door and ushered him into a dark room with a big bed under a huge mirrored ceiling.

Three moments later, they were both naked and aroused. She swept him up in her arms, tossed him onto the bed, and jumped in beside him. He spread his legs and lay on his back. She climbed on top of him, grasped his cock, mounted him, and slammed herself down onto his entire cock with one, smooth, wonderful movement.

Gasping at the feeling of having his entire shaft buried deep in the pussy of such a beautiful fem, he grabbed her firm ass, and they began a swift, almost brutally fast fuck.

He pulled her upper body down so that her breasts brushed his chest. Ignoring the allure of her slender, blood-red lips, he wrapped his arms around her back and sank his incisors deep into her neck, filling her pussy full of seed as her blood rushed into his mouth and down his throat.

She lay panting against his shoulder. "You sure know how to use that lethal cock of yours, boy. Give it me again. Bang me up, boy! Bust me open! Lord, I adore a young, handsome boy with a cock that stretches nearly down to his knee. Bang me, boy!"

He was too far gone to object to being called boy. As long as she allowed him to rut into her pussy without complaints, he didn't care how she addressed him.

They fucked on and on, hour after hour, sweet, addictive

fuck after addictive fuck, until Damon, annoyed at having been kept waiting all night, barged into the room at dawn. "Enough fucking! It's time to get down to business, Etienne!"

Feeling almost drunk, Etienne, lying on top of Kalista, rutting into her, reluctantly admitted that he had lost sight of his reason for going to the bar the night before.

Kissing the warm lips of the fem lying impaled on his cock, he shot his seed into her before pulling out of her. Shoving him none too gently as he pulled on his pants, Damon moved over to the bed and looked down at the fem, who had turned on her side and curled into a contented ball. "You owe us a name, fem."

She lifted her head and looked at him. Etienne felt his cock stirring as he looked in her eyes. "Come see me again, Etienne."

He nodded, breathing deeply.

She turned to look at Damon. "Check with the Defense League of the Brotherhood."

"Where can we find them?"

"They have headquarters all over the USA, but at the moment, I hear they are headquartered near the outskirts of Philadelphia. There is talk of Vitali Bourcaro recruiting the one you seek."

"What's his name?"

She looked at Etienne. "You want any more, I'll require another night of fucking as payment."

Etienne began to struggle out of his jacket.

"Oh, no you don't!" Damon snarled, grabbing his arm. "We'll learn his name on our own."

She waved a dismissal hand. "Suit yourself. Get out."

Etienne bent over the bed and stroked a hand down her back. She turned to look up at him. "Come back soon, handsome."

"Count on it," he promised, kissed her lips, and allowed

Damon to drag him from the room.

As they left the club, he raked a hand through his hair, realizing how tired he was. And now that he was away from Kalista, he still hungered for Raven. He handed Damon the keys to his SUV. "I'm too tired to drive."

"I wonder why the fuck that is!" Damon snatched the keys and rounded on him, his eyes dark with fury. "Etienne, if you're going to take care of business, do. This isn't going to work if you lose sight of our goal every time some female spreads her damned legs."

He sighed. "You're right. I'm sorry. It's just that—"

"That you need to bed Acier's woman and get the first taste for her out of your system."

He shook his head. "I can't, Damon!"

"You'll have to, Etienne. You cannot deny bloodlust. It doesn't work, Etienne."

Chapter Ten

ᔓ

Feeling adequately satisfied, Deoctra Diniti rose from the bed she had shared with her shifter lover. She stretched her slender, petite body, her dark eyes on the man still sleeping so soundly. Man? She recalled their sex of the night before with her on hands and knees and him behind her, fully shifted, growling and biting as he rutted into her like an animal.

He was definitely not a man. For all his animal-like passion, Leon was not as satisfying a lover as the Gautier brothers had been. Her pussy tingled and she shuddered, remembering Etienne Gautier making love to her and touching her feelings as only one vampire had never done, Mikhel Dumont, her former bloodlust.

Still, Leon was lusty and had a very respectable-sized cock. In his natural form, when he really pounded her pussy, his knot sometimes slipped inside her and drove her wild. He slept in his humanoid form. His hair was short and blond, his naked body well-built and pleasing. She and Den Alpha Leon de la Rocque had spent the last week fucking day and night.

Her thoughts again turned to the two hybrid shifters, Acier and Etienne Gautier, with whom she had spent an incredible night in this cabin. Between the two of them with their voracious appetite, they had succeeded in driving thoughts of Mikhel Dumont from her head, freeing her from years of slavery to her need for Mikhel.

Leon had proven to be slightly more than competent, but not particularly inspiring as a lover. The Gautiers, on the other hand, had been magnificent. Etienne in particular haunted her thoughts. When with Leon, she closed her eyes and imagined he was Etienne.

She showered quickly and dressed in a dark, one-piece catsuit. Walking back through the bedroom, she stiffened, sensing the presence of another vampire. She hesitated. Not long before, Vladimir Madison, half brother to Mikhel Dumont, had attacked and nearly killed her to avenge her attack of his younger sister, Katie Dumont.

In hindsight, she grudgingly allowed that she should not have tried to take out Katie Dumont. Two of her younger sisters had paid for that mistake with their lives at the hands of the Dumonts. She was determined to safeguard the lives of her remaining two sisters. Until her strength and her confidence returned, she would hide here. When she knew how things stood for her and she could ensure the safety of her family, she would call them to her.

Sensing that the vampire outside was not one of the Dumonts or the Madisons, she cast a quick look at Leon who still slept and walked out onto the porch of her remote cabin in the woods.

Standing across the clearing, just inside the tall trees on the other side of the road, stood a tall vampire with bronze colored skin, short, straight, salt and pepper hair, and very light brown eyes.

Although they had never met, Deoctra knew the striking vampire's identity. "Vitali Bourcaro. What brings the Defense League of The Brotherhood to my door?"

"Deoctra Diniti. I hear you are having vampire troubles." He beckoned to her. "Come. Walk with me and maybe we can come to an arrangement that will see the end of your troubles."

She wet her lips. "Are you offering me membership in the Brotherhood?" Such an invitation would be quite a coup and her troubles would surely be over. Even the Madison vampires wouldn't dare come after one shielded by the powerful and feared Brotherhood.

She frowned. "You know Vladimir Madison is one of the

vampires after me. I hear you have offered him membership in the league. How do I know he won't dispatch me if I join you?"

His eyes narrowed. "First you have not been asked to join us. Second, the Brotherhood is in the business of not only taking down those insidious half-human, half-vampire hunters, but discouraging infighting amongst ourselves. Now, come. Walk with me and we will see what transpires."

She crossed the road and turned into the woods with him.

* * * * *

Raven was alone in the trailer when she heard a car pull into the spot next to Steele's RV. She tossed the magazine she'd been flipping through aside and went to the front door as Abby alighted from her car.

Abby wore a dark, tailor-made suit that complimented her smooth, creamy skin. Her hair, short and dark, curled around her pretty face, highlighting her clear green eyes. A smile lit her face.

Raven stepped back from the doorway, beckoning. "Oh, Abb! Thanks for coming."

Abby entered and they embraced. As they broke apart, she placed her hands on Raven's arms. "Ravanni Monclair, born of Deliah, High Priestess of Modidsha, of the Barren Hills, I am Abigail, your clanswoman, chosen to guide you to your true destiny. Ask what you will and I will answer."

Raven felt as if a dam had burst inside her. Memories of her mother, telling her tales of a faraway world when she was very young, surfaced. "Abb...I'm human...I have a father and sisters. We're all human."

Abby lead her into the living area and sat with her on the sofa. "Can we talk?"

She nodded. Steele had taken his PDA, his folding keyboard, Pen and Drei and gone for a ride so she and Abby could talk uninterrupted. "You've had a long drive. Can I get you something? Coffee…something to eat?"

"Maybe after we've talked."

"Steele isn't human, Abb."

She nodded. "I know."

"How long have you known?"

"I had a vision last night."

"Well, he's not human, but I am."

Abby touched her cheek. "Your sisters are human, as is your father, but you are not."

"I am! We all have the same father and mother!" She bit her lip. "Well, I mean—"

"No. You have a different mother."

Raven moistened her lips. "You said have, not had."

"Their mother is dead. Yours is not."

Raven looked into Abby's green eyes and somehow knew she spoke the truth. "But…why did she leave me? Where is she?"

"What do you remember of what she told you of Aeolia?"

"How…how do you know she told me anything? I was very young when she…I was very young."

"A *Willoni* is never too young to hear and know of her true destiny. What do you remember?"

Raven closed her eyes and began to sway. "I remember stories of a planet called Aeolia, far from here. She said it had four fringe worlds and that our descendants were from one of those worlds called Boreias."

"And what do you know of Boreias?"

"It is the home world of the Keddi."

Abby's hand tightened on her arm. "You have seen the Keddi?"

She opened her eyes and looked at Abby. "Yes. Steele has two, Pen and Drei. The Alpha Supreme has one called

Dominator."

"Alpha Supreme?"

She nodded. "Steele and Etienne are shifters."

"Werewolves?"

Even though she sensed Abby already knew the answer to the questions, she answered anyway. "No. They are always sentient, even in their natural wolf form. They are not animals. Steele has a den of shifters he leads, but Alpha Supreme leads all of the dens. Steele is next in line for the position."

"Boreias is also the home world of The Barren Hills Clan...our clan. It is a huge world with many modern cities and some ancient towns, many ruled and governed by different authorities, some deities, some civil authorities. We are from the ancient town of Wind Swept Valley where Modidsha is Goddess of the *Willoni*. Wind Swept Valley covers a vast area of the planet Boreias. Deliah is now serving as High Priestess at the Temple on Stone Mountain in Wind Swept Valley."

"Why did she leave me?"

"It was her time to serve. Unlike the Goddess Caldara, who rules Denhari with an unkind hand, Modidsha is kind and gentle. She allowed Deliah to leave her duties at the temple so that she might know the joy of motherhood. Your mother picked your father carefully. She knew when she left that he would take very good care of you. And I was sent here from the temple to guide you."

"But we only met two years ago!"

Abby smiled. "Yes, but I have been close and have watched over you since Deliah returned to her duties. Two years ago, I felt the time was right to introduce myself to you. So I engineered our meeting at the film festival."

She didn't know if she liked the idea that nothing in her life had been left to chance or personal choice. "What is expected of me?"

"You are the daughter of a high priestess. One day you

will be called upon to serve in one of Modidsha's temples."

Raven blinked at her. "On…another world?"

"Modidsha has a small following on Earth, but a daughter of a high priestess will almost certainly be called to serve in Wind Swept Valley."

"What about my family? My sisters? Steele?"

"We of the Barren Hills Clan are your family, *Willoni*."

Raven shook her head and bolted to her feet. "No! I have a father and sisters who I love and who love me! I won't deny them! And I won't…I can't leave Steele."

Abby rose and faced her. "Ravanni Monclair, each *Willoni* has a destiny to which she must be true."

"I have a family and I finally have the man I love! I'm not leaving any of them to serve some Goddess who called my mother away from me!"

Abby sighed. "You are very young and—"

"I'm ten years younger than you, Abb! So come off this—"

Abby shook her head. "I am Abigail Valanti, sister of Belladonna, who serves the Goddess Caldara, here on Earth. Like my sister, I am far older than I look. I was guide to your mother when she was very young and I guided her mother before her."

Raven sucked in a breath. "Just how old are you?"

She smiled. "Very old. Old enough to know that young Earthborn *Willoni* always rebel when they first learn who and what they are. Unlike Caldara, Modidsha is a just and fair Goddess. You are not just a daughter of a high priestess, of which there are as many as there are temples, you are she who will one day command Bentia, the enchanted barrier. You will have a duty to which you must be true."

She shook her head again. The thought of leaving her family or Steele tore at her and yet she felt a calling…a whispering of the winds from the Valley where her mother had been born…urging her to come…home? "No," she whispered. Home was where her family and Steele was. She had no other destiny.

"Bentia has chosen you to command her, Ravanni. You must do your duty when you are called."

"Who is this Bentia that I should allow her to control my life?"

"Bentia is a living, sentient barrier spirit. She has no wish to control your life. She lives to serve the *Willoni* of her choosing. Sometimes she is dormant, spending many centuries alone in the canyons of the Valley…sometimes she emerges and chooses a *Willoni* to command her for a time. She has chosen you."

Raven longed to say none of what Abby said made sense and would not be governed by such nonsense, but she herself had said that she commanded Bentia. She knew Abby spoke the truth. And she sensed Bentia might be helpful in aiding Steele if and when he faced the Heoptin Shifter coming to menace him. More, she sensed a gentle loneliness inside herself she knew came not from her, but from Bentia.

"This is too much to handle, Abb."

Abby smiled. "That is why I am here, Ravanni. To guide you."

"Fine. You can start by calling me Raven or Rae, like you use to."

"You are about to come into your own, it is no longer appropriate to call you Rae."

She sighed. "I don't want our relationship to change, Abb."

"It has to in some ways. My primary objective now is not to be your friend. Sometimes I will say and do things you will say a friend would not do or say. I am your guide first and your friend…as circumstances allow."

"How do I control Bentia?"

Abby smiled. "No one controls one of Aeolia's living spirits, not even a Goddess."

"You mean there are more than one?"

"Yes…there are many. When one is chosen to command a living spirit for a time, one is honored but not in true control. Bentia will not be used for any but a true purpose."

"And what constitutes a true purpose?"

"Bentia will decide."

Charming. There was a living spirit inside her who had a mind of its own. "And how do this Bentia and I communicate?"

Abby shook her head. "It's difficult to say. The living spirits do not like to be categorized."

Raven frowned. These living spirits sounded like royal pains.

I am Bentia, living barrier spirit. I will do my best not to intrude on your life, Ravanni Monclaire. I seek nothing but your companionship. In return, I will assist you in any true purpose.

Raven stiffened and gave Abby a wide-eyed stare. "She just spoke to me!"

Abby smiled and rose. "Then I will leave you two alone to get acquainted. I will go to Philadelphia and remain close should you need me."

After she left, Raven sat on the sofa with her eyes closed, listening to the voice within her. As she and Bentia spoke to each other, she realized that Bentia had always been with her. Even as a young child, when she was the happiest, she had felt a sadness.

I had to wait until you were ready to learn who you were before I could communicate with you, Ravanni Monclaire. I spent a time with your great-great-grandmother Karmela and then I returned to live alone. When Flair, the living flame told me of Deliah's pregnancy, with her permission, I entered her body and was born with you. I have spent twenty-two silent years awaiting the time when we might be one for a time. Will you accept me, Ravanni

Monclaire?

Only vaguely aware of the great honor bestowed upon her, she nodded. "Yes…I think I will."

Her body tingled and a coil of energy filled her belly. *Then I grant you the authority to command me in any true purpose, Ravanni Monclaire.*

Raven took a deep breath. Her life had just become more complex, but she did not regret it. She was Ravanni Monclaire, she who commanded a living spirit. She bit her lip. Whether that was a good or a bad thing remained to be seen.

Chapter Eleven

ഔ

She was in the kitchen cooking when Steele returned with Pen and Drei. When the RV's door opened, she rushed to meet him, throwing his arms around his neck. "Welcome back, sweetie."

He slipped his arms around her waist and kissed her, biting into her bottom lip. She returned his kiss and felt his cock hardening against her. She drew back, arching a brow. "Someone is feeling horny."

He pulled her back into his arms, rubbing his cock against her. "Something smells delicious." His nostrils twitched. "Baked macaroni, collard greens…fried chicken…and cornbread?"

She nodded, a little apprehensively. As the youngest girl, she really hadn't been called upon to cook much, but she had learned to at least prepare what her sisters called a genuine down-home meal. "Does it smell okay?"

"It smells delicious." He licked her neck. "So do you."

"I didn't put on any perfume today."

"I said *you* smelled good, not your perfume. You have a natural, addictive scent all your own. Let's go to bed."

Her heart thumped at the idea of how easily they had become lovers. On some primal level, she had always known she loved him. Now she had to decide if she loved him enough to entrust her heart to him. That issue would be decided later. For now she was content to enjoy their current relationship as lovers. "The food will burn."

"I love burned food." He swept her off her feet and started towards the bedroom.

Peeking over his shoulder, she saw Drei shifting to humanoid form and moving towards the stove. Satisfied the RV wouldn't go up in flames while she and Steele made love, she settled against him, licking his chest. She loved how sometimes his chest was hairy, sometimes bare. Today it was bare.

In the bedroom, he kissed her and set her on her feet. His hands stroked over her shoulders and down her back, setting off tiny sensual fires in her. He drew her close, allowing her to feel his cock. A sudden longing to taste him overwhelmed her.

She pressed against his shoulders. "I want to undress you."

"I can't wait that long. I need you now." He swept her off her feet, laid her on the bed, opened her blouse, unzipped his pants and hers, and then slipped his cock into her already wet pussy.

She gasped, her hands curled into fists against his back as he slowly pushed into her body. He felt deliciously huge and thick invading her pussy. She closed her eyes and pushed her hips up against his. When she felt his pubic hair brushing against hers, he groaned and shuddered, burying his face against her neck.

"Oh, Petite, I've waited my entire life to meet you."

"You sweet-talking wolf, you." She stroked her palms down his back to his buns, reveling in the knowledge that every last hard inch of his cock was buried deep in her pussy — just where it belonged. "Hmmm. We make beautiful music together."

"The best ever." He brushed his lips, hot and hungry, against hers, kissing her with a passion and heat that almost robbed her of her ability to breathe. She felt icy chills everywhere his body touched hers. In the pit of her stomach, she felt a strange tingling sensation.

"Make love to me," she whispered against his mouth as he lay still on top of her, crushing her with his weight.

Keeping his mouth against hers, he slipped one hand under her to cup her butt. Even through her pants, his palm seemed to burn her skin. He moved in and out of her with long, leisurely strokes that sent fire all through her body and moisture rushing into her stuffed pussy.

His cock, so thick and hot, stretched and delighted her. In a frenzy of need, she wrapped her legs around him and thrust herself at him, her pussy clinging tightly around his cock, making him have to fight hard to remove a single inch of it from her body.

He responded by increasing the force and depth of his strokes. She felt the head of his cock brush against her cervix. Instead of pain, a jolt of unexpected and intense pleasure thundered up from her pussy and into her belly where it burned and caught fire.

Seconds later, raking her nails down over his shirt, they wildly fucked each other. She sobbed as the most exquisite climax, centered in her stomach, instead of her pussy, washed over her with the force of a tidal wave, dragging her under the surface to die a very happy and satisfied woman.

Good...so good.

The endless waves of orgasm were too much to bear. When her senses returned, she lay on her back with Steele kneeling beside her, stroking her hair away from her face. "Petite? Are you all right?"

Other than a strange hunger burning in her belly, she felt great. "Yes. Why do you ask?"

He pressed a gentle kiss against her lips, then slid down behind her, holding her body close to his. "You went wild and squeezed my cock so hard, I couldn't stop coming. Then you let out this...guttural moan and lost consciousness." He kissed the back of her ear. "I'm sorry. I didn't mean to hurt you, Petite."

She turned in his embrace, slipping her arms around his neck. "You didn't...okay, you did hurt me...but as before I loved it." She stroked her fingers through his hair and stared into his eyes. "I love you."

He shook his head and lowered it against her forehead. "You screamed and passed out…damn it! I didn't mean to hurt you like that. I'm so sorry."

"Steele!" She touched his face. "Please don't worry and don't be sorry. It felt so good. Honest."

His arms tightened and for the first time she realized he was trembling.

She pressed closer to him. "It's all right…I'm all right, Steele. Please don't worry."

"Petite, there was something wrong with what just happened between us."

She stiffened. "Didn't you…enjoy it?"

"I…on a physical level…yes, but Petite…it almost felt as if someone else was in the bed with us…in you."

She frowned. Just before she lost consciousness, she recalled an inner voice speaking… *Good…so good.* Oh, God! Bentia! Raven shuddered, realizing the spirit had taken control of her body as she and Steele had made love.

I am sorry, Ravanni. It will not happen again. It's been so long since I experienced passion of that magnitude. I lost momentary control of myself. It will not happen again.

It had better not or your butt is out of here! She warned. *He is mine and I will not share him, Bentia. Understand and believe that. Don't you ever come between us again.*

She experienced an upsurge of remorse. *It will not happen again. I give you my word.*

"Petite?"

She looked up and saw the worry in Steele's gray eyes. She kissed him. "Please don't worry, Steele. I'm fine and I enjoyed it." She kissed him again and reached down a hand to touch his cock and found it flaccid.

She looked up at him. "Steele?"

He shook his head and tightened his arms around her. "I just want to hold you tonight, Petite. No more sex."

She knew he was afraid of hurting her. "I love you and I loved what just happened between us."

"I'll be gentler the next time, Petite. I promise."

Damn, Bentia. "I don't want you to be gentle, Steele. I want you to be yourself with me. I want you to ravish me without worrying that you're hurting me. I'm not fully human. I can take whatever you dish out, Steele."

"I don't like the thought of rutting into you until you pass out."

That's exactly what he'd done the first time they made love. She didn't mention that because they both knew this time had been different. "I love everything about you…how you sound…how you feel…how you make love…how you fuck…how you change to your true self. Don't ever change or make any adjustments for me, Steele."

The arm around her waist shifted. The rest of his body did also until she found herself lying belly to belly with the big gray wolf with the gold eyes of her dreams. "Oh, Steele, I do love you!" Curling her body against his, she fell into a deep, but restless sleep.

* * * * *

It was nearly twilight. Raven stood alone in a field, miles from the nearest house, trying to pick up Steele's motorcycle which lay on its side. As she struggled to lift the heavy bike, Steele, Pen, Drei, two other shifters she had never seen, and the small, petite woman Steele and Tee had spent the night with in an earlier vision appeared.

Since the others did not seem aware of her presence, she renewed her efforts to lift the bike. For some reason she knew she had to get Steele's bike upright. She heard several grunts of pain. She looked up and froze. A Gray wolf held the limp bodies of Pen and Drei between his jaws. Steele stood with his back to the scene, talking to the woman.

She wanted to scream out a warning, but no sound left her mouth when she opened it. She could not move. She was powerless to do anything but watch in horror as another gray wolf, this one huge with green, menacing eyes, attacked the unsuspecting Steele from the rear, grabbing him by the neck. Although far stronger than a normal human, Steele, even after he shifted, was no match for the larger wolf who proceeded to toss him to his back and rip his throat open. Steele fought him off and rose. A soundless scream of anguish and despair filled the night as Steele wavered on his feet and sank to his kneels. Bleeding profusely, he fell forward on his face—dead. Beside him lay the lifeless bodies of Pen and Drei.

"No! Steele, no! Oh God, please, no! Don't let him die!"

"Raven! Petite. It's all right. It was just a dream."

Still sobbing, Raven opened her eyes and looked up at Steele, who sat on the side of the bed, holding her in his arms. "Steele? You're all right?"

"Yes." He kissed her forehead. "I'm fine, Petite."

She stoked a trembling hand down his throat. There was no gaping wound there…no precious blood spitting out on the field. "I…I thought you were… Oh, Steele, it was horrible…you, Pen, and Drei…all…dead!"

He pulled her close, rocking her. "Pen and Drei are fine and so am I." He slid down in the bed, pulling her down with him. "It was just a bad dream. Go back to sleep, love."

She pressed closer to him, wrapping her arms around his body, holding him close. Whatever she had seen, she knew it had been far more than a dream. She vowed that if necessary, she would surrender her life to prevent it from coming true.

Together, we will guard and protect he who brings such pleasure, Bentia vowed.

Earlier that night, Bentia's stated interest in Steele would have infuriated Raven. But after that vision, she feared she could not afford to risk alienating Bentia.

Yes, she whispered back. *We will protect him.*

* * * * *

When Raven woke again, it was daylight. She turned her head. Steele, wearing a pair of pajama bottoms, slept at the other end of the bed. She frowned, certain he had put on the pajamas on and moved to the other end of the bed because he worried that he had hurt her the last time they made love.

Thoughts of the vision-dream rushed at her and she sucked in an aching breath. *God, please, don't let that happen*, she prayed. Did vision-dreams become truth? She needed to find out.

She crawled out of bed. She found the matching top to the bottoms Steele wore, kissed his lips, and left the room, closing the doors behind her.

In the kitchen area, Pen and Drei hovered in the air in humanoid form, their lips puckered. She kissed them both and poured herself a glass of orange juice.

Breakfast? Drei asked.

She nodded and went into the living area. She sat on the sofa and reached for the cordless phone. Abby's answered on the fifth ring, her voice blurred.

"Abb, I'm sorry to wake you so early, but I have to talk to you as soon as possible."

"What is it? What's wrong?"

"I can't talk here," she said softly. "I'll give you time to get up and grab a bite to eat. I'll see you in about ninety minutes?"

"Yes. I'll be waiting."

She put down the phone. She turned and found Steele standing less than a foot away, watching her. "Why can't you talk here, Petite? That wasn't another man…was it?"

She stared at him, searching for signs that he was joking. She found none. "Steele, I gave my virginity to you. I love you.

259

How can you stand there and ask me if I've just made a date to meet another man?"

"Why can't you talk here, Petite?"

"That was Abby Valentine, my guide. I have to talk to her because what I saw last night was not a dream, Steele. You, Pen, and Drei are in mortal danger. I have to find a way to protect you."

He cupped her face between his palms. "Raven, I can take care of myself. So can Pen and Drei. They might seem small and helpless to you, but they are warrior-class Keddi. Both are quite capable of taking down a fully grown adult male in battle mode."

"What about a fully grown shifter in its natural form? Can they take down one of those?"

"If they have to…yes. Don't let their size and seeming defenselessness mislead you. Don't worry about them or me." He drew her into his arms and brushed his lips against hers. "Just love me, Petite, and leave the rest to me."

She stared up at him. "I do love you!"

"And you'll stay with me?"

"Yes!"

"For how long?"

"How long do you want me to stay, Steele?"

"I'm a shifter, Petite. We mate for life."

A lifetime with him sounded like a dream come true. Yet Abby had warned that one day she would be called away from Steele and her family. "I might not be able to stay that long, Steele."

He stared down at her. "You'll have to stay. You are mine and what I have I keep."

As his mouth crushed down on hers, she abandoned all thoughts of breakfast. What she needed and wanted was him.

"Let's go make love."

Not eat? Drei demanded when she led Steele through the kitchen area.

"Later," Steele said.

Want fuck too! Pen called out.

"No. Stay."

In the bedroom, Steele closed the doors before turning to smile at her. "Come to Daddy, baby."

She saw the gleam in his eyes and knew he had visions of fucking her until she could barely walk, but she had other ideas and not much time before she had to meet Abby.

She walked over to him. Instead of slipping into his arms, she placed her hands on his chest and kissed her way down his body. She paused with her lips poised at the top of his pajama bottoms and looked up at him. "I see something I'd love to taste and suck on."

He shook his head.

She pressed her cheek against his groin, feeling the beguiling bulge against her cheek. "Why not?"

"I don't want you sucking my cock, Petite."

"Why not?" She moved her mouth over his pajamas bottoms and lightly bit into his cock through the material before looking up at him again. "Don't you like it?"

He sucked in a breath and reached down a hand to pull her to her feet. "I don't want you sucking my cock."

"I heard that." She stroked her hands over his chest. "Why not? I thought all men loved getting a blowjob."

His eyes narrowed and darkened. "How would you know? How many men have you—?"

She balled her right hand into a fist and pressed the side of it against his lips. "How many pussies have you eaten?!" She jerked away from him and stalked over to the doors. "Jerk!"

"Raven!" He caught her hand.

Turning, she jerked it away, glaring at him. "Don't touch me, Steele! Who do you think you are? How dare you treat me like some back alley crack whore! I gave my virginity to you! Where the hell do you get off asking me how many men I've done anything with?!"

He raked a hand through his hair. "I'm sorry. It's just that—"

"You know what? I don't care! You think I waited four years and saved myself for you just so I could put up with your jealous shit?! To hell with you and your insecurities!"

"Raven! Wait a minute!"

As he reached for her again, she swung around, thrusting out her right hand. When he moved towards her, he came to an abrupt stop, a surprised look on his face. For a moment she didn't know why he'd stopped. Then she noted the emptiness in her belly and saw the almost transparent floor to ceiling barrier shimmering between them. Bentia.

"Stop whatever you're doing, Raven, and we'll talk about this."

"There's nothing to talk about. Even after I've given you my virginity, you still think I've been around."

"No, I don't!"

"Then why treat me as if you do?" She took a deep breath, pushing the hurt away. "I saw you with that woman…you and Tee…I got past that. Why are you trying to make me feel cheap? You don't want me here? You don't like that I said I loved you and wanted you to say you love me? Well, hell! This is all too weird to take in. You want me out of your life? I'm out of here!"

"No! Raven!"

He pushed against the barrier, then punched at it, but she knew he wouldn't be able to pierce Bentia. With him watching helplessly, she dressed quickly, grabbed her suitcases, and headed for the door.

"Raven!"

She yanked the doors open.

"Raven! Don't go!"

The desperation in his voice stopped her in her tracks. She closed her eyes briefly. Why couldn't she just walk away from him and not look back?

"Raven! Petite...please."

She sighed and turned to look at him, pushing against Bentia. He was arrogant, too quick to think the worst of her, and selfish. Tee admitted he loved her and sent her flowers and candy. Steele demanded blind obedience and insisted love was an empty word. The choice between the two of them should have been easy—Tee would be better for her emotional well-being, but she loved Steele so much she ached with it.

"Let him pass," she said softly.

Bentia dissolved quickly and silently and Raven felt the coil of energy lodge in her belly once again. With nothing between them, they stood staring at each other in silence.

She longed to rush into his arms and tell him all was forgiven, but she was determined not be taken for granted.

He swallowed several times before he spoke. "I...I've never met any woman I've wanted to spend more than a few weeks with...until you. This relationship stuff is very new...and scary for me. Bear with me, Petite?"

"I need to be loved, Steele."

He shrugged, his eyes narrowing. "Damn it, Raven! You have to accept me for who I am!"

"The hell I do!"

This time when she turned away, he moved so fast, that he had fastened his arms around her before Bentia could react. He stared down into her gaze. "Don't push me too far, Raven. I've tasted your passion and your blood. There's no way, living barrier or not, I'm letting you go. You are mine and I'm keeping you! You leave and I'll track you down and bring you back!"

"I'm not some possession you can lay claim to, Steele! I have a free will I intend to exercise!"

"You are mine! You gave up your free will to leave me when you seduced me!"

Before she could respond, his mouth crashed down on hers. Instead of struggling to break away, she parted her lips, and leaned into him, eagerly returning his kiss.

His mouth gentled on hers and he lifted his head and stared down at her. "I'm not going to allow you to leave me. You should know that. I don't care what happens. You are mine…for life."

"You want to own me but won't say you love me?"

"It's just a word, Raven. Why is it so important to you?"

"Why is it so unimportant to you?"

"Because it doesn't mean anything! No one in my life has ever loved me and not left me…except Etienne. Women want me for the size of my cock, but they don't really care about me as a person. I'm more than just a big dick!"

She stroked his face. "I love you for you. I know what you are and I still love you. All I ask is that you love me too."

He curled his fingers in her hair. "I want you…I need you…let that be enough."

It wasn't going to be enough in the long run. But for now she knew it was all he was capable of giving her. "I need to go talk to Abby. Will you be here when I come back?"

He nodded.

She kissed him, running her fingers through his long, dark hair. "I love you," she whispered against his lips.

"Don't ever do that again, Petite."

"Do what?"

"Put up a barrier between us."

"I didn't do it. Bentia did it on her own. She doesn't know you yet and your anger made her fearful for my safety."

"Then school her and tell her not to ever come between me and my woman again!"

"Don't worry about her. Treat me as an equal, Steele, and there will be less problems between us. I love you, but I am not one of your den members you can command and order around. Accept that and we'll be fine."

His eyes glittered with annoyance. "You are my woman…of course I command you."

She shoved against his shoulder. "In your dreams, buddy!"

His arms tightened around her. "Don't fight me, Petite. Living barrier or not, you won't win. You are mine. I will do my best to treat you with kindness and consideration, but you are mine."

Oh God, they were both hopeless. He insisted on thinking he could control her and she was half inclined to allow it.

She pulled away from him. "I'm going to talk to Abby. When I come back, you'd better be here…alone."

He laughed and dropped a quick kiss on her mouth.

She sighed. Damn she loved him. She looked up at him. "I never asked. What happened with your lost cub?"

He shrugged. "I called Xavier to send one of the den members to pick her up."

"What about her parents?"

"They're dead. Her father died in a…fight and her mother died when she was born. The den is her only family. She's our responsibility."

"How old is she?"

"Sixteen and feeling unloved."

"Why come to you?"

"As den Alpha, I am theoretically father to all the den members. Naturally if there are no birth parents, a troubled cub would seek me out."

"Will she be okay?"

"Yes. We love her and she knows that now. I have been remiss in not returning home more often so den members realize that they are still the most important elements in my life."

And just where the hell did that leave her?

She kissed his chest. "I have to shower and get ready."

Chapter Twelve

ഔ

Acier was in the bedroom working on his latest book when he sensed the presence of another shifter in the vicinity. He rose and left the bedroom. Pen and Drei met him in the kitchen area of the RV.

De la Rocque coming with others, Pen told him.

He nodded and opened the RV door. Leon, accompanied by Deoctra stood outside the door.

"I'm busy. What do you want now, Leon?"

"Aren't you going to invite us in, shifter?"

He cast a brief glance at Deoctra and shrugged. He stepped back, allowing them to enter.

"I'll come right to the point, Acier. We've come to appeal to you to step down from the position of Alpha-in-waiting."

"You've both wasted your breath. I am going to be the next Alpha Supreme, Leon and there's nothing either of you can do about it."

Deoctra walked over to him, stroking her hands down his chest. "It would be in your best interests to stand aside. You and your handsome brother gave me much pleasure and I would not like to see anything happen to either of you. Things have changed. I've made a new alliance that now extends to Leon. You cannot resist us, Gautier. To even try will result in pain and humiliation for you and your handsome brother."

He pushed her hands from his chest and stepped away from her. "The pack is mine and I have no intentions of giving up my rightful position. Aime chose me, Leon. You know the proper way to challenge me is not to bring outsiders into pack business."

Leon shook his head. "You just won't see reason, will you?" He looked at Deoctra. "I told you it would be useless to try to appeal to him. He's a half-breed who needs to be put in his place."

The words had barely left his mouth before he found himself lifted off the floor, struggling to peel Acier's fingers from around his neck.

"That will take someone far more powerful than you, de la Rocque!"

Deoctra flashed across the room to stare up at him. "Put him down now, shifter."

Without taking his gaze off Leon's, he clenched his free hand into a fist and backhanded her. "I warned you to stay out of pack business, fem!"

He made no effort to pull the blow and she flew across the room, landing in a heap against the sofa. She quickly vaulted to her feet...and found herself facing Pen and Drei, in full battle mode.

"Call them off, Gautier, or watch them die!" she warned.

He laughed and tightened his fingers around Leon's neck. "They are warrior-class Keddi, fem. Leon can tell you what that means. Try them and you will be surprised what they are capable of doing even to a vampire."

Do not challenge them, Deoctra, Leon warned. *They are nasty, vicious creatures bred for battle and capable of great destructive acts.*

"Call them off, release Leon, and we will leave, Gautier."

He stared up into Leon's eyes. "I will make no more allowances for old time's sake. The next time we meet, be prepared to bow to me or die, shifter." Without waiting for Leon's response, he opened his fingers and allowed Leon to fall to the floor in an ignominious heap. He looked at Pen and Drei, still menacing Deoctra. "Keddi, stand aside."

Deoctra gave him an angry look. "You have made a grave error, Gautier. I convinced Leon to come because I did not wish to see you or your brother hurt. You have insulted us both, Gautier. The next time we meet, it will be as enemies with no holds barred and no quarter given."

He picked Leon up by his collar and shoved him across the room at Deoctra, who had to dance out of the way to avoid being bowled over. "Get out and stay out of pack business or I will show you just what I think of vampires!"

She bared her incisors. "Fool! You've brought more trouble down on your head than you can imagine. I am Deoctra Diniti, of The Defense League of the Brotherhood. Fuck with me and you fuck with the whole Brotherhood."

"Fuck you and your brotherhood," he said coolly. "Now get out before I throw you both out!"

Eyes glowing and incisors bared, she turned and flashed out of the RV with Leon running behind her.

Acier locked the door and went back to writing.

Will be ready for fight, Drei said.

To death, Pen answered.

He sighed. If the little he had heard of the Defense League of the Brotherhood was accurate, he and his den might well have to fight to the death. It was time he prepared his den for what was coming. He phoned Xavier. "We have trouble coming, Xay. Gather the senior warriors of the den and meet me in Penny Pack woods tonight. I need to talk to them and you."

"I'll contact Etienne and—"

"No!"

"Acier?"

He shook his head. "This might be a fight to the death. If we do not prevail, dying will be easier knowing he will survive."

"I understand. We will meet you tonight, Alpha."

He nodded. "Good. And thanks for everything, Xay."

"No thanks are necessary. I live to serve, Alpha."

"I don't know if I've ever told you how…important you are to me and to Den Gautier, Xavier. Because of your loyalty and competence, I've been able to leave the den for long periods of time knowing I left everyone in excellent hands with you. If it looks like we will not prevail in the coming fight, you must withdraw, Xavier. If I perish, the den will need you more than ever."

"No, Alpha. If you perish, it will be after I and every warrior in the den have been dispatched first. Our prime duty is to safeguard your life. I live to serve and will gladly die to protect you, Alpha."

He heard the determination is Xavier's voice and knew nothing he could say would change the other shifter's mind. "God willing, we will all survive."

"We will survive or perish together, Alpha."

Damn if he would allow Xavier to die trying to protect him. "I'll see you later tonight, Xavier."

"Until then, Alpha."

He put the phone down. Damn this was a bad time for all this shit. Just when he and Raven had found each other. Damn!

Alpha will survive, Pen said.

He looked at Pen. "I don't want you or Drei dispatched, Pen. If I perish, Etienne will take very good care of you both."

If Alpha perishes, Keddi will die avenging, Pen vowed.

He shook his head. "No. I want you and Drei to live."

Will die protecting or avenging, Pen said stubbornly. *Will not live while Alpha dies.*

To have so many brave creatures willing to offer their lives on his behalf humbled him. It also gave him a new sense of commitment. Somehow, he had to prevail in the coming battle. He couldn't allow so many others to die trying to protect him.

* * * * *

Katie Dumont bolted into a sitting position, her heart pounding, her naked body covered with sweat. Trying to shake off the effects of her nightmare, she looked around. She was in her bedroom at the Dodge House. Mark was out of town at a conference. Instead of spending an entire weekend with his boring attorney friends, she had chosen to spend a few days at home in Boston with her parents. She would fly to L.A. on Friday night for the closing weekend activities.

She jumped out of bed and ran through the dark house. She threw a bedroom door open on the other side of the ranch house. "Mikhel! Mikhel, Dimitri's been poisoned!"

Her older brother, a full-blood vampire, Mikhel, sleeping with his wife, bolted out of the bed to stand in front of her. He grabbed her arms while Erica jumped out of bed and rushed across the large room to the bassinette where their son Dimitri slept.

"Katie. What is it? What's wrong?"

"It's Dimitri, Mik! He's been poisoned! We have to get Dr. Grinkolo here before it's too late!"

Mikhel released her and rushed over to Erica, who had Dimitri. They examined him carefully. After several moments, Mikhel turned to look at her. "He seems fine, Katie."

She shook her head. "He's not! A saw it. This big, horrible gray wolf attacked him, biting him…leaving his body riddled with poison."

"There's no sign he's been bitten, Katie," Mik told her gently.

"I know what I saw, Mik! Call Dr. Grinkolo before it's too late. Please or he'll die."

Twenty-four hours later, Dr. Grinkolo sat with her on the front porch of the Dodge House. After several tests, he had pronounced Dimitri poison free. "You are feeling stressed?"

"No!" She sighed. "I don't understand. I mean I'm delighted there's nothing wrong with Dimitri, but I don't understand. I know what I saw."

"Do you?"

"Of course I…" she paused. The dream-vision had been confusing. Dimitri had been much older with old dark hair and gray eyes instead of brown ones, but she had clearly seen her nephew getting bitten and poisoned. Since Dimitri was her only nephew, what she had seen must take place in the future.

"I've seen the future." She sighed. "I was confused about the place and time, but not about what happened. My nephew will be poisoned."

"If it's the future, what makes you think it was Dimitri you saw?"

She turned. Mikhel stood in the doorway, holding Dimitri against his shoulder.

"He's my only nephew."

He hesitated. "Actually, he's not."

"What?" She cast a quick look at the house. "Do you mean you have another son you haven't told us about?"

"No!" He sat beside her and looked at Dr. Grinkolo.

The doctor extended his arms. Mikhel kissed Dimitri and handed him to Dr. Grinkolo who disappeared into the house.

He took her hand in his. "This is just between us to ease your mind. Aleksei has a son. If you saw a vampire with gray eyes, maybe you saw his son."

"Why didn't he tell us?"

"He doesn't know much about him…not even his name. He just found out about him recently and has been searching for him."

She sucked in a breath, clutching his hand. "He must find him quick, Mik. He's going to be poisoned and he's not a vampire."

"Did you see anything that would help Aleksei identify him?"

She shook her head. "I just knew he was my nephew and he's going to die without Aleksei's help."

Mik's lips tightened. "Then we'll have to find him in time."

She closed her eyes, shaking her head. "Oh, Mik, that's not going to be easy."

"Maybe not, but we'll do it because we have no choice."

No. If they didn't find him soon, he'd die.

* * * * *

"And what makes you think this vampire is your father?"

Etienne considered the tall vampire with bronze colored skin, short, straight, salt and pepper hair, and very light brown eyes. He, Damon, and the vampire stood in the back room of yet another upscale nightclub. Vitali Bourcaro stared down at the detailed sketch Etienne had drawn from memory of their father. "My mother said so. He's my father. Do you know him?"

"I know many vampires. If this particular vampire was your father and he wanted anything to do with you, he would have been in contact. If I were you, I wouldn't try to force a meeting." Bourcaro cast a derisive look that encompassed him and Damon. "This vampire is not diurnal and not one for little pups like you two to try to corral. If you want my advice, stop looking now and consider him dead…if he is your father…or you may very well both wind up dead."

Etienne took a deep breath. This vampire's manner was sarcastic and superior. Small wonder Acier held such a poor opinion of that half of their heritage.

He snatched the paper from the other vampire's hand. "He's our father. My brother and I need his help. Do you know his name or not?"

"Of course I do. Am I going to tell you? Hell no!"

Etienne felt his incisors descending and his eyes glowing. He clenched a hand into a fist.

Damon grabbed him and spun him away from Bourcaro.

"Are you out of your mind, Etienne?" Damon pulled him across the room to the door.

"That's right, take your little puppy friend out of my sight before I decide to school you both."

Etienne looked over Damon's shoulder at the other vampire. "You tell him, whoever the hell he is, I'm going to find him. And when I do, he's going to have to account for leaving my mother and deserting us!"

"Considering who he is, you're lucky he didn't kill you, your brother, and your mother!"

The words spoken with a deep conviction stunned Etienne. Was it possible that he was wrong? Would they have to battle for their lives when they located their father?

Outside, Damon released his collar. "We'll find him, Etienne and regardless of what Bourcaro said, he won't be out to kill you and Acier."

"And how the hell do you know that?"

"I don't how I know," Damon admitted. "I just do."

Etienne raked a hand through his hair. "What do we do now?"

"Get out of here. We'll go back to your place and regroup."

They slid into Etienne's SUV. He put the key in the ignition and stiffened. He caught movement out of the corner of my eyes. He turned his head. A youngish vampire appeared near the driver's side of the SUV. He started the engine and rolled down his window. "What do you want?"

The vampire grinned. "To help. What else?"

"Why?"

"Why not? I have nothing against you. Like you, I went looking for my father one day too."

"And what happened when you found him?"

The vampire shrugged. "I had to kill him. What else?"

Etienne stared into the other vampire's eyes. "You killed him?"

"He had it coming for leaving me to fend for myself with no mother. And I'm thinking your papa has it coming too. I never liked that arrogant, murderous bastard."

"You know him?"

"Of course. Vitali's been recruiting him for years now. I really feel sorry for you. This father of yours is a first class nut case. You'll be sorry when you find him."

"What's his name?"

The vampire glanced over his shoulder and then quickly pushed a piece of paper into his hand. "This is the name of the vampire you're looking for. When you find him, make sure you give the bastard a slow and painful death."

With that he melted away. Etienne looked down at the piece of paper before handing it to Damon. "Have you ever heard of him?"

Damon nodded. "Oh, damn, Etienne! You and Acier are screwed. If you think my brothers are nuts, this vampire is certifiable."

He compressed his lips. "Maybe so and maybe that's just what we need to help us…a loony vampire."

He closed his eyes. *Father. We need you. You must help us or I'll be coming to call you to account for deserting us.*

* * * * *

Full-blood vampire Aleksei Madison stepped out of the elevator on the top floor of the office building and walked down a long hallway to the big oak doors at the end of the white corridor.

As he neared the door, it slid open. Inside behind a big mahogany desk sat a full-figured woman whom he always thought of as sweet as pie. She smiled and rose, opening her arms. "Aleksei, it's been too long, you well-hung, handsome vampire."

He engulfed her curvaceous body in a bear hug. "Sue! It's good to see you." He released her and stood back to smile at her. "How are you?"

She levitated off the floor several feet, swirling around, her arms spread wide. "Right as rain, as the humans say." She floated back to her seat. "And you? How is Luc's favorite escapee?"

Aleksei ran a hand over his long, silky dreads, a frown marring the bronzed skin of his face. After hundreds of years of heartache, he had found his bloodlust. They were going to have a child, his twin brother, Vlad no longer wished to kill their mother, and the vampire hunter who'd been after Vlad had seen the error of his ways. What should have been a happy time in Aleksei's life was marred by the fact that he no longer enjoyed the close relationship with Vlad he once had and he had a son he had to find.

He sighed. "Things could be better."

She rose and walked over to him, staring up at him. Without appearing to move, she cupped a hand over his cock. "Take me out to dinner and a movie and then tell me your troubles you over a little moonlight and pussy."

He sucked in a breath, his cock stirring. A hundred years earlier, he had spent one of the most magical nights of his life in her arms. She was fond of saying she had forgotten more ways to please a man than most women would ever know. And that was no exaggeration. She was an incredible lover and for months after that night, he had thought of the absolute joy of sliding into her tight, hot pussy. He looked at her mouth. She had such sweet lips. He swallowed, recalling the taste of her breasts in his mouth as he sucked her.

But he was no longer free to dally with every full-bodied charmer who aroused him. He eased her hand from his cock and stepped away from her. "That's a very temping offer, Sue, but I'm taken."

She sighed and returned to her chair. "Oh well, if she doesn't go a good job of letting you get your freak on... I'm here and always ready to service that big cock of yours, tall, dark, and delicious. So anytime you want some action on the side, handsome..."

Oh God, she was sweet and he loved when a woman talked dirty to him. He sighed. "I love her, Sue."

"Too bad you're the blasted true-blue kind."

He smiled. "I need Luc's help." He glanced at the big door behind Sue's desk. "Is he available?"

"He's always available for you. Go on. Try and surprise him."

How did one surprise an ancient being, who was but a few steps away from being a mighty god? Some called Luc a demon, but they didn't know him as Aleksei had come to know him. He nodded and walked around the desk. The door opened before he could touch the knob.

"Aleksei, come in, boy."

So much for surprising Luc. He walked through the door and into a big office that was empty except for a large marble desk and two black leather executive chairs, one on either side of the desk. Seated at the desk was a handsome blond with ice-blue eyes. He looked around twenty-five, but Aleksei knew the being who had taken him under his wing and been a second father to him, was ageless.

"What bring you to see me, Aleksei?"

Aleksei sat in the single black leather chair in front of Luc's desk. "I need your help. You have to at least tell me something to help me find my son."

Luc sighed and sank back against his chair. "I've been meaning to speak to you about that. I might have been mistaken."

Aleksei sat forward. "In what way?"

"You know I am not God."

He knew Luc was damn near being a god. "And?"

"There are actually two of them…both males…and they might not be your sons after all."

"What?! Ever since you had told me I had a son I didn't know about, I have spent all my free time searching out old lovers in an effort to figure out who had borne my son. And now you tell me you might have been mistaken?"

Luc shrugged. "As I said, I'm not God. I make the occasional mistake."

"How?"

"Very easily as it happens. They could be your sons…or they might be Vladimir's sons."

Aleksei felt as if he'd had a fist driven into his stomach. He and Dani had come to terms with the fact that he had a son he had to find. They had both figured the son was going to be angry and maybe even hostile when Aleksei finally located him. Now he was told there were two of them and they might be his nephews instead of his sons?

He wasn't sure how he felt. He couldn't quite imagine his identical twin as a father. Even now that Vlad had found his bloodlust in Adam, he was still wild and still had not made real peace with their mother, Palea Dumont. How would Vlad react to the knowledge that he might have two sons?

"Luc, I need to know. Are they my sons or are they Vlad's?"

Luc shook his head. "It's difficult to say. The past is not easily seen into and both of you slept with their mother."

That was not unusual. Part of the vampire culture to which he and Vlad belonged encouraged and expected siblings to bed each other's mates, whether bloodlusts or casual affairs. He couldn't recall any woman he'd slept with that Vlad had not also bedded at least once.

"What are their names? Where can I find them? We'll sort out which of us is their father after we find them."

"Aleksei, you are dearer to me than my own life, but there are limits to how far I'll go…even for you. If you want to know who they are, there's a price attached to that knowledge."

"And that would be?"

"Come back to me, Aleksei. Spend a few years with me here and I will tell you everything you long to know about them."

Long ago, when he was lost in a world of hate and rage centered around the mother he thought had deserted him and his siblings, he had met Luc. Luc had taken him in and treated him as a son and taught him many things, including black arts which made him far superior to ordinary vampires and almost impossible to kill.

It was finding his mother and discovering his younger brother, Mikhel, who had been five at the time, which had redeemed him. He had left Luc and returned to the world of mortals. Now he had a bloodlust who was pregnant with his baby. Nearly all his family had been restored to him. He could not return to Luc…not even to learn the identify of his sons or his nephews.

"I can't Luc. Dani is pregnant. She needs me and I need her. I can't come back here…even for a few years."

Luc sighed. "If I were not so fond of you, I would compel you to come."

The threat was an idle one. Although he knew Luc had a dark soul, he had never forced anything on Aleksei. "Luc, at least tell who their mother is."

"She is dead."

That didn't really help much. Many of his former human lovers were dead. "How long?"

"Not long."

Not long? That didn't help either. A hundred years was a short period of time to one such as Luc. "What was her name?"

"If you want her name…agree to spend but a single year

with me."

"I can't!"

"Then I cannot tell you her name, Aleksei."

There was a finality in his voice that Aleksei knew well. He would get nothing else from Luc. "I have to go." He rose and headed for the door.

"Come and see me again, Aleksei...sometime when you don't want anything but my company. Or is that asking too much of you?"

He heard the loneliness in Luc's voice and turned to face him. He owed Luc a lot and regretted that he could not spend more time with him. "I will." He spoke quietly. "I promise."

Luc frowned. "Aleksei, you and Vladimir will need to move quickly. The two sons will soon face a grave danger."

Oh, shit. "Will they survive, Luc?"

"It's difficult to say. The future, like the past, is not always easy to read. You know there are limits to how much I may interfere in human affairs. Do what you need to do to save them. If need be and the deck is stacked too heavily against you, I will intervene on your behalf."

"At what cost to yourself?"

"It will be...great, but you are the one being in all creation for whom I would gladly perish that you might live a happy life."

And yet he would not tell him the name of his sons. He would continue to think of them as his until he knew differently. He nodded, but was determined not to have to depend on Luc. If his sons or his nephews were in trouble, he wanted to be the one to save them. But first he'd have to find them and he had no idea how he was going to accomplish that. And now he had the added incentive of knowing that time was of the essence. He had to find Vlad. That wouldn't be difficult because if he were away, Vlad was sure to be at his house, bedding Dani.

His lips tightened as he thought of Vlad with his woman...his bloodlust and the mother of his unborn child. That shit had to stop. Damn if he was going to keep sharing her with Vlad. He thought of Vlad's bloodlust, Adam. His lip curled. Why the hell didn't Adam keep his man home and out of other men's beds?

"I will do my best not to require your assistance, Luc, and when I can, I will return for a visit. You have my word."

"And the word of Aleksei Madison is sufficient. Go, my Aleksei, knowing that as always, I will safeguard your back."

"Thank you...Luc."

Luc tilted his head, a longing in his blue eyes that troubled Aleksei. "Can you not find it in your heart after all this time to say it?"

He sighed. "It's just that...before you there were two mortal males who...nourished me."

"And saying it would tarnish their memories?"

"I didn't mean that." Oh, hell, how could someone as powerful as Luc be so damned needy? "I will come when I can...Father."

Luc's face literally glowed and he elevated out of his chair, flowing in the air in delight. "I ask little of life, Aleksei...except the love and affection of my one...son."

He inclined his head. "Father." He turned and left, knowing he left Luc much happier than when he'd arrived. In the outer office, he glanced at Sue, so lovely and sexy.

"Sue, have you and Luc ever...?"

She grinned. "No, but he has a cock to die for."

"How do you know if you and he have never fucked?"

"Some things a female knows, and I have ears, don't I?"

"Meaning?"

"Meaning I hear all the screams of passion and lust when he's with a female of any race or species."

"I've never heard them when I was here."

"Of course not. To him you're just his baby boy. You don't think he'd fuck around you, do you?"

The thought of Luc fucking boggled his mind. He leaned over and kissed Sue's sweet lips. "Why don't you go give him a fuck? He's lonely and he could probably use one."

She laughed and palmed his cock. "I'll give him one if you'll give me one."

"I can't."

"Then Luc will just have to find his own ho." She tossed back her head and laughed.

He kissed her cheek and left. He had a lot to accomplish in a short time.

* * * * *

Vladimir Madison, asleep behind the buxom pregnant woman lying with her back against his chest, came awake with a start, his senses alert. Without opening his eyes or moving, he scanned the room. They were alone. So what had disturbed his sleep?

Pressing a lingering kiss against the woman's exposed neck, he eased out of bed. He walked over to the window and stared out into the dark night, reaching out with his senses in an effort to find the source of his discomfort. Then he felt the words again.

Father. We need you. You must help us or I'll be coming to call you to account for deserting us.

The breath caught in his throat and his heart thundered. Father! Who the hell would be calling out to him and addressing him as father?

"Vlad? What's wrong?"

He turned and looked at the woman struggling to a sitting position in bed. She had short, dark hair and enchanting eyes. Her beautiful breasts bared and sagging made him ache to suck them. She was very pregnant and very desirable. They had spent the afternoon and the night making love. Yet he felt his cock hardening as he looked at her. He was going to need to leave soon and head home. Adam would be returning from a visit to his cousin on the West Coast and would expect a warm welcome.

"Nothing's wrong."

She smiled, extending a hand. "Then come back to bed and make love to me."

His cock leaking precum, he turned and walked back to the bed. He could smell her sweet fragrance and knew she was ready for him. Sliding behind her in the bed, he lifted one of her legs, pressed his cock at her entrance, and eased his aching shaft deep within her warm, welcoming pussy.

He slipped his arms around her, closed his eyes, and made gentle, hungry love to her. But even as his orgasm washed over him, all the sweeter because she belonged to his brother, he could still hear the voice in his head.

Father. We need you. You must help us or I'll be coming to call you to account for deserting us.

Holding Dani tight, he answered. *Whoever you are. Come. I await you.*

Chapter Thirteen

ဢ

Abby Valentine lay naked on her back in her hotel room. Legs spread wide, she watched the television set in front of the bed. On the screen, a talk, dark, breathtakingly handsome naked stud with silver-gray eyes, stood in the middle of a beautiful garden. He held an equally naked, tiny redhead in his arms. With his big hands cupping her ass, he eagerly fucked a large, thick cock in and out of the redhead's bare pussy. The redhead tossed her head back and arched her body, thrusting herself wildly on his cock and cried out.

On the bed, Abby gasped, imagining that lovely, naked shaft, coated with her juices sliding into her slick pussy, instead of the flesh-colored joy toy she moved between her legs in time with the hunk on the screen's movements. As the tiny redhead shuddered and came, Abby increased the thrusts of the shaft between her legs. When she saw Wyatt close his eyes, she knew he was about to come. She thrust hard on the vibrator and rubbed wildly at her clit. And just as she heard him call out and saw his seed seeping down the legs of the redhead, Abby shattered into a million happy pieces, whispering, "Wyatt…Wyatt… Oh, Wyatt!"

She lay whimpering with pleasure for a long time before she got up and went to shower. As the cool water poured over her, she closed he eyes and pressed her forehead against the shower stall tiles. It was unacceptable for her to pleasure herself at a time when Raven was finally maturing and would need her more than ever.

Raven was the last initiate she would have to guide before she would be allowed to indulge her own carnal desires for a time. As a seasoned *Willoni* who had aspirations to the priestesshood, she was required to put her own needs aside and concentrate fully on helping Raven. To lust after a man like Wyatt Diamond, whom she could never hope to have, was unacceptable.

Even as she admonished herself, she could feel her desire returning as she thought of the handsome man she couldn't stop thinking about. Somehow...someway she had to find a way to forget him. There could never be anything between them. While she was aware that there was something different about him, she would be called home once Raven no longer needed her.

The thought of never seeing Wyatt Diamond again, brought a rush of tears to her eyes. She stood in the shower, her arms wrapped around her body, sobbing. She sobbed for her lack of self-control, her selfish desires, and her endless ache for Wyatt Diamond.

* * * * *

Raven sat alone in the RV talking to her father when she heard a vehicle pulling into the space beside the RV. She glanced out the window and saw Tee's SUV. Her heart thudded. "Dad, I have to go."

"Acier...is he treating you well?"

"Yes, Daddy. Of course he is."

"He'd better or he will answer to me."

"I love him. Now I have to go. I'll call you later, Dad. I love you."

"I love you, baby!"

She hung up and went to admit Etienne. "Tee!"

He closed the door and hugged her close, brushing his lips lightly against hers. The muscles in her stomach tightened and she drew away from him, her face flushed.

He smiled. "Hi, honey. Where's Acier?"

"He took Pen and Drei and left a few hours ago. He said he would be back late tonight."

"Where did he go? It's important that I find him, Petite and he's not answering his cell phone."

She wrapped her arms around her body. "Tee, I'm afraid for him. I had a frightening…vision when I saw him and Pen and Drei dead."

Tee raked a hand through his hair. "Oh God! You saw it too?"

She nodded, her eyes filling with tears. "Yes and I'm so afraid for him."

He pulled her back into his arms and held her, this time his touch was comforting instead of arousing. "We're going to have some dark, scary times ahead, Petite, but we'll all come out of this somehow."

She knew she and Bentia and Tee would do all they could to protect Acier, but she was afraid that it might not be enough. She clung to him, pressing her cheek against his shoulder. "He has to be all right. He has to!"

He tipped up her chin and brushed her tears away. "He will be. I'll protect him somehow…even if I have to die doing it!"

"No!" She jerked away from him. "That would kill him! He adores you!"

"I know, but Petite…one of us might have to die. He's Alpha-in-waiting. Next to Aime, he's the most important person in the pack. He must survive for the good of the pack. I am expendable."

She balled a hand into a fist and hit it against his shoulder. "No! No, you are not expendable! Etienne! Please, don't talk of dying. There has to be a way for all of us to survive. There has to be."

He signed. "I don't know if there is, but I will not allow him to die…unless…"

"Unless what?"

He signed. "Unless we can locate our father…he's a full-blood vampire. He can help us."

"Will he?"

"He'll have to…or I'll kill him."

"Kill your own father?"

"Yes! If he'll stand by and watch us struggle when we need help! He's done nothing for us our whole life. When I needed a father, I had no one…except Acier…later there was Aime and your dad. But when we were young and afraid, we had no one but each other."

He stroked her cheeks. "Don't worry, Petite. He'll survive."

"And you think I'll be satisfied if he's alive and you're dead! No! No, Tee! We have to find a way for us all to survive."

She felt Bentia. *Fear not, Ravanni. We will find a way to save them both.*

How?

I do not know…but we will find a way.

She looked up at him. "Tee, please. Promise me you won't try to be noble and do something to get yourself killed! Neither Steele nor I could bear that. We both love you too much."

"I love you, too."

He touched her cheek and she swallowed hard. "Tee, I'm confused. How can I love Steele so much and yet want you so much at the same time? It makes me feel…cheap."

He cupped her face between his palms. "Cheap has nothing to do with it. You're Acier's bloodlust. I know he doesn't like to admit it, but we are part vampire and vampires have bloodlusts or perfect mates. You're his."

"Then why do I want you?"

"It's part of our vampire culture. One's bloodlust is always attracted to one's siblings. It's a fact of vampire life Acier is going to have a hard time accepting."

"He says he's not sharing me with you."

He stroked a finger down her cheek. "I know that." Something flickered in his eyes just before he bent his head.

She moistened her lips and pressed against his shoulders. "Tee…"

"I know, Petite… I just need a kiss…a few kisses."

She felt his cock, hard and long, pulsing against her leg. Her knees nearly buckled. "I want to, Tee, but I can't. Steele is—"

"Steel is right here!"

They both turned. Steele stood just inside the closed door.

Tee released her slowly and faced his brother. "This is not what it looks like, Sei."

Steele walked over to Tee and hugged him. "I know how you feel about her, Etienne. I wish I could share her with you, but I can't."

Tee pulled away and curled his fingers in his Steele's hair. "Acier, I feel like I'm going crazy! No matter who I'm with…I can't stop thinking about her. You have to help me."

He cupped Tee's face between his palms. "I would do anything for you, Etienne. Anything. You know that, but this is just too much. I can't share her."

She stood watching the two men she loved pleading for the other's understanding. Tears filled her eyes. She touched Acier's hand. "Steele…please."

"No! Shifters do not share mates."

"But you're part vampire and they do."

He shook his head. "Etienne…go get your own woman and leave Raven alone. Is that clear?"

Raven bit her lip as Tee nodded slowly. "Crystal." He took a deep breath and raked a hand through his hair. "I'm sorry, Sei. I'll leave now."

Acier cupped a hand over the back of Tee's neck and

hugged him. "Oh hell, Etienne, I didn't mean—"

Tee pulled away. "It's all right, Sei. You're perfectly within your rights. You know how to reach me if you need me." He looked at her and smiled. "Don't worry about me, Petite. I'll be fine. I promise."

But she doubted that. She could feel his need. She looked at Steele. Their gazes locked. After a moment, he gave a slight shrug and walked towards the back of the RV.

She smiled and walked over to Tee, linking her fingers through his. She walked outside to his SUV with him.

"Want a quickie?" she asked.

"Hell, yeah!" He glanced over his shoulder. "But Acier's just not ready to accept that part of our culture." He bent and kissed her cheek. "Just having him give his tacit approval is enough. I'll be all right. Now go back to him. He needs you and I have to find our father."

She placed her hands on his chest and kissed his chin. "I'm nuts about you."

"I love you too." He kissed her on the corner of her mouth and got in his SUV.

As she walked back to the RV, Pen and Drei seemingly appeared out of nowhere and kissed her on either cheek.

"Where have you two been?"

Getting laid! Drei told her happily.

She decided she probably didn't want to ask who they'd been with. Inside, she locked the door and went towards the bedroom.

Acier sat in the single chair in the bedroom, his jaw clenching. She walked over to him and sank in his lap, slipping her arms around his neck. "I love you."

He buried his face against her breasts. "Get on the phone and call him back. I can't stand how he's feeling. He needs you."

She stroked her fingers through his hair. "You are the

most considerate, loving brother in the world. Sitting here worrying about him. He'll be all right. I want to spend the night in your arms." She rose and tugged at his hand. "Come make love to me."

He rose and shook his head. "I want you to call Etienne back. I'll go spend the night in a hotel."

"Tee will be all right…tonight belongs to us, Acier."

"Acier? Oh, shit! You're going to leave me for him, aren't you?"

"How can a man as handsome and sexy as you be so insecure?" She sighed, stroking her fingers over his hair. "No other man could take your place with me, Acier. Not even Tee. I love you. I have since I was a child."

"Why are you calling me Acier all of a sudden?"

She smiled at him, rubbing her breasts against his chest. "It's what you said you wanted to be called."

"Not by you. You can call me anything you want…as long as you don't leave me."

She remembered Abby's words and sighed. "I would never willingly leave you again."

He relaxed against her, slipping his arms around her waist.

"There's something I'm dying to do to you."

His silver-gray eyes danced with wicked lights. "Fuck me?"

She kissed his bottom lip. "No. Take your clothes off for me, Acier."

"Steele. Call me Steele."

She kissed him slowly but drew her away when his lips parted against hers. "Take your clothes off for me. Strip for me, my handsome, sexy, Steele."

She didn't expect him to comply and was delighted when he began dancing around the bedroom, moving his lean hips suggestively as he slowly unbuttoned his shirt. She moistened her lips, her eager gaze moving rapidly from his face to his groin and back to his handsome face.

As he revealed his chest, her breathing quickened…hair. She licked her lips. She was going to enjoying running her fingers and lips over the silky dark strands. He rotated his hips and leisurely drew off his shirt, his gray gaze locking with hers. His shoulders were broad, his chest deep, his abs tight and so sexy, she went wet just looking at his bare torso. Her gaze slid down his body and locked on his groin. The breath left her lungs in almost painful gusts in time with the lengthening and thickening of his cock.

She still found it difficult to believe that she was able to take his entire length deep in her body. Her nipples tightened thinking about how good his huge shaft felt slowly pumping inside her slick pussy.

He tossed his shirt at her. She caught it and pressed it against her face, breathing in his scent.

Still dancing, he put one hand behind his head. She watched the muscles in his chest and shoulders ripple. With each ripple, her heartbeat increased. Cupping his free hand over his cock, he undulated his lower body. He slowly unzipped his pants. The breath caught in her throat. When he released the button at his waistband, he turned his back to her. Glancing at her over his shoulder, he inched the pants and his briefs over his hips, revealing his tight, hard buns with maddening slowness.

She had never seen such a breathtaking ass. She had to clench her hands into fists to keep from reaching out to touch him. With his back still to her, he removed his pants and briefs.

Her resolve and self-control snapped. She had to touch him. Heart thumping, she rushed over to him, dropped down to her knees, closed her hands on his hips, leaned forward, and rained small, biting kisses against his buns. His skin felt warm and tasted pungent against her mouth and tongue…delicious, but she needed more. Releasing his hips, she parted his cheeks, extended her tongue, and touched it against his asshole.

He made a small sound, a slight shiver dancing through his body. Emboldened, she leaned closer and licked and kissed the small tight hole. He groaned, a series of deep shudders shaking him. Loving the tension and desire she felt in him, she parted him further and pressed a hot, lustful kiss against him.

"Oh shit, Petite!"

Longing to please him and assure him that he was the only man for her, she parted his legs and touched the tip of her tongue against his balls. They were big and tight and thinking about him releasing their contents inside her, made her so hot, her pussy gushed. She had to have more.

She crawled between his legs, loving how his big cock and heavy balls bounced against her head. Still on her knees, but now in front of him, she looked up at him. "Steele...I love you."

His silver eyes swirled with lustful desire that fueled her passion. She had to taste him. Closing her hands over his hips, she leaned forward until her lips nearly touched the big, swollen head of his cock. She sucked in a deep breath and slowly closed her lips over the head of his shaft.

He groaned and shuddered. "Petite!"

Encouraged by the sound of pleasure-pain, she inched forward. His cock, hot, hard, and pulsing slid between her lips, over her tongue, and down into her throat. He was big and for a moment, she panicked, feeling as if she couldn't breathe.

You can do it. Suck him. Taste him. Pleasure him.

With Benita's lustful voice urging her on, she relaxed, gripped his lean hips, and began sucking him with a greedy pleasure she couldn't deny or control. His big hands settled on the back of her head. He rotated his hips as she increased the force of her sucks on his delicious cock.

He groaned and curled his fingers in her hair. "Oh shit, Petite! That feels so fucking good."

With her mouth and throat full of cock and the musky scent of his sex and pubic hair inflaming her senses, she was awash with pleasure. She shuddered and came, her pussy gushing. The unexpected climax crashed over her, leaving her feeling weak, her face pressed against his groin.

Keep sucking. He is almost there. Must give him pleasure.

Reaching down to fondle his balls, she began sucking him again, keeping her mouth closed over his shaft, as she deep-throated him.

"Oh shit!" Tightening his hands on her head, he shot his hips forward with a furious motion and began fucking his thick length down her throat with a force that threatened to cut off her ability to breathe. Just as she was about to panic, he shuddered, and came, shooting jets of seed down her throat. She couldn't taste it, but she felt the streams of his satisfaction sliding down her throat.

He seemed to come for a long time before he released his grip on the back of her head. When she removed her lips from his cock, he groaned and dropped to his knees, trembling. She put her arms around him and they tumbled to the floor together.

They lay for a long time, holding each other, whispering words of pleasure and contentment before he finally rose, lifted her in his arms, and carried her to bed. She turned on her side, pressing her cheek against the mattress. He moved behind her, licking at her neck.

A tingle of desire and lust shot through her. She moaned softly, pressing her butt back against him. Lord, she loved how he could stay hard for so long. She lifted her leg. "Love me."

He moved closer and his cock bumped against her butt. Reaching between her legs, she guided his shaft to the entrance of her pussy. He thrust forward, sinking his length balls deep with one lusty movement. Curling one hand over her breasts and the other over her pussy, he fucked her with a slow heat that made her burn for him.

She came twice before he finally rolled her onto her stomach, rose above her, and hammered into her until he called out her name and came, filling her with his seed.

Sated and happy, she quickly fell asleep with his cock still firmly embedded in her flooded pussy.

She woke several hours later to find him in his natural form, between her legs, licking her pussy. She smiled, sat up, and linked her arms around his neck. "Oh, Steele! Do you know how gorgeous you are in your natural form?"

Without waiting for his response, she kissed his mouth and wrapped her arms and legs around his flanks, her pussy but an inch away from his hot cock. He rotated his hips, found her opening, and slid home with one delicious plunge that made her come on his cock. Growling softly, his beautiful golden eyes alight with lust, he fucked her hard and deep until they both cried out with lust, love, and passion, and came together.

As she curled her body into his, she knew the last barrier between them had been removed. Now he was entirely hers.

* * * * *

The next morning, she woke alone in bed. Smelling coffee, she slipped on the shirt Steele had discarded the night before. Without bothering to button it, she made her way to the kitchen area. Steele, dressed in pajama bottoms sat at the table, reading a paper and sipping coffee.

He rose and slipped his arms around her waist. He brushed his lips against hers. "Hi."

She linked her arms around his neck, smiling up at him. "Hi. Where's Pen and Drei?"

"There are a few females from our den staying a few miles from here, they went to get laid."

"That's what they told me they did last night. Don't they ever get enough?"

"No!" He slid his hands under the shirt to fondle her butt. "My, what a nice, round ass you have."

She grinned and cupped her hands over his buns. "You have a rather nice set of buns yourself. The next time we make love, I'm going to finger fuck you there."

"Yeah?" He swept her off her feet. "Let's go make love now."

"Last night was incredible and I loved every second of it, but I'm a little on the sore side." She kissed his mouth. "Let's have breakfast now and save the night for love and lust."

He gave an exaggerated sigh and sat her on her feet. "Oh, hell. You're right. I guess I should concentrate on business for a while. Your dad will be expecting me to turn in my latest book soon. So after breakfast, I'll pick up Pen and Drei and we'll go find some place to write. How are you going to spend the day?"

"Trying to figure out how to make sure we all survive the coming troubles."

He stroked her cheek. "Don't worry, Petite. Somehow we'll be all right."

But his voice lacked conviction and she noted the worry in his gray gaze. Trouble was coming their way soon.

* * * * *

Whoever you are, come. I await you.

Etienne bolted up from a restless sleep as the words sounded in his head. He rose from the bed and went to stare out his bedroom window, his heart pounding. He heard the words, but felt nothing that made him welcome the coming confrontation with their father.

Whoever you are, come. I await you.

There was no warmth in the invitation. In fact, the words held a hint of menace.

He closed his eyes and leaned his head against his bedroom window. Damn! Why the hell did everything have to go wrong at the same time?

He straightened and opened his eyes. No matter what happened, he was determined that Acier would survive. If their errant father didn't help, then by god, he'd kill him or die trying.

I am coming, father. Whether you live or die depends on you.

* * * * *

Aleksei slipped out of his SUV in the main driveway of his 20-acre estate and headed towards the house he shared with his bloodlust, Dani Tyler. As his hand hovered over the doorknob, the door opened and he found himself facing his twin, Vlad.

His nostrils shivered and his lips tightened. He smelled the aroma of his woman on Vlad. He resisted the urge to grab Vlad by his collar and toss him out of the house on his ass. "We need to talk," he said coldly.

Vlad nodded. "Someone has been calling to me, Sei. In my mind…someone who calls me…Father."

Aleksei closed his eyes briefly, a wave of disappointment engulfing him. So Vlad was the twins' father. That should have made things easier for him. If the twins were his nephews instead of his sons, he could spend more time with Dani, who was due to deliver his child in two months. "I know. I've been to see, Luc. It would appear that you have two sons, Vlad."

Vlad's blue eyes glowed and his incisors descended. "One of them called out to me…they're in trouble, Aleksei. We have to help them."

For the first time in months, he felt close to Vlad. He clasped his hand on the back of Vlad's neck. "We will, but we'll have to find them first."

"Do you know who they are?"

"No. Luc wouldn't tell me, but if we can talk to them, we'll find them. We'll go see Katie. She can help."

Vlad's eyes darkened at the mention of their younger

sister's name. "Katie Dumont?"

Aleksei sighed. Although Vlad had finally been persuaded to give up his quest to kill their mother, Aleksei knew Vlad had not really forgiven or forgotten the heartache of their earlier years. It was going to take some time before Vlad was ready to accept their younger siblings without lingering bitterness.

"Yes. She has a form of second sight and we'll need all the help we can get."

Vlad raked a hand through his dreads, sighed, and finally gave a grudging nod. "Will she help us?"

"Of course she will. She's our sister." He glanced into the dark house behind Vlad. "Is Dani awake?"

Vlad shook his head. "No."

Aleksei clenched his jaw. Vlad had probably fucked her into a stupor. "I'm going to go speak to her for a while and then we'll go see Katie."

Vlad nodded and walked passed him.

He reached out and grabbed Vlad's shoulder, swinging him around. "Do me a favor, Vladimir."

"Of course, Sei. What is it?"

"Stay the fuck away from Dani or I'll kick your ass from here to New Jersey."

Vlad grinned and danced out of his reach. "You'd have to catch me first."

Snarling, he closed his front door with an exaggerated gentleness and rushed through the house, eager to spend a little quality time with Dani. He found her asleep in the big bed they shared.

He gently pulled back the cover and glanced down at her naked body. She was a beautiful, full-figured woman who had caught his eye the first night they meant. Naked and pregnant with his child, she took his breath away.

He bent his head and gently kissed her lips.

Without opening her eyes, she returned his kiss. "Sei. Darling, you're back. I've been lying here thinking about you and missing you."

"You had Vlad to keep you company," he pointed out.

She finally opened her eyes and reached for him. "For me there is no one but you, Aleksei. You are the love of my entire life. Without you, there would be little reason to live. Come make love to me, darling."

He thought briefly of Vlad as he tore off his clothes. It would do the bastard good to wait. Maybe he'd carry his sorry ass home to his own bloodlust.

Chapter Fourteen

Acier, sitting backward on his parked motorcycle typing on his folding keyboard, squinted at the small screen of his handheld computer. These weren't the ideal conditions in which to work on his latest book, but Raven needed to talk in private with her guide and Pen and Drei needed some fresh air.

He looked up from the small screen. Pen and Drei, in their natural forms, alternated between running through the relatively tall grass of the field and flying through the air. He could feel their contentment. They were very important to him and he was delighted they were happy.

Smiling, he turned his attention back to the screen and began typing again. He lost track of time until he realized that Pen and Drei were hovering beside his head in battle mode. He saved the manuscript on which he was working. "What is it?" he asked as he put his keyboard and handheld away.

De la Rocque with strange shifter, Alpha, Pen told him.

Acier rose and turned to face the road. For the first time he heard the sound of an approaching vehicle. Several minutes later, a big, dark SUV stopped on the side of the road. Both front doors opened and Leon, accompanied by a tall, heavily built shifter with long, wavy hair, chiseled features, and green eyes, alighted.

Acier immediately realized he faced the Heoptin Shifter about whom Aime had warned him. He tightened his lips. "de la Rocque. Why the hell are you involving outsiders in Pack affairs?"

"This is Tucker Falcone," Leon told him. "He has aligned himself with me."

"Afraid to face me alone, de la Rocque?"

A faint hint of color touched Leon's cheeks. "You are not fit to lead Pack Gautier, Acier. Step down or face Falcone."

Pen and Drei moved until they hovered in front of him. They bared their four-inch incisors and unsheathed their five-inch sharp claws, ready to give their faithful lives trying to protect him.

Keddi, stand down, he told them softly.

Won't let stranger hurt, Pen said.

Kill stranger and de la Rocque, Drei added.

Acier stepped around them and faced the Heoptin Shifter. Nearly as tall as Acier, the shifter was slightly heavier. His green eyes were cold and emotionless. "Gautier, stand aside and there will be no need for me to kill you."

"Fuck you!"

Falcone smiled. "Maybe I'll fuck you. I'm not averse to a little tight male ass. I'd love to fuck you."

Acier growled and flashed forward. He dropped to all fours and shifting to his natural form as he ran. Leon shifted and charged forward. Pen and Drei, their eyes flashing sped through the air towards Leon. Leaving them to keep Leon at bay, Acier continued moving towards Falcone.

Falcone shifted and rushed forward with a swiftness that surprised Acier. Deciding brute strength would not win the day, Acier waited until Falcone was but feet away before he returned to his human form. When Falcone leaped for his neck, his fangs bared, he shot his hands out, closing his fingers around Falcone's neck.

In his natural form, Falcone was strong and heavy. Acier struggled to lift him, while avoiding the other shifter's claws. He wasn't entirely successful. He gritted his teeth but remained silent as several of Falcone's claws raked across the left side of his face. Infuriated as blood gushed from the wounds, he tightened the fingers of one hand around Falcone's neck. With the other hand he reached down and shot his clenched fists into the other shifter's balls.

Falcone howled with rage and pain. Acier, nearly blinded by the blood rushing from his wounds, lifted Falcone off his feet, and tossed him several feet across the field.

He angrily wiped the blood from his face and cast a lightning-fast glance toward Leon. Pen and Drei were on either side of his blood-covered flanks, clawing and biting with a ferocity with which only a Keddi was capable.

As he brought his gaze back, Falcone leapt towards his neck. He fell backwards, tossing up his arm to protect his throat. He slammed onto his back with Falcone on top of him, his eyes glowing, his teeth sinking so deep, his upper and lower jaw met in Acier's arm.

Roaring with rage and pain, Acier shifted his head into his natural form, and buried his incisors in Falcone's neck, tearing and ripping. Screaming with pain, Falcone released his grip on Acier's arm. Aware that he needed to treat his injuries, Acier reluctantly removed his incisors from Falcone's neck. He didn't pursue when Falcone, howling with pain, fled across the field towards his SUV.

Realizing he was injured, Pen and Drei broke off their attack on Leon and flew to his side.

Acier lay on the ground gasping for breath.

Alpha hurt bad?

He heard the panic and fear in Drei's voice and struggled to sit up.

Tear both apart! Pen screamed with rage. *Kill!*

No! Let them go, Pen! Ignoring the pain in his arm, he sat up, afraid Pen would pursue Leon and Falcone and be killed.

Ignoring him, Pen flew through the air and sank his incisors in the back of Falcone's neck, tearing and ripping with a mad fury.

Falcone's right hand shot back to grab Pen.

Acier bolted to his feet and started to run across the field, sure he was about to witness Pen's death. But he had underestimated Pen. Just as Falcone's fingers were about to close over Pen's small body, Pen shot away from Falcone with an incredible burst of speed.

Drei flew in, slashed several claws across Falcone's face, and was gone in a blur before the shifter could respond. Then, still in full battle mode, Pen and Drei hovered in front of him. Acier swayed, fighting off the desire to lay down in the field and lose consciousness.

Leave before Keddi kill! Pen ordered.

Leave or die! Drei added.

Shifting back to humanoid form, Leon and Falcone stumbled back in the SUV and swiftly drove off.

Acier waited several moments, until he was sure they were not coming back, then he fell to his knees, and onto his face, unconscious.

When he woke several hours later, he lay in a different field behind an abandoned barn. Pen and Drei, still in battle mode, patrolled the area, guarding him. It didn't surprise him that they had managed to move him. The Keddi were loyal to death and when the need arose, they were capable of tremendous feats of strength in their efforts to protect those with whom they had aligned themselves.

He sat up, leaning his back against the barn. *Pen. Drei*, he called to them softly.

Keddi, go! Pen told Drei. *Pen still guard.*

Drei flew over to hover near his face. *Alpha better now?*

He felt his face and sighed when his fingers encountered no open, bleeding tissue. He looked down at his arm, although it ached, the wound had closed. "Yes. I'm better."

Drei's small body shook, then he tossed himself against Acier's shoulder, making high, whining sounds of distress and relief.

Acier held him in his palm, gently stroking a finger down

his back. "It's okay, Drei."

Thought Alpha dead. So sad!

"It'll take more than that to kill me. Thanks to you and Pen, I'm fine. I am so proud of you both. You were both so brave and fearless."

Not feel brave. Alpha fall. Not get up. Feel afraid.

"It's okay to be afraid some times, Drei. When I needed you most, you were brave and fearless. It's okay to be afraid now."

Drei pressed against his neck, still trembling.

He rose slowly, fighting off a lingering dizziness. Tilting his head to one side so that Drei would not be dislodged, he moved towards Pen. Although Pen was much older than Drei and was still in battle mode, he could feel Pen's concern for him.

"Thank you."

Pen turned to hover in front of him, his glowing eyes, making a quick, but thorough assessment of him. *Glad to see Alpha awake. Will kill both for hurting. Rip apart. Make bleed. Kill!*

Under Pen's rage, Acier sensed his fear. Neither he nor Drei had ever seen him in a fight in which he had not been the clear winner. He wondered if he had lost some of their respect.

No!

No!

Pen and Drei reassured him at the same time. He smiled. "I am very fortunate to have you two as my friends."

Be friend until dead, Pen told him.

Even then, Drei added.

He laughed. He looked around. "Where's my bike?"

Had to leave. Not far.

He glanced at his watch and groaned. Damn! It was after one a.m. Raven was going to kill him. Following Pen and Drei, he trotted back to his bike. It was on its side and he swore softly. Had someone vandalized it?

Knock over so not stole. Didn't hurt, Pen told him.

He looked at Pen. "Pen, you are one amazing Keddi."

Pen's chest swelled. *Duty to protect Alpha.*

"And you've both done it extremely well. Thank you."

As he lifted his bike, he heard a vehicle approaching. He straightened, tensing. Damn he hoped it wasn't Leon or Falcone returning because he was in no shape to face either one of them. Pen and Drei moved in front of him, in battle mode again. He didn't protest. He leaned back against his bike and waited. After a moment, a familiar and welcome scent spore assailed his nostrils. Both he and the Keddi relaxed.

Moments later, a big dark SUV stopped at the side of the road. Without turning off the engine, Etienne jumped out and two small balls of fury erupted from the open moon roof.

"Acier!" Accompanied by Slayer and Karol, Etienne raced to his side and wrapped his arms around him. "Are you all right?"

He felt Etienne tremble and returned his embrace briefly before pulling away to cup his face between his palms. "I'm...fine."

Etienne shook his head and pulled away from him. "No! You're not fine. You've been gravely injured!" His eyes glowed and his incisors descended. "I felt your injuries as if they were my own! I reached out to you, but there was nothing and I thought..."

Thought Alpha dead, Slayer said and Acier sensed the Keddi's rage and sorrow at the thought.

Came to avenge, Karol added.

"And to savage and destroy everyone responsible!" Etienne's voice cracked with the force of his emotions.

Acier watched tears of rage fill his brother's eyes and ached for the pain he knew Etienne had felt when he thought he was dead. "I was gravely injured," he admitted. "The shifter Leon has aligned himself with is more powerful than anyone we've ever faced. He nearly killed me."

Etienne clenched his hands into fists. "What's his name and where can we find him? Slayer, Karol, and I will go to call the bastard to account, but first we will kill Leon."

Rip de la Rocque to pieces, Slayer vowed.

Nothing left but blood when finished, Pen promised.

The desire of those surrounding him to protect him, humbled him, and made him fearful for their safety. Although he had no wish to die, to defend the Pack, he would surrender his life. But he had no wish for Etienne or their faithful Keddi to share the fate he might not be able to avoid.

It would take every ounce of strength and determination he possessed, but he was determined that he would kill Falcone. He doubted he could survive another confrontation with the other shifter, but he would take him to hell with him. His only consolation would be that Etienne and Raven would find comfort from their grief at his death in each other's arms.

"We have to proceed with caution." He frowned. He would have to find a way to face Falcone alone. Once he had killed the other shifter, the Pack would be safe. Etienne would comfort Raven, Xavier would become Alpha of Den Gautier, a new Alpha-in-waiting would be chosen, and Pen and Drei would be safe with Etienne and Raven. That was the best he could hope for.

Etienne stared into his eyes, shaking his head slowly. "I know what you're planning, Acier, and I will not allow it. You are Alpha-in-waiting. If you perish the entire Pack will be weakened and at a disadvantage. Slayer, Karol, and I will face this shifter."

He grabbed Etienne. "No! You have no idea how powerful he is!"

Etienne shook his hand off his arm. "And you have no idea of the power of a shifter who is half vampire. I will not allow you to face him alone, Acier."

"And you think I'll allow you to risk your life? No, Etienne! I am Alpha-in-waiting. It is my responsibility to face the Pack's enemies."

"Not alone!"

"I won't have you killed, damn it!"

"And I will not allow you to make my decisions for me, Acier! I am an adult! We will face this shifter together…just as we've always faced our challenges…or I'll face him alone."

He saw a determination in Etienne he had never seen before. He knew he was not going to be able to talk Etienne out of his resolve. As they stood trying to stare each other down, Acier tensed. He heard a voice. No, two different voices in his head. He closed his eyes.

My sons.

My nephews. We are coming. Hold on.

He opened his eyes. Etienne stood with his head tilted to one side, his eyes closed.

"Etienne? Did you…hear them?"

Etienne opened his eyes and nodded. "Yes. There are two of them. They are…twins."

"Do you know who they are?"

He nodded. "Yes. Our father and our uncle."

"Which one is our father?"

Etienne hesitated. "His name is Vladimir Madison. He and his brother are coming to help us, Sei. All will be well."

Acier recalled the loneliness and fear that had been an integral part of their childhood. This father of theirs had abandoned them when they'd needed him most. Now he was coming?

Etienne's hand tightened on his arm. "If we are to survive, we'll need their help, Acier. For the good of the pack and one of our lives, promise me you'll hear them out."

"I'll hear this Vladimir Madison out…for the good of the

pack. But eventually, he's going to have to die!"

To his surprise, Etienne nodded. "Yes and it will be no great loss. But first we will enlist his aid. It is the least he can do to atone for leaving us. Then, when the danger is past, we will kill him together."

They clasped hands. "Together," Acier repeated.

Etienne nodded. "Now we'll get your bike into the back of the SUV and I'll drive you home."

A mile down the dark, winding road, they encountered oncoming headlights. The driver of the convertible slammed on the brakes, stopped the car, hopped out, and dashed in front of the SUV. "Steele!"

Etienne slammed on his brakes. Almost before the SUV stopped, Acier pushed open the passenger door and jumped out the vehicle. He raced across the road and caught Raven in his arms.

She took one look at him and collapsed against him in a flood of tears. "Steele! Oh, Steele, you were dead! I saw you die!"

"I didn't die, Petite. I'm all right. It's all right, my love." Whispering softly to her, he lifted her into his arms and carried her back to her car. He put her in the passenger seat and slid into the driver's side. She buried her face against his shoulder, still sobbing.

Pen and Drei flew out of the open moon roof of Etienne's SUV and hovered in the air, just above the car, still in battle mood. He started the car, turned it around, and drove slowly behind Etienne, with one arm around Raven. He felt a dizzy and hot, but managed to make the drive back to the RV without losing consciousness.

It was as he alighted from the car that his knees buckled. He heard Raven's startled cry, made a grab for the car door, missed it, and fell to his knees. Raven, Etienne, and the Keddi rushed to his side. He looked up at Raven. "I love you," he whispered as the world went black.

When he woke, he lay in his bed in the RV. Etienne, Raven, and the Keddi were all crowed into the room, along with Dr. Softee, a shifter physician.

Raven bent over him and pressed a damp cheek against his. "Welcome back, sweetie."

He turned his head and brushed his lips against hers. "Don't cry. I'm all right."

"Okay. Everyone out. I need to examine him," Dr. Softee said.

When everyone had left, Dr. Softee closed the doors and took his pulse. "How are feeling?"

"A little disorientated, but otherwise fine. What happened to me?"

"You have a powerful poison in your system."

"Poison? How?"

"It must have been in the saliva of the shifter who bit you."

"But I've never been sick in my entire life!"

"You've never been bitten by an alien shifter. We nearly lost you, Alpha. In fact, you should be dead."

He swallowed and wet his lips. "Then why aren't I?"

"It's your vampire blood that saved you. It battled the infection in a way we never could. You're not completely out of the woods yet. Traces of the poison remain in your system."

"What?"

"It presents no immediate danger to you and you can resume your normal activities as soon as you like, but you're going to need to get all traces of poison out of your system eventually."

"How do we get rid of it?"

"You're going to need a transfusion of vampire blood."

"I'm sure Etienne will volunteer."

"He already has but it didn't work."

He blinked and sat up. "How long have I been unconscious?"

"Seven days."

Oh, hell! Just great. He sighed. "I'll ask Etienne to ask his friend Damon. He's a full-blood vampire."

Dr. Softee shook his head. "I'm afraid that won't do. You and Etienne have a very unique blood chemistry. You're going to need a transfusion from either your father or a close relative or his."

Oh, damn! His life now depended on the largess of a vampire who'd never given a damn about him.

Dr. Softee squeezed his shoulder. "As I said the immediate danger is passed. By the time you reach the point where you have to have the transfusion, you will have found him."

"How long before I reach that point?"

"It's difficult to say, Alpha…but I would hazard a guess you have several weeks…maybe several months before you need to be concerned."

He closed his eyes, considering his options. Several weeks. He would spend the next two weeks with Raven and then he would go in search of Falcone and kill him.

When he emerged from his bedroom ten minutes later, Raven threw her arms around his neck and tried to kiss him. He turned his head. He felt grubby and unpleasant to be around.

"Let me shower first, Petite."

Her arms tightened around his neck. "You think I care about anything but you?!" She curled the fingers of one hand in hair. "Kiss me!"

He heard the passion and near despair in her voice. He turned his head and allowed her to kiss his mouth briefly before he pulled away. He embraced Etienne, who stood nearby and allowed all four Keddi to bury their small bodies against his neck before making his way to the shower.

Ravenous after his shower, he dressed and made his way to the kitchen.

Raven, Etienne, and Xavier sat at the table. Xavier half rose, but he waved him back to his seat and sat at the remaining chair. Pen and Drei hovered around him, each finally landing on a shoulder. Slayer and Karol sat on the counter, their eyes trained on him.

Every pair of eyes in the RV centered on him, filled with worry and fear.

He sighed, wishing Dr. Softee had not shared his medical situation with them. "I'm fine," he said. He glanced out the kitchen window and noticed a faint glimmering like heat rising from a desert floor. He frowned. "What's that?"

"That's Bentia." Raven sighed. "She is distressed that we were not able to protect you. She has stationed herself around the RV so that no one may enter without permission."

He glanced at the window again, noting the barrier around the RV seemed…strained. "She must be tired. Tell her I am fine and I appreciate her efforts, but she should rest."

After several moments, the barrier around the RV vanished and he watched as Raven sucked in a short, quick breath.

"Xavier, I need you to return to the den. I don't think Falcone will attack there, but if he does, I need you to be ready and if necessary, flee. You must not allow yourself to be bitten, Xavier. The den needs you now more than ever."

"But Acier, I can't stand by while our warriors battle without joining them. They will expect—"

"I will expect you to survive for the good of the den, Xavier. You can do none of us any good dead. I want your word you will not endanger yourself."

"I cannot give it," Xavier said. "If the den is attacked, it is my responsibility as your second to defend the den with my life if necessary."

"If I perish, Xay, you must live. The den will not survive with both of us gone. You must obey me in this, Xavier."

"I cannot. Den Gautier is united on this point. We have talked about it and we have decided. We live with you, Alpha or we die with you…to the last cub."

Raven rose and linked her arms around his neck. "Bentia and I will also be at your side…to the death."

He looked across the table. Etienne said nothing, but he knew that he, like their Keddi would battle to the death with him. The thought of those he loved more than his own life dying sent a coil of rage and fear through him. He closed his eyes and reached out into the darkness.

Father! We face a grave danger. You have to help us! Please!

A quiet combined voice answered in his head.

Fear not. We are coming.

He opened his eyes and looked at Etienne. "They're coming."

* * * * *

Later that night, after the others left and Bentia had erected herself around the RV, he lay in bed, naked and aroused. Raven, wearing a provocative red teddy that exposed her hardened nipples and pussy, stood at the foot of the bed, slowly dancing in time with a soft, insidious jazz beat.

Each time she rotated her hips and thrust out her pussy, he felt his cock harden just a little more. Finally, when it felt like granite and she showed no signs of taking pity on him, he crawled across the bed, grabbed her hips, pulled her forward, and buried his face against her fragrant pussy. He licked and nipped at the slick folds of her sex, enjoying the taste of her.

"Oh, Steele!" Her soft hands tangled in his hair as she moved her hips closer.

He extended his tongue, shifted it, and slipped into her tight pussy.

"Ooooh, yeah, sweetie. That's what I'm talking about!"

Cupping his palms over her ass, he ate her with a hunger he couldn't control, biting, licking, and thrusting wildly into her honeyed warmth. Gasping and sobbing, she came. She grabbed his head and thrust his face against her, fucking herself against his plunging tongue. Pressing closer, he devoured the sweet, hot juices gushing from her climaxing pussy.

When she stopped coming, he lifted her in his arms and laid her on the bed. He stretched out beside her, running his fingers through her hair. He stroked a palm over her breasts, down her body to cup her mound. She turned and pressed him onto his back. She rose over him, settled between his legs, and paused with her pussy pressed against the head of his cock.

He slid his hands over her ass, palming the cheeks, left bare by the skimpy teddy. He stared up into her eyes. He shuddered at the look of love, lust, and need in her gaze. This woman was his. "Fuck me," he whispered.

Smiling, she eased forward. The tip of his cock slipped into her pussy. It felt so good, he fought the urge to close his eyes and just enjoy it. He wanted to watch the look on her face and in her eyes as they made love.

As she slid her pussy over his cock, she lowered her body. Her nipples came to rest against his chest just as the last few inches of his cock slid into her. He shuddered, tightened his hands on her ass, and thrust his hips upward, hard and fast, sending his shaft in and out of her tight, slick cunt. Damn, he'd never had better pussy than this or been so caught up in a woman…hell, who was he kidding? He was in love with her.

Her hair fell forward over his face and shoulders. He wrapped his arms around her waist, parted his legs, and fucked her hard and furiously. She shattered within moments, sobbing and muttering that she loved him against his lips.

His incisors descended, his eyes glowed. He bit into her

neck and drank her blood as he came, filling her tight, hot pussy with his seed. His orgasm rolled over him, keeping his feeling weak and almost incoherent.

She stiffened on him suddenly and lifted her head, staring down at him. "What? What did you say?"

He opened his eyes and blinked up at her. "What?"

She cupped her hands on his face. "Say it again."

"Say what again?"

"That you love me! You said you loved me, Steele! Finally. Didn't...you mean it?"

He felt a lump in his throat and hesitated. If he admitted how he felt, he'd be vulnerable. If he didn't, he risked losing her. "Yes."

She gulped in a deep breath, her eyes filling with tears. "Oh Steele, I never thought you'd say it."

He drew her back into his arms, holding her close. "It's all right, Petite."

"Do you really mean it? You're not just saying it because—"

"I said it because I mean it." He was still hard and still inside her. He gave a lazy thrust and shuddered with delight as she tightened her pussy around his shaft. "Oh, damn, I love you!"

She lifted her head, pressing her warm lips against his.

As they began to fuck again, he pushed thoughts of the trouble awaiting them out of his mind. Just for that night, he was going to enjoy being with the woman he now freely admitted he loved.

The future was filled with uncertainties and undeniable danger. But as long as he had this woman...his bloodlust and the one love of his life by his side, somehow things would work out.

Epilogue

🔊

We are here. Come.

Sometime later that night, Acier woke with a start. Raven slept soundly beside him. Pen and Drei slept on the dresser top. He slipped out of bed, uncertain what had disturbed him. He looked out the bedroom window and noted Bentia still shimmering around the RV. He opened the bedroom doors and made his way towards the front of the RV.

In the living room area he froze. A tall male with bronze skin, glowing blue eyes, and long dreadlocks stood just inside the closed and locked door. Acier recognized him immediately from the snapshot he carried in his wallet.

His feelings confused him. He had spent his entire life waiting for this moment. Now when the bastard who had sired and abandoned him stood within reach of his vengeance, he wanted to rush across the distance separating them and…

He sucked in a shuddering breath. *You came.*

The vampire inclined his head. *We both came, but my brother was not able to pass your living barrier. He is waiting outside.*

How did you get past?

The vampire smiled. *I am not an ordinary vampire. I am Aleksei Madison, but those I know and love insist on calling me Sei.*

Acier took a deep breath. Sei? That was the nickname Etienne had been calling Acier since they were cubs. He'd never particularly liked it. Now he knew why. It was *his* nickname. *You are the uncle?*

I am told I am the uncle. He crossed the floor and stood in front of him, a fist clenched against his chest. *But my heart tells me you are my son.* He curled his fingers in Acier's hair and looked into his eyes. *You are my son. My son. What is your name?*

Acier Gautier.

And your brother? What is he called and where is he?

Etienne. He is not far from here.

Is he well?

Yes.

He closed his eyes and touched his forehead against Acier's. *Acier. I've recently learned your mother is dead. That she died when you and Etienne were very young —*

Thanks to you she had a hard, miserable life! You didn't love her. He wanted this vampire to tell him he had loved his mother and that there had been some terrible misunderstanding.

I grieve for you and Etienne for the loss of your mother. Vladimir and I lost our mother when we were but ten, too. We had younger siblings who were but five when she was lost to us. I know your pain, my son.

Then why did you abandon her when she was pregnant?

I did not abandon her or you.

I don't believe you!

His fingers tightened in Acier's hair. *I do not lie.*

Then what happened between you and her?

I was called away and when I returned, she had fled.

Why? Where?

I don't know why or where.

Did you search for her like you claim you've been searching for us?

No, but had I known she was pregnant, I would have. I am so sorry for what you and your brother have endured. I had no reason to suppose she was pregnant.

And that was supposed to make everything all right? Acier's chest tightened and a lump formed in his throat. He felt rage, anger, and something else he did not want to feel for this…sorry bastard. Etienne had led him to believe their father was scum, but he felt none of the repulsion he had expected to feel.

The emotions welling in him made breathing difficult. He jerked away, clenching his hands into fists. *I was told our father was called Vladimir.*

He is my twin brother. Although my heart tells me you are my son, neither of us are sure which one of us is your father. But it doesn't matter if you are son or nephew. We have found you at last and those menacing you will soon know the folly of challenging a son or a nephew of Aleksei and Vladimir Madison. He curled his hands in Acier's hair again. *I am one of a family of eight full-blood vampires. Whatever or whoever has menaced you will soon be a threat no longer.*

There was an undeniable power emanating from the vampire. He would have to be an extraordinary individual to have penetrated Bentia's barrier without her knowledge. He exuded a confidence that he could handle any danger. Acier hated that just standing in this male's presence made him feel…inadequate and confident that the deck was no longer stacked against he and the pack.

Where the fuck have you been all our lives? Why did you desert us?

I did not desert you! I only learned of your existence a few months earlier and I have been searching for you since then.

Liar! The rage in Acier exploded. He jerked away, curled his hands into fists and struck out at the other male, raining furious blows on his face and shoulders. He stood under the blows, making no effort to deflect them or defend himself. When he'd had enough, his hands shot out with incredible speed and he closed powerful fingers around Acier's wrists, immobilizing them.

Even though he knew he would not be able to break the other male's hold, Acier attempted to yank away. The vampire easily overcame his resistance. He held both of Acier's wrists in one hand and drew him, struggling down to the floor.

Acier tensed, preparing to shift to his natural form to ward off the coming attack. Instead of retaliating, the vampire sat with his back against the sofa, and drew Acier into his arms. He felt the other male's lips against his hair.

Father or uncle, you and Etienne are no longer alone. You are now part of a big, loving family. Forgive me for what you've suffered. I will do my best to atone for your pain. He stroked his hand over Acier's hair and something inside him burst.

Acier burrowed against the other male, his throat tight with tears, breathing difficult. *I hate you!*

He felt a shudder shake the vampire's body. *I know you do, but I love you.*

He lifted his head and looked into the hated blue eyes. *You don't even know me.*

The vampire smiled. *I am a full-blood vampire, not some pitiful human male who doesn't know how he feels. You are a part of me…that's all I need to know to love you.*

Don't keep saying that.

You have a problem with love?

I have a problem with being abandoned! He took a deep breath. He didn't want to reveal all his hurts and pains to this male. But there was something about him that invited…almost demanded Acier's confidence. *You have no idea how much it hurt growing up knowing you didn't care about us! We are half-breeds. We grew up too vampire for the shifters and too shifter for the vampires. Do you have any idea what it's like to grow up in a world where no one wants or accepts you for what and who you are? You could have buffeted some of the pain.*

I would have, had I known. I am over 300 years old. Before I became a full-blood vampire, I grew up half-black and half-white in a white world that looked upon me as nothing! The humans who raised us did their best to shield us from the hate, but we always knew we didn't belong. Not in the black world with these blue eyes and this silky hair and not in the white world with this bronze colored skin. It was not until we became full-blood vampires that we were able to force people to treat us fairly or suffer the consequences.

My siblings and I know all too well the pain of being half-breeds and abandoned. We thought we had been abandoned and we spent years searching for our mother…hating her for well over 300 years. We were wrong. She had not abandoned us. Even if she had, I would never have abandoned you and your brother if I had known about you. I did not know your mother was pregnant.

I don't believe you and I hate you! If it's the last thing I do, I'm going to kill you!

He saw a glimmer of tears in the other male's eyes. *Don't you want to hear my side of the story?*

What side? When we needed you, where were you?

I am here now, my son.

My son. His entire life he had longed for a father to call him son and cherish him. Aime had been a father figure and then Mo. And he loved them both. But something had always been missing from his relationship with those two. With this male…he felt that missing something. *My son.* The words and the emotions he sensed bound up with them made his throat constrict.

When his vampire father/uncle pulled him back in his arms, he felt like a little lost boy. He told himself he submitted for the good of the pack. One day soon this male would pay the ultimate price for having deserted him. But the sense of belonging he felt could not be denied. This sense that this male would dare all to protect him even at the cost of his own life is what Acier had always longed for and never had—until now. But now was too late. He and Etienne and their mother had suffered too much. Some things were unforgivable.

Even if it turned out the other vampire, Vladimir was their father, he decided he would make this one pay…this vampire who had the power to make him feel like a little lost boy longing for his father would pay for all the heartache he and Etienne had suffered.

You are no longer alone. I know you hate me and I understand. But I am here now and I love you, my son. No matter what happens, know that you and Etienne are loved.

Acier, who had never wanted any more than the love of his father, was powerless to do anything but close his eyes and cling to his vampire father/uncle. The words *I love you, my son* echoed in his head and stroked a chord inside him.

The words *I forgive you, Father* trembled on his lips. Acier ruthlessly swallowed them. He would accept the help this vampire promised. He owned them that much. But he would never forgive or forget. When the danger was past, Aleksei Madison, father or uncle, would have to die. If his brother Vladimir took exception to his twin's death, he could bloody well join Aleksei in hell!

Why an electronic book?

We live in the Information Age—an exciting time in the history of human civilization, in which technology rules supreme and continues to progress in leaps and bounds every minute of every day. For a multitude of reasons, more and more avid literary fans are opting to purchase e-books instead of paper books. The question from those not yet initiated into the world of electronic reading is simply: *Why?*

1. *Price.* An electronic title at Ellora's Cave Publishing and Cerridwen Press runs anywhere from 40% to 75% less than the cover price of the exact same title in paperback format. Why? Basic mathematics and cost. It is less expensive to publish an e-book (no paper and printing, no warehousing and shipping) than it is to publish a paperback, so the savings are passed along to the consumer.

2. *Space.* Running out of room in your house for your books? That is one worry you will never have with electronic books. For a low one-time cost, you can purchase a handheld device specifically designed for e-reading. Many e-readers have large, convenient screens for viewing. Better yet, hundreds of titles can be stored within your new library—on a single microchip. There are a variety of e-readers from different manufacturers. You can also read e-books on your PC or laptop computer. (Please note that Ellora's Cave does not endorse any specific brands.

You can check our websites at www.ellorascave.com or www.cerridwenpress.com for information we make available to new consumers.)

3. *Mobility*. Because your new e-library consists of only a microchip within a small, easily transportable e-reader, your entire cache of books can be taken with you wherever you go.

4. ***Personal Viewing Preferences.*** Are the words you are currently reading too small? Too large? Too… ANNOYING? Paperback books cannot be modified according to personal preferences, but e-books can.

5. ***Instant Gratification.*** Is it the middle of the night and all the bookstores near you are closed? Are you tired of waiting days, sometimes weeks, for bookstores to ship the novels you bought? Ellora's Cave Publishing sells instantaneous downloads twenty-four hours a day, seven days a week, every day of the year. Our webstore is never closed. Our e-book delivery system is 100% automated, meaning your order is filled as soon as you pay for it.

Those are a few of the top reasons why electronic books are replacing paperbacks for many avid readers.

As always, Ellora's Cave and Cerridwen Press welcome your questions and comments. We invite you to email us at Comments@ellorascave.com or write to us directly at Ellora's Cave Publishing Inc., 1056 Home Avenue, Akron, OH 44310-3502.

COMING TO A BOOKSTORE NEAR YOU!

ELLORA'S CAVE

Bestselling Authors Tour

erridwen, the Celtic Goddess of wisdom, was the muse who brought inspiration to story-tellers and those in the creative arts. Cerridwen Press encompasses the best and most innovative stories in all genres of today's fiction. Visit our site and discover the newest titles by talented authors who still get inspired - much like the ancient storytellers did, once upon a time.

Discover for yourself why readers can't get enough
of the multiple award-winning publisher

Ellora's Cave.

Whether you prefer e-books or paperbacks,

be sure to visit EC on the web at
www.ellorascave.com

for an erotic reading experience that will leave you
breathless.